I0641490

The Little Lady of Lagunitas

Richard Henry Savage

Contents

THE LITTLE LADY
OF LAGUNITAS

BY

Richard Henry Savage

INTRODUCTION.

Forty-two years have passed since California's golden star first glittered in the flag of the United States of America.

Its chequered history virtually begins with the rush for gold in '48-'49.

Acquired for the evident purpose of extending slave-holding territory, it was occupied for years by a multitude of cosmopolitan "free lances," who swept away the defenceless Indians, and brutally robbed the great native families, the old "Dons."

Society slowly made headway against these motley adventurers. Mad riot, wildest excess, marked these earlier days.

High above the meaner knights of the "revolver and bowie knife," greater than card sharper, fugitive bravo, or sly wanton, giant schemers appeared, who throw, yet, dark shadows over the records of this State.

These daring conspirators dominated legislature and forum, public office and society.

They spoiled the Mexican, robbed the Indian, and paved the way for a "Lone Star Republic," or the delivering of the great treasure fields of the West to the leaders of Secession.

How their designs on this grand domain failed; what might have been, had the South been more active in its hour of primary victory and seized the Golden West, these pages may show.

The golden days of the "stars and bars" were lost by the activity of the Unionists and the mistaken policy at Richmond.

The utter demoralization of California by the "bonanza era" of silver discovery, the rise of an invincible plutocracy, and the second reign of loose luxury are herein set forth.

Scenes never equalled in shamelessness have disgraced the Halls of State, the Courts, and the mansions of the suddenly enriched.

The poor have been trampled by these tyrants for twenty years.

Characters unknown in the social history of any other land, have been evolved from this golden eddy of crime and adventure.

Not till all these men and women of incredibly romantic fortunes have passed away, will a firm social structure rise over their graves.

Throttled by usurers, torn by gigantic bank wars, its resources drained by colossal swindles, crouching yet under the iron rule of upstart land-barons, "dashing journalism," and stern railroad autocrats, the Californian community has gloomily struggled along.

Newer States have made a relative progress which shames California. Its future is yet uncertain.

The native sons and daughters of the golden West are the hope of the Pacific.

The homemakers may yet win the victory.

Some of the remarkable scenes of the past are herein portrayed by one who has seen this game of life played in earnest, the shadowed drama of California.

There is no attempt to refer to individuals, save as members of well-defined classes, in these pages. This book has absolutely no political bias.

THE AUTHOR.
NEW YORK CITY, May 15, 1892.

BOOK I.
THE LAST OF THE DONS BY THE BLUE PACIFIC.

CHAPTER I.

UNDER THE MEXICAN EAGLE.--EXIT THE FOREIGNER.--MONTEREY, 1840.

Caramba! Adios, Señores!" cried Captain Miguel Peralta, sitting on his roan charger on the Monterey bluffs. A white-sailed bark is heading southward for Acapulco. His vaqueros tossed up their sombreros, shouting, "Vive Alvarado! Muerte los estrangeros!"

The Pacific binds the hills of California in a sapphire zone, unflecked by a single sail in sight, save the retreating trader, which is flitting around "Punta de los Pinos."

It is July, 1840. The Mexican ensign flutters in the plaza of Monterey, the capital of Alta California.

Miguel Peralta dismounts and crosses himself, murmuring, "Sea por Dios y la Santissima Virgen."

His duty is done. He has verified the departure of the Yankee ship. It is crowded with a hundred aliens. They are now exiles.

Gathered in by General Vallejo, the "pernicious foreigners" have been held at Monterey, until a "hide drogher" comes into the port. Alvarado permits her to anchor under the guns of the hill battery. He then seizes the ship for his use.

Captain Peralta is given the honor of casting out these Ishmaels of fortune. He views calmly their exit. It is a land which welcomes not the "Gringo." The ship-master receives a draft on Acapulco for his impressed service. These pioneer argonauts are warned (on pain of death) not to return. It is a day of "fiesta" in Monterey. "Vive Alvarado!" is the toast.

So, when Captain Miguel dashes into the Plaza, surrounded with his dare-devil retainers, reporting that the vessel is off shore, the rejoicing is unbounded.

Cannons roar: the yells of the green jacket and yellow scrape brigade rise on the silent reaches of the Punta de los Pinos. A procession winds up to the Carmel Mission. Governor Alvarado, his staff, the leading citizens, the highest families, and the señoritas attend a mass of thanksgiving. Attired in light muslins, with here and there a bright-colored shawl giving a fleck of color, and silk kerchiefs --fleecy--the ladies' only other ornaments are the native flowers which glitter on the slopes of Monterey Bay. Bevies of dark-eyed girls steal glances at Andres, Ramon, or Jose, while music lends a hallowing charm to the holy father's voice as he bends before the decorated altar. Crowds of mission Indians fill the picturesque church. Every heart is proud. Below their feet sleeps serenely good Fray "Junipero Serra." He blessed this spot in 1770;--a man of peace, he hung the bells on the green oaks in a peaceful wilderness. High in air, to-day they joyously peal out a "Laus Deo." When the mystery of the mass rehearses the awful sacrifice of Him who died for us all, a silence broods over the worshippers. The notes of the choristers' voices slowly die away. The population leaves the church in gay disorder.

The Bells of the Past throw their spells over the mossy church--at once triumph, tomb, and monument of Padre Junipero. Scattered over the coast of California, the padres now sleep in the Lethe of death. Fathers Kino, Salvatierra, Ugarte, and sainted Serra left their beautiful works of mercy from San Diego to Sonoma. With their companions, neither unknown tribes, lonely coasts, dangers by land and sea, the burning deserts of the Colorado, nor Indian menaces, prevented the linking together of these outposts of peaceful Christianity. The chain of missions across New Mexico and Texas and the Mexican religious houses stretches through bloody Arizona. A golden circlet!

Happy California! The cross here preceded the sword. No blood stains the Easter lilies of the sacrifice. The Dons and Donnas greet each other in stately fashion, as the gathering disperses. Governor Alvarado gives a feast to the notables. The old families are all represented at the board. Picos, Peraltas, Sanchez, Pachecos, Guerreros, Estudillos, Vallejos, Alvarados, De la Guerras, Castros, Micheltorrenas, the descendants of "Conquistadores," drink to Mexico. High rises the jovial chatter. Good aguadiente and mission wine warm the hearts of the fiery Californian orators. A proud day for Monterey, the capital of a future Empire of Gold. The stranger is cast out. Gay caballeros are wending to the bear-baiting, the bull-fights, the "baile," and the rural feasts. Splendid riders prance along, artfully forcing their wild steeds into bounds and curvets with the rowels of their huge silver-mounted spurs.

Dark lissome girls raise their velvety eyes and applaud this daring horsemanship. Senioritas Luisa, Isabel, and Panchita lose no point of the display. In a land without carriages or roads, the appearance of the cavalier, his mount, his trappings, most do make the man shine before these fair slips of Mexican blue blood.

Down on the beach, the boys race their half-broken broncos. These lads are as lithe and lean as the ponies they bestride. Across the bay, the Sierras of Santa Cruz lift their virgin crests (plumed with giant redwoods) to the brightest skies on earth. Flashing brooks wander to the sea unvexed by mill, unbridged in Nature's unviolated freedom. Far to north and south the foot-hills stand shining with their golden coats of wild oats, a memorial of the seeds cast over these fruitful mesas by Governor Caspar de Portala. He left San Diego Mission in July, 1769, with sixty-five retainers, and first reached the Golden Gate.

Beyond the Coast Range lies a "terra incognita." A few soldiers only have traversed the Sacramento and San Joaquin. They wandered into the vales of Napa and Sonoma, fancying them a fairyland.

The sparkling waters of the American, the Sacramento, the Yuba, Feather, and Bear rivers are dancing silently over rift and ripple. There precious nuggets await the frenzied seekers for wealth. There are no gold-hunters yet in the gorges of these crystal streams. Down in Nature's laboratory, radiated golden veins creep along between feathery rifts of virgin quartz. They are the treasures of the careless gnomes.

Not till years later will Marshall pick up the first nugget of gleaming gold in Sutter's mill-race at Coloma. The "auri sacra fames" will bring thousands from the four quarters of the earth to sweep away "the last of the Dons."

A lovely land to-day. No axe rings in its forests. No steamboat threads the rivers. Not an engine is harnessed to man's use in this silent, lazy realm. The heart of the Sierras is inviolate. The word "Gold" must be whispered to break the charm.

The sun climbs to noon, then slowly sinks to the west. It dips into the silent sea, mirroring sparkling evening stars.

Stretching to Japan, the Pacific is the mysterious World's End.

Along the brown coast, the sea otter, clad in kingly robes, sports shyly in the kelp fields. The fur seals stream by unchased to their misty home in the Pribyloffs. Barking sea-lions clamber around the jutting rocks. Lazy whales roll on the quiet waters of the bay, their track an oily wake.

It is the land of siesta, of undreamed dreams, of brooding slumber.

The barbaric diversions of the day are done. The firing squad leave the guns. The twang of guitar and screech of violin open the fandango.

The young cavaliers desert the streets. Bibulous dignitaries sit in council around Governor Alvarado's table. Mexican cigars, wine in old silver flagons (fashioned by the deft workers of Chihuahua and Durango), and carafes of aguadiente, garnish the board.

The mahogany table (a mark of official grandeur), transported from Acapulco, is occupied (below the salt) by the young officers. Horse-racing, cock-fighting, and gambling on the combat of bear and bull, have not exhausted their passions. Public monte and faro leave them a few "doubloons" yet. Seated with piles of Mexican dollars before them, the young heroes enjoy a "lay-out." All their coin comes from Mexico. Hundreds of millions, in unminted gold and silver, lie under their careless feet, yet their "pieces of eight" date back to Robinson Crusoe! This is the land of "manana!" Had Hernando Cortez not found the treasures of Mexico, he might have fought his way north, over the Gila Desert, to the golden hoards of the sprites of the Sierras.

At the banquet fiery Alvarado counselled with General Vallejo. Flushed with victory, Captain Miguel was the lion of this feast. He chatted with his compadres.

The seniors talked over the expulsion of the strangers.

Cool advisers feared trouble from France, England, or the United States. Alvarado's instinct told him that foreigners would gain a mastery over the Dons, if permitted to enter in numbers. Texas was an irresistible warning. "Senores," said Alvarado, "the Russians came in 1812. Only a few, with their Kodiak Indians, settled at Bodega. Look at them now! They control beautiful Bodega! They are 800 souls! True, they say they are going, but only our posts at San Rafael and Sonoma checked them. A fear of your sword, General!" Alvarado drank to Vallejo.

Vallejo bowed to his Governor. "Senor," said he, "you are right. I have seen Mexico. I have been a scholar, as well as a soldier. I knew Von Resanoff's Russian slyness. My father was at the Presidio in 1807, when he obtained rights for a few fur hunters. Poor fellow! he never lived to claim his bride, but he was a diplomat."

"Foreigners will finally outroot us. Here is Sutter, building his fort on the Sacramento! He's a good fellow, yet I'll have to burn New Helvetia about his ears some day. Russian or Swiss, French or Yankee, it's all the same. The 'Gringo' is the worst of all. Poor Conception de Arguello. She waited long for her dead Russian lover."

"General, do you think the Yankees can ever attack us by land?" said Alvarado.

"Madre de Dios! No!" cried Vallejo, "we will drag them at our horses' tails!"

"Then, I have no fear of them," said Alvarado. "We occupy San Diego, Santa Barbara, Monterey, and San Francisco, the missions of San Juan Capistrano, Los Angeles, San Luis Obispo and Santa Clara, and help to control the Indians, but these home troubles have stopped their useful growth."

Governor Alvarado sighed. Governor Hijar in 1834 had desecularized the Catholic missions. Their cattle were stolen, their harvests and vineyards destroyed. The converts were driven off to seek new homes among the Utes, Yubas, Feather River, Napa, and Mohave tribes.

Pious Alvarado crossed himself. He glanced uneasily at Padre Castillo,--at the board. Only one or two priests were left at the beautiful settlements clustering around the old mission churches. To-day these are the only architectural ornaments of Alta California.

"I doubt the wisdom of breaking up the missions," said Alvarado, with gloomy brow. A skeleton was at this feast. The troubled Governor could not see the handwriting on the wall. He felt California was a priceless jewel to Mexico. He feared imprudent measures. Lying dormant, California slept since Cabrillo saw Cape Mendocino in 1542. After he turned his shattered prows back to Acapulco on June 27, 1543, it was only on November 10, 1602, that ambitious Viscaino raised the Spanish ensign at San Diego. He boldly claimed this golden land for Spain. Since that furtive visit, the lonely coast lay unsettled. It was only used as a haunt by wild pirates, lurking to attack the precious Philippine galleons sailing to Acapulco. For one hundred and sixty-eight years the land was unvisited. Spanish greed and iron rule satisfied itself with grinding the Mexicans and turning southward in the steps of Balboa and Pizarro.

Viscaino's neglected maps rotted in Madrid for two centuries. Fifty-five years of Spanish rule left California undeveloped, save by the gentle padres who, aided by their escort, brought in the domestic animals. They planted fruit-trees, grains, and the grape. They taught the peaceful Indians agriculture. Flax, hemp, and cotton supplanted the skins of animals.

Alvarado and Vallejo remembered the Spanish war in 1822. At this banquet of victory, neither thought that, a few years later, the rule of the Dons would be over; that their familiar places would know them no more. Just retribution of fate! The Dons drove out the friars, and recked not their own day was close at hand.

As the exultant victors stood drinking the toast of the day, "Muerte los estrangeros," neither crafty statesman, sly priest, fiery general, wise old Don, nor reckless caballero, could predict that the foreigners would return in two years. That they would come under protection of the conquering British flag.

Alvarado was excited by his feuds with Micheltorrena. The people were divided into clericals and anti-clericals. A time of "storm and stress" hung over all.

Wise in victory was Captain Miguel Peralta. His campaign against the foreigners marked the close of his service. Born in 1798, his family were lords of broad lands on the Alamedas of San Francisco Bay. He was sent to the city of Mexico and educated, serving in the army of the young republic. Returning to Alta California, he became a soldier.

Often had he sallied out to drive the warlike Indian toward the Sacramento. In watching his mustangs and cattle, he rode far to the slopes of the Sierra Nevadas. Their summits glittered under the blue skies, crowned with silvery snows, unprofaned by the foot of man.

A sturdy caballero, courtly and sagacious. His forty-two years admonished him now to settle in life. When Alvarado was in cheeriest mood, at the feast, the Captain reminded him of his promise to release him. This would allow Peralta to locate a new ten-league-square grant of lands, given him for past services to the State.

Graciously the Governor accorded the request. Noblesse oblige! "Don Miguel, is there any reason for leaving us besides your new rancho?" said Alvarado. The Captain's cheek reddened a little. "Senor Gobernador, I have served the State long," said he. "Juanita Castro waits for me at San Francisco. I will lay off my rancho on the San Joaquin. I move there in the spring."

Alvarado was delighted. The health of Senorita Juanita Castro was honored by the whole table. They drank an extra bumper for gallant Don Miguel, the bride-groom.

The Governor was pleased. Powerful Castros and Peraltas stretched from the Salinas, by San Jose and Santa Clara, to Martinez; and San Rafael as well as Sonoma. By this clan, both Sutter's Fort and the Russians could be watched.

This suitable marriage would bring a thousand daring horsemen to serve under the cool leadership of Don Miguel in case of war.

Peralta told the Governor he would explore the San Joaquin. He wished to locate his ranch where he could have timber, wood, water, game, and mountain air.

Don Miguel did not inform the chief of the state that in riding from San Diego to Cape Mendocino he had found one particular garden of Paradise. He had marked this for his home when his sword would be sheathed in honor.

"I will say, your Excellency," said the Captain, "I fear for the future. The Yankees are growing in power and are grasping. They have robbed us of lovely Texas. Now, it is still a long way for their ships to come around dreary Cape Horn. We had till late years only two vessels from Boston; I saw their sails shining in the bay of San Francisco when I was five years old. I have looked in the Presidio records for the names. The Alexander and the Aser, August 1st, 1803. Then, they begged only for wood and water and a little provision. Now, their hide-traders swarm along our coast. They will by and by come with their huge war-ships. These trading-boats have no cannon, but they are full of bad rum. Our coast people will be cleared out. Why, Catalina Islands," continued the Captain, "were peopled once densely. There are yet old native temples there. All these coast tribes have perished. It is even worse since the holy fathers were robbed of their possessions."

The good soldier crossed himself in memory of the wise padres. They owned the thousands of cattle, sheep, and horses once thronging the oat-covered hills. Theirs were the fruits, grains, and comforts of these smiling valleys, untrodden yet by a foreign foe.

"Your Excellency, when the Yankee war-ships have come, we cannot resist them. Our batteries are old and poor, we have little ammunition. Our arms are out of repair. The machete and lasso are no match for their well-supplied men-of-war. I shall locate myself so far in the interior that the accursed Gringos cannot reach me with their ships or their boats. The trappers who straggle over the deserts from Texas our horsemen will lasso. They will bring them in bound as prisoners."

"Miguel, mi compadre," said the Governor, "do you think they can cross the deserts?" He was startled by Peralta's views of the future.

"Senor," said the Captain, "I saw the first American who came overland. The wanderer appeared in 1826. It was the 20th of December. He was found half starved by our vaqueros. I have his name here on a piece of paper. I have long carried it, for I was a guard over him."

Miguel slowly spelled off the detested Yankee name, Jedediah S. Smith, from a slip of cartridge paper in his bolsa. Glory be to the name of Smith!

"Where THAT one Yankee found a way, more will come, but we will meet and fight them. This is our OWN land by the right of discovery. The good King Philip II. of Spain rightfully claimed this (from his orders to Viceroy Monterey in 1596). We get our town name here in his honor. We will fight the English, and these accursed Yankees. They have no right to be here. This is our home," cried fiery Miguel, as he pledged the hospitable Governor. He passed out into the dreaming, starry night. As he listened to the waves softly breaking on the sandy beach, he thought fondly of Juanita Castro. He fumbled over the countersign as the sentinel presented his old flint-lock musket.

Both Governor and Captain sought the repose of their Spartan pillows. The Captain forgot, in his zeal for Spanish dominion, that daring Sir Francis Drake, in days even then out of the memory of man, piloted the "Golden Hind" into Drake's Bay. He landed near San Francisco in 1578, and remained till the early months of 1579. Under the warrant of "good Queen Bess" he landed, and set up a pillar bearing a "fair metal plate" with a picture of that antiquated but regal coquette. He nailed on the pillar a "fair struck silver five-pence," saluting the same with discharge of culverins, much hearty English cheer and nautical jollity. The land was English--by proscription.

Sir Francis, gallant and courtly, was, like many travellers, as skilful at drawing the long bow as in wielding the rapier. He was not believed at home.

Notwithstanding, he tarried months and visited the inland Indians, bringing home many objects of interest, announcing "much gold and silver," his voyage was vain. His real discovery was deemed of no practical value. The robust Indians swarmed in thousands, living by the watersides in huts, wearing deerskin cloaks and garments of rushes. Hunters and fishers were they. They entertained the free-booter, and like him have long since mouldered to ashes. Along the Pacific Coast great mounds of shells, marking their tribal seaside feasts, are now frequently un-earthed. Their humble history is shadowed by the passing centuries. They are only a memory, a shadow on Time's stream. Good Queen Bess sleeps in the stately fane of Westminster. Sir Francis's sword is rusted. The "brazen plate" recording that date and year is of a legendary existence only. "Drake's Bay" alone keeps green the memory of the daring cruiser. Even in one century the Spanish, Russian, Mexican, and American flags successively floated over the unfrequented cliffs of California. Two hundred years before, the English ensign kissed the air in pride, unchallenged by the haughty Spaniard.

Miguel Peralta was happy. He had invited all the officials to attend the nuptials by the Golden Gate. Venus was in the ascendant. The red planet of Mars had set, he hoped, forever. The officers and gentry contemplated a frolicsome ride around the Salinas bend, over the beautiful passes to Santa Clara valley and the town of Yerba Buena.

Peralta's marriage was an excuse for general love making. A display of all the bravery of attire and personal graces of man and maid was in order.

The soldier drifted into the land of dreams haunted by Juanita Castro's love-lit eyes and rare, shy smile. No vision disturbed him of the foothold gained in Or-egon by the Yankees. They sailed past the entrance of San Francisco Bay, on the Columbia, in 1797, but they found the great river of the northwest. They named it after their gallant bark, said to be the legal property of one General Washington of America.

The echoes of Revolutionary cannon hardly died away before the eagle-guided Republic began to follow the star of empire to the Occident.

Had the listless mariners seen that obscured inlet of the Golden Gate, they had never braved the icy gales of the Oregon coast. Miguel Peralta's broad acres might have had another lord. Bishop Berkeley's prophecy was infallible. A fatal remissness seemed to characterize all early foreign adventure on Californian coasts.

Admiral Vancouver in 1793 visited Monterey harbor, and failed to raise the Union Jack, as supinely as the later British commanders in 1846. French commanders, technically skilful and energetic, also ignored the value of the western coast. As a result of occasional maritime visits, the slender knowledge gained by these great navigators appears a remarkable omission.

The night passed on. Breezes sweeping through the pines of Monterey brought no murmur from the south and east of the thunder crash of cannon on the unfought fields of Mexico.

No drowsy vaquero sentinel, watching the outposts of Monterey, could catch a sound of the rumbling wheels and tramping feet of that vast western immigration soon to tread wearily the old overland and the great southern route.

The soldier, nodding over his flint-lock as the white stars dropped into the western blue, saw no glitter of the sails of hostile Yankee frigates. Soon they would toss in pride at anchor here, and salute the starry flag of a new sovereignty. The little twinkling star to be added for California was yet veiled behind the blue field of our country's banner.

Bright sun flashes dancing over the hills awoke the drowsy sacristan. The hallowed "Bells of Carmel" called the faithful to mass.

Monterey, in reverse order of its social grades, rose yawning from the feast. Fandangos and bailes of the day of victory tired all. Lazy "mozos" lolled about the streets. A few revellers idly compared notes of the day's doings.

In front of the government offices, squads of agile horses awaited haughty riders. A merry cavalcade watched for Captain Miguel Peralta. He was to be escorted out of the Pueblo by the "jeunesse doree" of Alta California.

Clad in green jackets buttoned with Mexican dollars, riding leggings of tiger-cat skin seamed with bullion and fringed with dollars, their brown faces were surmounted by rich sombreros, huge of rim. They were decorated in knightly fashion with silver lace. The young caballeros awaited their preux chevalier. Saddle and bridle shone with heavy silver mountings. Embossed housings and "tapadero," hid the symmetry of their deer-like coursers.

Pliant rawhide lassos coiled on saddle horns, gay serapes tied behind each rider, and vicious machetes girded on thigh, these sons of the West were the pride of the Pacific.

Not one of them would be dismayed at a seven days' ride to Los Angeles. A day's jaunt to a fandango, a night spent in dancing, a gallop home on the morrow, was child's play to these young Scythians.

Pleasure-loving, brave, and courteous; hospitable, and fond of their lovely land--they bore all fatigue in the saddle, yet despised any manual exertion; patricians all, in blood.

So it has been since man conquered the noblest inferior animal. The man on the horse always rides down and tramples his brother on foot. Life is simply a struggle for the saddle, and a choice of the rarest mount in the race. To-day these gay riders are shadows of a forgotten past.

Before noon Captain Peralta receives the order of the Governor. It authorizes him to locate his military grant. General Vallejo, with regret, hands Miguel an order relieving him from duty. He is named Commandante of the San Joaquin valley, under the slopes of the undefiled Sierras.

Laden with messages, despatches, and precious letters for the ranches on the road to the Golden Gate, he departs. These are entrusted to the veteran sergeant, major-domo and shadow of his beloved master. Miguel bounds into the saddle. He gayly salutes the Governor and General with a graceful sweep of his sombrero. He threads the crowded plaza with adroitness, swaying easily from side to side as he greets sober friend or demure Donna. He smiles kindly on all the tender-eyed senoritas who admire the brave soldier, and in their heart of hearts envy Juanita Castro, the Rose of Alameda.

Alert and courteous, the future bright before him, Peralta gazes on the Mexican flag fluttering in the breeze. A lump rises in his throat. His long service is over at last. He doffs his sombrero when the guard "turns out" for him. It is the last honor.

He cannot foresee that a French frigate will soon lie in the very bay smiling at his feet, and cover the returning foreigner with her batteries.

In two short years, sturdy old Commodore Jones will blunder along with the American liners, CYANE and UNITED STATES, and haul down that proud Mexican ensign. He will hoist for the first time, on October, 19, 1842, the stars and stripes over the town. Even though he apologizes, the foreigners will troop back there like wolves around the dying bison of the west. The pines on Santa Cruz whisper of a coming day of change. The daybreak of the age of gold draws near.

Steadily through the live-oaks and fragrant cypress the bridegroom rides to the wedding. A few days' social rejoicings, then away to the beautiful forests of his new ranch. It lies far in the hills of Mariposa. There, fair as a garden of the Lord, the grassy knolls of the foothills melt into the golden wild-oat fields of the San Joaquin.

Behind him, to the east, the virgin forest rises to the serrated peaks of the Nevada. He drops his bridle on his horse's neck. He dreams of a day when he can visit the unknown canons beyond his new home.

Several Ute chiefs have described giant forests of big trees. They tell of a great gorge of awful majesty; that far toward the headwaters of the American are sparkling lakes fed by winter snows.

His escort of young bloods rides behind him. They have had their morning gymnastics, "a cheval," to edify the laughing beauties of the baile of last night. The imprisoned rooster, buried to the neck in soft earth, has been charged on and captured gaily. Races whiled away their waiting moments.

Then, "adios, senoritas," with heart-pangs in chorus. After a toss of aguardiente, the cigarito is lit. The beaux ride out for a glimpse of the white cliffs of the Golden Gate. The sleeping Monterey belles dream yet of yester-even. Nature smiles, a fearless virgin, with open arms. Each rancho offers hospitality. Money payments are unknown here yet, in such matters.

Down the Santa Clara avenue of great willows these friends ride in the hush of a starry evening. As the mission shows its lights, musical bells proclaim the vesper service. Their soft echoes are wafted to the ears of these devotees.

Devoutly the caballeros dismount. They kneel on the tiled floor till the evening service ends.

Miguel's heart sinks while he thinks of the missions. He bows in prayer. Neglected vineyards and general decay reign over the deserted mission lands.

It is years since Hijar scattered the missions, He paralyzed the work of the Padres. Already Santa Clara's gardens are wasted. Snarling coyotes prowl to the very walls of the enclosures left to the Padres.

Priest and acolytes quit the altar. Miguel sadly leaves the church. Over a white stone on the sward his foot pauses. There rests one of his best friends--Padre Pacheco--passed beyond these earthly troubles to eternal rest and peace. The mandate of persecution can never drive away that dead shepherd. He rests with his flock around him.

Hijar seized upon the acres of the Church. He came down like the feudal barons in England. Ghostly memories cling yet around these old missions.

> "When the lord of the hill, Amundeville,
> Made Norman church his prey,
> And expelled the friars, one friar still
> Would not be driven away."

So here the sacred glebe was held by a faithful sentinel. His gravestone flashed a white protest against violence. In the struggle between sword and cowl, the first victory is with the sword; not always the last. Time has its revenges.

Padre Hinojosa, the incumbent, welcomes the Captain. There is cheer for the travellers. Well-crusted bottles of mission claret await them. The tired riders seek the early repose of primitive communities.

Beside the fire (for the fog sweeps coldly over the Coast Range) the priest and his guest exchange confidences. Captain Peralta is an official bulletin. The other priest is summoned away to a dying penitent. The halls of the once crowded residence of the clergy re-echo strangely the footsteps of the few servants.

By the embers the man of the sword and he of the gown lament these days. They are pregnant with trouble. The directing influence of the Padres is now absent. Peralta confides to Hinojosa that jealousy and intrigue will soon breed civil warfare. Micheltorrena is now conspiring against Alvarado. Peralta seeks a secluded home in the forests of Mariposa. He desires to gain a stronghold where he can elude both domestic and foreign foes.

"Don Miguel," the padre begins, "in our records we have notes of a Philippine galleon, the SAN AUGUSTIN, laden with the spoils of the East. She was washed ashore in 1579, tempest tossed at the Golden Gate. Viscaino found this wreck in

1602. Now I have studied much. I feel that the Americans will gradually work west, overland, and will rule us. Our brothers destroyed the missions. They would have Christianized the patient Indians, teaching them industries. Books tell me even the Apaches were peaceful till the Spanish soldiers attacked them. Now from their hills they defy the whole Mexican army." The good priest sighed. "Our work is ruined. I shall lay my bones here, but I see the trade of the East following that lonely wrecked galleon, and a young people growing up. The Dons will go." Bestowing a blessing on his guest, the padre sought his breviary. Priest and soldier slept in quiet. To-day the old padre's vision is realized. The treasures of the East pour into the Golden Gate. His simple heart would have been happy to know that thousands of Catholics pause reverently at his tomb covered with the roses of Santa Clara.

CHAPTER II.

AT THE PRESIDIO OF SAN FRANCISCO.---WEDDING CHIMES FROM
THE MISSION DOLORES.---LAGUNITAS RANCHO.

Golden lances pierced the haze over the hills, waking the padre betimes next morning. Already the sacristan was ringing his call.
The caballeros were kneeling when the Indian choir raised the chants. When mass ended, the "mozos" scoured the potrero, driving in the chargers. Commandante Peralta lingered a half hour at the priest's house. There, the flowers bloom in a natural tangle.

The quadrangle is deserted; while the soldier lingers, the priest runs over the broken chain of missions. He recounts the losses of Mother Church---seventeen missions in Lower California, twenty-one all told in Alta California, with all their riches confiscated. The "pious fund"--monument of the faithful dead--swept into the Mexican coffers. The struggle of intellect against political greed looks hopeless.

The friends sadly exchange fears. The bridegroom reminds the priest that shelter will be always his at the new rancho.

Peralta's plunging roan frets now in the "paseo." After a blessing, the Commandante briskly pushes over the oak openings, toward the marshes of the bay. His shadow, the old sergeant, ambles alongside. Pearly mists rise from the bay. Far to the northeast Mount Diablo uplifts its peaked summit. From the western ridges balsamic odors of redwoods float lightly.

Down by the marshes countless snipe, duck, geese, and curlew tempt the absent sportsman.

The traveller easily overtakes his escort. They have been trying all the arts of the vaquero. Past hills where startled buck and doe gaze until they gracefully bound into the covert, the riders pursue the lonely trail. Devoid of talk, they follow the shore, sweeping for six hours over the hills, toward the Mission Dolores. Another hour brings them to the Presidio.

This fort is the only safeguard of the State; a battery of ship guns is a mere symbol of power.

In the quadrangle two companies of native soldiers and a detachment of artillery constitute the feeble garrison. Don Miguel Peralta canters up to the Commandante's residence.

Evening parade is over. Listless sentinels drag over their posts with the true military laziness.

Peralta is intent upon affairs both of head and heart. His comrade, the Commandante, sits late with him in sage counsel. A train follows from Monterey, with stores for the settlement. Sundry cargoes of gifts for the fair Juanita, which the one Pacific emporium of Monterey alone could furnish, are moving. Miguel bears an order for a detail of a sergeant and ten men, a nucleus of a force in the San Joaquin. Barges and a shallop are needed to transport supplies up the river. By couriers, invitations are to be sent to all the clans not represented at the Monterey gathering.

The priests of the mission must also be visited and prepared for the wedding. Miguel's heart softens. He thinks of his bright-eyed Californian bride waiting in her home, soon to be Seftora Peralta.

In twenty days Don Miguel arranges his inland voyage. While his assistants speed abroad, he pays visits of ceremony to the clergy and his lovely bride.

The great day of his life arrives. Clad in rich uniform, he crosses to the eastern shore. A breeze of morning moves. The planet of love is on high. It is only the sun tinting the bay with golden gleams. Never a, steamer yet has ploughed these silent waters.

Morning's purple folds Tamalpais in a magic mantle. Rolling surges break on the bar outside the Golden Gate. Don Miguel, attended by friends, receives his bride, the Rose of Alameda. Shallops wait. The merry party sails for the western shore. Fluttering flags decorate this little navy of San Francisco.

Merry laughter floats from boat to boat. The tinkle of the guitar sounds gaily. Two hours end this first voyage of a new life.

At the embarcadero of Yerba Buena the party descends. They are met by a procession of all the notables of the mission and Presidio. Hardy riders and ladies, staid matrons and blooming senoritas, have gathered also from Santa Clara, Napa, and Sonoma. The one government brig is crowded with a merry party from Monterey.

The broad "camino real" sweeps three miles over sand dunes to the mission. Past willow-shaded lakes, through stunted live-oak groves, the wedding cavalcade advances. The poverty of the "mozo" admits of a horse. Even the humblest admirer of Don Miguel to-day is in the saddle. No one in California walks.

With courtly grace the warrior rides by his bride. Juanita Castro is a true Spanish senorita. Blest with the beauty of youth and the modesty of the Castilian, the Rose of Alameda has the blush of her garden blossoms on her virgin cheek. She walks a queen. She rides as only the maids of Alta California can.

The shining white walls of the mission are near. Eager eyes watch in the belfry whence the chimes proclaim the great event. To the west the Coast Range hides the blue Pacific. Rolling sand hills mask the Presidio. East and south the panorama of shore and mountain frames the jewel of the West, fair San Francisco bay.

Soldiers, traders, dull-eyed Indians, and joyous retainers crowd the approaches.

The cortege halts at the official residence. Soon the dark-eyed bride is arrayed in her simple white robes. Attended by her friends, Juanita enters the house of the Lord. Don Luis Castro supports the bride, who meets at the altar her spouse. Priests and their trains file in. The fateful words are said.

Then the girl-wife on her liege lord's arm enters the residence of the Padres; a sumptuous California breakfast awaits the "gente de razon."

Clangor of bells, firing of guns, vivas and popular clamor follow the party.

The humbler people are all regaled at neighboring "casas."

In the home of the Padres, the nuptial feast makes glad the gathered notables. The clergy are the life of this occasion. They know when to lay by the austerity of official robes. From old to young, all hearts are merry.

Alcaldes, officials, and baronial rancheros--all have gathered for this popular wedding.

Carrillos, Del Valles, Sepulvedas, Arguellos, Avilas, Ortegas, Estradas, Martinez, Aguirres and Dominguez are represented by chiefs and ladies.

Beakers of mission vintages are drained in honor of the brave and fair. When the sun slopes toward the hills, the leaders escort the happy couple to the Presidio. The Commandante and his bride begin their path in life. It leads toward that yet unbuilt home in the wild hills of Mariposa. With quaint garb, rich trappings, and its bright color, the train lends an air of middle-age romance to the landscape.

Knightly blood, customs, and manners linger yet in the "dolce far niente" of this unwaked paradise of the Occident. Sweetly sound the notes of the famous sacred mission bell. It was cast and blessed at far Mendoza in Spain, in 1192. Generations and tens of generations have faded into shadowy myths of the past since it waked first the Spanish echoes. Kings and crowns, even countries, have passed into history's shadowy night since it first rang out. The cunning artificer, D. Monterei, piously inscribed it with the name of "San Franisco." Mingled gold and silver alone were melted for its making. Its sacred use saved the precious treasure many times from robbers. Six hundred and fifty years that mellow voice has warned the faithful to prayer. Pride and treasure of the Franciscans, it followed the "conquistadores" to Mexico. It rang its peal solemnly at San Diego, when, on July 1, 1769, the cross of the blessed Redeemer was raised. The shores of California were claimed for God by the apostolic representative, sainted Friar Junipero Serra. In that year two babes were born far over the wild Atlantic, one destined to wrap the world in flame, and the other to break down the mightiest modern empire of the sword. It was the natal year of Napoleon Bonaparte, the child imperially crowned by nature, and that iron chief, Arthur Wellesley, the Duke of Wellington.

The old bell sounded its first call to the faithful on San Francisco Bay, in 1776. It was but a few months after the American colonists gave to wondering humanity their impassioned plea for a world's liberty--the immortal Declaration of the Fourth of July.

No merrier peal ever sounded from its vibrant throat than the rich notes following Miguel Peralta and his lovely Rose of Alameda.

Revelry reigns at the Presidio; Commandante Peralta's quarters are open. Music and brightest eyes mark the closing of this day. In late watches the sentinels remember the feast as they pace their rounds, for none are forgotten in largesse.

Fair Juanita learns to love the dainty title of Senora. Light is her heart as she leaves for the Hills.

Don Miguel's barges already are on the San Joaquin. The cattle have reached their potreros on the Mariposa. Artificer and "peon" are preparing a shelter for the lord of the grant.

Donna Juanita waves her hand in fond adieu as the schooner glides across to Alameda. Here Commandante Miguel has a report of the arrival of his trains.

From the Castros' home, Juanita rides out toward the San Joaquin. Great commotion enlivens the hacienda. Pack-trains are laden with every requisite--tents, hammocks, attendants, waiting-women and retainers are provided.

Winding out of the meadows of the Alameda, eastwardly over the Coast Range defiles, the train advances. Even here "los ladrones" (thieves of animals) are the forerunners of foreign robbers. Guards watch the bride's slumbers.

Star-lit nights make the journey easy. It is the rainless summer time; no sound save the congress of the coyotes, or the notes of the mountain owl, disturbs the dreams of the campers.

Don Miguel, in happiest mood, canters beside his wife. The party has its scouts far in advance. Resting places in fragrant woods, with pure brooks and tender grass, mark the care of the outriders.

Over the Coast Range Juanita finds a land of delightful promise. Far away the rich valley of the San Joaquin sweeps. Rolling hills lie on either side, golden tinted with the ripening wild oats. Messengers join the party with auspicious reports.

Down the San Joaquin plains the train winds. Here Senora Peralta is in merry mood; hundreds of stately elk swing tossing antlers, dashing away to the willows. Gray deer spring over brook and fallen tree, led by some giant leader. Pigeons, grouse, doves, and quail cleave the air with sudden alarm. Gorgeous in his painted plumage, the wood duck whirrs away over the slow gliding San Joaquin. Swan and wild geese cover the little islands.

There are morning vocal concerts of a feathered orchestra. They wake the slumbering bride long before Don Miguel calls his swarthy retainers to the day's march.

By night, in the valley, the sentinels watch for the yellow California lions, who delight to prey on the animals of the train. Wild-cats, lynx, the beaver and raccoon scuttle away surprised by this invasion of Nature's own game preserves.

It is with some terror that the young wife sees a display of native horsemanship. Lumbering across the pathway of the train a huge grizzly bear attracts the dare-devils. Bruin rises on his haunches; he snorts in disdain. A quickly cast lariat encircles one paw. He throws himself down. Another lasso catches his leg. As he rolls and tugs, other fatal loops drop, as skilfully aimed as if he were only a helpless bullock. Growling, rolling, biting, and tearing, he cannot break or loosen the rawhide ropes. When he madly tries to pull in one, the agile horses strain upon the others. He is firmly entangled. The giant bear is tightly bound.

Donna Juanita, her lord by her side, laughs at the dreaded "oso." She enjoys the antics of the horsemen. They sport with their enemy. After the fun ends, Bruin receives a gunshot. Choice cuts are added to the camp menu.

The bear, panther, and rattlesnake are the only dangers of the Californian woods.

Days of travel bring the hills of Mariposa into view. Here the monarchs of the forest rise in air; their wild harps are swept by the cool breezes of the Sierras. Tall, stately redwoods, swathed in rich, soft, fibrous bark, tower to the skies. Brave oaks spread their arms to shelter the doe and her fawns. The madrona, with greenest leaf and pungent berry, stands here. Hazels, willows, and cottonwoods follow the water. Bald knolls are studded with manzanita, its red berry in harvest now. Sturdy groves of wild plum adorn the hillsides. Grouse and squirrel enjoy their annual feast.

The journey is over. When the train winds around a sweeping range, Don Miguel nears his wife. The San Joaquin is studded with graceful clumps of evergreen. In its bosom a lake shines like a diamond. The Don uncovers smilingly. "Mi querida, there lies your home, Lagunitas," he murmurs.

Sweet Juanita's eyes beam on her husband. She says softly, "How beautiful!"

It is truly a royal domain. From the lake the ten leagues square of the Commandante's land are a panorama of varying beauties. Stretching back into the pathless forests, game, timber, wood, and building stones are at hand; a never-failing water supply for thousands of cattle is here. To the front, right, and left, hill pastures and broad fields give every variety of acreage.

Blithely the young wife spurs her favorite steed over the turf. She nears the quarters. The old sergeant is the seneschal of this domain. He greets the new arrivals.

With stately courtesy the Commandante lifts his bride from her charger. The hegira is over. The occupation of arranging abodes for all is the first task. Already the cattle, sheep, and horses are fattening on the prairie grasses. Peons are sawing lumber. A detachment is making bricks for the houses. These are one-storied mansions with wide porches, beloved by the Californians; to-day the most comfortable homes in the West. Quaintly superstitious, the natives build so for fear of earthquakes. Corrals, pens, and sheds have been first labors of the advance guard. The stores and supplies are all housed.

Don Miguel left the choice of the mansion site to his Juanita. Together they visit the different points of vantage. Soon the hacienda rises in solid, fort-like simplicity.

The bride at Lagunitas strives to aid her companion. She shyly expresses her preferences. All is at her bidding.

Don Miguel erects his ranch establishment in a military style. It is at once a square stronghold and mansion shaded with ample porches. Corrals for horses, pens for sheep, make up his constructions for the first year. Already the herds are increasing under the eyes of his retainers.

The Commandante has learned that no manual work can be expected of his Californian followers, except equestrian duties of guarding and riding.

A flash of mother-wit leads him to bring a hundred mission Indians from the bay. They bear the brunt of mechanical toil.

Autumn finds Lagunitas Rancho in bloom. Mild weather favors all. Stores and supplies are brought from San Francisco Bay.

Don Miguel establishes picket stations reaching to the Castro Rancho.

Save that Juanita Peralta sees no more the glories of the Golden Gate, her life is changed only by her new, married relation. A few treasures of her girlhood are the sole reminders of her uneventful springtime.

Rides through the forests, and canters over the grassy meadows with her beloved Miguel, are her chiefest pleasures. Some little trading brings in the Indians of the Sierras. It amuses the young Donna to see the bartering of game, furs, forest nuts, wild fruits and fish for the simple stores of the rancho. No warlike cavaliers of the plains are these, with Tartar blood in their veins, from Alaskan migration or old colonization. They have not the skill and mysterious arts of the Aztecs.

These Piute Indians are the lowest order of indigenous tree dwellers. They live by the chase. Without manufactures, with no language, no arts, no agriculture, no flocks or herds, these wretches, clad in the skins of the minor animals, are God's meanest creatures. They live on manzanita berry meal, pine-nuts, and grasshoppers. Bows and flint-headed arrows are their only weapons. They snare the smaller animals. The defenceless deer yield to their stealthy tracking. The giant grizzly and panther affright them. They cannot battle with "Ursus ferox."

Unable to cope with the Mexican intruders, these degraded tribes are also an easy prey to disease. They live without general intercourse, and lurk in the foothills, or hide in the canons.

Juanita finds the Indian women peaceable, absolutely ignorant, and yet tender to their offspring. The babes are carried in wicker baskets on their backs. A little weaving and basket-making comprise all their feminine arts. Rudest skin clothing covers their stunted forms.

Don Miguel encourages the visits of these wild tribes. He intends to use them as a fringe of faithful retainers between him and the Americans. They will warn him of any approach through the Sierras of the accursed Yankee.

The Commandante, reared in a land without manufactures or artisans, regarding only his flocks and herds, cherishes his military pride in firmly holding the San Joaquin for the authorities. He never turns aside to examine the resources of his domain. The degraded character of the Indians near him prevents any knowledge of the great interior. They do not speak the language of his semi-civilized mission laborers from the Coast Range. They cannot communicate with the superior tribes of the North and East. All their dialects are different.

Vaguely float in his memory old stories of the giant trees and the great gorge of the Yosemite. He will visit yet the glistening and secret summits of the Sierras.

Weeks run into months. Comfort and plenty reign at Lagunitas. With his wife by his side, Miguel cons his occasional despatches. He promises the Seflora that the spring shall see a chapel erected. When he makes the official visit to the Annual Council, he will bring a padre, at once friend, spiritual father, and physician. It is the first sign of a higher life--the little chapel of Mariposa.

Winter winds sway the giant pines of the forests. Rains of heaven swell the San Joaquin. The summer golden brown gives way to the velvety green of early spring.

Juanita meekly tells her beads. With her women she waits the day when the bell shall call to prayer in Mariposa.

Wandering by Lagunitas, the wife strays in fancy to far lands beyond the ocean. The books of her girlhood have given her only a misty idea of Europe. The awe with which she has listened to the Padres throws a glamour of magic around these recitals of that fairy world beyond the seas.

Her life is bounded by the social horizon of her family circle; she is only the chatelaine. Her domain is princely, but no hope clings in her breast of aught beside a faded middle age. Her beauty hides itself under the simple robe of the Californian matron. Visitors are rare in this lovely wilderness. The annual rodeo will bring the vaqueros together. Some travelling officials may reach the San Joaquin. The one bright possibility of her life is a future visit to the seashore.

Spring casts its mantle of wild flowers again over the hillocks. The rich grass waves high in the potreros; the linnets sing blithely in the rose-bushes. Loyal Don Miguel, who always keeps his word, girds himself for a journey to the distant Presidio. The chapel is finished. He will return with the looked-for padre.

Leaving the sergeant in command, Don Miguel, with a few followers, speeds to the seashore. Five days' swinging ride suffices the soldier to reach tide-water. He is overjoyed to find that his relatives have determined to plant a family stronghold on the San Joaquin. This will give society to the dark-eyed beauty by the Lagunitas who waits eagerly for her Miguel's return.

At the Presidio the Commandante is feasted. In a few days his business is over. Riding over to the Mission Dolores, he finds a missionary priest from Acapulco. He is self-devoted to labor. Father Francisco Ribaut is only twenty-five years of age. Born in New Orleans, he has taken holy orders. After a stay in Mexico, the young enthusiast reaches the shores of the distant Pacific.

Commandante Miguel is delighted. Francisco Ribaut is of French blood, graceful and kindly. The Fathers of the mission hasten to provide the needs of Lagunitas chapel.

The barges are loaded with supplies, councils and business despatched. Padre Francisco and Don Miguel reach the glens of Mariposa in the lovely days when bird, bud, and blossom make Lagunitas a fairyland. In the mind of the veteran but one care lingers--future war. Already the feuds of Alvarado and Micheltorrena presage a series of domestic broils. Don Miguel hears that foreigners are plotting to return to the coast; they will come back under the protection of foreign war-ships. As his horse bounds over the turf, the soldier resolves to keep out of this coming conflict; he will guard his hard-won heritage. By their camp fire, Padre Francisco has told him of the Americans wrenching Texas away from Mexico. The news of the world is imparted to him. He asks the padre if the Gringos can ever reach the Pacific.

"As sure as those stars slope to the west," says the priest, pointing to Orion, gleaming jewel-like in the clear skies of the Californian evening.

The don muses. This prophecy rankles in his heart. He fears to ask further. He fears these Yankees.

Joy reigns at Lagunitas! A heartfelt welcome awaits the priest, a rapturous greeting for Don Miguel. The grassy Alamedas are starred with golden poppies. Roses adorn the garden walks of the young wife. Her pensive eyes have watched the valley anxiously for her lord.

Padre Francisco hastens to consecrate the chapel. The Virgin Mother spreads her sainted arms on high. A school for the Indians soon occupies the priest.

Months roll around. The peace and prosperity of the rancho are emulated by the new station in the valley.

Don Miguel rides over the mountains often in the duties of his position. Up and down the inland basin bronzed horsemen sweep over the untenanted regions, locating new settlements. San Joaquin valley slowly comes under man's dominion.

Patriot, pioneer, and leader, the Commandante travels from Sutter's Fort to Los Angeles. He goes away light-hearted. The young wife has a bright-eyed girl to fondle when the chief is in the saddle.

Happiness fills the parents' hearts. The baptism occasions the greatest feast of Lagunitas. But, from the coast, as fall draws near, rumors of trouble disturb the San Joaquin.

Though the Russians are about to leave the seacoast, still Swiss Sutter has taken foothold on the Sacramento. The adherents of Micheltorrena and Alvarado are preparing for war in the early spring. To leave Lagunitas is impossible. The Indian tribes are untrustworthy. They show signs of aggressiveness. Father Ribaut finds the Indians of the Sierras a century behind those of the coast. They are devoid of spiritual ideas. Contact with traders, and association with wild sea rovers, have given the Indians of the shore much of the groundwork of practical civilization.

To his alarm, Don Miguel sees the Indians becoming treacherous. He discovers they make voyages to the distant posts, where they obtain guns and ammunition.

In view of danger, the Commandante trains his men. The old soldier sighs to think that the struggle may break out between divided factions of native Californians. The foreigners may gain foothold in California while its real owners quarrel.

The second winter at Lagunitas gives way to spring. Rapidly increasing herds need for their care all the force of the ranch.

From the coast plentiful supplies provided by the Commandante arrive. With them comes the news of the return of the foreigners. They are convoyed by a French frigate, and on the demand of the British consul at Acapulco they are admitted. This is grave news.

Donna Juanita and the padre try to smooth the gloomy brow of Don Miguel. All in vain. The "pernicious foreigner" is once more on the shores of Alta California. The Mexican eagle flutters listlessly over the sea gates of the great West. The serpent coils of foreign conspiracy are twining around it.

CHAPTER III.

A MISSING SENTINEL.---FREMONT'S CAMP.

Quien Vive!" A sentinel's challenge rings out. The sounds are borne away on the night wind sweeping Gavilan Peak. No response. March breezes drive the salty fog from Monterey Bay into the eyes of the soldier shivering in the silent hours before dawn.

"Only a coyote or a mountain wolf," mutters Maxime Valois. He resumes his tramp along the rocky ramparts of the Californian Coast Range. His eyes are strained to pierce the night. He waits, his finger on the trigger of his Kentucky rifle.

Surely something was creeping toward him from the chaparral. No: another illusion. Pride keeps him from calling for help. Three-score dauntless "pathfinders" are sleeping here around intrepid Fremont.

It is early March in 1846. Over in the valley the herd-guard watch the animals. "No, not an Indian," mutters the sentinel. "They would stampede the horses at once. No Mexican would brave death here," muses Valois.

Only a boy of twenty, he is a veteran already. He feels for his revolver and knife. He knows he can defy any sneaking Californian.

"It must be some beast," he concludes, as he stumbles along the wind-swept path. Maxime Valois dreams of his far-away home on the "Lower Coast," near New Orleans. He wanders along, half asleep. This hillside is no magnolia grove.

It is but a year since he joined the great "Pathfinder's" third voyage over the lonely American Desert. He has toiled across to the Great Salt Lake, down the dreary Humboldt, and over the snowy Sierras.

Down by Walker's Lake the "pathfinders" have crept into the valley of California. As he shields his face from biting winds, he can see again the panorama of the great plains, billowy hills, and broad vistas, tantalizing in their deceptive nearness. Thundering herds of buffalo and all the wild chivalry of the Sioux and Cheyennes sweep before him. The majestic forests of the West have darkened his way. The Great Salt Lake, a lonely inland sea; Lake Tahoe, a beautiful jewel set in snowy mountains; and its fairy sisters near Truckee--all these pass before his mental vision.

But the youth is tired. Onward ever, like the "Wandering Jew," still to the West with Fremont.

Pride and hot southern blood nerve him in conflicts with the fierce savages. Dashing among the buffalo, he has ridden in many a wild chase where a single stumble meant death. His rifle has rung the knell of elk and bear, of wolf and panther.

These varied excitements repaid the long days of march, but the Louisianian is mercurial. Homeward wander his thoughts.

Hemmed in, with starvation near, in the Sierras, he welcomes this forlorn-hope march to the sea. Fremont with a picked squad has swept down to Sutter's Fort to send succor to the remaining "voyageurs."

But the exploring march to Oregon, and back East by the southern road, appalls him. He is tired now. He would be free. As a mere volunteer, he can depart as soon as the frigate PORTSMOUTH arrives at Monterey. He is tired of Western adventures. Kit Carson, Aleck Godey, and Dick Owens have taught him their border lore. They all love the young Southerner.

The party are now on the defensive. Maxime Valois knows that General Jose Castro has forbidden them to march toward Los Angeles. Governor Pio Pico is gathering his army to overawe "los Americanos."

Little does Valois think that the guns of Palo Alto and Resaca de la Palma will soon usher in the Mexican war. The "pathfinders" are cut off from home news. He will join the American fleet, soon expected.

He will land at Acapulco, and ride over to the city of Mexico. From Vera Cruz he can reach New Orleans and the old Valois plantation, "Belle Etoile." The magnolias' fragrance call him back to-night.

Another rustle of the bushes. Clinging to his rifle, he peers into the gloom. How long these waiting hours! The gleaming stars have dipped into the far Pacific.

The weird hours of the night watch are ending. Ha! Surely that was a crouching form in the arroyo. Shall he fire? No. Another deception of night. How often the trees have seemed to move toward him! Dark beings fancifully seemed to creep upon him. Nameless terrors always haunt these night hours.

To be laughed at on rousing the camp? Never! But his inner nature tingles now with the mysterious thrill of danger. Eagerly he scans his post. The bleak blasts have benumbed his senses.

Far away to the graceful groves and Gallic beauties of Belle Etoile his truant thoughts will fly once more. He wonders why he threw up his law studies under his uncle, Judge Valois, to rove in this wilderness.

Reading the exploits of Fremont fascinated the gallant lad.

As his foot falls wearily, the flame of his enthusiasm flickers very low.

Turning at the end of his post he starts in alarm. Whizz! around his neck settles a pliant coil, cast twenty yards, like lightning. His cry for help is only a gurgle. The lasso draws tight. Dark forms dart from the chaparral. A rough hand stifles him. His arms are bound. A gag is forced in his mouth. Dragged into the bushes, his unknown captors have him under cover.

The boy feels with rage and shame his arms taken from his belt. His rifle is gone. A knife presses his throat. He understands the savage hiss, "Vamos adelante, Gringo!" The party dash through the chaparral.

Valois, bruised and helpless, reflects that his immediate death seems not to be his captors' will. Will the camp be attacked? Who are these? The bitter words show them to be Jose Castro's scouts. Is there a force near? Will they attack? All is silent.

In a few minutes an opening is reached. Horses are there. Forced to mount, Maxime Valois rides away, a dozen guards around him. Grim riders in scrapes and broad sombreros are his escort. The guns on their shoulders and their jingling machetes prove them native cavalry.

For half an hour Valois is busy keeping his seat in the saddle. These are no amiable captors. The lad's heart is sad. He speaks Spanish as fluently as his native French. Every word is familiar.

A camp-fire flickers in the live-oaks. He is bidden to dismount. The lair of the guerillas is safe from view of the "pathfinders."

The east shows glimmers of dawn. The prisoner warms his chilled bones at the fire. He sees a score of bronzed faces scowling at him. Preparations for a meal are hastened. A swarthy soldier, half-bandit, half-Cossack in bearing, tells him roughly to eat. They must be off.

Maxime already realizes he has been designedly kidnapped. His capture may provide information for Castro's flying columns. These have paralleled their movements, from a distance, for several weeks. Aware of the ferocity of these rancheros, he obeys instantly each order. He feigns ignorance of the language. Tortillas, beans, some venison, with water, make up the meal. It is now day. Valois eats. He knows his ordeal. He throws himself down for a rest. He divines the journey will be hurried. A score of horses are here tied to the trees. In a half hour half of these are lazily saddled. Squatted around, the soldiers keep a morose silence, puffing the corn-husk cigarette. The leader gives rapid directions. Valois now recalls his locality as best he can. Fremont's camp on Gavilan Peak commands the Pajaro, Salinas, and Santa Clara. A bright sun peeps over the hills. If taken west, his destination must be Monterey; if south, probably Los Angeles; and if north, either San Francisco Bay or the Sacramento, the headquarters of the forces of Alta California.

Dragged like a beast from his post, leaving the lines unguarded! What a disgrace! Bitterly does he remember his reveries of the home he may never again see.

The party mounts. Two men lead up a tame horse without bridle. The leader approaches and searches him. All his belongings fill the saddle-pouches of the chief. A rough gesture bids him mount the horse, whose lariat is tied to a guard's saddle. Valois rages in despair as the guard taps his own revolver. Death on the slightest suspicious movement, is the meaning of that sign.

With rough adieus the party strike out eastwardly toward the San Joaquin. Steadily following the lope of the taciturn leader, they wind down Pacheco Pass. Valois' eyes rove over the beautiful hills of the Californian coast. Squirrels chatter on the live-oak branches, and the drumming grouse noisily burst out of their manzanita feeding bushes.

Onward, guided by distant peak and pass, they thread the trail. No word is spoken save some gruff order. Maxime's captors have the hang-dog manner of the Californian. They loll on their mustangs, lazily worrying out the long hours. A rest is taken for food at noon. The horses are herded an hour or so and the advance resumed.

Nightfall finds Valois in a squalid adobe house, thirty miles from Gavilan Peak. An old scrape is thrown him. His couch is the mud floor.

The youth sleeps heavily. His last remembrance is the surly wish of a guard that Commandante Miguel Peralta will hang the accursed Gringo.

At daybreak he is roused by a carelessly applied foot. The dejected "pathfinder" begins his second day of captivity. He fears to converse. He is warned with curses to keep silent. In the long day Maxime concludes that the Mexicans suspect treachery by Captain Fremont's "armed exploration in the name of science."

These officials hate new-comers. Valois had been, like other gilded youth of New Orleans, sent to Paris by his opulent family. He knows the absorbing interest of the South in Western matters. Stern old Tom Benton indicated truly the onward march of the resistless American. In his famous speech, while the senatorial finger pointed toward California, he said with true inspiration: "There is the East; there is the road to India."

All the adventurers of the South are ready to stream to the West. Maxime knows the jealous Californian officials. The particulars of Fremont's voyage of 1842 to the Rockies, and his crossing to California in 1843, are now history. His return on the quest, each time with stronger parties and a more formidable armament, is ominous. It warns the local hidalgos that the closed doors of the West must yield to the daring touch of the American---manifest destiny.

The enemy are hovering around the "pathfinders" entrenched on the hills; they will try to frighten them into return, and drive them out of the regions of Alta California. Some sly Californian may even contrive an Indian attack to obliterate them.

Valois fears not the ultimate fate of the friends he has been torn away from. The adventurous boy knows he will be missed at daybreak. The camp will be on the alert to meet the enemy. Their keen-eyed scouts can read the story of his being lassoed and carried away from the traces of the deed.

The young rover concludes he is to be taken before some superior officer, some soldier charged with defending Upper California. This view is confirmed. Down into the valley of the San Joaquin the feet of the agile mustangs bear the jaded travellers.

They cross the San Joaquin on a raft, swimming their horses. Valois sees nothing yet to hint his impending fate. Far away the rich green billows of spring grass wave in the warm sun. Thousands of elk wander in antlered armies over the meadows. Gay dancing yellow antelope bound over the elastic turf. Clouds of wild fowl, from the stately swan to the little flighty snipe, crowd the tule marshes of this silent river. It is the hunter's paradise. Wild cattle, in sleek condition, toss their heads and point their long, polished horns. Mustangs, fleet as the winds, bound along, disdaining their meaner brethren, bowing under man's yoke. At the occasional mud-walled ranches, vast flocks of fat sheep whiten the hills.

Maxime mentally maps the route he travels. Alas! no chance of escape exists. At the first open attempt a rifle-ball, or a blow from a razor-edged machete, would end his earthly wanderings. Despised, shunned by even the wretched women at the squalid ranchos, he feels utterly alone. The half-naked children timidly flee from him. The wicked eyes of his guards never leave him. He knows a feeling animates the squad, that he would be well off their hands by a use of the first handy limb and a knotted lariat. The taciturn chief watches over him. He guards an ominous silence.

The cavalcade, after seven days, are in sight of the purpled outlines of the sculptured Sierras. They rise heavenward to the sparkling crested pinnacles where Bret Harte's poet fancy sees in long years after the "minarets of snow." Valley oaks give way to the stately pines. Olive masses of enormous redwoods wrap the rising foothills. Groves of laurel, acorn oak, and madrona shelter the clinging panther and the grim warden of the Sierras, the ferocious grizzly bear.

Over flashing, bounding mountain brooks, cut up with great ledges of blue bed rock, they splash. Here the silvery salmon and patrician trout leap out from the ripples to glide into the great hollowed pools, yet the weary cavalcade presses on. Will they never stop?

Maxime Valois' haggard face looks back at him from the mirrored waters of the Cottonwood, the Merced, and the Mariposa. The prisoner sees there only the worn features of his strangely altered self. He catches no gleam of the unreaped golden harvest lying under the feet of the wild mustangs. These are the treasure channels of the golden West.

The mountain gnomes of this mystic wilderness are already in terror lest some fortunate fool may utter the one magic word, "Gold." It will call greedy thousands from the uttermost parts of the earth to break the seals of ages, and burrow far below these mountain bases. Through stubborn granite wall, tough porphyry, ringing quartz, and bedded gnarled gneiss, men will grope for the feathery, fairy veins of the yellow metal.

A feverish quest for gold alone can wake the dreamy "dolce far niente" of the Pacific. God's fairest realm invites the foot of man in vain. Here the yellow grains will be harvested, which buy the smiles of beauty, blunt the sword of justice, and tempt the wavering conscience of young and old. It will bring the human herd to one grovelling level--human swine rooting after the concrete token of power. Here, in later years, the wicked arm of power will be given golden hammers to beat down all before it. Here will that generation arise wherein the golden helmet can dignify the idle and empty pate.

Maxime, now desperate, is ready for any fate. Only let this long ride cease. Sweeping around the hills, for the first time he sees the square courtyard, the walled casas of the rancho of Lagunitas.

By the shores of the flashing mountain lake, with the rich valley sweeping out before it, it lies in peace. The fragrant forest throws out gallant flanking wings of embattled trees. It is the residence of the lord of ten leagues square. This is the great Peralta Rancho.

In wintering in the San Joaquin, Maxime has often heard of the fabulous wealth and power of this inland chieftain. Don Miguel Peralta is Commandante of the San Joaquin. By a fortunate marriage he is related to Jose Castro, the warlike Commandante general of Pio Pico--a man of mark now. Thousands of cattle and horses, with great armies of sheep, are herded by his semi-military vaqueros. The young explorer easily divines now the reason of his abduction.

The party dismounts. While the sergeant seeks the major-domo, Valois' wondering eye gazes on the beauties of lake and forest. Field and garden, bower and rose-laden trellises lie before him. The rich autumn sun will ripen here deep-dyed clusters of the sweet mission grapes. It is a lordly heritage, and yet his prison. Broad porches surround the plaza. There swinging hammocks, saddled steeds, and waiting retainers indicate the headquarters of the Californian Don.

Maxime looks with ill-restrained hatred at his fierce guards. They squat on the steps and eye him viciously. He is under the muzzle of his own pistol. It is their day of triumph.

Dragging across the plaza, with jingling spur, trailing leggings, and sombrero pushed back on his head, the sergeant comes. He points out Maxime to a companion. The new-comer conducts the American prisoner to a roughly furnished room. A rawhide bed and a few benches constitute its equipment. A heavy door is locked on him. The prisoner throws himself on the hard couch and sleeps. He is wakened by an Indian girl bringing food and water. Some blankets are carelessly tossed in by a "mozo." The wanderer sleeps till the birds are carolling loudly in the trees.

Hark! a bell! He springs to the window. Valois sees a little chapel, with its wooden cross planted in front. Is there a priest here? The boy is of the old faith. He looks for a possible friend in the padre. Blessed bell of peace and hope!

Sturdy and serious is the major-domo who briskly enters Valois' room.

"Do you speak Spanish?" he flatly demands in that musical tongue.

"Yes," says Maxime, without hesitation. He knows no subterfuge will avail. His wits must guard his head.

"Give me your name, rank, and story," demands the steward.

Valois briefs his life history.

"You will be taken to the Commandante. I advise you not to forget yourself; you may find a lariat around your neck." With which admonition the major-domo leaves. He tosses Maxime a bunch of cigaritos, and offers him a light ere going, with some show of courtesy.

Valois builds no fallacious hopes on this slender concession. He knows the strange Mexicans. They would postpone a military execution if the condemned asked for a smoke.

Facing his fate, Maxime decides, while crossing the plaza, to conceal nothing. He can honorably tell his story. Foreigners have been gathering in California for years. The Commandante can easily test his disclosures, so lying would be useless. He believes either a British or American fleet will soon occupy California. The signs of the times have been unmistakable since the last return of the foreigners. Will he live to see the day? "Quien sabe?"

Maxime sees a stern man of fifty seated in his official presence room. Commandante Miguel Peralta is clad in his undress cavalry uniform. The sergeant captor is in attendance, while at the door an armed sentinel hovers. This is the wolf's den. Maxime is wary and serious.

"You are a Yankee, young man," begins the soldier. Maxime Valois' Creole blood stirs in his veins.

"I am an American, Senor Commandante, "from New Orleans. No Yankee!" he hotly answers, forgetting prudence. Peralta opens his eyes in vague wonder. No Yankee? He questions the rash prisoner. Valois tells the facts of Fremont's situation, but he firmly says he knows nothing of his future plans.

"Why so?" demands Peralta. "Are you a common soldier?" Maxime explains his position as a volunteer.

A pressing inquest follows. Maxime's frankness touches the Commandante favorably. "I will see you in a day or so. I shall hold you as a prisoner till I know if your chief means war. I may want you as an interpreter if I take the field."

"Sergeant," he commands.

The captor salutes his chief.

"Has this young man told me the truth?"

"As far as I know, Senior Don Miguel," is the reply.

"See that he has all he wants. Keep him watched. If he behaves himself, let him move around. He is not to talk to any one. If he tries to escape, shoot him. If he wants to see me, let me know."

The Commandante lights a Mexican cigar, and signs to the sergeant to remove his prisoner. Maxime sees a score of soldiers wandering around the sunny plaza, where a dozen fleet horses stand saddled. He feels escape is hopeless. As he moves to the door, the chapel bell rings out again, and with a sudden inspiration he halts.

"Senior Commandante, can I see the priest?" he asks.

"What for?" sharply demands the officer.

"I am a Catholic, and would like to talk to him."

Don Miguel Peralta gazes in wonder. "A Gringo and a Catholic! I will tell him to see you."

Valois is reconducted to his abode. He leaves a puzzled Commandante, who cannot believe that any despised "Gringo" can be of the true faith. He has only seen the down-east hide traders, who are regarded as heathen by the orthodox Dons of the Pacific.

Don Miguel knows not that the mariners from Salem and the whalers of New England hold different religious views from the impassioned Creoles of the Crescent City.

The prisoner's eye catches the black robe of the priest fluttering among the rose walks of the garden. Walking with him is a lady, while a pretty girl of seven or eight years plays in the shady bowers.

The sergeant gruffly fulfils the orders of his chief. Maxime is given the articles needed for his immediate use. He fears now, at least, a long captivity, but a war may bring his doom suddenly on him.

There is an air of authority in Miguel Peralta's eye, which is a guarantee of honor, as well as a personal menace. His detention will depend on the actions of the besieged Fremont.

Valois prays that bloodshed may not occur. His slender chances hang now on a peaceable solution of the question of this Yankee visit.

There have been days in the dreary winter, when Maxime Valois has tried to divine the future of the magnificent realm he traverses. His education and birth gave him the companionship of the scientific subordinates of the party. His services claimed friendly treatment of the three engineer officers in command. That the American flag will finally reach the western ocean he doubts not. Born in the South, waited upon by patrimonial slaves, he is attached to the "peculiar institution" which throws its dark shadow on the flag of this country. Already statesmen of the party have discussed the question of the extension of slavery. Maxime Valois knows that the line of the Missouri Compromise will here give a splendid new southern star to the flag south of 36 deg 30 min. In the long, idle hours of camp chat, he has laughingly pledged he would bring a band of sable retainers to this western terra incognita. He dreamed of establishing a great plantation, but the prison cell shatters these foolish notions.

He marvels at his romantic year's experience. Was it to languish in a lonely prison life on the far Pacific, that he left the gay circle at far-off Belle Etoile? Worn with fatigue, harassed with loneliness, a prisoner among strangers, Maxime Valois' heart fails him. Sinking on the couch, he buries his head in his hands.

No present ray of hope cheers the solitary American. He raises his eyes to see the thoughtful face of a young priest at the door of his prison room.

CHAPTER IV.

HELD BY THE ENEMY.--"THE BEAR FLAG."

The padre bends searching eyes on the youth as the door opens. The priest's serious face heightens his thirty-five years. He is worn by toil as a missionary among the tribes of the Gila--the Apaches and the wild and brutal Mojaves. Here, among the Piute hill dwellers, his task is hopeless. This spiritual soil is indeed stony. Called from the society of Donna Juanita and his laughing pupil, merry Dolores, he comes to test the religious faith of the young freebooter--Yankee and Catholic at once.

Maxime's downcast appearance disarms the padre. Not such a terrible fire-eater! He savors not of infidel Cape Cod.

"My son, you are in trouble," softly says the padre. It is the first kind word Maxime has heard. The boy's heart is full, so he speaks freely to the mild-mannered visitor. Padre Francisco listens to the recital. His eyes sparkle strangely when Valois speaks of New Orleans.

"Then you understand French?" cries the padre joyously.

"It is my native tongue," rejoins Valois proudly.

"My name before I took orders was Francois Ribaut," says the overjoyed father. "Hold! I must see Don Miguel. I am a Frenchman myself." He flies over the plaza, his long robe fluttering behind him. His quickened steps prove a friendly interest. Maxima's heart swells within him. The beloved language has unlocked the priestly heart.

In five minutes the curate is back. "Come with me, 'mon fils,'" he says. Guided by the priest, Maxime leaves his prison, its unlocked door swinging open. They reach the head of the square.

By the chapel is Padre Francisco's house, school-room, and office. A sacristy chamber connects chapel and dwelling.

The missionary leads the way to the chancel, and points to the altar rails.

"I will leave you," he whispers.

There, on his knees, where the wondering Indians gaze in awe of the face on the Most Blessed Virgin, Maxime thanks God for this friend raised up to him in adversity.

He rejoins the missionary on the rose-shaded porch. In friendly commune he answers every eager query of the padre. The priest finds Maxime familiar with Paris. It is manna in the wilderness to this lonely man of God to speak of the beloved scenes of his youth.

After the Angelus, Maxime rests in the swinging hammock. The priest confers with the Commandante. His face is hopeful on returning. "My poor boy," he says, "I gained one favor. Don Miguel allows me to keep you here. He loves not the American. Promise me, my son, on the blessed crucifix, that you will not escape. You must not aid the American troops in any way; on this hangs your life."

These words show that under the priest's frock beats yet the gallant heart of the French gentleman. Maxima solemnly promises. The good father sits under the vines, a happy man.

Day by day the new friends stroll by the lake. Seated where below them the valley shines in all its bravery of spring, surrounded with the sighing pines, Padre Francisco tells of the resentment of the Californians toward all Americans. They are all "Gringos," "thieving Yankees."

"Be careful, my son, even here. Our wild vaqueros have waylaid and tortured to death some foreigners. The Diggers, Utes, and Hill Indians butcher any wanderer. Keep closely under my protection. Don Miguel adores Donna Juanita, sweet Christian lady! She will lend me aid; you are thus safe. If your people leave the Hawk's Peak without a battle, our cavalry will not take the field; we expect couriers momentarily. Should fighting begin, Don Miguel will lead his troops. He will then take you as guide or interpreter; God alone must guard you." The man of peace crosses himself in sadness. "Meanwhile, I will soften the heart of Don Miguel."

Maxime learns of the padre's youth. Educated for the Church after a boyhood spent in Paris, he sailed for Vera Cruz. He has been for years among the Pacific

Indians. He familiarized himself with the Spanish language and this western life in Mexico. Stout-hearted Padre Francisco worked from mission to mission till he found his self-chosen field in California.

The "pathfinder" sees the decadence of priestly influence. Twenty-one flourishing missions have been secularized by Governor Hijar since 1834. Now the superior coast tribes are scattered, and the civilizing work since 1769 is all lost to human progress. In glowing words Padre Francisco tells of idle farms, confiscated flocks, and ruined works of utility. Beautiful San Luis Rey is crumbling to decay. Its bells hang silent. The olive and vine scatter their neglected fruits. The Padres are driven off to Mexico. The pious fund is in profane coffers. San Juan Capistrano shines out a lonely ruin in the southern moonlight. The oranges of San Gabriel now feed only the fox and coyote. Civil dissension and wars of ambitious leaders follow the seizure of the missions. Strangers have pillaged the religious settlements. All is relapsing into savagery. In a few stations, like Monterey, Santa Clara, Santa Barbara, and Yerba Buena, a lonely shepherd watches a diminished flock; but the grand mission system is ruined.

"Does not the Government need the missions?" queries Maxime.

"Ah! my son, Sonoma and San Rafael are kept up to watch the Russians at Fort Ross. Sutter menaces us at New Helvetia. I can see the little cloud of the future, which will break one day in storm."

"Whence comes it, father?" queries the prisoner.

"From the United States," replies the padre. "Our whole political system is paralyzed. The Americans have supported the Texans in battle. That splendid land is dropping away from Mexico. We will lose this glorious land, and our beloved flag will go down forever. The Government sleeps, and the people will be ruined. There are two thousand scattered foreigners here to-day. They gain daily: we weaken hourly. When your people in numbers follow such leaders as your gallant captain over the plains, we will lose this land also."

The padre sighed. His years of hard endeavor are wasted, the fruits are wanting, his labor is vain.

"Why is not your Government more vigorous?" says the stranger.

"My son, our pastoral life builds up no resources of this great land. The young men will not work; they only ride around. Flocks and herds alone will not develop this paradise. The distance from Mexico has broken the force of the laws. In fifty-five years of Spanish rule and twenty-three more of Mexican, we have had twenty-two different rulers. The old families have lost their loyalty, and they now fight each other for supremacy. All is discord and confusion in Alta California."

"And the result?" questions Maxime.

"Either England or the United States will sweep us off forever," mourns the padre. He addresses himself to his beads. Bright sunlight wakes Maxime with the birds. The matin bell rings out. He rises refreshed by the father's hospitality.

During the day Valois measures the generosity of Padre Francisco. A few treasured books enable Maxime to amuse himself. As yet he dares not venture out of the garden.

The sound of clattering hoofs causes the prisoner to drop his volume. He sits enjoying a flask of ripe claret, for he is broken down and needs recruiting.

A courier spurs his foam-covered horse up to the Commandante's porch. Panting and staggering, the poor beast shows the abuse of a merciless rider. The messenger's heels are adorned with two inch spiked wheels, bloody with spurring the jaded beast.

Peace or war? Maxime's heart beats violently. He prudently withdraws. The wild soldiery gather on the plaza. His guards are there with his own weapons, proudly displayed.

The Southerner chafes in helplessness. Could he but have his own horse and those weapons, he would meet any two of them in the open. They are now clamoring against the Gringos. Soon the courier reappears. All is bustle and shouting. Far away, on the rich knolls, Maxime sees fleet riders gathering up the horses nearest the ranch. When Padre Francisco arrives from his morning lessons, a troop of vaqueros are arrayed on the plaza.

"The news?" eagerly queries Maxime.

"Thanks be to God!" says the padre, "Fremont has broken camp after five days' stay at the Hawk's Peak. He is moving north. There has been skirmishing, but no battle. Don Miguel is sending a company to watch their march, and will attack if they menace any of our sentinels. The Americans may, however, go into Oregon, or back over the mountains. The Commandante will keep his main force in the valley. If they turn back, he will dispute their passage. You will be kept here."

Valois gazes on the departure. He takes an informal adieu of those trusty weapons which have been with him in so many scenes of danger.

The last files sweep down the trail. Lagunitas Lake smiles peacefully from its bowers. The war clouds have rolled north.

As days glide by, the priest and his youthful charge grow into each other's hearts. Padre Francisco is young enough still to have some flowers of memory blossoming over the stone walls of his indomitable heart. Maxime learns the story of his early life. He listens to the padre's romantic recitals of the different lands he has strayed over. Couriers arrive daily with news of Fremont's whirling march northward. The explorer travels like a Cossack in simplicity. He rides with the sweep of the old Tartars. Cool, wary and resolute, the "Pathfinder" manoeuvres to baffle clumsy Castro. He may yet elude his pursuers, or cut his way out.

Don Miguel steadily refuses to see Maxime. Through the padre, Maxime receives any necessary messages or questions.

The Louisianian learns that all the foreigners are in commotion. Peralta's spies bring rumors of war vessels expected, both English and American.

In New Helvetia, in Sonoma, at Monterey, and in Yerba Buena, guided by the most resolute, the aliens are quietly arming; they are secretly organizing.

March wears away into April. The breath of May is wafted down in spicy odors from the forests.

Fremont is away hiding where the great Sacramento River mountains break into the gorgeous canyons of its headwaters. Will he never turn?

The padre, now unreservedly friendly, tells Maxime that Castro fears to attack Fremont in the open field. He has sent Indian runners to stir up the wild Klamath, Snake River, and Oregon Indians against the Americans. This is serious. Should the explorers receive a check there, they would retreat; then the guerillas would cut them off easily.

Padre Francisco fears for the result. He tells Maxime that bands of fierce vaqueros are riding the roads; they have already butchered straggling foreigners. A general war of extermination may sweep from Sonoma to San Diego.

Valois' weary eyes have roved from mountain to valley for many days. Will he ever regain his liberty? A few morning walks with the padre, and a stroll by the waters of Lagunitas, are his only liberties.

The priest is busy daily with the instruction of little Dolores. The child's sweet, dancing eyes belie her mournful name. Valois has passed quiet Donna Juanita often in the garden walks. A light bending of her head is her only answer to the young man's respectful salutation. She, too, fears and distrusts all Americans.

The roses have faded from her cheeks too early. It is the hard lot of the California lady. Though wealth of lands in broad leagues dotted with thousands of cattle, horses, and sheep is hers, this daughter of an old feudal house has dreamed away a lonely life. It is devoid of all social pleasures since she became the first lady of Lagunitas.

Colorless and sad is her daily life. Denied society by her isolation, she is yet too proud to associate with her women dependants.

Her lord is away often in the field. His days are spent galloping over his broad domains. There is no intellectual life, no change of day and day. The years have silently buried themselves, with no crown of happy memories. She left her merry home at the Alameda shore of the great bay to be the lonely lady of this distant domain. Her narrow nature has settled into imitative and mechanical devotion, a sad, cold faith.

Youthful lack of education has not been repaired by any individual experience of life. Maternity has been a mere physical epoch of her dreary womanhood. The current of her days in narrow channels sluggishly flows toward its close.

Even the laughing child runs away from the young "pathfinder." She furtively peers at him from the shelter of the graceful vines and rose bowers of her playground.

Maxime has exhausted the slender library of his friend. In the peaceful evening hours he listens to weird stories of the lonely land of the Far West--early discovery, zealous monkish exploration, daring voyages in trackless unknown seas, and the descent of curious strangers. Bold Sir Francis Drake, Cabrillo, Viscaino, Portala, the good Junipero Serra of sainted memory, live again in these recitals.

Day by day passes. No news from the Americans at bay in the wilds of the Klamath. By courier the Don has heard of Castro's feeble moves. He toils along with his cavalry, guns, and foot soldiers, whom Fremont defied from behind the rocky slopes of Hawk's Peak. The foreigners are all conspiring.

A cloud of government agents are scouring the valleys for aid to send a column to attack Fremont. It had been a pride of Don Miguel's military career to assist war-like Vallejo to drive the foreigners from Monterey in 1840. He is ready for the fray again.

The Commandante gnashed his teeth when he heard, in 1842, at Lagunitas, that the strangers had returned. He remembers the shameful day of October 19, 1842, when the Yankee frigates covered Monterey with their guns, while Commodore Jones hoisted the stars and stripes for a day or so. Always before the English.

Though it was disowned, this act showed how easily the defenceless coast could be ravaged. Many times did he thank the Blessed Virgin that his domain was far away in the inland basin. There his precious herds are safe from the invader.

There is danger for Valois in the Commandante's scowl when the saddest May day of his life comes. A rider on relay horses hands him a fateful despatch.

"Curse the, Gringos!" He strikes his table till the glasses ring.

There are five huge Yankee war vessels in Monterey harbor. It is too true. This time they have come to stay. Padre Francisco softly makes his exit. He keeps Maxime in cover for a day or so.

Bit by bit, the details come to light. The SAVANNAH, PORTSMOUTH, CYANE, LEVANT, and CONGRESS bear the flag of Commodore Sloat. This force can crush any native army. All communication by sea with Mexico is now cut off. The Californian Government is paralyzed.

Worse and worse, the wild Klamath warriors have failed in their midnight dash on Fremont. He is now swinging down the valley--a new danger to Maxime.

What means all this? The perplexed Don knows not what to do. From his outposts come menacing news. The battery of the PORTSMOUTH commands the town of Yerba Buena. San Diego, too, is under American guns. The CYANE is victorious there, and the CONGRESS holds San Pedro. The political fabric is so slight that its coming fall gives no sign. The veteran Commandante receives an order to march, with every available man, to join General Castro. He feels even his own domains are now in danger. He communes long with the padre. He musters every vaquero for their last campaign under the Mexican eagle.

Miguel Peralta growls with rage. He learns the English liner COLLINGWOOD has arrived, a day or so too late--only another enemy. Still, better temporary English rule than the long reign of the grasping Yankee. The Don's self-interest, in alarm, is in the logical right this time.

How shall he protect his property? What will he do with his family? He knows that behind him the great Sierras wall the awful depths of the Yosemite. The gloomy forests of the big trees appall the stray traveller. The Utes are merciless in the day of their advantage, and the American war vessels cut off all escape by sea to Mexico. All the towns near the ocean are rendezvous of defiant foreigners, now madly exultant. To the north is the enemy he is going out to fight.

Padre Francisco advises him to leave the rancho in his charge. He begs him to even let the young American prisoner remain.

Lagunitas may be seized, yet private property will be respected. Young Valois may be a help to considerate treatment. After council with his frightened spouse, Don Miguel rides off to the rendezvous near Santa Clara. He curbs his passion from prudence only, for he was on the point of making Valois a human tassel for a live-oak limb.

The padre breaths freer.

Day after day elapses. Under a small body-guard both the padre and Maxime ride the domain in freedom. Juanita Peralta shuts herself up in the gloomy mansion, where she tells her beads in the shadow of the coming defeats.

Rich and lovely Lagunitas is yet out of the theatre of action. Its lonely inhabitants hear of the now rapid march of events, but only defeated riders wander in with heavy tidings.

Fremont has whirled back once more and controls Suiter's Fort and Sonoma. The ablest general of California is powerless. Gallant Vallejo is now a prisoner. His scanty cannons and arms are all taken. Castro's cavalry are broken up or captured. Everywhere the foreigners gather for concerted action. It is a partisan warfare.

Don Miguel's sullen bulletins tell of Castro's futile attempt to get north of the bay. Since Cabrillo was foiled in landing at Mendocino in 1543, the first royal flag floating over this "No Man's Land" was Good Queen Bess's standard, set up in 1579 by dashing Sir Francis Drake. He landed from the Golden Hind. In 1602 the Spanish ensign floated on December 10 at Monterey; in 1822 the third national ensign was unfurled, the beloved Mexican eagle-bearing banner. It now flutters to its downfall.

Don Miguel warns the padre that the rude "bear flag" of the revolted foreigners victoriously floats at Sonoma. It was raised on July 4, 1846. Castro and Pio Pico are driven away from the coast. They only hold the Santa Clara valley and the interior. There is but one depot of arms in the country now; it is a hidden store at San Juan. Far away in Illinois, a near relative of the painter and hoister of the "bear flag" is a struggling lawyer. Todd's obscure boyhood friend, Abraham Lincoln, is destined to be the martyr ruler of the United States. A new star will shine in the stars and stripes for California, in a bloody civil war, far off yet in the mystic future.

In the narrow theatre where the decaying Latin system is falling, under Anglo-Saxon self-assertion, the stern logic of events teaches Don Miguel better lessons. His wild riders may as well sheathe their useless swords as fight against fate.

The first blood is drawn at Petaluma. A declaration of independence, rude in form, but grimly effective in scope, is given out by the "bear flag" party. Fremont joins and commands them. The Presidio batteries at San Francisco are spiked by Fremont and daring Kit Carson, The cannon and arms of Castro are soon taken. On July 7, Captain Mervine, with two hundred and fifty blue-jackets, raises the flag of the United States at Monterey. Its hills reecho twenty-one guns in salvo from Sloat's squadron.

On the 8th, Montgomery throws the national starry emblem to the breeze at the Golden Gates of San Francisco. The old PORTSMOUTH'S heavy cannon roar their notes of triumph.

Valois remains lonely and inactive at Lagunitas. His priestly friend warns him that he would be assassinated at any halting place if he tried to join his friends. In fact, he conceals his presence from any wayfaring, Yankee-hunting guerillas.

Don Miguel is bound by his military oath to keep the field. A returning straggler brings the crushing news that the San Juan military depot has been captured by a smart dash of the American volunteers under Fremont and Gillespie. And San Diego has fallen now. The bitter news of the Mexican War is heard from the Rio Grande. A new sorrow!

Broken-hearted Don Miguel bravely clings to his flag. He marches south with Castro and Pico, The long weeks wear along. The arrival of General Kearney, and the occupation of San Diego and Los Angeles, are the prelude to the last effort made for the honor of the Mexican ensign. Months drag away. The early winter finds Don Miguel still missing. Commodore Stockton, now in command of the powerful fleet, reinforces Fremont and Gillespie. The battles of San Gabriel and the Mesa teach the wild Californians what bitter foes their invaders can be. The treaty of Coenga at last ends the unequal strife. The stars and stripes wave over the yet unmeasured boundaries of the golden West. The Dons are in the conquerors' hands. After the fatal day of January 16, 1847, defeated and despairing of the future of his race, war-worn Miguel Peralta, Commandante no longer, with a few followers rides over the Tehachape. He descends the San Joaquin to his imperilled domain.

With useless valor he has thrown himself into the fire of the Americans at the battles near Los Angeles, but death will not come to him. He must live to be one of the last Dons. The defeats of Mexico sadden and embitter him. General Scott is fighting up to the old palaces of the Montezumas with his ever victorious army.

In these stormy winter days, when the sheeted rain drives down from the pine-clad Sierras, Donna Juanita day by day turns her passive face in mute inquiry to the padre. She has the sense of a new burden to bear. Her narrow nature contracts yet a little with a sense of wounded native pride.

In all her wedded years her martial lord has always returned in victory. Fandango and feast, "baile" and rejoicings, have made the woodland echoes ring.

The growing Dolores mopes in the lonely mansion. She demands her absent father daily.

Before the troopers of Lagunitas return with their humbled chieftain, a squad of mounted American volunteers ride up and take possession. For the first time in its history the foreigner is master here, Though personally unknown to these mixed revolutionists, Maxime Valois is free to go in safety.

While he makes acquaintance with his fellow "patriots," the advance riders of Don Miguel announce his home-coming. It is a sad day when the Commandante dismounts at his own door. There is a sentinel there. He lives to be only a sullen, brooding protest in the face of an accidental progress.

Standing on his porch he can see the "mozos," under requisition, gathering up his choicest horses by the fifties. They are destined for the necessary remount of the victors.

After greeting his patient helpmeet, henceforth to be the partner of his sorrows, he sends for the padre and his major-domo. He takes on himself the only dignity left to his defeated pride, practical self-isolation.

He bears in his bosom this rankling thorn--the hated Fremont he rode out to bring in a captive, is now "His Excellency John C. Fremont," the first American governor of California.

With his flocks and herds scattered, his cattle and horses under heavy requisition, his cup is full. He moodily curses the Gringo, and wishes that the rifle-ball which wounded him at San Gabriel had reached the core of his proud old heart.

From all sides come fugitives with news of the Americanization of the towns. The inland communities are reorganized. His only friend is the Padre, to whose patient ear he confides the story of the hopeless campaign. With prophetic pessimism he sees the downfall of the native families.

Three months have made Larkin, Redding, Ide, Sutter, Semple, Merritt, Bidwell, Leese, and Lassen the leading men of the day. The victorious military and naval chiefs, Sloat, Stockton, Montgomery, Fremont, Kearney, Halleck, and Gillespie are now men of history. All the functions of government are in the hands of American army or navy officers. The fall of the beloved Mexican banner is as light and unmarked as the descent of the drifting pine-needles torn from the swaying branches of the storm-swept forest kings around him.

His settled gloom casts a shadow over Lagunitas. The padre has lost his scholars. The converts of the dull Indian tribes have fled to the hills, leaving the major-domo helpless. All is in domestic anarchy. At last the volunteers are leaving.

When the detachment is ready to depart, Maxime Valois is puzzled. The Mexican War raging, prevents his homeward voyage as planned. It will be months before the war vessels will sail. If allowed to embark on them, he will be left, after doubling Cape Horn, a stranger in the north, penniless. Why not stay?

Yet the shelter of Lagunitas is his no more. The maddened Don will not see an American on the bare lands left to him. His herds and flocks are levied on to feed the troops.

Many an hour does the youth confer with Francois Ribaut. The priest is dependent on his patron. The Church fabric is swept away, for Church and state went down together. With only one friend in the State, Valois must now quit his place of enforced idleness.

The meagre news tells him the Fremont party is scattered. He has no claims on the American Government. But Fremont has blossomed into a governor. He will seek him. Happily, while Maxime Valois deliberates, the question decides itself. He is offered the hospitality of an escort back to Santa Clara, from whence he can reach Monterey, San Francisco, or Los Angeles. In the new State no present avenues are open to a castaway. His education is practically useless. He is forced to consider the question of existence. The utmost Padre Francisco can do is to provide him horse and gear. A few Mexican dollars for the road are not lacking. The lot of fate is drawn for him by necessity. For the present he must be a Californian. He cannot leave until the future provides the means.

When the vigil of the departure comes, the young man is loath to leave his friend. In their companionship they have grown dear to each other.

The camp of the volunteers is ready for the next day's march. At their last dinner, the simple cheer of the native wine and a few cigaritos is all the padre can display.

"Maxime, listen. You are young and talented," the padre begins. "I see a great community growing up here, This is a land of promise. The termination of the war ends all tumult. Your fleet holds the coast. Mexico seems to be under the talons of your eagle. Your nation is aggressive. It is of high mechanical skill. Your people will pour into this land and build here a great empire. Your busy Yankees will never be satisfied with the skeleton wealth of a pastoral life. They will dig, hew, and build. These bays and rivers will be studded with cities. Go, my dear friend, to Yerba Buena. I will give you letters to the fathers of the Mission Dolores. Heaven will direct you after you arrive. You can communicate with me through them. I shall remain here as long as my charge continues. If driven out, I shall trust God to safely guide me to France. When I am worn out, I shall die in peace under the shadows of Notre Dame."

At the hour of mass Maxime kneels to receive the blessing of the Church.

The volunteers are in the saddle. It is the man, not the priest, who embraces the freed "pathfinder." Valois' eyes are dim with tears as he waves the adieu to the missionary. Not a word does Don Miguel vouchsafe to the departing squad. The aversion of the dwellers in Lagunitas is as great as their chief's.

Maxime joins the escort on the trail. Runaway sailors, voyageurs, stray adventurers are they--queer flotsam on the sea of human life. He learns from them the current stories of the day. He can trace in the mysterious verbal "order to return," and that never-produced "packet" given to Fremont by Gillespie, a guiding influence from afar. The appearance of the strong fleet and the hostilities of Captain Fremont are mysteriously connected. Was it from Washington these wonders were worked? As they march, unopposed, over the alamedas of San Joaquin, bearing toward the Coast Range, they pass under overhanging Mount Diablo. The Louisianian marvels at the sudden change of so many peaceful explorers into conquering invaders. Valois suspects Senator Benton of intrigues toward western conquest. He knows not that somewhere, diplomatically lost between President Polk and Secretaries Buchanan, Marcy, and Bancroft, is the true story of this seizure of California. Gillespie's orders were far in advance of any Mexican hostilities. The fleet and all the actions of the State, War, and Navy departments prove that some one in high place knew the Pacific Coast would be subdued and held.

Was it for slavery's added domains these glorious lands were destined?

Maxime is only a pawn in that great game of which the annexation of Texas, the Mexican War, and California conquest are moves.

Wise, subtle, far-seeing, and not over-scrupulous, the leaders of southern sentiment, with prophetic alarm, were seeking to neutralize free-State extension in the Northwest. They wished to link the warmer climes, newly acquired, to the Union by negro chains. Joying in his freedom, eager to meet the newer phases of Californian life under the stars and stripes, Valois rides along. Restored in health, and with the light heart and high hopes of twenty, he threads the beautiful mountain passes; for the first time he sees the royal features of San Francisco Bay, locked by the Golden Gates.

BOOK II.
GOLD FOR ALL.--A NEW STAR IN THE FLAG.

CHAPTER V.

THE GOLDEN MAGNET.--FREE OR SLAVE?

Maxine Valois marvels not that the old navigators missed the Golden Gate. It was easy to pass the land-locked bay, with its arterial rivers, the Sacramento and San Joaquin. Fate hung a foggy curtain on the outside bar. Greenest velvet sward now carpets the Alameda hills. It is a balmy March day of 1847. The proceeds of his horse and trappings give the youth less than a hundred dollars--his whole fortune.

The Louisianian exile, with the world before him, is now a picture of manly symmetry. Graceful, well-knit physique, dark hair and eyes, and his soft, impassioned speech, betray the Franco-American of the Gulf States. While gazing on the glories of Tamalpais and the wooded mountains of Marin, he notes the little mission under the Visitacion hills. It's a glorious scene. All the world's navies can swing at ease in this superb bay. The only banner floating here is the ensign at the peak of the frigate Portsmouth. Interior wanderings give him a glimpse of the vast areas controlled by this noble sheet of water. Young and ardent, with a superior education, he may be a ruling spirit of the new State now about to crystallize. His studies prove how strangely the finger of Fortune points. It turned aside the prows of Captain Cook, La Perouse, Vancouver, and the great Behring, as well as the bold Drake, who tarried within a day's sail at his New Albion. Frenchman, Englishman, and Russian have been tricked by the fairy goddess of the mist. The Golden Gates in these later days are locked by the Yankees from the inside.

Leaping from the boat, Valois tosses his scanty gear on the strand. It is a deep, curving bay, in later years to be covered with stately palaces of commerce, far out to where the Portsmouth now lies.

A few huts make up the city of Yerba Buena. Reflecting on his status, he dares not seek the alcalde, Lieut. Washington Bartlett of the navy. From his escort he has heard of the many bickerings which have involved Sloat, Stockton, Fremont, and Kearney.

Trusting to Padre Francisco's letters, he hires a horse of a loitering half-breed. This native pilots him to the mission.

The priests receive him with open arms. They are glad for news of their brother of the Sierras. Maxime installs himself as a guest of the priests. Some current of life will bear him onward--whither he knows not.

Idle days run into weeks. A motley five or six hundred whites have gathered. The alcalde begins to fear that the town limits are crowded.

None of the wise men of the epoch dare to dream that in less than three years two hundred vessels will lie tossing, deserted in the bay; that the cove will be filled with ships from the four corners of the earth in five years.

Frowning hills and rolling sand dunes are to be thrown bodily into the reentrant bay. They are future coverings for sunken hulks. Where for twenty square miles coyote and fox now howl at night, the covert oaks and brambles will be shaved off to give way to a city, growing like a cloud-land vision.

Active and energetic, Valois coasts down to Monterey. He finds Fremont gone, already on his way east. His soldier wrists are bound with the red tape of arrest. The puppet of master minds behind the scenes, Fremont has been a "pathfinder" for others.

Riding moodily, chafing in arrest, at the rear of the overland column, the explorer receives as much as Columbus, Pizarro, or Maluspina did--only obloquy. It is the Nemesis of disgrace, avenging the outraged and conquered Californians.

A dark shade of double dealing hangs around the glories of the capture of California. The methods used are hardly justified, even by the national blessings of extension to this ocean threshold of Asian trade. The descent was planned at Washington to extend the domineering slave empire of the aspiring South. The secret is out. The way is clear for the surplus blacks of the South to march in chains to the Pacific under the so-called "flag of freedom."

Valois discovers at Monterey that no man of the staff of the "Pathfinder" will be made an official pet, They are all proscribed. The early fall finds him again under the spell of the bells of the Mission Dolores. Whither to turn he knows not.

Averse to manual labor, like all Creoles, the lad decides to seek a return passage on some trader. This will be hardly possible for months. The Christmas chimes of 1848 sound sadly on his ears.

With no home ties but his uncle, his memories of the parents, lost in youth, fade away. He feels the bitterness of being a stranger in a strange land. He is discouraged with an isolated western empire producing nothing but hides and tallow. He shares the general opinion that no agriculture can succeed in this rainless summer land of California. Hardly a plough goes afield. On the half-neglected ranchos the owners of thousands of cattle have neither milk nor butter. Fruits and vegetables are unattainable. The mission grapes, olives, and oranges have died out by reason of fourteen years' neglect. The mechanic arts are absent. What shall the harvest of this idle land be?

Valois knows the interior Indians will never bear the strain of development. Lazy and ambitionless, they are incapable of uniting their tribal forces. Alas for them! They merely cumber the ground.

At the end of January, 1848, a wild commotion agitates the hamlet of San Francisco. The cry is "Gold! Gold everywhere!" The tidings are at first whispered, then the tale swells to a loud clamor. In the stampede for the interior, Maxime Valois is borne away. He seeks the Sacramento, the Feather, the Yuba, and the American. He too must have gold.

A general hegira occurs. Incoming ships, little settlements, and the ranches are all deserted, for a wondrous golden harvest is being gleaned. The tidings go forth over the whole earth. Sail and steam, trains of creaking wagons, troops of hardy horsemen, are all bent Westward Ho! Desertion takes the troops and sailors from camp and fleet pell-mell to the Sacramento valley. A shabby excrescence of tent and hut swells Yerba Buena to a town. In a few months it leaps into a city's rank. Over the prairies, toward the sandy Humboldt, long emigrant trains are crawling toward the golden canyons of the Sierras. The restless blood of the Mexican War pours across the Gila deserts and the sandy wastes of the Colorado.

The Creole boy learns that he, too, can work with pick, pan, cradle, rocker, at the long tom, sluice, and in the tunnel drift. The world is mad for gold. New York and New Orleans pour shiploads of adventurers in by Panama and Nicaragua. Sailing vessels from Europe, fleets around the Horn, vessels from Chile, Mexico, Sandwich Islands, and Australia crowd each other at the Golden Gates.

In San Francisco six months show ten thousand madmen. Tent, hut, shanty, shed, even pretentious houses appear. Uncoined nuggets, glittering gold dust in grains and powder, prove the harvest is real.

The Indians and lazy Californians are crowded out of the diggings. The superior minds among the priests and rancheros can only explain the long ignorance of the gold deposits by the absolute brutishness of the hill tribes. Their knowledge of metals was absolutely nothing. Beyond flint-headed spears, their bows and arrows, and a few mats, baskets, and skin robes, they had no arts or useful handicraft. Starving in a land of plenty, their tribal career never lifted itself a moment from the level of the brute. And yet gold was the Spaniards' talisman.

The Mexican-descended rancheros should have looked for gold. The traditions even indicated it. Their hold on the land was only in the footprints of their horses and cattle.

Had the priests ever examined the interior, had a single military expedition explored the State with care, the surface gold deposits must have been stumbled on.

It remains an inexplicable fact, that, as early as 1841, gold was found in the southern part of the State. In 1843, seventy-five to one hundred ounces of dust were obtained from the Indians, and sent to Boston via the Sandwich Island trading ships. Keen old Sir Francis Drake's reports to good Queen Bess flatly spoke of these yellow treasures. They, too, were ignored. English apathy! Pouring in from the whole world, bursting in as a flood of noisy adventurers on the stillness of the lazy land of the Dons, came the gold hunters of California.

Already, in San Francisco, drinking booth, gambling shop, and haunts of every villany spring up--the toadstools of a night.

Women throng in to add the incantations of the daughters of Sin to this mad hurly-burly. Handsome Mexicans, lithe Chilenas, escaped female convicts, and women of Australia were reinforced by the adventuresses of New Orleans, Paris,

New York, and Liverpool--a motley crowd of Paphian dames.

Maxime Valois, reaching Suiter's Fort by a launch, falls in with a lank Missouri lad. His sole property in the world is a rifle and his Pike county name of Joe Woods. A late arrival with a party of Mexican war strays, his age and good humor cause the Creole to take him as valuable, simply because one and one make two. He is a good-humored raw lad. Together in the broiling sun, half buried under bank or in the river-beds, they go through the rough evolution of the placer miner's art.

The two thousand scattered foreigners of the State are ten thousand before the year is out. Through the canyons, troops of gold seekers now wander. Sacramento's lovely crystal waters, where the silvery salmon leap, are tinged with typical yellow colors, deepening every month. Tents give way to cabins; pack trains of mules and horses wind slowly over the ridges. Little towns dot the five or six river regions where the miners toil, and only the defeated are idle.

From San Diego to Sonoma the temporary government is paralyzed. It loses all control except the fulmination of useless orders.

Local organization occurs by the pressure of numbers. Quaint names and queer local institutions are born of necessity.

At San Francisco the tower of Babel is duplicated. Polyglot crowds arrive in the craziest craft. Supplies of every character pour in. Shops and smiths, workmen of all trades, appear. Already an old steamboat wheezes on the Sacramento River. Bay Steamers soon vex the untroubled waters of the harbor. They appear as if by magic.

A fever by day, a revel by night, San Francisco is a caravansera of all nations. The Argonauts bring with them their pistols and Bibles, their whiskey and women, their morals and murderers. Crime and intrigues quickly crop out. The ready knife, and the compact code of Colonel Colt in six loaded chapters, are applied to the settlement of all quarrels.

While Valois blisters his hands with the pick and shovel, a matchless strain of good blood is also pouring westward. Young and daring men, even professional scholars, cool merchants, able artisans, and good women hopeful of a golden future, come with men finally able to dragoon these varied masses into order.

Regular communications are established, presses set up, and even churches appear. Post-office, banks, steamer and freight lines spring up within the year of the reign of gold. Disease raises its fevered head, and the physician appears by magic. The human maelstrom settles into an ebb and flood tide to and from the mines.

All over California keen-eyed men from the West and South begin to appropriate land. The Eastern and Middle States pilgrims take up trades and mechanical occupations. All classes contribute recruits to the scattered thousands of miners. Greedy officials and sly schemers begin to prey on the vanishing property rights of the Dons. A strange, unsubstantial social fabric is hastily reared. It clusters around the western peaks by the Golden Gate.

Missouri, Texas, Arkansas, and Louisiana are sending great contingents. Mere nearness, with a taste for personal adventure, causes the southern border element to brave the overland journey. The northwestern overland travellers are more cautious. They have longer roads to drag over. They come prepared for farming or trade, as well as rude mining. As soon as the two lines of Eastern steamers are established, the Eastern and Middle States send heavy reinforcements. They are largely traders or permanent settlers. From the first day, the ambitious, overbearing men of the slave States take the lead in politics. They look to the extension of their gloomy "institution," negro slavery.

Valois keeps much to himself. Resolutely he saves his golden gleanings. He avoids the gambling tables and dance-houses. Joe Woods works like a horse, from mere acquisitiveness. He fondly looks back to a certain farm in Missouri, where he would fain squire it when rich. Public rumor announces the great hegira of gold seekers. The rush begins. Horse stealing, quarrels over claims, personal encounters, rum's lunacy, and warring opinion cause frequent bloody affrays.

Already scattered mounds rudely marked prove the reign of grim King Death. His dark empire stretches even here unstayed, unchallenged. Winter approaches; its floods drive the miners out of the river beds. Joe Woods has aggregated several Pike County souls, whose claims adjoin those of the two young associates. Wishing to open communication with Judge Valois at Belle Etoile, Maxime ceases work. He must recruit for hardships of the next season. He leaves all in the hands of "partner Joe," who prefers to camp with his friends, now the "Missouri Company." Valois is welcome at the Mission Dolores. He can there safely deposit his splendid savings.

Provided with ample funds of gold dust, in heavy buckskin sacks, to send up winter supplies, Valois secures his half of the profits. It is in rudely sealed tin cans of solid gold dust. He is well armed and in good company. He gladly leaves the human bee-hive by the terrific gorges of the American River. He has now learned every trick of the mines. By pack train his treasure moves down to Sacramento. Well mounted, Maxime is the companion of a score of similarly fortunate returning miners. Name, nationality, and previous history of these free lances of fortune have been dropped, like Christian's bundle, on climbing these hills. Every man can choose for himself a new life here, under the spicy breezes of the Sierras. He is a law unto himself.

The young gold hunter sees, amazed, a cantonment of ten thousand people at the bay. He safely conveys his treasure to the priests at the mission. They are shaken from slumber of their religious routine by eager Argonauts. Letters from Padre Francisco at Lagunitas prove the formation of bands of predatory Mexicans. These native Californians and Indian vagabonds are driving away unguarded stock. They mount their fierce banditti on the humbled Don's best horses. Coast and valley are now deserted and ungoverned. The mad rush for gold has led the men northward.

No one dreams as yet of the great Blue Cement lead, which, from Sierra to Mariposa, is to unbosom three hundred millions from the beds of the old, covered geologic rivers. Ten thousand scratch in river bank and bed for surface gold. Priest and layman, would-be scientist and embryo experts, ignore the yellow threaded quartz veins buttressing the great Sierras. He would be a madman now who would think that five hundred millions will be pounded out of the rusty rocks of these California hills in less than a score of years.

The toilers have no curiosity as to the origin or mother veins of the precious metal sought.

Maxime Valois sits under the red-tiled porches of the mission in January, 1849. He has despatched his first safe consignment of letters to Belle Etoile. He little cares for the events which have thrown the exhaustless metal belt of the great West into the reserve assets of the United States. He knows not it is destined within fifty years to be the richest land in the world. The dark schemes of slavery's lord-like statesmen have swept these vast areas into our map. The plotters have ignored the future colossal returns of gold, silver, copper, and lead.

Not an American has yet caught the real value of the world's most extensive forests of pine and redwood. They clothe these western slopes with graceful, unmutilated pageantry of green.

Fisheries and fields which promise great gains are passed unnoticed. It is a mere pushing out of boundary lines, under the political aggression of the South.

Even Benton, cheering the departing thousands Westward, grumbles in the Senate of the United States, on January 26, 1840. As the official news of the gold discoveries is imparted, the wise senators are blind in the sunlight of this prosperity. "I regret that we have these mines in California," Benton says; "but they are there, and I am in favor of getting rid of them as soon as possible." Wise senator!

Neither a prophet nor the son of a prophet is he. He cannot see that these slighted mines in the future will be the means of sustaining our country's credit in a great war. This gold and silver will insure the construction of the overland railroads. The West and Northwest, sealed to the Union by bands of steel, will be the mainstay of the land. They will equalize a broader, grander Union than he ever dreamed of.

Benton little thinks he has found the real solution of the wearying strife of North and South. Turning the surplus population of these bitterly opposed sections to the unpeopled West solves the problem. His son-in-law, Governor Fremont, has been a future peacemaker as well as a bold pathfinder. For it is on the track of Fremont that thousands are now tramping west. Their wheels are bearing the household gods. Civilization to be is on the move. Gold draws these crowds. The gulfs of the Carribean, even the lonely straits of Magellan and the far Pacific, are furrowed now by keels seeking the happy land where plentiful gold awaits every daring adventurer. Martinet military governors cannot control this embryo empire. Already in Congress bills are introduced to admit California into the Union. A rising golden star glitters in the West; it is soon to gild the flag of the Union with a richer radiance.

Great leaders of the sovereign people struggle at Washington in keen debate, inspired by the hostile sections of the Union. They quarrel over the slavery interests in the great West. Keen Tom Corwin, loyal Dix, astute Giddings, Douglass the little giant, and David Wilmot fight freedom's battle with the great apostle of State rights, Calhoun. He is supported by President Polk, the facile Secretary of State Buchanan, and that dark Mississippi man of destiny, Jefferson Davis. The fiery Foote and all the ardent knights of the day champion the sunny South. Godlike Daniel Webster pours forth for freedom some of his greatest utterances. William H. Seward, prophet, seer, statesman, and patriot, with noble inspirations cheers on freedom's army. Who shall own bright California, the bond or the free? While these great knights of our country's round table fight in the tourney of the Senate over this golden prize, Benton sends back the "pathfinder" Fremont. He is now freed from the army by an indignant resignation. He bears a letter to Benton's friends in the West to organize the civil community and prepare a constitution.

While Valois watches for news, the buds and blossoms of early spring call him back to the American River. The bay whitens with the sails of arriving thousands. Political combinations begin everywhere. Two years have made Fremont, Kearney, Colonel Mason, General P. F. Smith, and General Bennett Riley temporary military governors. Maxime leaves with ample stores; he rejoins the "Missouri Company," already reaping the golden harvest of the golden spring.

Sage counsel reaches him from Padre Francisco. He hears with delight of the youth's success in the mines. The French missionary, with a natural love of the soil, advises Valois to buy lands as soon as good titles can be had.

The Mexican War ends in glory to the once despised Gringos. Already the broad grants of the Dons are coveted by the officials of the military regency. Several of the officers have already served themselves better than their country. The entanglements of a new rule amount to practical confiscation of the lands of the old chieftains. What they saved from the conqueror is destined later to fatten greedy lawyers.

The spoliated Church is avenged upon the heirs of those who worked its temporal ruin. For here, while mad thousands delve for the gold of their desire, the tramping feet of uncontrolled hosts are heard at the gates of the Sierras. When the fleets give out their hordes of male and female adventurers, there is no law but that of force or duplicity; no principle but self-interest. Virtue, worth, and desert meekly bow to strength. Wealth in its rudest form of sacks of uncoined gold dust rules the hour.

The spring days lengthen into summer. Maxime Valois recoils from the physical toil of the rocky bars of the American. His nature is aristocratic; his youthful prejudices are averse to hand work. Menial attendance, though only upon himself, is degrading to him. The rough life of the mines becomes unbearable. A Southerner, par excellence, in his hatred of the physical familiarity of others, he avails himself of his good fortune to find a purchaser for his interests. The stream of new arrivals is a river now, for the old emigrant road of Platte and Humboldt is delivering an unending human current. Past the eastern frontier towns of Missouri, the serpentine trains drag steadily west; their camp fires glitter from "St. Joe" to Fort Bridger; they shine on the summit lakes of the Sierras, where Donner's party, beset in deepest snows, died in starvation. They were a type of the human sacrifices of the overland passage. Skeletons dot the plains now.

By flood and desert, under the stroke of disease, by the Indian tomahawk and arrow, with every varied accident and mishap, grim Death has taken his ample toll along three thousand miles. Sioux and Cheyenne, Ute and Blackfoot, wily Mormon, and every lurking foe have preyed as human beasts on the caravans. These human fiends emulate the prairie wolf and the terrific grizzly in thirst for blood.

The gray sands of the burning Colorado desert are whitening with the bones of many who escaped Comanche and Apache scalping knives, only to die of fatigue.

By every avenue the crowd pours in. Valois has extended his acquaintance with the leading miners. He is aware of the political organization about to be effected. He has now about forty thousand dollars as his share of gold dust. An offer of thirty thousand more for his claim decides him to go to San Francisco. He is fairly rich. With that fund he can, as soon as titles settle, buy a broad rancho. His active mind suggests the future values of the building lots in the growing city.

He completes the rude formalities of his sale, which consist of signing a bill of sale of his mining claim, and receiving the price roughly weighed out in gold. He hears that a convention is soon to organize the State. On September i, 1849, at Monterey, the civil fabric of government will be planned out.

Before he leaves he is made a delegate. Early July, with its tropical heat, is at hand. The camp on the American is agitated by the necessity of some better form of government. Among others, Philip Hardin of Mississippi, a lawyer once, a rich miner now, is named as delegate.

At Sacramento a steamer is loaded to the gunwales with departing voyagers. Maxime meets some of his fellow delegates already named. Among them is Hardin of Mississippi. Philip Hardin is a cool, resolute, hard-faced man of forty. A lawyer of ability, he has forged into prominence by sheer superiority. The young Creole is glad to meet some one who knows his beloved New Orleans. As they glide past the willow-shaded river banks, the two Southerners become confidential over their cigars.

Valois learns, with surprise, that President Polk sent the polished Slidell confidentially to Mexico in 1846, and offered several millions for a cession of California. He also wanted a quit-claim to Texas. This juggling occurred before General Taylor opened the campaign on the Rio Grande. In confidential relations with Sidell, Hardin pushed over to California as soon as the result of the war was evident. Ambitious and far-seeing, Philip Hardin unfolds the cherished plan of extending slavery to the West. It must rule below the line of the thirty-sixth parallel. Hardin is an Aaron Burr in persuasiveness. By the time the new friends reach San Francisco, Maxime has found his political mentor. Ambition spurs him on.

Wonders burst upon their eyes. Streets, business houses and hotels, dwellings and gaudy places of resort, are spread over the rolling slopes. Valois has written his friends at the mission to hold his letters. He hastens away to deposit his treasures and gain news of the old home in the magnolia land.

Hardin has the promise of the young Louisianian to accompany him to Monterey. A preliminary conference of the southern element in the convention is arranged. They must give the embryo State a pro-slavery constitution. He busies himself with gaining a thorough knowledge of the already forming cabals. Power is to be parcelled out, places are to be filled. The haughty Mississippian cares more for this excitement than digging for mere inert treasure. His quick eye catches California's splendid golden star in the national constellation.

Valois finds he must wait the expected letters. He decides to take no steps as to investment until the civil power is stable.

With a good mustang he rides the peninsula thoroughly. He visits the old Presidio on the outskirts of the growing city. He rides far over the pass of Lake Merced, to where the broken gap in the coast hills leaves a natural causeway for the railway of the future.

Philip Hardin, fisher of men, is keeping open house near the plaza. Already his rooms are the headquarters of the fiery chivalry of the South. Day by day Valois admires the self-assertion of the imperious lawyer. The Mississippian has already plotted out the situation. He is concert with leaders like himself, who are looking up and drawing in their forces for the struggle at the convention.

Valois becomes familiar with the heads of the Northern opposition. Able and sturdy chiefs are already marshalling the men who come from the lands of the northern pine to meet in the peaceful political arena the champions of the palmetto land. Maxime's enthusiasm mounts. The young Southerner feels the pride of his race burning in his veins.

In his evening hours, under the oaks of the Mission Dolores, he bears to the calm priests his budget of port and town. He tells of the new marvellous mines, of the influx of gold hunters. He cannot withhold his astonishment that the priest-hood should not have discovered the gold deposits. The astute clergy inform him calmly that for years their inner circles have known of considerable gold in the possession of the Indians. It was a hope of the Church that some fortunate turn of Mexican politics might have restored their sway. Alas! It was shattered in 1834 by the relentless Hijar.

"Hijo mio!" says an old padre. "We knew since 1838 that gold was dug at Fran-scisquita canyon in the south. If we had the old blessed days of Church rule, we could have quietly controlled this great treasure field. But this is now the land of rapine and adventure. First, the old pearl-fishers in the gulf of California; then the pirates lurking along the coast, watching the Philippine galleons. When your Americans overran Texas, and commenced to pour over the plains here, we knew all was lost. Your people have fought a needless war with Mexico; now they are swarming in here--a godless race, followed by outcasts of the whole of Europe. There is no law here but the knife and pistol. Your hordes now arriving have but one god alone--gold."

The saddened old padre sighs as he gathers his breviary and beads, seeking his lonely cloister. He is a spectre of a day that is done.

CHAPTER VI.

LIGHTING FREEDOM'S WESTERN LAMP.

Bustling crowds confuse Valois when he rides through San Francisco next day. One year's Yankee dominion shows a progress greater than the two hundred and forty-six years of Spanish and Mexican ownership. The period since Viscaino's sails glittered off Point Reyes has been only stagnation.

Seventy-three years' droning along under mission rule has ended in vain repetition of spiritual adjurations to the dullard Indians. To-day hammer and saw, the shouts of command, the din of trade, the ships of all nations, and the whistle, tell of the new era of work. The steam engine is here. The age of faith is past. "Laborare est orare" is the new motto. Adios, siesta! Enter, speculation.

Dreamy-eyed senoritas in amazement watch the growing town. Hundreds are throwing the drifted sand dunes into the shallow bay to create level frontage. Swarthy riders growl a curse as they see the lines of city lot fences stretching toward the Presidio, mission, and potrero.

Inventive Americans live on hulks and flats, anchored over water lots. The tide ebbs and flows, yet deep enough to drown the proprietors on their own tracts, purchased at auction of the alcalde as "water lots."

Water lots, indeed! Twenty years will see these water lots half a mile inland.

Masonry palaces will find foundations far out beyond where the old CYANE now lies. Her grinning ports hold Uncle Sam's hushed thunder-bolts. It is the downfall of the old REGIME.

Shed, tent, house, barrack, hut, dug-out, ship's cabin--everything which will cover a head from the salt night fog is in service. The Mexican adobe house disappears. Pretentious hotels and storehouses are quickly run up in wood. The mails are taking orders to the East for completed houses to come "around the Horn." Sheet-iron buildings are brought from England. A cut stone granite bank arrives in blocks from far-off China.

Vessels with flour from Chile, goods from Australia, and supplies from New York and Boston bring machinery and tools. Flour, saw, and grist mills are provided. Every luxury is already on the way from Liverpool, Bordeaux, Havre, Hamburg, Genoa, and Glasgow. These vessels bring swarms of natives of every clime. They hasten to a land where all are on an equal footing of open adventure, a land where gold is under every foot.

Without class, aristocracy, history, or social past, California's "golden days" are of the future.

Strange that in thirty years' residence of the sly Muscovites at Fort Ross, in the long, idle leisure of the employees of the Hudson Bay station at Yerba Buena Cove from 1836 to 1846, even with the astute Swiss Captain Sutter at New Helvetia, all capacities of the fruitful land have been so strangely ignored.

The slumber of two hundred and fifty years is over. Frenchman, Russian, Englishman, what opiate's drowsy charms dulled your eager eyes so long here? Thousands of miles of virgin lands, countless millions of treasures, royal forests and hills yet to grow under harvest of olive and vine--all this the mole-like eyes of the olden days have never seen.

Even the Mormons acted with the supine ignorance of the foreigners. They scorned to pick this jewel up. Judicious Brigham Young from the Great Salt Lake finally sends emissaries to spy and report. Like the wind his swift messengers go east to divert strong battalions of the Mormon converts from Europe, under trusted leaders, to San Francisco. Can he extend his self-built empire to the Pacific Slope? Brigham may be a new Mahomet, a newer Napoleon, for he has the genius of both.

Alas! when the Mormon bands arrive, Sam Brannard, their leader, abandons the new creed of "Mormon" for the newer creed of "Mammon." He becomes a mercantile giant. The disciples scatter as gold-seekers. California is lost to the Mormons. Even so! Fate, providence, destiny, or some cold evolution of necessary order, draws up the blue curtains of the West. It pins them to our country's flag with a new, glittering star, "California."

With eager interest Valois joins Philip Hardin. There is a social fever in the air. His friends are all statesmen in this chrysalis of territorial development. They are old hands at political intrigue. They would modestly be senators, governors, and rulers. They would cheerfully serve a grateful State.

A band of sturdy cavaliers, they ride out, down the bay shores. They cross the Santa Clara and Salinas valleys toward Monterey.

Valois' easy means enable him to be a leader of the movement. It is to give a constitution and laws to the embryo State.

Hardy men from the West and South are taking up lands. Cool traders are buying great tracts. Temporary officials have eager eyes fixed on the Mexican grants. At all the landings and along the new roads, once trails, little settlements are springing up, for your unlucky argonaut turns to the nearest avocation; inns, stables, lodging-houses and trading-tents are waited on by men of every calling and profession. Each wanderer turns to the easiest way of amassing wealth. The settlers must devise all their own institutions. The Mexicans idly wrap their serapes around them, and they avoid all contact with the hated foreigner. Beyond watching their flocks and herds, they take no part in the energetic development. Cigarito in mouth, card playing or watching the sports of the mounted cavaliers are their occupations. Dismounted in future years, these queer equestrian natures have never learned to fight the battle of life on foot. The law of absorption has taken their sad, swarthy visages out of the social arena.

The cavalcade of Southerners sweeps over the alamedas. They dash across the Salinas and up to wooded Monterey. There the first constitutional convention assembles.

Their delighted eyes have rested on the lovely Santa Cruz mountains, the glorious meadows of Santa Clara, and the great sapphire bay of Monterey. The rich Pajaro and Salinas valleys lie waiting at hand. Thinking also of the wondrous wealth of the Sacramento and San Joaquin, of the tropical glories of Los Angeles, Philip Hardin cries: "Gentlemen, this splendid land is for us! We must rule this new State! We must be true to the South!"

To be in weal and woe "true to the South" is close to the heart of every cavalier in Philip Hardin's train.

The train arrives at Monterey, swelled by others faithful to that Southern Cross yet to glitter on dark fields of future battle.

The treaty of Guadalupe Hidalgo closed a bloody Conflict on February 2, 1848. It is the preamble to a long struggle. It is destined in the West to be bloodless until the fatal guns trained on Fort Sumter bellow out their challenge to the great Civil War. It is only then the mighty pine will swing with a crash against the palm.

Hardin knows that recruits, true of blood, are hastening to the new land of El Dorado. As he leads his dauntless followers into Monterey his soul is high. He sees the beloved South sweeping in victory westward as proudly as her legions rolled over the fields of Monterey and Buena Vista.

The convention assembles. All classes are represented on September 1, 1849. The first legal civil body is convoked west of the Rockies. Men of thought are here. Men destined to be world-famous in the unknown future. Settlers, hidalgos, traders, argonauts, government officials of army and navy, and transient adventurers of no mean ability. A little press already works with its magical talking types. A navy chaplain is the Franklin of the West. Some order and decorum appear. The calm voice of prayer is heard. The mingled amens of the conquerors thank God for a most unjustifiable acquisition of the lands of others. They are ours only by the right of the strong against the weak--the world's oldest title.

The South leads in representative men. Ready to second the secret desires of Polk, Buchanan, and Calhoun is the astute and courtly Gwin, yet to be senator, duke of Sonora, and Nestor of his clan. Moore of Florida, Jones of Louisiana, Botts, Burnett, and others are in line. On the Northern side are Shannon, an adopted citizen; wise Halleck; polished McDougall; gifted Edward Gilbert, and other distinguished men--men worthy of the day and hour.

As independent members, Sutter, General Vallejo, Thomas O. Larkin, Dr. Semple, Wright, Hastings, Brown, McCarver, Rodman S. Price, Snyder, and others lend their aid. From the first day the advocates of slavery and freedom battle in oratorical storm. The forensic conflict rages for days; first on the matter of freedom, finally on that of boundary.

Freedom's hosts receive a glorious reinforcement in the arrival of John C. Fremont.

After bitter struggles the convention casts the die for freedom. The Constitution of the State is so adopted. While the publicists, led by Fremont and Gwin, seek to raise the fabric of state, the traders and adventurers, the hosts of miners springing to life under the chance touch of James W. Marshall's finger, on January 24, 1848, are delving or trading for gold.

Poor, ill-starred Marshall! He wanders luckless among the golden fields. He gains no wealth. He toils as yet, unthinking of his days of old age and lonely poverty. He does not look forward to being poor at seventy-three years, and dying in 1885 alone. The bronze monument over his later grave attests no fruition of his hopes. It only can show the warm-hearted gratitude of children yet unborn, the Native Sons of the Golden West. Cool old borderers like Peter Lassen, John Bidwell, P. B. Redding, Jacob P. Leese, Wm. B. Ide, Captain Richardson, and others are grasping broad lands as fair as the banks of Yarrow. They permit the ill-assorted delegates to lay down rules for the present and laws for the future. The State can take care of itself. Property-holders appear and aid. Hensley, Henley, Bartlett, and others are cool and able. While the Dons are solemnly complimented in the convention, their rights are gracefully ignored.

The military governor, General Bennett Riley, stands back. He justly does not throw his sword into the scales. Around him are rising men yet to be heroes on a grander field of action than the mud floors of a Monterey adobe. William T. Sherman, the only Northern American strategist, is a lieutenant of artillery. Halleck, destined to be commander-in-chief of a million men, is only a captain of engineers and acting Secretary of State. Graceful, unfortunate, accomplished Charles P. Stone is a staff officer. Ball's Bluff and Fort Lafayette are far in the misty unknown.

The convention adjourns SINE DIE n October 13, 1849. It has settled the great point of freedom on the Pacific Coast. It throws out the granite Sierras as an eternal bulwark against advancing slavery. The black shame is doomed never to cross the Rockies, and yet the great struggle for the born nobility of manhood has been led by Shannon, an alien Irishman. The proudest American blood followed Dr. Gwin's pro-slavery leading. The two senators named are Gwin and the hitherto unrewarded Fremont. Wright and Gilbert are the two congressmen. Honest Peter H. Burnett, on November 13, is elected the first governor of California. He is chosen by the people, and destined to live to see nearly fifty years of peaceful prosperity on the golden coast.

While this struggle is being waged on the Pacific, at Washington the giant statesmen of those famous ante-bellum days close in bitter strife. The political future of the great West, now known to be so rich, is undecided. It is the desperate desire of the South to keep California out of the Union, unless the part falling under the Wilmot proviso act south of 36 deg 30 min is given to slavery.

The national funds to pay for the "Gadsden purchase" will be withheld unless slavery can be extended. The great struggle brings out all the olden heroes of the political arena. Benton, Webster, Clay, Calhoun, Davis, King, Sam Houston, Foote, Seward, John Bell, and Douglas, are given a golden prize to tourney for. In that press of good knights, many a hard blow is struck. The victor and vanquished stand to-day, looming gigantic on the dim horizon of the past. It is the dark before the dawn of the War of the Rebellion.

It was before these days of degenerated citizenship, when the rising tide of gold floats the corrupt millionnaire and syndicate's agent into the Senate. The senator's toga then wrapped the shoulders of our greatest men. No bonanza agents--huge moral deformities of heaped-up gold--were made senatorial hunchbacks by their accidental millions.

No vulgar clowns dallied with the country's interests in those old days when Greek met Greek. It was a gigantic duel of six leaders: Webster, Seward, and Clay, pitted against Calhoun, Davis, and Foote. Pausing to refresh their strength for the final struggle, the noise of battle rolled away until the early days of 1850. California was kept out.

The delegates at Monterey hastened home to their exciting callings. Philip Hardin saw the wished-for victory of the South deferred. Gnashing his teeth in rage, he rode out of Monterey. Maxime Valois now is the ardent "Faust" to whom he plays "Mephisto." His following had fallen away. Hardin, cold, profound, and deep, was misunderstood at the Convention. He wished to gain local control. He knew the overmastering power of the pro-slavery administration would handle the main issue later--if not in peace, then in war.

As the red-tiled roofs of Monterey fade behind them, Hardin unbosoms himself to his young comrade. Maxime Valois has been a notable leader in the Convention. He was eager and loyal to the South. He extended many acquaintances with the proud chivalry element of the new State. His short experience of public life feeds his rising ambition. He determines to follow the law; the glorious profession which he laid aside to become a pathfinder; the pathway to every civic honor.

"Valois," says Hardin, "these people are too short-sighted. Our Convention leaders are failures. We should have ignored the slavery fight as yet. Thousands of Southern voters are coming to us within six months from the border States. Our friends from the Gulf are swarming here. The President will fill all the Federal offices with sound Southern Democrats. The army and navy will be in sympathy with us. With a little management we could have got slavery as far as 36 deg 30 sec. We could work it all over the West with the power of our party at the North. We could have controlled the rest of this coast by the Federal patronage, keeping the free part out of the Union as territories. Then our balance of power would be stable. It is not a lost game. Wait! only wait!"

Maxime agrees. Philip Hardin opens the young politician's eyes with a great confidence.

"Maxime, I have learned to like you and depend on you. I will give you a proof of it. We of the old school are determined to rule this country. If Congress admits California as a free State, there will yet be a Lone Star republic covering this whole coast. The South will take it by force when we go out."

The Louisianian exclaims, "Secession!"

"Yes, war even. Rather war than the rule of the Northern mud-sill!" cries Hardin, spurring his horse, instinctively. "Our leading men at home are in thorough concert day by day. If the issue is forced on us the whole South will surely go out. But we are not ready yet. Maxime, we want our share of this great West. We will fill it with at least even numbers of Southern men. In the next few years the West will be entirely neutral in case of war or unless we get a fair division. If we re-elect a Democrat as President we will save the whole West."

"War," muses Valois, as they canter down the rich slopes toward the Salinas River, "a war between the men who have pressed up Cerro Gordo and Chepultepec together! A war between the descendants of the victorious brothers of the Revolution!" It seems cold and brutal to the young and ardent Louisianian. An American civil war! The very idea seems unnatural. "But will the Yankees fight?" queries Valois. Hardin replies grimly: "I did not think we would even be opposed in this Convention. They seemed to fight us pretty well here. They may fight in the field-

-when it comes."

For Philip Hardin is a wise man. He never under-estimates his untried enemy.

Valois smiles. He cannot control a sneer. The men who are lumber-hewers, dirt-diggers, cod-fishers and factory operatives will never face the Southern chivalry. He despises the sneaking Yankees. Traders in a small way arouse all the arrogance of the planter. He cannot bring any philosophy of the past to tell him that the straining, leaky Mayflcnver was the pioneer of the stately American fleets now swarming on every sea. The little wandering Boston bark, Otter, in 1796 found her way to California. She was the harbinger of a mighty future marine control. The lumbering old Sachem (of the same Yankee borough) in 1822 founded the Pacific hide and tallow trade as an earnest of the sea control. Where one Yankee shows the way thousands may follow, yet this Valois ignored in his scorn of the man who works.

Maxime could not dream that the day could ever come when thousands of Yankees would swarm over entrenchments, vainly held by the best blood of the sunny South.

As the two gentlemen ride on, Hardin uses the confidential loneliness of the trip to prove to the Creole that war and separation must finally come.

"We want this rich land for ourselves and the South." The young man's blood was up.

"I know the very place I want!" cries Valois.

He tells Hardin of Lagunitas, of its fertile lands sweeping to the San Joaquin. He speaks of its grassy, rolling hills and virgin woods.

Philip Hardin learns of the dashing waters of the Merced and Mariposa on either side. He hears of the glittering gem-like Lagunitas sparkling in the bosom of the foot-hills. Valois recounts the wild legends, caught up from priest and Indian, of that great, terrific gorge, the Yosemite. Hardin allows much for the young man's wild fancy. The gigantic groves of the big trees are only vaguely described. Yet he is thrilled.

He has already seen an emigrant who wandered past Mono Lake over the great Mono notch in the Sierras. There it rises eleven thousand feet above the blue Pacific--with Castle Dome and Cathedral Peak, grim sentinels towering to the zenith.

"It must really be a paradise," muses Hardin.

"It is," cries the Creole; "I intend to watch that region. If money can make it mine, I will toil to get it."

Philip Hardin, looking through half-closed eyes at Valois, decides to follow closely this dashing adventurer. He will go far.

"Valois," he slowly says, "you have seen these native land-barons at the Convention. A few came in to join us. The rest are hostile and bitter. They can never stand before us. The whole truth is, the Mexican must go! We stopped the war a little too soon here. They are now protected by the treaty, but we will litigate them out of all their grants. Keep your eye on Lagunitas. It may come into the market. Gold will be the fool's beacon here for some time. These great valleys will yet be the real wealth of the new State. Land is the rock of the wealth to come. Get land, my boy!" he cries, with the lordly planter's instinct.

Valois admires the cold self-confidence of the sardonic Hardin. He opens his heart. He leans upon the resolute Mississippian.

It takes little to make Maxime joyfully accept Philip Hardin's invitation to share his office. They will follow the fortunes of the city by the Golden Gates.

On riding down the Visitacion valley their eyes are greeted with the sight of the first ocean steamers. A thousand new-comers throng the streets.

Maxime finds a home in the abode of Hardin. His cottage stands on a commanding lot, bought some time before.

Letters from "Belle Etoile" delight the wanderer. He learns of the well-being of his friends. Judge Valois' advice to Maxime decides him to cast his lot in with the new State. It is soon to be called California by legal admission.

Philip Hardin is a leader of the embryo bar of the city. Courts, books, two newspapers and the elements of a mercantile community are the newest signs of a rapid crystallization toward order. With magic strides the boundaries of San Francisco enlarge. Every day sees white-winged sails fluttering. Higher rises the human tumult. From the interior mines, excited reports carry away half the arrivals. They are eager to scoop up the nuggets, to gather the golden dust. New signs attract the eye: "Bank," "Hotel," "Merchandise," "Real Estate." Every craft and trade is represented. It is the vision of a night.

Already a leader, Hardin daily extends his influence as man, politician, and counsellor.

The great game is being played at the nation's capital for the last sanction to the baptism of the new star in the flag.

California stands knocking at the gates of the Union, with treasure-laden hands. In Congress the final struggle on admission drags wearily on. Victorious Sam Houston of Texas, seconded by Jefferson Davis, fresh laurelled from Buena Vista, urges the claims of slavery. Foote "modestly" demands half of California, with a new slave State cut out from the heart of blood-bought Texas. But the silver voice of Henry Clay peals out against any extension of slave territory. Proud King of Alabama appeals in vain to his brethren of the Senate to discipline the two ambitious freemen of the West, by keeping them out of the Union.

Great men rally to the bugle notes of their mighty leaders.

The gallant son of the South, General Taylor, finds presidential honors following his victories. In formal message he announces on February 13, 1850, to Congress that the new State waits, with every detail of first organization, for admission.

Stern Calhoun, chief of the aspiring Southerners, proudly claims a readjustment of the sectional equality thus menaced. Who shall dare to lift the gauntlet thrown down by South Carolina's mighty chieftain?

In the hush of a listening Senate, Daniel Webster, the lion of the North, sounds a noble defiance. "Slavery is excluded from California by the law of nature itself," is his warning admonition.

With solemn brow, and deep-set eyes, flashing with the light of genius, he appeals to the noblest impulses of the human heart. Breathless senators thrill with his inspired words. "We would not take pains to reaffirm an ordinance of nature," he cries, and, as his grave argument touches the listeners, he reverently adds, "nor to re-enact the will of God."

Mighty Seward rises also to throw great New York's gauntlet in the teeth of slavery.

Taunted with its legal constitutional sanction, he exclaims grandly, "There is a higher law than the Constitution."

Long years have passed since both the colossus of the North and the great Governor entered into the unbroken silence of the grave. Their immortal words ring still down the columned years of our country's history. They appeal to noble sons to emulate the heroes of this great conflict. Shall the slave's chains clank westward?

No! Above the din of commoner men, the logic of John Bell, calm and patriotic, brings conviction. The soaring eloquence of Stephen A. Douglas claims the Western shores for freedom.

Haughty Foote and steadfast Benton break lances in the arena.

Kentucky's greatest chieftain, whose gallant son's life-blood reddened Buena Vista's field, marshals the immortal defenders of human liberty. Henry Clay's paternal hand is stretched forth in blessing over the young Pacific commonwealth. All vainly do the knights of the Southern Cross rally around mighty Calhoun, as he sits high on slavery's awful throne.

Cold Davis, fiery Foote, ingenious Slidell, polished and versatile Soule, ardent King, fail to withstand that mighty trio, "Webster, Seward, and Clay," the immortal three. The death of the soldier-President Taylor calms the clamor for a time. The struggle shifts to the House. Patriotic Vinton, of Ohio, locks the door on slavery. On the 9th day of September, 1850, President Millard Fillmore signs the bill which limits the negro hunter to his cotton fields and cane brakes at home. The representatives of the new State are admitted. A new golden star shines unpolluted in the national constellation.

Westward the good news flies by steamer. All the shadows on California's future are lifted.

While wearied statesmen rest from the bitter warfare of two long years, from North and South thousands eagerly rush to the golden land.

The Southern and Border States send hosts of their restless youths.

From the Northwest sturdy freemen, farmers with families, toil toward new homes under freedom's newest star. The East and Middle States are represented by all their useful classes.

The news of California's admission finds Hardin and Valois already men of mark in the Occidental city.

Disappointed at the issue, Hardin presses on to personal eminence; he turns his energies to seeking honors in the legal forum.

Maxime Valois, quietly resuming his studies for the bar, guards his funds, awaiting opportunity for investment. He burns the midnight oil in deep studies. The two men wander over the growing avenues of the Babel of the West. Every allurement of luxury, every scheme of vice, all the arts of painted siren, glib knave, and lurking sharper are here; where the game is, there the hunter follows. Rapidly arriving steamers pour in hundreds. The camp followers of the Mexican war have streamed over to San Francisco. The notable arrival of the steamer California brings crowds of men, heirs to future fame, and good women, the moral salt of the new city. It also has its New York "Bowery Boys," Philadelphia "Plug Uglies," Baltimore "Roughs," and Albany "Strikers."

By day, new occupations, strange callings, and the labor of organizing a business community, engage all men. The ebb and flow of going and returning miners excite the daylight hours. From long wharves, river steamers, laden to the gunwales, steam past the city shores to Sacramento. At night, deprived of regular homes, the whole city wanders in the streets, or crowds flashy places of amusement. Cramped on the hilly peninsula, there are no social lines drawn between good and bad. Each human being is at sea in a maelstrom of wild license.

The delegated representatives of the Federal Government soon arrive. Power is given largely to the Southern element. While many of the national officials are distinguished and able, they soon feel the inspiring madness of unrebuked personal enjoyment.

Money in rough-made octagonal fifty-dollar slugs flows freely. Every counter has its gold-dust scales. Dust is current by the ounce, half ounce, and quarter ounce. The varied coins of the whole world pass here freely. The months roll away to see, at the end of 1850, a wider activity; there is even a greater excitement, a more pronounced madness of dissipation. Speculation, enterprise, and abandonment of old creeds, scruples, and codes, mark the hour.

The flying year has brought the ablest and most daring moral refugees of the world to these shores, as well as steady reinforcements of worthy settlers. Pouring over the Sierras, and dragging across the deserts, the home builders are spreading in the interior. The now regulated business circles, extending with wonderful elasticity, attract home and foreign pilgrims of character. Though the Aspasias of Paris, New Orleans, and Australia throng in; though New York sends its worthless womanhood in floods, there are even now worthy home circles by the Golden Gate. Church, school, and family begin to build upon solid foundations. All the government bureaus are in working order. The Custom House is already known as the "Virginia Poor House." The Post-Office and all Federal places teem with the ardent, haughty, and able ultra Democrats of the sunny South. The victory of the Convention bids fair to be effaced in the high-handed control of the State by Southern men. As the rain falleth on the just and unjust, so does the tide of prosperity enrich both good and bad. Vice, quickly nourished, flaunts its early flowers. The slower growth of virtue is yet to give golden harvest of gathered sheaves in thousands of homes yet to be in the Golden State. Long after the maddened wantons and noisy adventurers have gone the way of all "light flesh and corrupt blood," the homes will stand. Sailing vessels stream in from the ports of the world. On the narrow water-front, Greek and Lascar, Chinaman and Maltese, Italian and Swede, Russian and Spaniard, Chileno and Portuguese jostle the men of the East, South, and the old country. Fiery French, steady German, and hot-headed Irish are all here, members of the new empire by the golden baptism of the time.

Knife and revolver, billy and slung-shot, dirk and poniard, decide the ARGUMENTUM AD HOMINEM.

In the enjoyment of fraternal relations with the leaders of the dominant party East, Philip Hardin becomes a trusted counsellor of the leading officials. He sees the forum of justice opened in the name of Union and State. He ministers at the altars of the Law. He gains, daily, renown and riches in his able conduct of affairs.

Hardin's revenue rises. He despises one of the State judgeships easily at his hand. As his star mounts, his young neophyte, Maxime Valois, shares his toils and enjoys his training. Under his guidance he launches out on the sea of that professional legal activity, which is one continued storm of contention.

Valois has trusted none of the mushroom banks. He keeps his gold with the Padres. He makes a number of judicious purchases of blocks and lots in the city, now growing into stable brick, stone, and even iron.

CHAPTER VII.

THE QUEEN OF THE EL DORADO.--GUILTY BONDS.

In the dreary winter of 1850-51, there are luxurious resting places for the crowds driven at night from the narrow plank sidewalks of the Bay City. Rain torrents make the great saloons and gambling houses the only available shelter.

Running east and west, Sacramento, Clay, Washington, and Jackson Streets rise in almost impracticable declivity to the hills. Their tops, now inaccessible, are to be the future eyries of self-crowned railroad nobs and rude bonanza barons.

Scrubby chaparral, tenanted by the coyote, fox, and sand rabbit, covers these fringing sand hills. North and south, Sansome, Montgomery, Kearney, Dupont, Stockton, and a faint outline of Powell Street, are roadways more or less inchoate. An embryo western Paris.

Around the plaza, bounded by Clay, Washington, Dupont, and Kearney, the revelry of night crystallizes. It is the aggregating sympathy of birds of a feather.

The peculiar unconquered topography makes the handcart, wheelbarrow, and even the Chinaman's carrying poles, necessary vehicles of transit.

Water, brought in iron boats from Sansalito, is dragged around these knobby hills in huge casks on wheels. The precious fluid is distributed in five-gallon tin buckets, borne on a yoke by the dealer, who gets a dollar for two bucketfuls. No one finds time to dig for water. All have leisure to drink, dance, and gamble. They face every disease, danger, and hardship. They breast the grizzly-bear-haunted canyons in search of gold. No one will seek for water. It is the only luxury. The incoming and outgoing merchandise moves only a few rods from the narrow level city front. At the long wharves it is transshipped from the deep-water vessels, across forty feet of crazy wooden pier, to the river steamers. Lighters in the stream transfer goods to the smaller vessels beginning to trade up and down the coast.

In the plaza, now dignified by the RAFFINE name of "Portsmouth Square," the red banners of vice wave triumphant over great citadels of sin. Virtue is pushed to the distant heights and knolls. The arriving families, for sheer self-protection, avoid this devil's maelstrom. It sucks the wide crowd into the maddened nightly orgies of the plaza.

In the most pretentious buildings of the town, the great trinity of unlawful pleasures holds high carnival. Day and night are the same: drink, gaming, and women are worshipped. For the average resident there is no barrier of old which has not been burned away in the fever of personal freedom and the flood of gold.

A motley mass of twenty thousand men and women daily augments. They are all of full capacity for good and evil. They are bound by no common ties. They serve no god but pleasure. They fear no code. With no intention to remain longer than the profit of their adventures or the pleasures of their wild life last, they catch the passing moment.

Immense saloons are made attractive by displays of gaudy luxuries, set out to tempt the purses of the self-made autocrats of wealth. Gambling houses here are outvying in richness, and utter wantonness of wasted expense, anything yet seen in America. They are open always. Haunts abound where, in the pretended seclusion of a few yards' distance, rich adventurers riot with the beautiful battalions of the fallen angels. It were gross profanation to the baleful memories of Phryne, Aspasia, and Messalina to find, from all the sin-stained leaves of the world's past, prototypes of these bold, reckless man-eaters. They throng the softly carpeted, richly tapestried interiors of the gilded hells of Venus.

Drink and play. Twins steeds of the devil's car on the road to ruin. They are lashed on by wild-eyed, bright, beautiful demons. All follow the train of the modern reigning star of the West, Venus.

Shabby dance-halls, ephemeral Thespian efforts, cheap dens of the most brutal vice, and dark lairs abound, where sailors, laborers, and crowding criminals lurk, ready for their human prey. Their female accomplices are only the sirens watching these great strongholds of brazen vice. A greater luxury only gilds a lower form of human abasement. The motley horde, wallowing on the "Barbary Coast" and in the mongrel thieves' haunts of "Pacific Street," the entrenched human devils on "Telegraph Hill" are but natural prey of the coarsest vices.

The ready revolver, Colt's devilish invention, has deluged the West and South with blood. Murder's prime minister hangs in every man's belt. Colonel James Bowie's awful knife is a twin of this monstrous birth. In long years of dark national shame our country will curse the memory of the "two Colonels." They were typical of their different sectional ideas. These men gave us the present coat of arms of San Francisco: the Colt's revolver and the Bowie knife.

Yes, thousands of yet untenanted graves yawn for the future victims of these mechanical devices. The skill of the Northern inventor, and the devilish perfection of the heart-cleaving blade of the Southern duellist are a shame to this wild age.

The plaza with impartial liberality yields up its frontages to saloon, palace of play, and hotels for the fair ministers of His Satanic Majesty. It is the pride of the enterprising "sports" and "sharpers," who represent the baccalaureate degree of every known vice. On the west, the "Adelphi" towers, with its grand gambling saloon, its splendid "salle a manger," and cosey nooks presided over by attractive Frenchwomen. Long tables, under crystal chandeliers, offer a choice of roads to ruin. Monte, faro, rouge et noir, roulette, rondo and every gambling device are here, to lure the unwary. Dark-eyed subtle attendants lurk, ready to "preserve order," in gambling parlance. At night, blazing with lights, the superb erotic pictures on the walls look down on a mad crowd of desperate gamesters. Paris has sent its most suggestive pictures here, to inflame the wildest of human passions. Nymph and satyr gleam from glittering walls; Venus approves with melting glances, from costliest frames, the self-immolation of these dupes of fortune. Every wanton grace of the artist throws a luxurious refinement of the ideal over the palace of sin and shame.

Long counters, with splendid mirrors, display richest plate. They groan with costliest glass, and every dark beverage from hell's hottest brew. Card tables, and quiet recesses, richly curtained, invite to self-surrender and seclusion. The softest music breathes from a full orchestra. Gold is everywhere, in slugs, doubloons, and heaps of nuggets. Gold reigns here. Silver is a meaner metal hardly attainable. Bank notes are a flimsy possibility of the future. Piles of yellow sovereigns and the coinage of every land load the tables. Sallow, glittering-eyed croupiers sweep in, with affected nonchalance, this easy-gained harvest of chance or fraud.

As the evening wears on, these halls fill up with young and old. The bright face of youth is seen, inflamed with every burning passion, let loose in the wild uncontrolled West. It is side by side with the haggard visage of the veteran gamester. Every race has its representatives. The possession of gold is the cachet of good-fellowship. Anxious crowds criticise rapid and dashing play. The rattle of dice, calls of the dealers, shouts of the attendants ring out. The sharp, hard, ringing voices of the fallen goddesses of the tables rise on the stifling air, reeking of smoke and wine. Dressed with the spoils of the East, bare of bosom, bright of eye, hard of heart, glittering in flashing gems, and nerved with drink, are these women. The painted sirens of the Adelphi smile, with curled carmine lips which give the lie to the bold glances of the wary eyes of those she-devils.

With a hideous past thrown far behind them, they fear no future. Desperate as to the present, ministering to sin, inciting to violence, conspiring to destroy body and soul, these beautiful annihilators of all decency vie in deviltry only with each other.

They flaunt, by day, toilettes like duchesses' over the muddy streets; their midnight revels outlast the stars sweeping to the pure bosom of the Pacific. The nightly net is drawn till no casting brings new gudgeons. An unparalleled display of wildest license and maddest abandonment marks day and night.

Across the square the Bella Union boasts similar glories, equal grandeur, and its own local divinities of the Lampsacene goddess.

It is but a stone's throw to the great Arcade. From Clay to Commercial Street, one grand room offers every allurement to hundreds, without any sign of over-crowding. The devil is not in narrow quarters.

On the eastern front of the plaza, the pride of San Francisco towers up: the El Dorado. Here every glory of the Adelphi, Arcade, and Bella Union is eclipsed. The unrivalled splendor of rooms, rich decorations, and unexcelled beauty of pictures excite all. The rare liveliness of the attendant wantons marks them as the fairest daughters of Beelzebub. The world waves have stranded these children of Venus on the Pacific shores. Music, recalling the genius of the inspired masters, sways the varying emotions of the multitude. The miners' evenings are given up to roaming from one resort to another. Here, a certain varnish of necessary politeness restrains the throng of men; they are all armed and in the flush of physical power; they dash their thousands against impregnable and exciting gambling combinations at the tables. With no feeling of self-abasement, leading officials, merchants, bankers, judges, officers, and professional men crowd the royal El Dorado. Here they relax the labors of the day with every distraction known to human dissipation.

Staggering out broken-hearted, in the dark midnight, dozens of ruined gamesters have wandered from these fatal doors into the plaza. The nearest alley gives a shelter; a pistol ball crashes into the half-crazed brain.

Suicide!--the gambler's end! Already the Potter's Field claims many of these victims. The successful murderers and thugs linger in the dark shadows of Dupont Street. They crowd Murderer's Alley, Dunbar's Alley, and Kearney Street.

When the purse is emptied, so that the calculating women dealers scorn to notice the last few coins, they point significantly to the outer darkness. "Vamos," is the word. A few rods will bring the plucked fool to the "Blue Wing," the "Magnolia," or any one of a hundred drinking dens. Here the bottle chases away all memories of the night's play.

In utter defiance of the decent community, these temples of pleasure, with their quick-witted knaves, and garrisons of bright-eyed bacchanals, ignore the useful day; at night, they shine out, splendid lighthouses on the path to the dark entrance of hell. By mutual avoidance, the good and bad, the bright and dark side of human effort rule in alternation the day and night. Sin rests in the daytime.

In the barracks, where the serried battalions of crime loll away the garish day, silence discreetly rules. Sleep and rest mark the sunlit hours. The late afternoon parade is an excitant.

All over San Francisco, in its queerly assorted tenancy, church and saloon, school and opium den, thieves' resort and budding home, are placed side by side. Vigorous elbowing of the criminal and base classes finally forces all that is decent into a semi-banishment. Decency is driven to the distant hills, crowned with their scrubby oaks. Vice needs the city centre. It always does.

Philip Hardin is cynical and without family ties. Able by nature, skilled in books, and a master of human strategy he needs some broader field for the sweep of his splendid talents than the narrowed forum of the local courts. Ambition offers no immediate prize to struggle for. The busy present calls on him for daily professional effort. Political events point to an exciting struggle between North and South in the future; but the hour of fate is not yet on the dial.

In the Southerner's dislike of the contact of others, looking to his place as a social leader of the political element, Philip Hardin lives alone; his temporary cottage is planted in a large lot removed from the immediate danger of fires. His quick wit tells him they will some day sweep the crowded houses in the eastern part of the city, as far as the bay. The larger native oaks still afford a genial shade. Their shadows give the tired lawyer a few square rods of breathing space. Books and all the implements of the scholar are his; the interior is crowded with those luxuries which Hardin enjoys as of right. Deeply drinking the cup of life, even in his social vices, Philip Hardin aims at a certain distinction.

Around his table gather the choicest knights-errant of the golden quest. Maxime Valois here develops a social talent as a leader of men, guided by the sardonic Mephisto of his young life.

Still the evening hours hang heavily on the hands of the two lawyers. When the rapidly arriving steamers bring friends, with letters or introductions, they have hospitality to dispense. The great leaders of the South are now systematically colonizing California. Guests abound at these times at Hardin's board. Travel, mining, exploration, and adventure carry them away soon; extensive tours on official duty draw them away. As occupations increase, men grow unmindful of each other and meet more rarely.

For the saloons, rude hotels, gaming palaces, and resorts of covert pleasures are the usual rendezvous of the men of fortune and power. In such resorts grave intrigues are planned; future policies are mapped out; business goes on under the laughter of wild-eyed Maenads; secrets of state are whispered between glass and glass.

Family circles, cooped up, timid and distant, keep their doors closed to the general public. No one has yet dared to permanently set up here their Lares and Penates. The subordination of family life to externals, and insincerity of social compacts, are destined to make California a mere abiding place for several generations. The fibres of ancestry must first knit the living into close communion with their parents born on these Western shores. Hardin's domineering nature, craving excitement and control over others, carries him often to the great halls of play; cigar in mouth, he stands unmoved; he watches the chances of play. Nerved with the cognac he loves, he moves quickly to the table; he astonishes all by the deliberate daring of his play. His iron nerve is unshaken by the allurements of the painted dancers and surrounding villains. Towering high above all others, the gifted Mississippian nightly refreshes his jaded emotions. He revels in the varying fortunes of the many games he coolly enjoys. Unheeding others, moving neither right nor left at menace or danger, Hardin scorns this human circus, struggling far below his own mental height.

Heartless and unmoved, he smiles at the weaknesses of others. The strong man led captive in Beauty's train, the bright intellect sinking under the craze of drink, the weak nature shattered by the loss of a few thousands at play--all this pleases him. He sees, with prophetic eye, hundreds of thousands of future dwellers between the Sierras and the sea. His Southern pride looks forward to a control of the great West by the haughty slave-owners.

This Northern trash must disappear! To ride on the top wave of the future successful community, is his settled determination. Without self-surrender, he enjoys every draught of pleasure the cup of life can offer. Without scruple, void of enthusiasm, his passionless heart is unmoved by the joys or sorrows of others. His nature is as steady as the nerve with which he guides his evening pistol practice. The welcome given to Maxime Valois by him arises only from a conviction of that man's future usefulness. The general acceptability of the young Louisianian is undoubted. His blood, creed, and manners prove him worthy of the old Valois family. Their past glories are well known to Philip Hardin. "Bon sang ne peut mentir." Hardin's legal position places him high in the turmoils of the litigations of the great Mexican grants. Already, over the Sonoma, Napa, Santa Clara, San Joaquin and Sacramento valleys all is in jeopardy. The old Dons begin to seek confirmations of the legal lines, to keep the crowding settlers at bay. The mining, trading, and land-grabbing of the Americans are pushed to the limits of the new commonwealth. A backward movement of the poor Mexican natives carries them between the Americans and the yet powerful land barons of their own race. Harassed, unfit to work, unable to cope with the intruders, the native Californians become homeless rovers. They are bitter at heart. Many, in open resentment, rise on the plains or haunt the lonely trails. They are now bandits, horse-thieves, footpads and murderers. True to each other, they establish a chain of secret refuges from Shasta to San Diego. Every marauder of their own blood is safe among them from American pursuers.

Every mining camp and all the settlements are beginning to send refugees of the male foreign criminal classes to join these wandering Mexican bands.

With riot in the camps, licentiousness ruling the cities, and murder besetting every path, there is no safety for the present. California sees no guarantee for the future. Judge Lynch is the only recognized authority. He represents the rough justice of outraged camps and infuriated citizens. Unrepressed violent crimes lead to the retaliatory butchery of vigilance committees. Innocent and guilty suffer without warrant of law. Foreign criminal clans herd together in San Francisco for mutual aid. The different Atlantic cities are separately represented in knots of powerful villains. Politics, gambling, and the elements of wealth flourishing in dens and resorts, are controlled by organized villains. They band together against the good. Only some personal brawl throws them against each other.

Looking at the dangerous mass of vicious men and women, Valois determines that the real strength of the land will lie in the arrivals by the overland caravans. These trains are now filling the valleys with resolute and honest settlers.

His determination holds yet to acquire some large tract of land where he may have a future domain. On professional visits to Sacramento, Stockton, and San Jose he notes the rising of the agricultural power in the interior. In thought he yearns often for the beauties of splendid Lagunitas. Padre Ribaut writes him of the sullen retirement of Don Miguel. He grows more morose daily. Valois learns of the failing of the sorrow-subdued Donna Juanita. The girlish beauty of young Dolores is pictured in these letters. She approaches the early development of her rare beauty. Padre Francisco has his daily occupation in his church and school. The higher education of pretty Dolores is his only luxury. Were it not for this, he would abandon the barren spiritual field and return to France. Already in the canyons of the Mariposa, Fresno, and in the great foot-hills, miners are scratching around the river beds. Hostile settlers are approaching from the valley the Don's boundaries. These signs are ominous.

Padre Francisco writes that as yet Don Miguel is sullenly ferocious. He absolutely refuses any submission of his grant titles to the cursed Gringos. Padre Francisco has not been able to convince the ex-commandante of the power of the great United States. He knows not it can cancel or reject his title to the thousands of rich acres where his cattle graze and his horses sweep in mustang wildness. Even from his very boundaries the plough can now be seen breaking up the breast of the virgin valley. The Don will take no heed. He is blinded by prejudice. Maxime promises the good priest to visit him. He wonders if the savage Don would decline a word. If the frightened, faded wife would deign to speak to the Americano. If the budding beauty would now cast roses slyly at him from the bowers of her childhood.

Maxime's heart is young and warm. He is chilled in his affections. The loss of his parents made his life lonely. Judge Valois, his uncle, has but one child, a boy born since Maxime's departure on the Western adventure. Between Hardin and himself is a bar of twenty years of cool experience. It indurates and blunts any gracefulness Hardin's youth ever possessed. If any man of forty has gained knowledge of good and evil, it is the accomplished Hardin. He is a law unto himself.

Fearing neither God nor man, insensible to tenderness, Philip Hardin looks in vain to refresh his jaded emotions by the every-day diversions of the city by the sea. The daily brawls, the excited vigilance committee of the first winter session of popular justice, and partial burning of the city, leave Hardin unmoved. It is a dismal March night of 1851 when he leaves his residence for a stroll through the resorts of the town. Valois listlessly accompanies him. He does not gamble. To the El Dorado the two slowly saunter. The nightly battle over the heaps of gold is at its height. At the superb marble counter they are served with the choicest beverages and regalias of Vuelta Abajos' best leaf. The human mob is dense. Wailing, passionate music beats upon the air. There is the cry of lost souls in its under-toned pathos. Villany and sentiment go hand in hand at the El Dorado. The songs of old, in voice and symphony, unlock the gates of memory. They leave the lingerers, disarmed, to the tempting allurements of beauty, drink, and gaming.

There is an unusual crowd in the headquarters of gilded folly. Maxime, wandering alone for a few minutes, finds a throng around a table of rouge et noir. It is crowded with eager gamesters. Nodding to one and another, he meets many acquaintances--men have no real friends as yet in this egoistic land. The Louisianian moves toward the goal whither all are tending. Jealous glances are cast by women whose deserted tables show their charms are too well known. All swarm toward a new centre of attraction. Cheeks long unused to the blush of shame are reddened with passion, to see the fickle crowd surge around the game presided over by a new-comer to the sandy shores of San Francisco. She is an unknown goddess.

"What's all this?" asks Maxime, of a man he knows. He is idling now, with an amused smile. He catches a glimpse of the tall form of Philip Hardin in the front row of players, near the yellow bulwarks of gold.

"Why, Valois, you are behind the times!" is the reply. "Don't you know the 'Queen of the El Dorado'?"

"I confess I do not," says the Creole. He has been absent for some time from this resort of men with more gold than brains. "Who is she? What is she?" continues Maxime.

His friend laughs as he gaily replies, "As to what she is, walk up to the table. Throw away an ounce, and look at her. It's worth it. As to who she is, she calls herself Hortense Duval." "I suppose she has as much right to call herself the daughter of the moon as to use that aristocratic name." "My dear boy, she is, for all that--" "Queen Hortense?" "Queen of the El Dorado." He saunters away, to allow Valois a chance to edge his way into the front row. There the dropping gold is raked in by this fresh siren who draws all men to her.

Dressed in robes of price, a young woman sits twirling the arrow of destiny at the treasure-laden table. Her exquisite form is audaciously and recklessly exposed by a daring costume. Her superb arms are bared to the shoulder, save where heavy-gemmed bracelets clasp glittering badges of sin around her slender wrists. An indescribable grace and charm is in every movement of her sinuous body. Her well-poised head is set upon a neck of ivory. The lustrous dark eyes rove around the circle of eager betters with languishing velvety glances. A smile, half a sneer, lingers on the curved lips. Her statuesque beauty of feature is enhanced by the rippling dark masses of hair crowning her lovely brows. In the silky waves of her coronal, shines one diamond star of surpassing richness. In all the pride and freshness of youth her loveliness is unmarred by the tawdry arts of cosmetic and make-up. Unabashed by the admiration she compels, she calmly pursues her exciting calling. The newcomer is well worthy the rank, by general acclaim, of "Queen of the El Dorado." In no way does she notice the eager crowd. She is an impartial priestess of fortune. Maxime waits only to hear her speak. She is silent, save the monosyllabic French words of the game. Is she Cuban, Creole, French, Andalusian, Italian, or a wandering gypsy star? A jewelled dagger-sheath in her corsage speaks of Spain or Italy. Maxime notes the unaccustomed eagerness with which Hardin recklessly plays. He seems determined to attract the especial attention of the divinity of the hour. Hardin's color is unusual. His features are sternly set. Near him stands "French Charlie," one of the deadliest gamesters of the plaza. Equally quick with card, knife, or trigger, the Creole gambler is a man to be avoided. He is as dangerous as the crouching panther in its fearful leap.

Hardin, betting on black, seems to win steadily. "French Charlie" sets his store of ready gold on the red. It is a reckless duel of the two men through the medium of the golden arrow, twirled by the voluptuous stranger.

A sudden idea strikes Valois. He notes the ominous sparkle of "French Charlie's" eye. It is cold as the depths of a mountain-pool. Is Hardin betting on the black to compliment the presiding dark beauty? Murmurs arise among the bystanders. The play grows higher. Valois moves away from the surging crowd, to wait his own opportunity. A glass of wine with a friend enables him to learn her history. She has been pursued by "French Charlie" since her arrival from Panama by steamer. No one knows if the reigning beauty is Havanese or a French Creole. Several aver she speaks French and Spanish with equal ease. English receives a dainty foreign accent from the rosebud lips. Her mysterious identity is guarded by the delighted proprietors. The riches of their deep-jawed safes tell of her wonderful luck, address, or skill.

Charlie has in vain tried to cross the invisible barrier which fences her from the men around her. To-night he is as unlucky in his heavy play, as in arousing any passion in that wonderful beauty of unexplained identity. The management will answer no questions. This nightly excitement feeds on itself. "French Charlie" has been drinking deeply. His play grows more unlucky. Valois moves to the table, to quietly induce Hardin to leave. Some inner foreboding tells Valois there is danger in the gambling duel of the two men he watches. As he forces his way in, Charlie, dashing a last handful of gold upon the red, turns his ferocious eyes on Hardin. The lawyer calmly waits the turn of the arrow. Some quick presentiment reaches the mind of the woman. Her nerves are shaken with the strain of long repression. The arrow trembles on the line in stopping. The queen's eyes, for the first time, catch the burning glances of Philip Hardin. "French Charlie," with an oath, grasps the hand of the woman. She is raking in his lost coins before paying Hardin's bet. It is his last handful of gold.

Maddened with drink and his losses, Charlie yields to jealousy of his victorious neighbor. "French Charlie" roughly twists the wrist of the woman. With a sharp shriek, she snatches the dagger from her bosom. She draws it over the back of the gambler's hand. He howls with pain. Like a flash he tears a knife from his bosom. He springs around the table toward the woman. With a loud scream, she jumps back toward the wall. She seeks to save herself, casting golden showers on the floor, in a rattling avalanche. Before the ready hireling desperadoes of the haunt can seize Charlie, the affrighted circle scatters. Valois' eye catches, the flash of a silver-mounted derringer. Its barking report rings out as "French Charlie's" right arm drops to his side. His bowie-knife falls ringing on the floor. A despairing curse is heard. The Creole gambler snatches, with the other hand, a pistol. He springs like a lion on Philip Hardin. One step back Hardin retreats. No word comes from his closed lips. The mate of the derringer rings out loudly Charlie's death warrant. The gambler crashes to the floor. His heart's blood floods the scattered gold. The pistol is yet clenched in his stiffened left hand. Valois rushes to Hardin. He brushes him aside, and springs to the side of the "Queen of the El Dorado." She falls senseless in his arms. In a few moments the motley crowd has been hurried from the doors. The great entrances are barred. The frightened women dealers seek their dressing-rooms. All fear the results of this brawl. Their cheeks are ashy pale under paint and powder. The treasures are swiftly swept from the gaming tables by the nimble-witted croupiers. Hardin and Valois are left with the unconscious fallen beauty. A couple of the lately organized city police enter and take charge. Even the blood stained gold is gathered from the floor. Light after light is turned out. The main hall has at last no tenants but the night watchman and the police, waiting by the dead gambler. He lies prone on the floor, awaiting his last judge, the city coroner. This genial official is sought from his cards and cups, to certify the causes of death of the outcast of society. A self-demonstrating problem. The gaping wound tells its story.

Valois is speechless and stunned with the quickness of the deadly quarrel. He gloomily watches Hardin supporting the fainting woman. Slowly her eyes unclose. They meet Hardin's in one long, steadfast, inscrutable glance. She shudders and says, "Take me away." She covers her siren face with her jewelled hands, to avoid the sight of the waxy features and stiffening form of the thing lying there. Ten minutes ago it was the embodiment of wildest human passion and tiger-like activity.

Vale, "French Charlie."

Hardin has quickly sent for several influential friends. On their arrival he is permitted to leave, escorted by a policeman. The shaken sorceress, whose fatal beauty has thrown two determined men against each other in a sudden duel to the death, walks at his side. There is a bond of blood sealed between them. It is the mere sensation of a night; the talk of an idle day. On the next evening the "El Dorado" is thronged with a great multitude. It is eager to gaze on the wondrous woman's face, for which "French Charlie" died. Their quest is vain. Another daughter of the Paphian divinity presides at the shrine of rouge et noir. The blood-stains are effaced from the floor. A fresh red mound in the city cemetery is the only relic of French Charlie. Philip Hardin, released upon heavy bail, awaits a farcical investigation. After a few days he bears no legal burden of this crime. Only the easy load upon his conscience. Although the mark of Cain sets up a barrier between him and his fellows, and the murder calls for the vengeance of God, Philip Hardin goes his way with unclouded brow. His eyes have a strange new light in them.

The "Queen of the El Dorado" sits no more at the wheel of fortune. Day succeeds to day. Nightly expectation is balked. Her absent charms are magnified in description. The memory of the graceful, dazzling Hortense Duval fades from the men who struggle around the gaming boards of the great "El Dorado." She never shows her charming face again in the hall.

The secret of the disappearance of this mysterious sovereign of chance is known to but few. It is merely surmised by others. To Maxime Valois the bloody occurrence has borne fruits of importance. As soon as some business is arranged, the shadowy barrier of this tragedy divides the two men. Though slight, it is yet such that Valois decides to go to Stockton. The San Joaquin valley offers him a field. Land matters give ample scope to his talents. The investment in lands can be better arranged from there. The Creole is glad to cast his lot in the new community. By sympathy, many Southerners crowd in. They gain control of the beautiful prairies from which the herds of elk and antelope are disappearing.

Philip Hardin's safety is assured. With no open breach of friendship between them, Maxime still feels estranged. He visits the scene of his future residence. His belongings follow him. It was an intuition following a tacit understanding. Man instinctively shuns the murderer.

Maxime never asked of the future of the vanished queen of the El Dorado. In his visits to San Francisco he finds that few cross Philip Hardin's threshold socially. Even these are never bid to come again. Is there a hidden queen in the house on the hill? Rumor says so.

Rising in power, Philip Hardin steadily moves forward. He asks no favors. He seeks no friends. All unmindful is he of the tattle that a veiled lady of elegant appearance sometimes walks under the leafy bowers shading his lovely home.

The excitable populace find new food for gossip. There are more residences than one in San Francisco, where dreamy luxury is hidden within the unromantic wooden boxes called residences.

Fair faces gleam out furtively from these casements. At open doors, across whose thresholds no woman of position ever sets a foot, wealth stands on guard. Silence seals the portals. The vassals of gold wait in velvet slippers. The laws of possession are enforced by the dangers of any trespass on these Western harems.

While the queen city of the West rises rapidly it is only a modern Babylon on the hills of the bay. The influx augments all classes. Every element of present and future usefulness slowly makes headway against the current of mere adventure. Natural obstacles yield to patient, honest industry. California begins in grains, fruits, and all the rich returns of nature, to show that Ceres, Flora, and Pomona are a trinity of witching good fairies. They beckon to the world to wander hither, and rest under these blue-vaulted balmy skies. Near the splendid streams, picturesque ridges, and lovely valleys of the new State, health and happiness may be found, even peace.

The State capital is located, drawn by the golden magnet, at Sacramento. The only conquest left for the dominating Americans, is the development of this rich landed domain. Here, where the Padres dreamed over their monkish breviaries, where the nomad native Californians lived only on the carcasses of their wild herds, the richest plains on earth invite the honest hand of the farmer.

The era of frantic dissipation, wildest license, insane speculation, and temporary abiding wears away. Bower and blossom, bird and bee, begin to adorn the new homes of the Pacific.

Mighty-hearted men, keen of vision, strong of purpose, appear. The face of nature is made to change under the resolute attacks of inventive man. Roads and bridges, wharves and storehouses, telegraph lines, steamer routes, express and stage systems, banks and post-offices, courts, churches, marts and halls, all come as if at magic call. The school-master is abroad. Public offices and records are in working order. Though the fierce hill Indians now and then attack the miners, they are driven back toward the great citadel of the Sacramento River. The huge mountain ranges on the Oregon border are their last fastnesses.

In every community of the growing State, the law is aided by quickly executed decrees of vigilance committees. Self-appointed popular leaders, crafty politicians, scheming preachers, aspiring editors, and ambitious demagogues crop up. They are the mushroom growth of the muck-heap of the new civilization.

Hardin gathers up with friendships the rising men of all the counties. At the newly formed clubs of the city his regular entertainments are a nucleus of a socio-political organization to advance the ambitious lawyer and the cause of the South.

Men say he looks to the Senate, or the Supreme Bench. Maxime Valois, rising in power at Stockton, retains the warmest confidence of Hardin. He knows the crafty advocate is the arch-priest of Secession. Month by month, he is knitting up the web of his dark intrigues. He would unite the daring sons of the South in one great secret organization, ready to strike when the hour of destiny is at hand. It comes nearer, day by day. Here, in this secret cause of the South, Valois' heart and soul go out to Hardin. He feels the South was juggled out of California. Both he and his Mephisto are gazing greedily on the wonderful development of the coast. Even adjoining Arizona and New Mexico begin to fill up. The conspirators know the South is handicapped in the irrepressible conflict unless some diversion is made in the West. They must secure for the states of the Southern Republic their aliquot share of the varied treasures of the West. The rich spoil of an unholy war.

Far-seeing and wise is the pupil of Calhoun and Slidell. He is the coadjutor of the subtle Gwin. Hardin feeds the flame of Maxime Valois' ardor. The business friendship of the men continues unabated. They need each other. With rare delicacy, Valois never refers to the blood-bought "beauty of the El Dorado." Her graceful form never throws its shadow over the threshold of the luxurious home of the lawyer. On rare visits to the residence of his friend, Valois' quick eye notes the evidence of a reigning divinity. A piano and a guitar, a scarf here, a few womanly treasures there, are indications of a "manage a deux." They prove to Maxime that the Egeria of this intellectual king lingers near her victim. He is still under her mystic spell. Breasting the tide of litigation in the United States and State courts, popular and ardent, the Louisianian thrives. He rises into independent manhood. He is toasted in Sacramento, where in legislative halls his fiery eloquence distinguishes him. He is the king of the San Joaquin valley.

Preserving his friendship with the clergy, still warmly allied to Padre Francisco, Maxime Valois gradually gains an unquestioned leadership. His friends at New Orleans are proud of this young pilgrim from "Belle Etoile." Judge Valois hopes that the coming man will return to Louisiana in search of some bright daughter of that sunny land, a goddess to share the honors of the younger branch of the old Valois family. Rosy dreams!

Maxima, satisfied, yet not happy, sees a great commonwealth grow up around him. Looking under the tides of the political struggles, he can feel the undertow of the future. It seems to drag him back to the old Southern land of his birth, "Home to Dixie."

CHAPTER VIII.

JOAQUIN, THE MOUNTAIN ROBBER.--THE DON'S PERIL.

The leaders of the San Joaquin meet at the office of Counsellor Maxime Valois. He is the rising political chief. While multitudes yet delve for gold, Valois wisely heads those who see that the miners are merely nomadic. They are all adventurers. The great men of the coast will be those who control its broad lands, and create ways of communication. The men who develop manufactures, start commercial enterprises, and the farmers, will develop resources of this virgin State. The thousand vocations of civilization are building up a solid fabric for future generations.

True, the poet, the story-writer, and the careless stranger will be fascinated by the heroes of camp and glen. High-booted, red-shirted, revolver-carrying, bearded argonauts are they, braving all hardships, enjoying sudden wealth, and leading romantic lives. Stories of camp and cabin, with brief Monte-Cristo appearances at San Francisco, are the popular rage. These rough heroes are led captive, even as Samson was betrayed by Delilah. The discovery of quartz mining leads Valois to believe that an American science of geologic mining will be a great help in the future. Years of failure and effort, great experience, with associated capital, will be needed for exploring the deep quartz veins. Their mysterious origin baffles the scientist.

Long after the individual argonauts have laid their weary brows upon the drifted pine needles in the deep eternal sleep of Death, the problem will be solved. When their lonely graves are landmarks of the Sierras; when the ephemeral tent towns have been folded up forever, the broad lands of California will support great communities. To them, these early days will be as unreal as the misty wreaths clinging around the Sierras.

The romance of the Gilded Age! Each decade throws a deeper mantle of the shadowy past over the struggles of fresh hearts that failed in the mad race for gold.

Their lives become, day by day, a mere disjointed mass of paltry incident. Their careers point no moral, even if they adorn the future tale. The type of the argonaut itself begins to disappear. Those who returned freighted with gold to their foreign homes are rich, and leading other lives far away. Those who diverted their new-found wealth into industries are prospering. They will leave histories and stable monuments of their life-work. But the great band of placer hunters have wandered into the distant territories of the great West. They leave their bones scattered, under the Indian's attack, or die on distant quests. They drop into the stream of unknown fate. No moral purpose attended their arrival. No high aim directed their labors. As silently as they came, the rope of sand has sifted away. Their influence is absolutely nothing upon the future social life of California. Even later Californian society owes nothing of its feverish strangeness to these gold hunters. They toiled in their historic quest. The prosaic results of the polyglot settlement of the new State are not of their direction.

The bizarre Western character is due to an admixture of ill-assorted elements. Not to gold itself or the lust of gold. The personal history of the gold hunters is almost valueless. No hallowed memory clings to the miner's grave. No blessing such as hovers over the soldier, dead under his country's banner.

The early miners fell by the way, while grubbing for gold. Their ends were only selfish gain. Their gold was a minister of vilest pleasures. A fool's title to temporary importance.

Among them were many of high powers and great capacity, worthy of deeds of derring-do, yet it cannot be denied that the narrowest impulses of human action drove the impetuous explorers over the high Sierras. Gain alone buried them in the dim canons of the Yuba and American. The sturdy citizens pouring in with their families, seeking homes; those who laid the enduring foundations of the social fabric, the laws and enterprises of necessity, pith, and moment, are the real fathers of the great Golden State. In the rapidity of settlement, all the manifold labors of civilization began together. Laus Deo! There were hands, brains, and hearts for those trying hours of the sudden acquisition of this royal domain.

The thoughtful scholar Nevins, throwing open the first public school-room to a little nursery-like brood, planted the seeds of a future harvest, far richer than the output of the river treasuries.

A farmer's wife toiling over the long plains, caring for two beehives, mindful of the future, introduced a future wealth, kinder in prophetic thought, than he who blindly stumbled on a bonanza.

Humble farmer, honest head of family, intelligent teacher, useful artisan, wise doctor, and skilled mechanic, these were the real fathers of the State.

The sailor, the mechanic, and the good pioneer women, these are the heroes and heroines gratefully remembered now. They regulated civilization; they stood together against the gold-maddened floating miners; they fought the vicious camp-followers.

Maxime Valois, learned in the civil law of his native State, speaking French and Spanish, soon plunged in the vexatious land litigation of his generation. Mere casual occupancy gave little color of title to the commoner Mexicans. Now, the great grant owners are, one by one, cited into court to prove their holdings; many are forced in by aggressive squatters.

While gold still pours out of the mines, and the young State feels a throbbing life everywhere, the native Californians are sorely pressed between the land-getting and the mining classes. Wild herds no longer furnish them free meat at will. The mustangs are driven away from their haunts. Growing poverty cuts off ranch hospitality. Without courage to labor, the poorer Mexicans, contemptuously called Greasers, go to the extremes of passive suffering. All the occupations of the vaqueros are gone. These desperate Greasers are driven to horse-stealing and robbery.

Expert with lasso, knife, and revolver, they know every trail. These bandits mount themselves at will from herds of the new-comers.

The regions of the north, the forests of the Sierras, and the lonely southern valleys give them safe lurking-places. Wherever they reach a ranch of their people, they are protected; the pursuers are baffled; they are misled by the sly hangers-on of these gloomy adobe houses.

In San Joaquin, the brigands hold high carnival; they sally out on wild rides across the upper Sacramento. The mining regions are in terror. Herds of stolen horses are driven by the Livermore Pass to the south. Cattle and sheep are divided; they are used for food. Sometimes the brands are skilfully altered by addition or counterfeit.

Suspicious Mexicans are soon in danger. Short shrift is given to the horse-thief. The State authorities are powerless in face of the duplicity of these native residents. They feel they have been enslaved by the treaty of Guadalupe Hidalgo. The roads became unsafe. Travellers are subject to a sudden volley from ambush. The fatal lasso is one trick; the midnight stab, when lodging in Mexican wayside houses, is another. There is no longer safety save in the large towns. From San Diego to Shasta, a chain of criminals leaves a record of bloody deeds. There are broader reasons than the mere friction of races. The native Californians are rudely treated in the new courts; their personal rights are invaded; their homes are not secure; their women are made the prey of infamous attack.

A deadly feud now rises between the Mexicans and Americans. These brutal encroachments of the new governing race bring reprisals in chance duels and secret crimes. This organized robbery is a return blow. The Americans are forced to travel in posses. They reinforce their sheriffs. They establish armed messengers. In town and county they execute suspects by a lively applied Lynch law.

All that is needed to create a general race-war is a determined leader.

As months roll on, the record of violence becomes alarming. Small stations are attacked, many desperate fights occur. Dead men are weltering in their blood, on all the trails. A scheming intelligence seems now to direct the bandits. Pity was never in the Mexican heart. But now unarmed men are butchered while praying for mercy. Their bodies are wantonly gashed. Droves of poor, plodding, unarmed Chinese miners are found lying dead like sheep in rows. Every trail and road is unsafe. Different bodies of robbers, from five to twenty, operate at the same time. There is no telegraph here as yet, to warn the helpless settlers. The following of treasure trains shows that spies are aiding the bandits.

The leading men of the new State find this scourge unbearable. Lands are untenanted, cattle and herds are a prey to the robbers. Private and public reward has failed to check this evil. Sheriff's posses and occasional lynching parties shoot and hang. Still the evil grows. It is an insult to American courage. As 1852 is ushered in, there are nearly two hundred and fifty thousand dwellers in the new State. Still the reign of terror continues. One curious fact appears. All of the bandits chased south toward Monterey or Los Angeles are finally driven to bay, killed, or scattered as fugitives. In the middle regions, the organization of the Mexican murderers seems to be aided by powerful friends. They evidently furnish news, supplies, and give concealment to these modern butchers. They are only equalled by the old cutthroats of the Spanish main.

A meeting of citizens is called at Stockton. It is privately held, for fear of betrayal. Maxime Valois is, as usual, in the van. His knowledge of the country and his renown as a member of Fremont's party fit him to lead. A secret organization is perfected. The sheriff of the county is made head of it. He can use the power of posse and his regular force. The plundered merchants agree to furnish money as needed. Maxime Valois is needed as the directing brain. In study over news and maps, the result proves that the coast and south are only used for the sale of stock or for refuge.

The extreme north of the State shows no prey, save the starving Klamath Indians. It is true the robbers never have cursed the upper mountains. Their control sweeps from Shasta to Sonoma, from Marysville and Nevada as far as the gates of Sacramento, and down to the Livermore Pass. Mariposa groans under their attacks.

Valois concludes this bloody warfare is a logical result of the unnecessary conquest of California. To lose their nationality is galling. To see Mexico, which abandoned California, get $15,000,000 in compensation for the birthright of the Dons is maddening. It irritates the suspicious native blood. To be ground down daily, causes continual bickering. Ranch after ranch falls away under usury or unjust decisions. In this ably planned brigandage, Valois discerns some young resentful Californian of good family has assisted. The terrific brutality points also to a relentless daring nature, aroused by some special wrong.

Valois muses at night in his lonely office. His ready revolvers are at hand. Even here in Stockton a Mexican, friendly to the authorities, has been filled with bullets by a horseman. The assailant was swathed to his head in his scrape. He dashed away like the wind. There is danger everywhere.

The young lawyer pictures this, the daring bravo--hero by nature--made a butcher and a fiend by goading sorrows. It must be some one who knows the Americans, who has travelled the interior, and has personal wrongs to avenge.

These dark riders strike both innocent and guilty. They kill without reason, and destroy in mere wantonness. The band has never been met in its full muster. The general operations are always the same. It seems to Valois that there are two burning questions:

First--Who is the leader?

Second--Where is the hiding-place or stronghold?

To paralyze the band, this master intelligence must be neutralized by death. To finish the work, that stronghold must be found or destroyed.

There is as yet no concurrent voice as to their leader. Maxime Valois is positive, however, that the stronghold is not far from the slopes of Mariposa. The deadly riders seem to disappear, when driven towards Stockton. They afterwards turn up, as if sure shelter was near.

But who will hound this fiend to his lair? Valois sends for the sheriff. They decide to organize a picked corps of men. They will ride the roads, with leaders selected from veteran Indian fighters. Others are old soldiers of the Mexican war. The heaviest rewards are offered, to stimulate the capture of the bandit chiefs. Valois knows, though, that money will never cause a Mexican to betray any countryman to the Americans. A woman's indiscretion, yes, a jealous sweetheart's bitter hatred might lead to gaining the bandit chief's identity. But gold. Never! The Mexicans never needed it, save to gamble. Judas is their national scapegoat.

The sheriff has collated every story of attack. Valois draws out the personality of the leading actor in this revelry of death. A superb horseman, of medium size, who handles his American dragoon revolvers with lightning rapidity. A young man in a yellow, black-striped scrape. He is always superbly mounted. He has curling blackest hair. Two dark eyes, burning under bushy brows, are the principal features. This man has either led the murderers or been present at the fiercest attacks. In many pistol duels, he has killed some poor devil in plain sight of his comrades.

Valois decides to search all towns where Spanish women abound, for such a romantic figure. This bandit must need supplies and ammunition. He must visit women, the fandango, and the attractions of monte. He must have friends to give him news of treasure movements. Valois watches secretly the Spanish quarters of all the mountain towns and the great ranchos.

The Louisianian knows that every gambling-shop and dance-house is a centre of spies and marauders. The throngs of unnoticed Mexicans, in a land where every traveller is an armed horseman, enable these robber fiends to mingle with the innocent. The common language, hatred of the Americans, the hospitality to criminals of their blood, and the admiration of the sullen natives for these bravos, prevent any dependence on the Mexican population.

The pursuers have often failed because of lack of supplies, and worn-out steeds. The villains are secretly refitted by those who harbor them. An hour suffices to drive up the "caballada," and remount the bandits at any friendly interior ranch.

Obstinate silence is all the roadside dwellers' return to questions.

Valois cons over the bloody record of the last two years. The desperate crimes begin with Andres Armijo and Tomas Maria Carrillo. They were unyielding ex-soldiers. Both of these have been run to earth. Salamon Pico, an independent bandit, of native blood, follows the same general career. John Irving, a renegade American, has held the southern part of the State. With his followers, he murdered General Bean and others. He was only an outcast foreigner.

Maxime Valois knows that Irving and his band have been butchered by savage Indians near the Colorado. Yet none of these have killed for mere lust of blood. This mysterious chieftain who murders for personal vengeance, is soon known to the determined Louisianian. In the long trail of tiger-like assassinations, the robber is disclosed by his unequalled thirst for blood.

"Joaquin Murieta, Joaquin the Mountain Robber, Joaquin the Yellow Tiger." He flashes out from the dark shades of night, or the depths of chaparral and forest. His insane butchery proves Valois to be correct.

Dashing through camps, lurking around towns, appearing in distant localities, he robs stages, plunders stations, and personally murders innocent travellers. Express riders are ambushed. The word "Joaquin," scrawled on a monte card, and pinned to the dead man's breast, often tells the tale. Lonely men are found on the trails with the fatal bullet-hole in the back of the head, shot in surprise. Sometimes he appears with followers, often alone. Now openly daring individual conflict, then slinking at night and in silence. Sneak, bravo, and tiger. He is a Turpin in horsemanship. A fiend in his thirst for blood. A charmed life seems his. On magnificent steeds, he rides down the fleeing traveller. He coolly murders the exhausted "Gringo," taunting his hated race with cowardice. Sweeping from north to south, five hundred miles, this yellow-clad fiend always keeps the Sacramento or San Joaquin between him and the coast. Men shudder at the name of Joaquin Murieta.

Valois sees that the robber chief's permanent haunt is somewhere in the Sierras. This must be found. The sheriffs of Placer, Nevada, Sierra, El Dorado, Tuolumne, Calaveras, and Mariposa counties are in the field with posses. Skirmish after skirmish occurs. All doubtful men are arrested. Yet the red record continues. Doubling on the pursuers, hiding, the bandit whirls from Shasta to Tehama, from Oroville to Sacramento, from Marysville to Placerville. Stockton, San Andreas, Sonora, and Mariposa are terrorized. Plundered pack-trains, murdered men, and robbed wayfarers prove that Joaquin Murieta is ever at work. His swoop is unerring. The yellow serape, black banded, the dark scowling face, and the battery of four revolvers, two on his body, two on his saddle, soon make him known to all the State.

The Governor offers five thousand dollars State reward for Joaquin's head. County rewards are also published. Valois watches all the leading Mexican families. Some wild son or member must be unaccounted for. No criminal has yet appeared of good blood, save Tomas Maria Carrillo. But he has been dead a year, shot in his tracks by a brave man. The bandits hover around Stockton. The Americans go heavily armed, and only travel in large bodies. Public rage reaches its climax, when there is found pinned on the body of a dead deputy-sheriff a printed proclamation of the Governor of $5,000 for Joaquin's head.

Under the printed words is the scrawl:

"I myself will give ten thousand.

"JOAQUIN."

The passions of the Americans break loose. Innocent Mexicans are shot and hanged; all stragglers driven out.

The San Joaquin valley becomes a theatre of continued conflict.

"Claudio," another dark chief, ravages the Salinas. He is the robber king of the coast. The officers find a union between the coast and inland bandits. Now the manly settlers of the San Joaquin rise in wrath. Texan rangers, old veterans, heroes of Comanche and Sioux battles, all swear to hunt Joaquin Murieta to death.

Maxime Valois takes the saddle. He posts strong forces in the defiles opening to the coast. A secret messenger leaves for Monterey. A vigorous attack on the coast bandits drives them toward the inland passes.

"Claudio" and his followers are killed, after a bitter hand-to-hand duel. One or two are hanged. Sheriff Cocks is the hero of the coast. Maxime Valois calls his ablest men together.

Dividing the main forces into several bodies, a leader is selected for each squad. Scouts are thrown out. They report daily to the heads of divisions. The moving forces are ready to close in and envelop their hated enemy.

Learning of the death of "Claudio," and that a strong body of Southern settlers is also in the field, Maxime Valois feels the band of Joaquin is cut off in the square between Placerville and Sonora, Stockton and the Sierras. It is agreed that the fortunate division striking the robbers, shall follow the warm trail to the last man and horse. Reinforcements will push after them.

The sheriff has charge of one, Maxime Valois of another, Captain Harry Love, a swarthy long-haired Texan ranger, of the third. Love's magnificent horsemanship, his dark features, drooping mustache and general appearance, might class him as a Spaniard. Blackened with the burning sun of the plains, the deserts, and tropic Mexico, his cavalier locks sweep to his shoulders. The heavy Kentucky rifle, always carried across his saddle, proves him the typical frontiersman and ranger. He is a dead shot. Many a Comanche and guerilla have fallen under the unerring aim of Harry Love. His agile frame, quickness with the revolver, and nerve with the bowie-knife, have made him equally feared at close quarters.

In the dark hours of a spring morning of 1854, the main command breaks into its three divisions. The sheriff covers the lines towards the north and San Andreas. Maxime skirts the Sierras. Harry Love, marching silently and at night, hiding his command by day, marches towards Sonora. He sweeps around and rejoins Valois' main body. The net is spread.

Scouts are distributed over this region. The mad wolf of the Sierras is at last to be hunted to his lair.

The unknown retreat must be in the Sierras. He determines to throw his own command over the valley towards the unvisited Lagunitas rancho. Padre Francisco will be there, a good adviser. Valois, the rich and successful lawyer, is another man from the penniless prisoner of seven years before. Knowing the hatred of Don Miguel for the Americans, he has never revisited the place. Still he would like to meet the beloved padre again. He will not uselessly enrage the gloomy lord of Lagunitas. Don Miguel is a hermit now.

Three days' march, skilfully concealed, brings him to the notched pass, where Lagunitas lies under its sentinel mountains.

Brooding over the past, thinking of the great untravelled regions behind the grant, stories from the early life of Don Miguel haunt the sleepless hours of the anxious young Southern leader. He lies under the stars, wrapped in his blankets. Lagunitas, once more!

Up before day, filing through light forest and down the passes of the foothills, the command threads its way. Valois calls his leading subordinates together. He arranges the visit to the ranch. He sends a squad of five to ride down the roads a few miles, and meet any scouts or vedettes of the other Southern party. Valois directs his men where to rejoin him. He points out, a few miles ahead, a rocky cliff, behind which the rolling hills around Lagunitas offer several hidden approaches to the rancho. Cautiously leading his men, to avoid a general alarm, he skirts the woods. The party rides in Indian file, to leave a light trail only.

Before the frowning cliff is neared, Valois' keen eye sees his scouts straggling back. They are galloping at rapid speed, making for the cliff. The whole command, with smoking steeds, soon joins the scouts. With them are two of Love's outriders. The bandits are near at hand. For the scouts, riding up all night from Love's body, have taken the main road. Within ten miles they find several dead men--the ghastly handiwork of Joaquin. Their breathless report is soon over. Detaching ten fresh men, with one of the news-bearers, to join Love and bring him up post-haste, Maxime Valois orders every man to prepare his girths and arms for action. Guided by the other scouts, the whole command pricks briskly over to the concealment of a rolling valley. There is but one ridge between it, now, and Lagunitas.

Maxime calls up his aids. He gives them his rapid directions. Only the previous knowledge of the ex-pathfinder enabled him to throw his men behind the sheltering ridge, unseen from the old Don's headquarters.

In case of meeting any robbers, the subordinates are to seize and hold the ranch with ten determined men. He throws the rest out in a strong line, to sweep east and south, till Love's column is met. Winding into the glen, Valois takes five men and mounts the ridge.

He now skilfully nears the crest of the ridge. The main command is moving slowly, a few hundred yards below. With the skill of the old scout of the plains, he brings his little squad up to the shoulder of the ridge to the south of the rancho. Dismounting, Indian-like, he crawls up to the summit, from which the beautiful panorama of glittering Lagunitas lies before him. By his side is a tried friend. A life and death supporter.

Lagunitas again! It is backed by the forest, where swaying pines are singing the same old song of seven long years ago. His eye sweeps over the scene.

Quick as a flash, Valois springs back to the horses. Two mounted cavaliers, followed by a serving man, can be seen smartly loping away to the southeast. They are bending towards the region where Love's course, the trail of the bandits, and Maxime's march intersect. Is it treachery? Some one to warn the robbers!

Not a moment to lose! "Harris," cries Valois to his companion, "lead the main command over to that mountain. Be ready to strike any moment. Send Hill and ten men to capture the ranch by moving over the ridge. Keep every one there. Hold every human inmate. I'll cut these men off." Away gallops Harris. Valois leads the four over the other spur. They drop down the eastern slope of the point. The riders have to pass near. In rapid words he orders them to throw themselves quickly, at a dead run, ahead of the travellers. He waits till, six or eight hundred yards away, the strange horsemen pass the lowest point of the ridge. The first three scouts are now well across the line of march of the quick-moving strangers. Then, with a word, "Now, boys, remember!" Valois spurs his roan out into the open. At a wild gallop he cuts off the retreat of the horsemen.

Ha! one turns. They are discovered. In an instant the wild mustangs are racing south. Valois dashes along in pursuit. He has warned his men to use no firearms till absolutely necessary. He shouts to his two followers to wait till the last. He would capture, not kill, these three spies.

Out from the slopes below, the main column, at a brisk trot, cross the valley. They are led by the quick-eyed scout, who knows how to throw them on the narrowing suspected region. Love's men and the band of Joaquin, if here, must soon meet. The three men in advance ride up at different points. They have seen pursuer and pursued galloping madly towards them. Instantly the man following the first rider darts northward, and spurring up a ridge disappears, followed by two of the three scouts in advance. The other rider draws up and stands his ground with his servant. As Valois and his companions ride up, the crack, crack, crack, of heavy dragoon revolvers is wafted over the ridge. It is now too late for prudence. The horseman at bay has wheeled. Maxime recognizes the old Don.

Miguel Peralta is no man to be bearded in his own lair, unscathed. He spurs his horse back towards the ranch. He fires rapidly into the three pursuers as he darts by. He is a dangerous foe yet.

Valois feels a sharp pang in his shoulder. He reels in his saddle. His revolver lies in the dust. The ringing reports of his body-guard peal out as they empty their pistols at fleeing horse and man, The servant runs up, thoroughly frightened.

Don Miguel's best horse has made its last leap. It crashes down, pinioning the old soldier to the ground. A bullet luckily has pierced its brain.

Before the old ranchero can struggle to his feet, his hands are twisted behind his back. A couple of turns of a lariat clamp his wrists with no fairy band. A cocked pistol pressed against his head tells him that the game is up.

Valois drops, half fainting, from his horse, while his men disarm and bind the sullen old Mexican. The blood pouring from Valois' shoulder calls for immediate bandaging. The two pursuers of the other fugitive now ride smartly back.

One lags along, with a torn and shattered jaw. His companion is unhurt. He bears across his saddle bow a well-known emblem, the yellow and black scrape of Joaquin Murieta. Several ball holes prove it might have been his shroud. Valois quickly interrogates the two; after a hasty pistol duel, in which the flowing serape misled the two practised shots, the fugitive plunged down a steep slope, with all the recklessness of a Californian vaquero. It was Joaquin!

When the pursuers reached the trail, it was marked by the abandoned blanket. A heavy saddle also lay there, cut loose. Joaquin Murieta was riding away on the wings of the wind, but unwittingly into the jaws of death. Two or three from the main body took up the trail. The whole body pushed ahead on the track of the flying bandit--ready for fight.

With failing energies, Valois directs the unwounded pursuer to rejoin the column. He sends stern orders to Harris, to spare neither man nor beast, to follow the trail to the last. Even to the heart of the gloomy forests, this great human vampire must be hounded on his lonely ride to death.

In the saddle, held up by his men, Maxime Valois toils slowly towards Lagunitas. Beside him the wounded scout, pistol in hand, rides as a body-guard. In charge of growling old Don Miguel, a man leads him, dismounted, by a lariat. His horse and trappings lie on the trail, after removing all the arms. He is sullen and silent. His servant is a mere human animal. Cautiously approaching, the plaza lies below them. In the square, the horses of the captors can be seen peacefully grazing. Sentinels are mounted at several places. Valois at last reenters the old hacienda, wounded, but in pride, as a conqueror.

He is met at the priest's door by Padre Francisco. Don Miguel Peralta, the last of the land barons of the San Joaquin, is now a prisoner in the sacristy of the church. Time has its revenges. The turns of fortune's wheel. Padre Francisco assembles the entire population of the home ranch by the clanging of the church bell. In a few words he explains the reasons of the occupancy. He orders the hired men to remain in the enclosure under the guard of the sentinels. He dresses skilfully the wound of Maxime. He patches up the face of the wounded scout, whose proudest future boast will be that Joaquin Murieta gave him those honorable scars.

Maxime, worn and faint, falls into a fevered sleep. His subordinate holds the ranch, with all the force ready for any attack. The afternoon wears on. In sleep Valois forgets both the flying bandit and his fate. The old Don, his eyes filled with scalding tears, rages in his bonds. Pale, frightened Donna Juanita clasps her hands in the agony of prayer before the crucifix in the chapel. Beside her stands Dolores, now a budding beauty, in radiant womanhood. The dark-eyed young girl is mute. Her pathetic glances are as shy as a wounded deer's dying gaze. "The dreaded Americanos."

Over the beautiful hills, fanned by the breezes of sunset, the softened shadows fall. Twilight brings the hush and rest of early evening. The stars mirror themselves in the sparkling bosom of Lagunitas.

Watching the wounded leader, Padre Francisco's seamed, thoughtful face is very grave. His thin fingers tell the beads of the rosary. Prayer after prayer passes his moving lips.

The shadow of sorrow, sin, and shame is on Lagunitas. He fears for the future of the family. There has been foul play. There the tiger of Sonora has made his lair in the trackless canons and rich valleys of the foot-hills. The old Don must have known all.

Prayers for the dead and dying fall on the silence of the night. They are roughly broken by the trampling of horses' feet. The priest is called out by the sentinel. By the dim light of the stars, he sees two score shadowy horsemen. Between their lines, several poor wretches are bound and shivering in captivity.

A swarthy figure swings from the saddle. Captain Harry Love springs across the threshold. Unmindful of the warning of the priest, he rouses Valois. He cries exultantly, "We have him this time, squire!" Lying on the portico, tied in the sack, in which it swung at the ranger's saddle-horn, is the head of Joaquin Murieta. Valois struggles to his feet. Surrounded by the victors, by the light of a torch, he gazes on the awful token of victory. As the timid priest sees the fearful object, he cries, "Joaquin Carrillo!"

It is indeed he. The disgraced scion of an old and proud line. The good priest shudders as Harry Love, leaning on the rifle which sent its ball into Joaquin's heart, calmly says, "That thing is worth ten thousand dollars to me to-night, Valois!"

Already, swift riders are bringing up the forces of the sheriff. In the morning the history is known. The converging columns struck the bandits, who scattered. The work of vengeance was quick. "Three-fingered Jack," the murderous ancient of the bandit king, is killed in the camp. Several fugitives are captured. Several more hung. Joaquin Murieta, exhausted in the flight of the morning, his horse tired and wounded, drops from the charger, at a snap shot of the intrepid ranger, Love. The robber has finished his last ride.

Valois recovers rapidly. He has much to do to stem the resentment of the pursuers. The head of Joaquin and the hand of Three-fingered Jack are poor, scanty booty. Not as ghastly as the half-dozen corpses swinging on Lagunitas' oaks, and ghastly trophies of a chase of months. The prisoners are lynched. Far and wide, cowardly avengers butcher suspected Mexicans. California breathes freely now. Joaquin Murieta Carrillo will weave no more guerilla plots.

The padre and Valois commune with the frightened lady of the hacienda. Donna Juanita implores protection. Shy Dolores puts her slender hand in his, and begs him to protect her beloved father.

Maxime, in pity for the two women, conceals the history gathered from honorable Francois Ribaut. Joaquin played skilfully upon Don Miguel's hatred of the Americans. He knew of the lurking places behind Lagunitas. From these interior fastnesses, known to Don Miguel from early days, Joaquin could move on several short lines. He thus appeared as if by magic. With confederates at different places, his scattered bands had a rendezvous near Lagunitas. His followers mingled with different communities, and were picked up here and there on his raids. Special attacks were suggested by treasure movements. The murdering was not executed by the general banditti, but by Joaquin alone, and one or two of his special bravos. Examining the captives, Padre Francisco, by the agency of the Church, learned that, a few years before, a lovely Mexican girl, to whom Joaquin was bound by a desperate passion, was the victim of foul outrage by some wandering American brutes. Her death, broken-hearted, caused the desperado to swear her grave should be watered with American blood. Pride of race, and a bitter thirst for revenge, made Joaquin Murieta what he was,--a human scourge. His boyhood, spent roaming over the interior, rendered him matchless in local topography.

It was possible to disguise the fact of supplies being drawn from Lagunitas. Don Miguel was a great ranchero. As days rolled on, the plunder of the bandits was brought to the rancho. Joaquin's mutilated body was a prey to the mountain wolf. The ghastly evidences of victory were sent to San Francisco, where they remained for years, a reminder of bloody reprisal.

Padre Francisco saw with fear the rising indignation against Don Miguel. A clamor for his blood arose. Maxime Valois plead for the old Commandante. He had really imagined Joaquin's vendetta to be a sort of lawful war.

The forces began to leave Lagunitas. Only a strong escort body remained. Valois prepares his departure.

In a last interview, with Padre Francisco present, the lawyer warned Don Miguel not to leave his hacienda for some time. His life would surely be sacrificed to the feelings of the Americans. Thankful for their safety, the mother and sweet girl Dolores gratefully bid adieu to Maxime. He headed, himself, the last departing band of the invaders. The roads were safe to all. No trace of treasures of Joaquin was found. Great was the murmuring of the rangers. Were these hoards concealed on the rancho? Search availed nothing. Valois spurs down the road. Lagunitas! He breathes freer, now that the avengers are balked, at Lagunitas. They would even sack the rancho. Camping twenty miles away, Maxime dreams of his Southern home, as the stars sweep westward.

In the morning, a rough hand rouses him. It is the sentinel.

"Captain, wake up!"

He springs to his feet. "What is it?" he cries.

"Half the men are gone, sir. They have stolen back to hang the old Spaniard. They think he has concealed Joaquin's treasures."

Valois rouses several tired friends.

"My horse!" he yells.

As he springs to the saddle, the sentinel tells him a friend disclosed the plot. Fear kept him silent till the mutineers stole away.

"There are yet two hours to day. Is there time?" Maxime stretches out in the gallop of a skilled plainsman. He must save the priest and the women at least.

The mutineers will wait till daylight for their swoop. They are mad with the thirst for the lost treasures of Joaquin.

On, on, with the swing of the prairie wolf, the young leader gallops. He rides down man after man. As he gallops he thinks of Senora Juanita, the defenceless priest, the wounded old Commandante, and the sweet blossoming beauty of the Sierras, star-eyed young Dolores. They must be saved. On, on!

Day points over the hills as Maxime dashes into the unguarded plaza of the ranch. There are sounds of shots, yells, and trampling feet. He springs from his exhausted steed. The doors of the ranch-house give way. He rushes to the entrance, to find the rooms empty. In a moment he realizes the facts. He reaches the priest's house. Beating on the door, he cries: "Open quick! It is Valois." Springing inside he finds Padre Francisco, his eyes lit up with the courage of a gallant French gentleman.

"They are all here," he gasps. "Safe?" queries Valois. "Yes." "Thank God!" Maxime cries. "Quick! Hurry them into the church. Hold the sacristy door."

Maxime's two or three friends have followed him. The doors are closed behind them. The heavy adobe walls are shot-proof. The refuge of the church is gained none too soon.

The mutineers spread through the padre's house. Pouring in through the sacristy passage, they are faced in the gray dawn by Valois, his eyes blazing. He holds a dragoon revolver in each hand. He is a dead shot. Yet the mutineers are fearless.

"Give up the Greaser robber!" is their mad yell.

"Never!" cries Valois. "He is old and foolish, but he shall not be abused. Let him answer to the law."

"Captain," cries one, "we don't want to hurt you, but we are going to find Joaquin's plunder."

"The first man who moves over this threshold is a dead man!" cries Valois.

No one cares to be first, but they rage wildly. They all gather for a rush. Weapons are ominously clicking. As they come on, Padre Francisco stands before them, pale and calm in the morning light.

"Kill me first, my friends," he says. His body covers Valois.

The knot of desperate men stand back. They cannot shoot an unarmed priest, yet growling murmurs are heard: "Burn them out," "Go ahead,"

"Shoot the old Greaser."

A sound of trampling hoofs drowns their cries. The main body of the detachment, stung with shame, have galloped back to rescue Valois. It is over. The mutineers sullenly retire in a body.

Three hours later the detachment rides off. The rebels have wandered away. Guarded by the friends of the wild night-ride, Valois remains at Lagunitas.

Under questioning of the padre, whose honorable French blood boils at the domain being made a nest of assassins, the Don describes Joaquin's lurking-places. With one or two mozos, Valois visits all the old camps of the freebooters, within seventy-five miles. He leaves his men at Lagunitas for safety. He threads the fastnesses of the inviolate forests. They stretch from Shasta to Fresno, the great sugar pines and redwoods of California.

The axe of man has not yet attacked them. No machinery, no tearing saws are in these early days destroying their noble symmetry. But they are doomed. Fires and wanton destruction are yet to come, to leave blackened scars over once lovely areas. Man mutilates the lovely face of Nature's sweetest sylvan retreats. Down the great gorge of the Yosemite, Valois rides past the giant Big Trees of Calaveras. He finds no hidden treasures, no buried deposits. The camps near Lagunitas disclose only some concealed supplies. No arms, valuables, and treasures, torn from the murdered travellers, in the two years' red reign of Joaquin, the Mountain Tiger.

Valois concludes that Joaquin divided the gold among his followers. He must have used it largely to purchase assistance from his spies, scattered through the interior.

The stolen animals were undoubtedly all scattered over the State. The weapons, saddlery, and gear, booty of the native horse-thief bands, have been sent as far as Chihuahua in Mexico. Valuable personal articles were scarce. Few trophies were ever recovered. The gold-dust was unrecognizable. Valois reluctantly gives up the search. He returns convinced that mere lust of blood directed Joaquin Murieta Carrillo.

The bandits under him represented the native discontent. Their acts were a protest against the brutal Americans. They were goaded on by the loss of all property rights. This harshness drove the Indians, decimated, drunken, and diseased, from their patrimonial lands. It has effected the final ruin of the native Californians. Frontier greed and injustice have done a shameful work.

Maxime Valois blushes for his own nation. He realizes that indigenous dwellers must go to the wall in poverty, to their death. They go down before the rush of the wolf pack, hunting gold, always gold.

Taking the precaution to leave men to bear to him any messages from the padre, Maxime leaves Lagunitas for Stockton. The affairs of the community call him home. Property, covered by his investments, has been exposed to fire and flood at Sacramento. Sari Francisco has been half destroyed by a great conflagration. These calamities make thousands penniless.

Before he rides away, old Don Miguel comes to say adieu to his savior, once his prisoner. "Senor Americano," he murmurs, "be pleased to come to my house." Followed by the padre, Valois enters. There Don Miguel bids Donna Juanita and Dolores thank the man who saved his life.

"I shall not be here long, Senor Abogado," he says; "I wish you and the padre to watch over my wife and child. YOU are a 'caballero' and 'buen Cristiano.'"

Padre Francisco has proved that the young leader is a true child of the Church.

The finest horse on the rancho is led to the door. It is trapped with Don Miguel's state equipment. With a wave of the hand, he says:

"Senor, vayase V. con Dios. That horse will never fail you. It is the pride of the Lagunitas herds."

Maxime promises to aid in any future juncture. He rides out from lonely Lagunitas, near which tradition to-day locates those fabulous deposits, the vanished treasures of Joaquin, the mountain robber.

A generation glides away. The riches, long sought for, are never found. This blood-stained gold may lie hidden beneath the soil of Mariposa, but it is beyond human ken.

There are wild rejoicings at Stockton. Harry Love, splendid in gayest trappings, is the hero of the hour. The dead mountain tiger was the last leader of resistance to the Americans. The humbled Mexicans sink into the condition of wandering helots. The only possession left is their unconquerable pride, and the sadness which wraps them in a gloomy mantle.

CHAPTER IX.

THE STRANGER'S FOOT AT LAGUNITAS. VALOIS' SPANISH BRIDE.

Through the mines runs a paean of rejoicing. The roads are free; Joaquin is slain at last. Butcher bravos tire of revenging past deeds of blood. They slay the helpless Indians, or assassinate the frightened native Californians. This rude revenge element, stirred up by Harry Love's exploit, reaches from Klamath to the Colorado. Yet the unsettled interior is destined to keep up the sporadic banditti of the valleys for years. Every glen offers an easy ambush. In the far future only, the telegraph and railway will finally cut up the great State into localized areas of civilization.

All the whiskey-drinking and revolver-carrying bravos must be swept into obscure graves before crime can cease. It becomes, however, occasional only. While bloody hands are ready, the plotting brain of Joaquin Murieta never is equalled by any future bandit.

Coming years bring Francisco Garcia, Sebastian Flores, and the "Los Manilas" gang, whose seventeen years of bloodshed end finally at the gallows of Los Angeles. Varrella and Soto, Tiburcio Vasquez, Santos Lotello, Chavez, and their wild Mexican brothers, are all destined to die by shot or rope.

"Tom Bell," "Jack Powers," and other American recruits in the army of villany, have only changed sides in their crimes. All these wretches merit the deaths awaiting them. The last purely international element of discord vanishes from the records of crime.

Wandering Americans aptly learn stage-robbing. They are heirs of the old riders. The glories of "Black Bart," the lone highwayman of eighty stage-robberies, and the "train robbers," are reserved for the future. But Black Bart never takes life. He robs only the rich.

Valois appreciates that the day has arrived when legal land spoliation of the Mexicans will succeed these violent quarrels. Nothing is left to steal but their land. That is the object of contention between lawyers, speculators, squatters, and the defenceless owners. Their domains narrow under mortgage, interest, and legal (?) robbery.

"Vae victis!" The days of confiscation follow the conquest.

Hydraulic mining, quartz processes, and corporate effort succeed the earlier mining attempts. Two different forces are now in full energy of action.

Hills are swept bodily into the river-beds, in the search for the underlying gold. Rivers and meadows are filled up, sand covered, and ruined. Forests are thrown down, to rot by wholesale. Tunnels are blasted out. The face of nature is gashed with the quest for gold. Banded together for destruction, the miners leave no useful landmark behind them. All is washed away and sent seaward in the choking river-channels.

The home-makers, in peaceful campaigns of seed-time and harvest, develop new treasures. Great interests are introduced. The gold of field, orchard, and harvest falls into the hands of the industrious farmers. These are the men whose only weapons are scythe and sickle. They are the real Fathers of the Pacific. Roving over the interior, the miners leave a land as nearly ruined as human effort can render it. In the wake of these nugget-hunters, future years bring those who make the abandoned hills lovely with scattered homes. They are now hidden by orchards, vineyards, and gardens. Peaceful flocks and herds prove that the Golden Age of California is not to be these wild days of the barbaric Forty-niner.

Maxime Valois sees the land sweeping in unrivalled beauty to the Colorado. Free to the snowy peaks of the Sacramento, the rich plains roll. He knows that there will be here yet,

"Scattered cities crowning these, Whose far white walls along them shine, With fields which promise corn and wine."

He realizes that transient California must yield to stable conditions. Some civilized society will succeed the masses as lacking in fibre as a rope of sand. Already the days of roving adventure are over. There are wanderers, gamblers, fugitives, ex-criminals, and outcasts enough within the limits of the new land. Siren and adventuress, women of nameless history and gloomy future, yet abound. They throng the shabby temporary camps or tent cities. He knows there is no self-perpetuation in the mass of men roving in the river valleys. Better men must yet rule.

A visit to San Francisco and other large places proves that the social and commercial element is supplied from the Northern, Eastern, and Middle States. Their professional men will be predominant also.

In the interior, the farmers of the West and the sagacious planters of the South control.

As May-day approaches, Valois, at San Francisco in 1853, sees a procession of growing children. There, thousands of happy young faces of school-children, appear bearing roses in innocent hands.

Philip Hardin gives him the details of the coming struggle of North and South. It is a battle for the coast from Arizona to Oregon. Lost to England, Russia, and France, lost to the Mormons by stupidity or neglect, this West is lost to the South by the defeat of slavery. Industrious farmers come, in fairly equal numbers, from the Northern and Southern agricultural States. The people of the Atlantic free States come with their commerce, capital, and institutions. The fiat of Webster, Clay, and Seward has placed the guardian angel of freedom at the gates and passes of California. The Southerner cannot transfer his human slave capital to the far West. The very winds sing freedom's song on the wooded heights of the Sierras.

Philip Hardin sighs, as he drains his glass, "Valois, our people have doomed the South to a secondary standing in the Union. This fatal blunder in the West ruins us. Benton and Fremont's precipitancy thwarted our statesmen. This gold, the votes of these new States, the future commerce, the immense resources of the West, all are cast in the balance against us. We must work for a Western republic. We must wait till we can fight for Southern rights. We will conquer these ocean States. We will have this land yet."

The legal Mephisto and his pupil are true to the Southern cause. Neither of them can measure the coming forces of Freedom. Rosalie Leese, the pioneer white child of California, born in 1838, at Yerba Buena, was the first of countless thousands of free-born American children. In the unpolluted West the breath of slavery shall never blight a single human existence. Old Captain Richardson and Jacob Leese, pioneers of the magic city of San Francisco, gaze upon the beautiful ranks of smiling school-children, in happy troops. They have no regrets, like the knights of slavery, to see their places in life filled by free-born young pilgrims of life. All hail the native sons and daughters of the Golden West!

But the Southern politicians forge to the front. The majority is still with them. They carry local measures. Their hands are only tied by the admission of California, as a free State. Too late! On the far borders of Missouri, the contest of Freedom and Slavery begins. It excites all America. Bleeding Kansas! Hardin explains that the circle of prominent Southerners, leading ranchers, Federal officials, and officers of the army and navy, are relied on for the future. The South has all the courts. It controls the legislature. It seeks to cast California's voice against the Union in the event of civil war. As a last resort they will swing it off in a separate sovereignty--a Lone Star of the West.

"We must control here as we did in Texas, Valois. When the storm arises, we will be annexed to the Southern Confederacy."

Even as he spoke, the generation of the War was ripening for the sickle of Death. Filled with the sectional glories of the Mexican war, Hardin could not doubt the final issue.

"Get land, Valois," he cries. "Localize yourself. When this State is thrown open to slavery, you will want your natural position. Maxime, you ought to have a thousand field-hands when you are master at Lagunitas. You can grow cotton there."

Valois muses. He revolves in his mind the "Southern movement." Is it treason? He does not stop to ask. As he journeys to Stockton he ponders. Philip Hardin is about to accept a place on the Supreme Bench of the State. Not to advance his personal fortunes, but to be useful to his beloved South.

While the banks, business houses and factories are controlled by Northern men: while the pothouse politicians of Eastern cities struggle in ward elections, the South holds all the Federal honors. They govern society, dominate in the legislature and in the courts. They dictate the general superior intercourses of men. The ardent Southrons rule with iron hand. They are as yet only combated by the pens of Northern-born editors, and a few fearless souls who rise above the meekly bowing men of the free States.

All see the approaching downfall of lawless pleasure and vicious license in San Francisco. Slowly the tide of respectable settlement rises. It bears away the scum of vice, swept into the Golden Gates in the first rush. The vile community of escaped convicts and mad adventurers cannot support itself. "The old order changeth, yielding slowly to the new."

At the head of all public bodies, the gentleman of the South, quick to avenge his personal honor, aims, with formal "code," and ready pistol, to dragoon all public sentiment. He is sworn to establish the superiority of the cavalier.

The first Mayor of San Francisco, a Congressman elect, gifted editor Edward Gilbert, has already fallen in an affair of honor. The control of public esteem depends largely on prowess in the duelling field. Every politician lives up to the code.

Valois ponders over Hardin's advice. Averse to routine business, fond of a country life, he decides to localize himself. His funds have increased. His old partner, Joe Woods, is now a man of wealth at Sacramento. Maxime has no faith in quartz mines. He has no desires to invest in ship, or factory. He ignores commerce. To be a planter, a man of mark in the legislature, to revive the glories of the Valois family, is the lawyer's wish. While he passes the tule-fringed river-banks, fate is leading him back to Lagunitas. He has led a lonely life, this brilliant young Creole. In the unrest of his blood, under the teachings of Hardin, Valois feels the future may bear him away to unfought fields. The grandsons of those who fought at New Orleans, may win victories, as wonderful, over the enemies of that South, even if these foes are brothers born.

Gliding towards his fate, the puppet of the high gods, Maxime Valois may dream of the surrender of Fort Sumter, and of the Southern Cross soaring high in victory. Appomattox is far hidden beyond battle-clouds of fields yet to come! The long road thither has not yet been drenched with the mingled blood of warring brethren. Dreams! Idle dreams! Glory! Ambition! Southern rights!

At Stockton, Valois receives tidings from Padre Francisco. Clouds are settling down on Lagunitas. Squatters arc taking advantage of the defenceless old Mexican. If the Don would save his broad acres, he must appear in the law-courts of the conquerors.

Alas! the good old days are gone, when the whole State of California boasted not a single lawyer. These are new conditions. The train of loyal retainers will never sweep again out of the gates of Lagunitas, headed by the martial Commandante, in all the bravery of rank and office. It is the newer day of gain and greed.

Prospecting miners swarm over Mariposa. The butterflies are driven from rocky knoll and fragrant bower by powder blasts. The woods fall under the ringing axe of the squatter. Ignorant of new laws and strange language; strong only in his rights; weak in years, devoid of friends, Don Miguel's hope is the sage counsel of Padre Francisco. The latter trusts to Valois' legal skill.

As adviser, Valois repairs to Lagunitas. Old patents, papers heavy with antique seal and black with stately Spanish flourish, are conned over. Lines are examined, witnesses probed, defensive measures taken.

Maxime sits; catechizes the Don, the anxious Donna Juanita, and the padre. Wandering by the shores of Lagunitas, Valois notes the lovely reflection of the sweet-faced Dolores in the crystal waters. The girl is fair and modest. Francois Ribaut often wonders if the young man sees the rare beauty of the Spanish maiden. If it would come to pass!

Over his beads, the padre murmurs, "It may be well. All well in time."

The cause drags on slowly. After months, the famous case of the Lagunitas rancho is fought and won.

But before its last coil has dragged out of the halls of justice, harassed and broken in spirit, Don Miguel closes his eyes upon the ruin of his race. Born to sorrow, Donna Juanita is a mere shade of womanly sorrow. She is not without comfort, for the last of the Peraltas has placed his child's hand in that of Maxime Valois and whispered his blessing.

"You will be good to my little Dolores, amigo mio," murmurs the old man. He loves the man whose lance has been couched in his behalf. The man who saved his life and lands.

Padre Francisco is overjoyed. He noted the drawing near of the young hearts. A grateful flash, lighting the shining eyes of Dolores, told the story to Maxime. His defence of her father, his championship of the family cause, his graceful demeanor fill sweet Dolores' idea of the perfect "caballero."

The priest with bell, book, and candle, gives all the honors of the Church to the last lord of Lagunitas. Hard by the chapel, the old ranchero rests surrounded by the sighing forest. It is singing the same unvarying song, breathing incense from the altars of nature over the stout soldier's tomb.

He has fought the fight of his race in vain. When the roses' leaves drift a second time on the velvet turf, Maxime Valois receives the hand of Dolores from her mother. The union is blessed by the invocation of his priestly friend. It is a simple wedding. Bride and groom are all in all to each other. There are none of the Valois, and not a Peralta to join in merrymaking.

Padre Francisco and Donna Juanita are happy in the knowledge that the shy bird of the mountains is mated with the falcon-eyed Creole. He can defend the lordly heritage of Lagunitas. So, in the rosy summer time, the foot of the stranger passes as master over the threshold of the Don's home. The superb domain passes under the dominion of the American. One by one the old holdings of the Californian families pass away. The last of the Dons, sleeping in the silence of the tomb, are spared the bitterness of seeing their quaint race die out. The foreigner is ruling within their gates. Their unfortunate, scattered, and doomed children perish in the attrition of a newer civilization.

Narrow-minded, but hospitable; stately and loyal; indifferent to the future, suspicious of foreigners, they are utterly unable to appreciate progress. They are powerless to develop or guard their domains. Abandoned by Mexico, preyed on by squatters, these courtly old rancheros are now a memory of the past.

This wedding brings life to Lagunitas. The new suzerain organizes a working force. It is the transition period of California. Hundreds of thousands of acres only wait for the magic artesian well to smile in plenty. Valois gathers up the reins. Only a few pensioners remain. The nomadic cavalry of the natives has disappeared. The suggestion of "work" sets them "en route." They drift towards the Mexican border. The flocks and herds are guarded by corps of white attendants. The farm succeeds the ranch.

Maxime Valois gives his wife her first sight of the Queen City. The formalities of receiving the "patent" call him to San Francisco.

Padre Francisco remains with Donna Juanita. The new rule is represented by "Kaintuck," an energetic frontiersman, whose vast experience in occasional warfare and frequent homicide is a guarantee of finally holding possession. This worthy left all his scruples at home in Kentucky, with his proper appellation. He is a veteran ranger.

As yet the lands yield no regular harvests. The ten-leagues-square tract produces less fruit, garden produce, and edibles, than a ten-acre Pennsylvania field in the Wyoming. But the revenue is large from the cattle and horses. The cattle are as wild as deer. The horses are embodiments of assorted "original sin," and as agile as mountain goats. Valois knows, however, the income will be ample for general improvements.

His policy matures. He encourages the settlement of Southerners. He rents in subdivisions his spare lands.

The Creole, now a landlord, hears the wails of short-sighted men. They mourn the green summers, the showery months of the East. Moping in idleness, they assert that California will produce neither cereal crops, fruits, nor vegetables. Prophets, indeed! The golden hills look bare and drear to strangers' eyes. The brown plains please not.

In the great realm, apples, potatoes, wheat, corn, the general cereals and root crops are supposed to be impossible productions. Gold, wild cattle, and wilder mustangs are the returns of El Dorado. Cultivation is in its infancy.

The master departs with the dark-eyed bride. She timidly follows his every wish. Dolores has the education imparted by gentle Padre Francisco. It makes her capable of mentally expanding in the experiences of the first journey. The gentle refinement of her race completes her charms.

To the bride, the steamer, the sights of the bay, crowded with shipping, and the pageantry of the city are dazzling. The luxuries of city life are wonders. Relying on her husband, she glides into her new position. Childishly pleased at the jewels, ornaments, and toilets soon procured in the metropolis, Donna Dolores Valois is soon one of Eve's true daughters, arrayed like the lily.

Months roll away. The stimulus of a brighter life develops the girl wife into a sweetly radiant woman.

Maxime Valois rejoins Philip Hardin. He is now a judge of the Supreme Court. Stormy days are these of 1855 and the spring of 1856.

Deep professional intrigues busy Valois. Padre Francisco and "Kaintuck" announce the existence of supposed quartz mines on the rancho. Valois will not pause in his occupations to risk explorations.

For the Kansas strife, the warring of sections, and the growing bitterness of free and slave State men make daily life a seething cauldron. Southern settlers are pouring into the interior. They shun the cities. In city and country, squatter wars, over lot and claim, excite the community. San Francisco is a hotbed of politicians and roughs of the baser sort. While the Southerners generally control the Federal and State offices, Hardin feels the weakness in their lines has been the journalistic front of their party. Funds are raised. Pro-slavery journals spring into life. John Nugent, Pen Johnston, and O'Meara write with pens dipped in gall, and the ready pistol at hand. Tumult and fracas disgrace bench, bar, legislature, and general society. The great wars of Senators Gwin and Broderick precede the separation of Northern and Southern Democrats. As the summer of 1856 draws on, corruption, violence, and sectional hatred bitterly divide all citizens. School and Church, journal and law-giver, work for the right. The strain on the community increases. While the coast and interior is dotted with cities and towns, and the Mint pours out floods of ring-ing gold coins, there is no confidence. Farm and factory, ship and wagon train, new streets, extension of the city and material progress show every advancement. But a great gulf yawns between the human wave of old adventurers, and the home-makers, now sturdily battling for the inevitable victory.

The plough is speeding in a thousand furrows everywhere. Cattle and flocks are being graded and improved. Far-sighted men look to franchise and public associa-tion. The day dawns when the giant gaming hells, flaunting palaces of sin, and the violent army of miscreants must be suppressed.

Everywhere, California shows the local irritation between the buccaneers of the first days, and the resolute, respectable citizens. The latter are united in this lo-cal cause, though soon to divide politically on the battle-field.

Driven from their lucrative vices of old, the depraved element, at the polls, overawes decency. San Francisco's long wooden wharves, its precipitous streets, its crowded haunts of the transient, and its flashy places of low amusement harbor a desperate gang. They are renegades, deserters, and scum of every seaport--graduates of all human villany. Aided by demagogues, the rule of the "Roughs" nears its cul-mination. Fire companies, militia, train bands, and the police, are rotten to the core. In this upheaval, affecting only the larger towns, the higher classes are powerless.

Cut off, by the great plains, from the central government, the State is almost devoid of telegraphs and has but one little railroad. It has hostile Indians yet on its borders. The Chinese come swarming in like rats. The situation of California is critical.

Personal duels and disgraceful quarrels convulse high life. The lower ranks are ruled only by the revolver. The criminal stalks boldly, unpunished, in the streets.

The flavor of Americanism is no leaven to this ill-assorted population. The exciting presidential campaign, in which Fremont leads a new party, excites and divides the better citizens of the commonwealth.

Though the hills are now studded with happy homes and the native children of the Golden West are rising in promise, all is unrest. A local convulsion turns the anger of better elements into the revolution of the Vigilance Committee of 1856. James Casey's pistol rang out the knell of the "Roughs" when he murdered the fearless editor of the leading journal.

Valois, uninterested in this urban struggle, returns to Lagunitas. His domain rewards his energy.

All is peace by the diamond lake. Senora Dolores, her tutor, Padre Francisco, and the placid Duenna Juanita make up a pleasant home circle. It is brightened by luxuries provided by the new lord. Maxime Valois' voice is heard through the valleys. He travels in support of James Buchanan, the ante-bellum President. For is not John C. Breckinridge, the darling son of the South, as vice-president also a promise of Southern success?

San Francisco throws off its criminals by a spasmodic effort. The gallows tree has borne its ghastly fruit. Fleeing "Roughs" are self-expatriated. Others are unceremoniously shipped abroad. The Vigilance Committee rules. This threshing out of the chaff gives the State a certain dignity. At least, an effort has been made to purge the community. All in all, good results--though a Judge of the Supreme Court sleeps in a guarded cell as a prisoner of self-elected vindicators of the law.

When the excitement of the presidential election subsides, Maxime Valois joins the banquets of the Democratic victors. The social atmosphere is purer. Progress marks the passing months. The State springs forward toward the second decade of its existence. There is local calm, while the national councils potter over the Pacific railways. Valois knows that the great day of Secession approaches. The Sons of the South will soon raise the banner of the Southern Cross. He knows the purposes of the cabinet, selected by the conspirators who surround Buchanan. Spring sees the great departments of the government given over to those who work for the South. They will arrange government offices, divide the army, scatter the navy, juggle the treasury and prepare for the coming storm. The local bitterness heightens into quarrels over spoils. Judge Philip Hardin, well-versed in the Secession plots, feeds the ever-burning pride of Valois. From Kansas, from court and Congress, from the far East, the murmur of the "irrepressible conflict" grows nearer. Maxime Valois is in correspondence with the head of his family. While at Lagunitas, the Creole pushes on his works of improvement. He dreams at night strange dreams of more brilliant successes. Of a new flag and the triumph of the beloved cause. He will be called as a trusted Southron into the councils of the coast. Will they cut it off under the Lone Star flag? This appeals to his ambition.

There are omens everywhere. The Free-State Democrats must be suppressed. The South must and shall rule.

He often dreams if war and tumult will ever roll, in flame and fire, over the West. The mists of the future veil his eyes. He waits the signal from the South. All over California, the wealth of the land peeps through its surface gilding. There are no clouds yet upon the local future. No burning local questions at issue here, save the aversion of the two sections, distrustful of each other.

It needs only the mad attack of John Brown upon Virginia's slave-keepers to loose the passions of the dwellers by the Pacific. Martyr or murderer, sage or fanatic, Brown struck the blows which broke the bonds of the brotherhood of the Revolution. From the year 1858, the breach becomes too great to bridge. Secretly, Southern plans are perfected to control the West. While the conspiracy slowly moves on, the haughtiness of private intercourse admits of no peaceable reunion. Active correspondence between officials, cool calculations of future resources, and the elevation to prominent places of men pledged to the South, are the rapid steps of the maturing plans. On the threshold of war.

For the senators, representatives, and agents in Washington confidentially report that the code of honor is needed to restrain the Northerners under personal dragooning. Yankee self-assertion comes at last.

Around the real leaders of thought their vassals are ranged. Davis, Toombs, Breckinridge, Yancey, Pryor, Wigfall, Wise, and others direct. Herbert, Keith, Lamar, Brooks, and a host of cavaliers are ready with trigger and cartel. The tone at Washington gives the keynote to the Californian agents of the Southern Rights movement. There are not enough Potters, Wades, and Landers, as yet. The Northern mind needs time to realize the deliberation of Secession.

The great leaders of the free States are dead or in the gloomy retirement of age. Webster and Clay are no more. There are yet men of might to fight under the banners streaming with the northern lights of freedom. Douglas, Bell, Sumner, Seward, and Wade are drawing together. Grave-faced Abraham Lincoln moves out of the background of Western woods into the sunrise glow of Liberty's brightest day.

On the Pacific coast, restraint has never availed. Here, ancestry and rank go for naught. Here, men meet without class pride. The struggle is more equal.

California's Senator, David C. Broderick, was the son of an humble New York stone-cutter. He grapples with his wily colleague, Senator Gwin.

It is hammer against rapier. Richard and Saladin. Beneath the banners of the chieftains the free lances of the Pacific range themselves. Neither doubts the courage of the opposing forces. The blood of the South has already followed William Walker, the gray-eyed man of destiny, to Sonora and Nicaragua. They were a splendid band of modern buccaneers. Henry A. Crabbe found that the Mexican escopetas are deadly in the hands of the maddened inhabitants of Arispe. Raousset de Boulbon sees his Southern followers fall under machete and revolver in northern Mexico. The Southern filibusters are superbly reckless. All are eager to repeat the glories of Texas and Mexico. They find that the Spanish races of Central America have learned bitter lessons from the loss of Texas. They know of the brutal conquest of California. The cry of "Muerte los Americanos!" rings from Tucson to Darien. The labors of conquest are harder now for the self-elected generalissimos of these robber bands. "Extension of territory" is a diplomatic euphemism for organized descents of desperate murderers. The wholesome lessons of the slaughter in Sonora, the piles of heads at Arispe, and the crowded graves of Rivas and Castillo, with the executions in Cuba, prove to the ambitious Southrons that they will receive from the Latins a "bloody welcome to hospitable graves."

As the days glide into weeks and months, the thirst for blood of the martial generation overcrowding the South is manifest. On the threshold of grave events the leaders of Southern Rights restrain further foreign attempts. The chivalry is now needed at home. Foiled in Cuba and Central America, restrained by the general government from a new aggressive movement on Mexico, they decide to turn their faces to the North. They will carve out a new boundary line for slavery.

The natural treasury of the country is an object of especial interest. To break away peaceably is hardly possible. But slavery needs more ground for the increasing blacks. It must be toward the Pacific that the new Confederacy will gain ground. Gold, sea frontage, Asiatic trade, forests and fisheries,--all these must come to the South. It is the final acquisition of California. It was APPARENTLY for the Union, but REALLY for the South, that the complacent Polk pounced upon California. He waged a slyly prepared war on Mexico for slavery.

As the restraints of courtesy and fairness are thrown off at Washington, sectional hostilities sweep over to the Western coast. The bitterness becomes intense. Pressing to the front, champions of both North and South meet in private encounters. They admit of neither evasion nor retreat.

Maxime Valois is ready to shed his blood for the land of the palmetto. But he will not degrade himself by low intrigue or vulgar encounter.

He learns without regret of the extinction of the filibusters in Sonora, on the Mexican coast, Cuba, and Central America. He knows it is mad piracy.

Valois sorrows not when William Walker's blood slakes the stones of the plaza at Truxillo. A consummation devoutly to be wished.

It is for the whole South he would battle. It is the glorious half of the greatest land on the globe. For HER great rights, under HER banner, for State sovereignty he would die. On some worthy field, he would lead the dauntless riflemen of Louisiana into the crater of death.

THERE, would be the patriot's pride and the soldier's guerdon of valor. He would be in the van of such an uprising. He scorns to be a petty buccaneer, a butcher of half-armed natives, a rover and a robber. In every scene, through the days of 1859, Valois bears himself as a cavalier. Personal feud was not his object.

In the prominence of his high position, Valois travels the State. He confers with the secret councils at San Francisco. He is ready to lead in his regions when needed. The dark cabal of Secession sends out trusty secret agents, even as Gillespie and Larkin called forth the puppets of Polk, Buchanan and Marcy to action. Valois hopes his friends can seize California for the South. Fenced off from Oregon and the East by the Sierras, there is the open connection with the South by Arizona.

A few regiments of Texan horse can hold this great gold-field for the South. Valois deems it impossible for California to be recaptured if once won. He knows that Southern agents are ready to stir up the great tribes of the plains against the Yankees. The last great force, the United States Navy, is to be removed. Philip Hardin tells him how the best ships of the navy are being dismantled, or ordered away to foreign stations. Great frigates are laid up in Southern navy-yards. Ordnance supplies and material are pushed toward the Gulf. Appropriations are expended to aid these plans. The leaders of the army, now scattered under Southern commanders, are ready to turn over to the South the whole available national material of war. Never dreaming of aught but success, Valois fears only that he may be assigned to Western duties. This will keep him from the triumphal marches over the North. He may miss the glories of that day when Robert Toombs calls the roll of his blacks at Bunker Hill Monument. In the prime of life and vigor of mind, he is rich. He has now a tiny girl child, gladdening sweet Senora Dolores. His domain blossoms like the rose. Valois has many things to tie him to San Joaquin. His princely possessions alone would satisfy any man. But he would leave all this to ride with the Southern hosts in their great northward march. Dolores sits often lonely now, on the porch of the baronial residence which has grown up around the Don's old adobe mansion. Her patient mother lies under the roses, by the side of Don Miguel.

Padre Francisco, wearied of the mental death in life of these lonely hills, has delayed his return to France only by the appeals of Maxime Valois. He wants a friend at Lagunitas if he takes the field. If he should be called East, who would watch over his wife and child? Francois Ribaut, a true Frenchan at heart, looks forward to some quiet cloister, where he can see once more the twin towers of Notre Dame. The golden dome of the Invalides calls him back. He sadly realizes that his life has been uselessly wasted. The Indians are either cut off, chased away, or victims of fatal diseases. The Mexicans have fallen to low estate. Their numbers are trifling. He has no flock. He is only a lonely shepherd. With the Americans his gentle words avail nothing. The Catholics of the cities have brought a newer Church hierarchy with them. "Home to France," is his longing now.

In the interior, quarrels bring about frequent personal encounters between political disputants. The Northern sympathizers, stung by jeer, and pushed to the wall, take up their weapons and stand firm--a new fire in their eyes. The bravos of slavery meet fearless adversaries. In the cities, the wave of political bitterness drowns all friendly impulses. Every public man takes his life in his hand. The wars of Broderick and Gwin, Field and Terry, convulse the State. Lashed into imprudence by each other's attacks, David C. Broderick and David S. Terry look into each other's pistols. They stand face to face in the little valley by Merced Lake. Sturdy Colton, and warm-hearted Joe McKibbin, second the fearless Broderick. Hayes and the chivalric Calhoun Benham are the aids of the lion-hearted Terry. It is a meeting of giants. Resolution against deadly nerve. Brave even to rashness, both of them know it is the first blood of the fight between South and North. Benham does well as, with theatrical flourish, he casts Terry's money on the sod. The grass is soon to be stained with the blood of a leader. This is no mere money quarrel. It is a duel to the death; a calm assertion of the fact that neither in fray, in the forum, nor on the battle-field, will the North go back one inch. It is high time.

Broderick, the peer of his superb antagonist, knows that the pretext of Terry's challenge is a mere excuse. It is first blood in the inevitable struggle for the western coast. With no delay, the stout-hearted champions, friends once, stand as foes in conflict. David Terry's ball cuts the heart-strings of a man who had been his loving political brother. His personal friend once and a gallant comrade. Broderick's blood marks the fatal turning-off of the Northern Democrats from their Southern brothers. As Terry lowers his pistol, looking unpityingly at the fallen giant, he does not realize he has cut the cords tying the West to the South. It was a fatal deed, this brother's murder. It was the mistake of a life, hitherto high in purpose. The implacable Terry would have shuddered could he have looked over the veiled mysteries of thirty years to come. It was beyond human ken. Even he might have blenched at the strange life-path fate would lead him over. Over battle-fields where the Southern Cross rises and falls like Mokanna's banner, back across deserts, to die under the deadly aim of an obscure minion of the government he sought to pull down. After thirty years, David S. Terry, judge, general, and champion of the South, was destined to die at the feet of his brother-judge, whose pathway inclined Northwardly from that ill-starred moment.

Maxime Valois saw in the monster memorial meeting on the plaza, that the cause of the South was doomed in the West. While Baker's silver voice rises in eulogy over Broderick, the Louisianian sees a menace in the stern faces of twenty thousand listeners. The shade of the murdered mechanic-senator hovers at their local feast, a royal Banquo, shadowy father of political kings yet to be.

The clarion press assail the awful deed. Boldly, the opponents of slavery draw out in the community. There is henceforth no room for treason on the Western coast. Only covert conspiracy can neutralize the popular wave following Broderick's death. Dissension rages until the fever of the Lincoln campaign excites the entire community. The pony express flying eastward, the rapidly approaching telegraph, the southern overland mail with the other line across the plains, bring the news of Eastern excitement. Election battles, Southern menace, and the tidings of the triumph of Republican principles, reach the Pacific. Abraham Lincoln is the elected President.

Valois is heavy-hearted when he learns of the victory of freedom at the polls. He would be glad of some broad question on which to base the coming war. His brow is grave, as he realizes the South must now bring on at moral disadvantage the conflict. The war will decide the fate of slavery. Broderick's untimely death and the crushing defeat of the elections are bad omens. It is with shame he learns of the carefully laid plots to seduce leading officers of the army and navy. The South must bribe over officials, and locate government property for the use of the conspirators. It labors with intrigue and darkness, to prepare for what he feels should be a gallant defiance. It should be only a solemn appeal to the god of battles.

He sadly arranges his personal affairs, to meet the separations of the future. He sits with his lovely, graceful consort, on the banks of Lagunitas. He is only waiting the throwing-off of the disguise which hides the pirate gun-ports of the cruiser, Southern Rights. The hour comes before the roses bloom twice over dead Broderick, on the stately slopes of Lone Mountain.

BOOK III
GOING HOME TO DIXIE: STARS AND STRIPES, OR STARS AND BARS?

CHAPTER X

A LITTLE DINNER AT JUDGE HARDIN'S.--THE KNIGHTS OF THE GOLDEN CIRCLE.

The rain drips drearily around Judge Hardin's spacious residence in San Francisco. January, 1861, finds the sheltering trees higher. The embowered shade hides to-night an unusual illumination. Winter breezes sigh through the trees. Showers of spray fall from acacia and vine. As the wet fog drives past, the ship-lights on the bay are almost hidden. When darkness brings out sweeping lines of the street-lamps, many carriages roll up to the open doors.

A circle of twenty or thirty intimates gathers in the great dining-room. At the head of the table, Hardin welcomes the chosen representatives of the great Southern conspiracy in the West. His residence, rarely thrown open to the public, has grown with the rise of his fortunes. Philip Hardin must be first in every attribute of a leading judge and publicist. Lights burn late here since the great election of 1860. Men who are at the helm of finance, politics, and Federal power are visitors. Editors and trusted Southrons drop in, by twos and threes, secretly. There is unwonted social activity.

The idle gossips are silent. These visitors are all men, unaccompanied by their families. Woman's foot never crosses this threshold. In the wings of the mansion, a lovely face is sometimes seen at a window. It is a reminder of the stories of that concealed beauty who has reigned years in the mansion on the hill.

Is it a marriage impending? Is it some great scheme? Some new monetary institution to be launched?

These vain queries remain unanswered. There is a mystic password given before joining the feast. Southerners, tried and true, are the diners. Maxime Valois sits opposite his associate. It is not only a hospitable welcome the Judge extends, but the mystic embrace of the Knights of the Golden Circle. In feast and personal enjoyment the moments fly by. The table glitters with superb plate. It is loaded with richest wines and the dainties of the fruitful West. The board rings under emphatic blows of men who toast, with emphasis, the "Sunny South." In their flowing cups, old and new friends are remembered. There is not one glass raised to the honor of the starry flag which yet streams out boldly at the Golden Gate.

The feast is of conspirators who are sworn to drag that flag at their horses' heels in triumph. Men nurtured under it.

Judge Hardin gives the signal of departure for the main hall. In an hour or so they are joined by others who could not attend the feast.

The meeting of the Knights of the Golden Circle proceeds with mystic ceremony. The windows, doors, and avenues are guarded. In the grounds faithful brothers watch for any sneaking spy. Every man is heavily armed. It would be short shrift to the foe who stumbles on this meeting of deadly import.

It is the supreme moment to impart the last orders of the Southern leaders. The Washington chiefs assign the duties of each, in view of the violent rupture which will follow Lincoln's inauguration.

Fifty or sixty in number, these brave and desperate souls are ready to cast all in jeopardy. Life, fortune, and fame. They represent every city and county of California.

Hardin, high priest of this awful propaganda, opens the business of the session with a cool statement of facts. Every man is now sworn and under obligation to the work. Hardin's eye kindles as he sees these brothers of the Southern Cross. Each of them has a dozen friends or subordinates under him. To them these tidings will be only divulged under the awful seal of the death penalty. There are scores of army and navy officers with high civil officials on the coast whose finely drawn scruples will keep them out until the first gun is fired, Then these powerful allies, freed by resignation, can come in. They are holding places of power and immense importance to the last. The Knights are wealthy, powerful, and desperate.

As Valois hears Hardin's address, he appreciates the labor of years, in weaving the network which is to hold California, Arizona, and New Mexico for the South. Utah and Nevada are untenanted deserts. The Mormon regions are neutral and only useful as a geographical barrier to Eastern forces. Oregon and Washington are to be ignored. There the hardy woodsmen and rugged settlers represent the ingrained "freedom worship" of the Northwest. They are farmers and lumbermen. All acknowledge it useless to tempt them out of the fold. Oregon's star gleams now firmly fixed in the banner of Columbia. And the great Sierras fence them off.

The speaker announces that each member of the present circle will be authorized, on returning, to organize and extend the circles of the Order. Notification of matters of moment will be made by qualified members, from circle to circle. Thus, orders will pass quickly over the State. The momentous secrets cannot be trusted to mail, express, or the local telegraphs.

Hardin calls up member after member, to give their views. The general plan is discussed by the circle. Keen-eyed secretaries note and arrange opinions and remarks.

Hardin announces that all arrangements are made to use all initiated members going East as bearers of despatches. They are available for special interviews, with the brothers who are in every large Northern city and even in the principal centres of Europe.

Ample funds have been forthcoming from the liberal leaders of the local movement. Millions are already promised by the branches at the East.

Wild cheers hail Judge Hardin's address. He outlines the policy, so artfully laid out, for the cut-off Western contingent. In foaming wine, the fearless coterie pledges the South till the rafters ring again. The "Bonnie Blue Flag" rings out, as it does in many Western households, with "Dixie's" thrilling strains.

The summing up of Hardin is concise: "We are to hold this State until we have orders to open hostilities. Our numbers must not be reduced by volunteers going East. Our presence will keep the Yankee troops from going East. We want the gold of the mines here, to sustain our finances. We have as commanding General, Albert

Sidney Johnston, the ideal soldier of America, who will command the Mississippi. Lee, Beauregard, and Joe Johnston will operate in the East. The fight will be along the border lines. We will capture Washington, and seize New York and Philadelphia. A grand Southern army will march from Richmond to Boston. Another from Nashville to Cincinnati and Chicago. Johnston will hold on here, until forced to resign. Many officers go with him. We shall know of this, and throw ourselves on the arsenals and forts here, capturing the stores and batteries. The militia and independent companies will come over to us at once. With Judge Downey, a Democratic governor, no levies will be called out against us. The navy is all away, or in our secret control. Once in possession of this State, we will fortify the Sierra Nevada passes. We are prepared. Congress has given us $600,000 a year to keep up the Southern overland mail route. It runs through slave-holding territory to Arizona. Every station and relay has been laid out to suit us. We will have trusty friends and supplies, clear through Arizona and over the Colorado. At the outbreak, we will seize the whole system. It is the shortest and safest line."

Hardin, lauding the skilful plans of a complacent Cabinet officer, did not know that the Southern idea was to connect Memphis direct with Los Angeles.

It was loyal John Butterfield of New York, who artfully bid for a DOUBLE service from Memphis and St. Louis, uniting at Fort Smith, Arkansas, and virtually defeated this sly move of slavery.

Judge Hardin, pausing in pride, could not foresee that Daniel Butterfield, the gallant son of a loyal sire, would meet the chivalry of the South as the Marshal of the greatest field of modern times--awful Gettysburg!

While Hardin plotted in the West, Daniel Butterfield in the East personally laid out every detail of this great service, so as to checkmate the Southern design, were the Mississippi given over to loyal control.

The afterwork of Farragut and Porter paralyzed the Southern line of advance; and on the Peninsula, at Fredericksburg, at Resaca and Chancellorsville, Major-General Daniel Butterfield met in arms many of the men who listened to Hardin's gibes as to the outwitted Yankee mail contractors.

Hardin, complacent, and with no vision of the awful fields to come, secure in his well-laid plans, resumes:

"Thus aided through Arizona we will admit a strong column of Texan dragoons. We shall take Fort Yuma, Fort Mojave, and the forts in Arizona, as well as Forts Union and Craig in New Mexico. We will then be able to control the northern overland road. We will hold the southern line, and our forces will patrol Arizona. Mexico will furnish us ports and supplies.

"Should the Northerners attempt to push troops over the plains, we will attack them, in flank, from New Mexico. We can hold, thus, New Mexico, Arizona, southern Utah, and all of California, by our short line from El Paso to San Diego. We are covered on one flank by Mexico."

The able brethren are ready with many suggestions. Friendly spies in the Department at Washington have announced the intended drawing East of the regular garrisons. It is suggested that the forts, and in fact the whole State, be seized while the troops are in transit.

Another proposes the fitting out of several swift armed steam letters-of-marque from San Francisco, to capture the enormous Yankee tonnage now between China, Cape Horn, Australia, and California. The whaling fleet is the object of another. He advises sending a heavily armed revenue cutter, when seized, to the Behring Sea to destroy the spring whalers arriving from Honolulu too late for any warning, from home, of the hostilities.

A number of active committees are appointed. One, of veteran rangers, to select frontiersmen to stir up the Indians to attack the northern overland mail stations. Another, to secretly confer with the officers of the United States Mint, Custom-House, and Sub-Treasury. Another, to socially engage the leading officers of the army and navy, and win them over, or develop their real feelings. Every man of mark in the State is listed and canvassed.

The "high priest" announces that the families of those detailed for distant duty will be cared for by the general committee. Each member receives the mystic tokens. Orders are issued to trace up all stocks of arms and ammunition on the coast.

The seizure of the Panama Railroad, thus cutting off quick movement of national troops, is discussed. Every man is ordered to send in lists of trusty men as soon as mustered into the new mystery. Convenient movements of brothers from town to town are planned out. Only true sons of the sunny South are to be trusted.

In free converse, the duty of watching well-known Unionists is enjoined upon all. Name by name, dangerous men of the North are marked down for proscription or special action. "Removal," perhaps.

With wild cheers, the Knights of the Golden Circle receive the news that the South is surely going out. The dream long dear to the Southern heart! Any attempt of the senile Buchanan to reinforce the garrisons of the national forts will be the signal for the opening roar of the stolen guns. They know that the inauguration of Lincoln on March 4, 1861, means war without debate. He dare not abandon his trust. He will be welcomed with a shotted salute across the Potomac.

When the move "en masse" is made, the guests, warmed with wine and full of enthusiasm, file away. Hardin and Valois sit late. The splashing rain drenches the swaying trees of the Judge's hillside retreat.

Lists and papers of the principal men on both sides, data and statistics of stock and military supplies, maps, and papers, are looked at. The deep boom of the Cathedral bell, far below them, beats midnight as the two friends sit plotting treason.

There is something mystical in the exact hour of midnight. The rich note startles Hardin. Cold, haughty, crafty, and able, his devotion to the South is that of the highest moral courage. It is not the exultation which culminates rashly on the battle-field. These lurid scenes are for younger heroes.

His necessary presence in the West, his age and rank, make him invaluable, out of harness. His scheming brain is needed, not his ready sword.

He pours out a glass of brandy, saying, "Valois, tell me of our prospects here. You know the interior as well as any man in the State."

Maxime unburdens his mind. "Judge, I fear we are in danger of losing this coast. I have looked over the social forces of the State. The miners represent no principle. They will cut no figure on either side. They would not be amenable to discipline. The Mexicans certainly will not sympathize with us. We are regarded as the old government party. The Black Republicans are the 'liberals.' The natives have lost all, under us. We will find them fierce enemies. We cannot undo the treatment of the Dons." Hardin gravely assents.

"Now, as to the struggle. Our people are enthusiastic and better prepared. The nerve of the South will carry us to early victory. The North thinks we do not mean fight. Our people may neglect to rush troops from Texas over through Arizona. We should hold California from the very first. I know the large cities are against us. The Yankees control the shipping and have more money than we. We should seize this coast, prey on the Pacific fleets, strike a telling blow, and with Texan troops (who will be useless there) make sure of the only gold-yielding regions of America. Texas is safe. We hold the Gulf at New Orleans. Yankee gunboats cannot reach the shallow Texas harbors. Unless we strike boldly now, the coast is lost forever. If our people hold the Potomac, the Ohio, and the Missouri (after a season's victories), without taking Cincinnati and Washington, and securing this coast, we will go down, finally, when the North wakes up. Its power is immense. If Europe recognizes us we are safe. I fear this may not be."

"And you think the Northerners will fight," says Hardin.

"Judge," replies Valois, "you and I are alone. I tell you frankly we underestimate the Yankees. From the first, on this coast we have lost sympathy. They come back at us always. Broderick's death shows us these men have nerve. "Valois continues: "That man is greater dead than alive. I often think of his last words, 'They have killed me because I was opposed to a corrupt administration and the extension of slavery.'"

Hardin finishes his glass. "It seems strange that men like Broderick and Terry, who sat on the bench of the Supreme Court (a senator and a great jurist), should open the game. It was unlucky. It lost us the Northern Democrats. We would have been better off if Dave Terry had been killed. He would have been a dead hero. It would have helped us."

Valois shows that, in all the sectional duels and killings on the coast, the South has steadily lost prestige. The victims were more dangerous dead than alive. Gilbert, Ferguson, Broderick, and others were costly sacrifices.

Hardin muses: "I think you are right, Maxime, in the main. Our people are in the awkward position of fighting the Constitution, and the old flag is a dead weight against us. We must take the initiative in an unnecessary war. This Abe Lincoln is no mere mad fool. I will send a messenger East, and urge that ten thousand Texan cavalry be pushed right over to Arizona. We must seize the coast. You are right! There is one obstacle, Valois, I cannot conquer."

"What is that?" says Maxime.

"It is Sidney Johnston's military honor," thoughtfully says Hardin. "He is no man to be played with. He will not act till he has left the old army regularly. He will wait his commission from our confederacy. He will then resign and go East."

"It will be too late," cries Valois. "We will be forgotten, and so lose California."

"The worst is that the coast will stand neutral," says Hardin.

"Now, Judge," Valois firmly answers, "I have heard to-night talk of running up the 'bear flag,' 'the lone star,' 'the palmetto banner,' or 'the flag of the California Republic,' on the news of war. I hope they will not do so rashly."

"Why?" says Hardin.

"I think they will swing under the new flags on the same pole," cries Valois, pacing the room. "If there is failure here, I shall go East. Judge Valois offers me a Louisiana regiment. If this war is fought out, I do not propose to live to see the Southern Cross come down."

The Creole pauses before the Judge, who replies, "You must stay here; we must get California out of the Union."

"If we do not, then the cause lies on Lone Mountain," says Valois, pointing westward toward the spot where a tall shaft already bears Broderick's name.

Hardin nods assent. "It was terrific, that appeal of Baker's," he murmurs.

Both felt that Baker (now Senator from Oregon) would call up the mighty shade of the New York leader. Neither could foresee the career of the eulogist of Broderick, after his last matchless appeals to an awakening North. That denunciation in the Senate sent the departing Southern senators away, smarting under the scorpion whip of his peerless invective. Baker was doomed to come home cold in death from the red field of Ball's Bluff, and lie on the historic hill, beside his murdered friend.

The plotters in the cold midnight hours then, the glow of feeling fading away, say "Good-night." They part, looking out over twinkling lights like the great camps soon to rise on Eastern plain and river-bank. Will the flag of the South wave in TRIUMPH HERE? Ah! Who can read the future?

Cut off from the East, the excited Californians burn in high fever. The grim dice of fate are being cast. Slowly, the Northern pine and Southern palm sway toward the crash of war. As yet only journals hurl defiance at each other. Every day has its duties for Hardin and Valois; they know that every regimental mess-room is canvassed; each ship's ward-room is sounded; officers are flattered and won over; woman lends her persuasive charms; high promised rank follows the men who yield.

In these negotiations, no one dares to breed discontent among the common soldiers and sailors. It is madness to hope to turn the steady loyalty of the enlisted men. They are as true in both services as the blue they wear. Nice distinctions begin at the epaulet. Hardin and Valois are worn and thoughtful. The popular tide of feelings is not for the South. Separation must be effective, to rouse enthusiasm. The organization of the Knights of the Golden Circle proceeds quickly, but events are quicker.

The seven States partly out of the Union; the yet unfinished ranks of the Southern Confederacy; the baffling questions of compromise with the claims and rights of the South to national property are agitated. The incredulous folly of the North and the newspaper sympathy of the great Northern cities drag the whole question of war slowly along. In the West (a month later in news), the people fondly believe the bonds of the Union will not be broken.

Many think the South will drop out quietly. Lincoln's policy is utterly unknown. Distance has dulled the echo of the hostile guns fired at the STAR OF THE WEST by armed traitors, on January 9, at Charleston.

Jefferson Davis's shadowy Confederacy of the same fatal date is regarded as only a temporary menace to the Union. The great border States are not yet in line.

Paltering old President Buchanan has found no warrant to draw the nation's sword in defence of the outraged flag.

Congress is a camp of warring enemies. Even the conspirators cling to their comfortable chairs.

It is hard to realize, by the blue Pacific, that the flag is already down. No one knows the fatal dead line between "State" and "Union."

So recruits come in slowly to the Knights of the Golden Circle, in California. Secession is only a dark thunder-cloud, hanging ominously in the sky. The red lightning of war lingers in its sulphury bosom.

Hardin, Valois, and the Knights toil to secure their ends. They know not that their vigorous foes have sent trusted messengers speeding eastward to secure the removal of General Albert Sidney Johnston. There is a Union League digging under their works!

The four electoral votes of California cast for Lincoln tell him the State is loyal.

An accidental promotion of Governor Latham to the Senate, places John G. Downey in the chair of California. If not a "coercionist," he is certainly no "rebel." The leaders of the Golden Circle feel that chivalry in the West is crushed, unless saved by a "coup de main." McDougall is a war senator. Latham, ruined by his prediction that California would go South or secede alone, sinks into political obscurity. The revolution, due to David Terry's bullet, brought men like Phelps, Sargent, T. W. Park, and John Conness to the front. Other Free-State men see the victory of their principles with joy. Sidney Johnston is the last hope of the Southern leaders. The old soldier's resignation speeds eastward on the pony express. Day by day, exciting news tells of the snapping of cord after cord. Olden amity disappears in the East. The public voice is heard.

The mantle of heroic Baker as a political leader falls upon the boy preacher, Thomas Starr King. He boldly raises the song of freedom. It is now no time to lurk in the rear. Men, hitherto silent; rally around the flag.

The "Union League" grows fast, as the "Golden Circle" extends. All over California, resolute men swear to stand by the flag. Stanford and Low are earning their governorships. From pulpit and rostrum the cry of secession is raised by Dr. Scott and the legal meteor Edmund Randolph, now sickening to his death. Randolph, though a son of Virginia, with, first, loyal impulses, sent despatches to President Lincoln that California was to be turned over to the South. He disclosed that Jefferson Davis had already sent Sidney Johnston a Major-General's commission. Though he finally follows the course of his native State, Randolph rendered priceless service to the Union cause in the West. General Edward V. Sumner is already secretly hurrying westward. He is met at Panama by the Unionist messengers. They turn back with him. In every city and county the Unionists and Southerners watch each other. While Johnston's resignation flies eastward, Sumner is steaming up the Mexican coast, unknown to the conspirators.

In the days of March and April, 1861, one excited man could have plunged the Pacific Coast into civil warfare. All unconscious of the deadly gun bellowing treason on April 12th at Charleston, as the first shell burst over Sumter, the situation remained one of anxious tension in California. The telegraph is not yet finished. On April 19th, General Sumner arrived unexpectedly. He was informed of local matters by the loyalists. General Sidney Johnston, astonished and surprised, turned over his command at once. Without treasonable attempt, he left the Golden Gate. When relieved, he was no longer in the service. Speeding over the Colorado deserts to Texas, the high-minded veteran rode out to don the new gray uniform, and to die in the arms of an almost decisive victory at Shiloh.

Well might the South call that royal old soldier to lead its hosts. Another half hour of Albert Sidney Johnston at Shiloh, and the history of the United States might have been changed by his unconquered sword. Lofty in his aims, adored by his subordinates, he was a modern Marshal Ney. The Southern cypress took its darkest tinge around his untimely grave. Sidney Johnston had all the sterling qualities of Lee, and even a rarer magnetism of character.

Honor placed one fadeless wreath upon his tomb. He would not play the ignoble part of a Twiggs or a Lynde. He offered a stainless sword to the Bonnie Blue Flag.

The gravity of his farewell, the purity of his private character, the affection of his personal friends, are tributes to the great soldier. He nearly crushed the Union army in his tiger-like assault at Shiloh. By universal consent, the ablest soldier of the "old army," he was sacrificed to the waywardness of fate. Turns of Fortune's wheel.

California was stunned by the rapidity of Sumner's grasp of the reins of command. Before the Knights of the Golden Circle could move, the control of the State and the coast was lost to them forever. Forts and arsenals, towns and government depositories, navy-yards and vessels, were guarded.

Following this action of Sumner, on May 10th the news of Sumter, and the uprising of the North, burst upon friend and foe in California. The loyal men rallied in indignation, overawing the Southern element. The oath of fealty was renewed by thousands. California's star was that day riveted in the flag. An outraged people deposed Judge Hardy, who so feebly prosecuted the slayer of Broderick. Every avenue was guarded. Conspiracy fled to back rooms and side streets. Here were no Federal wrongs to redress. On the spot where Broderick's body lay, under Baker's oratory, the multitude listened to the awakened patriots of the West. The Pacific Coast was saved.

The madness of fools who fluttered a straggling "bear flag," "palmetto ensign," or "lone star," caused them to flee in terror.

Stanley, Lake, Crockett, Starr King, General Shields, and others, echoed the pledges of their absent comrades in New York. Organization, for the Union, followed. Even the maddest Confederate saw the only way to serve the South was to sneak through the lines to Texas. The telegraph was completed in October, 1861. The government had then daily tidings from the loyal sentinels calling "All's well," on fort and rampart, from San Juan Island to Fort Yuma.

Troops were offered everywhere. The only region in California where secessionists were united was in San Joaquin.

While public discussion availed, Hardin and Valois listened to Thornton, Crittenden, Morrison, Randolph, Dr. Scott, Weller, Whitesides, Hoge, and Nugent. But the time for hope was past. The golden sun had set for ever. Fifteen regiments of Californian troops, in formation, were destined to hold the State. They guarded the roads to Salt Lake and Arizona. The arsenals and strongholds were secured. The chance of successful invasion from Texas vanished. It was the crowning mistake of the first year of secession, not to see the value of the Pacific Coast. From the first shot, the Pacific Railroad became a war measure. The iron bands tied East and West in a firm union.

Gwin's departure and Randolph's death added to the Southern discomfiture. No course remained for rebels but to furtively join the hosts of treason. Flight to the East.

In the wake of Sidney Johnston went many men of note. Garnett, Cheatham, Brooks, Calhoun, Benham, Magruder, Phil Herbert, and others, with Dan Showalter and David Terry, each fresh from the deadly field of honor. Kewen, Weller, and others remained to be silenced by arrest. All over the State a hegira commenced which ended in final defeat. Many graves on the shallow-trenched battle-fields were filled by the Californian exiles. Not in honor did these devoted men and hundreds of their friends leave the golden hills. Secretly they fled, lest their romantic quest might land them in a military prison. Those unable to leave gave aid to the absent. Sulking at home, they deserted court and mart to avoid personal penalties.

It was different with many of the warm-hearted Californian sons of the South who were attached to the Union. Cut off in a distant land, they held aloof from approving secession. Grateful for the shelter of the peaceful land in which their hard-won homes were made, it was only after actual war that the ties of blood carried them away and ranged them under the Stars and Bars. When the Southern ranks fell, in windrows, on the Peninsula, hundreds of these manly Californians left to join their brethren. They had clung to the Union till their States went out one by one. They sadly sought the distant fields of action, and laid down their lives for the now holy cause.

The attitude of these gallant men was noble. They scorned the burrowing conspirators who dug below the foundations of the national constitution. These schemers led the eager South into a needless civil war.

The holiest feelings of heredity dragged the Southerners who lingered into war. It was a sacrifice of half of the splendid generation which fought under the Southern Cross.

When broken ranks appealed for the absent, when invaded States and drooping hopes aroused desperation, the last California contingents braved the desert dangers. Indian attack and Federal capture were defied, only to die for the South on its sacred soil. "Salut aux braves!" The loyalists of California were restrained from disturbing the safe tenure of the West by depleting the local Union forces. Abraham Lincoln saw that the Pacific columns should do no more than guard the territories adjacent. To hold the West and secure the overland roads was their duty. To be ready to march to meet an invasion or quell an uprising. This was wisdom.

But the country called for skilled soldiers and representative men to join the great work of upholding the Union. A matchless contingent of Union officers went East.

California had few arms-bearing young Americans to represent its first ten years of State existence. But it returned to the national government men identified with the Pacific Coast, who were destined to be leaders of the Union hosts.

Grant, Sherman, Sheridan, Thomas, Halleck, Hancock, Hooker, Keyes, Naglee, Baker, Ord, Farragut (the blameless Nelson of America), Canby, Fremont, Shields, McPherson, Stoneman, Stone, Porter, Boggs, Sumner, Heintzelman, Lander, Buell, with other old residents of the coast, drew the sword. Wool, Denver, Geary, and many more, whose abilities had been perfected in the struggles of the West, took high rank.

Where the young were absent (by reason of the infancy of the State), these men were returned to the government. They went with a loyalty undimmed, in the prime of their powers. Even the graceful McClellan was identified with the Pacific Railway survey. Around the scenes of their early manhood, the halo of these loyal men will ever linger, and gild the name of "Pioneer." It can never be forgotten that without the stormy scenes of Western life, without the knowledge of the great golden empire and the expansion of powers due to their lessons on plain and prairie, many of these men would have relapsed into easy mediocrity.

The completed telegraph, military extension of lines, and the active Union League, secured California to the Union.

The gigantic game of war rolled its red pageantry over Eastern fields. Bull Run fired the Southern heart. Hardin and Valois learned the Southern Government would send a strong expedition to hold New Mexico and Arizona. Local aid was arranged by the Knights of the Golden Circle to, at last, seize California. It was so easy to whip Yankees. The Knights were smiling.

At the risk of their lives, two Southern messengers reached San Francisco. One by Panama. The other crossed Arizona and examined the line of march. He rode, warning sympathizers to await the Confederate flag, which now waved in triumph at Munson's Hill, in plain sight of the guarded capitol.

Valois fears this Western raid may be too late. For the Navy Department reinforces the Pacific fleet. Valois explains to Hardin that his prophecy is being realized. The Confederates, with more men than are needed, hold their lines of natural defence. The fruits of Bull Run are lost. While letters by every steamer come from Northern spies, Washington friends, and Southern associates, the journals tell them of the deliberate preparation of the North for a struggle to the death. The giant is waking up.

Valois mourns the madness of keeping the flower of the South inactive. A rapid Northern invasion should humble the administration. The ardent Texans should be thrown at once into California, leaving New Mexico and Arizona for later occupation.

There is no reason why the attack should not be immediate. Under the stimulus of Bull Run the entire Southern population of California would flock to the new standard. Three months should see the Confederate cavalry pasturing their steeds in the prairies of California.

The friends sicken at the delay, as weary months drag on. Sibley's Texans should be now on the Gila. They have guides, leaders, scouts, and spies from the Southern refugees pouring over the Gila. Every golden day has its gloomy sunset. Hardin's brow furrows with deep lines. His sagacity tells him that the time has passed for the movement to succeed.

And he is right. Sibley wearies out the winter in Texas. The magnet of Eastern fields of glory draws the fiery Texans across the Mississippi. The Californian volunteers are arming and drilling. They stream out to Salt Lake. They send the heavy column of General Carleton toward El Paso.

The two chiefs of the Golden Circle are unaware of the destination of Carleton. Loyalty has learned silence. There are no traitor department clerks here, to furnish maps, plans, and duplicate orders.

Canby in New Mexico, unknown to the secessionists of California, aided by Kit Carson, gathers a force to strike Sibley in flank. It is fatal to Californian conquest. Hardin and Valois learn of the lethargy of the great Confederate army, flushed with success. Sibley's dalliance at Fort Bliss continues.

The "army of New Mexico," on September 19, 1861, is only a few hundreds of mounted rangers and Texan youth under feeble Sibley.

From the first, Jefferson Davis's old army jealousies and hatred of able men of individuality, hamstring the Southern cause. A narrow-minded man is Davis, the slave of inveterate prejudice. With dashing Earl Van Dorn, sturdy Ben Ewell, and dozens of veteran cavalry leaders at his service, knowing every foot of the road, he could have thrown his Confederate column into California. Three months after Sumter's fall, California should have been captured. Davis allows an old martinet to ruin the Confederate cause in the Pacific.

The operation is so easy, so natural, and so necessary, that it looks like fatuity to neglect the golden months of the fall of 1861.

Especially fitted for bold dashes with a daring leader, the Texans throw themselves, later, uselessly against the flaming redoubts of Corinth. They are thrown into mangled heaps before Battery Robinett, dying for the South. Their military recklessness has never been surpassed in the red record of war.

Though gallant in the field, President Jefferson Davis, seated on a throne of cotton, gazes across the seas for England's help. He craves the aid of France. He allows narrow prejudice to blind him to any part of the great issue, save the military pageantry of his unequalled Virginian army. It is the flower of the South, and moves only on the sacred soil of Virginia. Davis, restrained by antipathies, haughty, and distant, is deaf to the thrilling calls of the West for that dashing column. It would have gained him California. Weakness of mind kept him from hurling his victorious troops on Washington, or crossing the Ohio to divide the North while yet unprepared. Active help could then be looked for from Northern Democrats. But he masses the South in Virginia.

As winter wears on the movement of Carleton's and Canby's preparations are disclosed by Southern friends, who run the gauntlet with these discouraging news.

Sibley lingered with leaden heels at Fort Bliss. The Confederate riders are not across the Rio Grande. Valois grows heartsick.

Broken in hopes, wearied with plotting, mistrusted by the community, Hardin knows the truth at last. The words, "Too late!" ring in his ears.

It will be only some secret plot which can now hope to succeed in the West.

Davis and Lee are wedded to Virginia. The haughty selfishness of the "mother of presidents" demands that every interest of the Confederacy shall give way to morbid State vanity. Virginia is to be the graveyard of the gallant Southern generation in arms.

Every other pass may be left unguarded. The chivalry of the Stars and Bars must crowd Virginia till their graves fill the land. Unnecessarily strong, with a frontier defended by rivers, forests, and chosen positions, it becomes Fortune's sport to huddle the bulk of the Confederate forces into Lee's army.

It allows the Border, Gulf, and Western States to fall a prey to the North. The story of Lee's ability has been told by an adoring generation. The record of his cold military selfishness is shown in the easy conquests of the heart of the South. Their natural defenders were drafted to fill those superb legions, operating under the eyes of Davis and controlled by the slightest wish of imperious Lee.

Albert Sidney Johnston, Beauregard, and the fighting tactician, Joe Johnston, were destined to feel how fatal was the military favoritism of Jefferson Davis. Davis threw away Vicksburg, and the Mississippi later, to please Lee. All for Virginia.

Stung with letters from Louisiana, reproaching him for inaction while his brethren were meeting the Northern invaders, Valois decides to go East. He will join the Southern defence. For it is defence--not invasion--now.

Directing Hardin to select a subordinate in his place, Valois returns to Lagunitas. He must say farewell to loving wife and prattling child. Too well known to be allowed to follow Showalter, Terry, and their fellows over the Colorado desert, he must go to Guaymas in Mexico. He can thus reach the Confederates at El Paso. From thence it is easy to reach New Orleans. Then to the front. To the field.

Valois feels it would be useless for him to go via Panama. The provost-marshal would hold him as a "known enemy."

With rage, Valois realizes a new commander makes latent treason uncomfortable in California. He determines to reach El Paso, and hurl the Texans on California. Should he fail, he heads a Louisiana regiment. His heart tells him the war will be long and bloody. Edmund Randolph's loyalty, at the outbreak, prevented the seizure of California. Sibley's folly and Davis's indifference complete the ruin of the Western plan of action.

"Hardin, hold the Knights together. I will see if I can stop a Yankee bullet!" says Valois. He notifies Hardin that he intends to make him sole trustee of his property in his absence.

Hardin's term on the bench has expired. Like other Southerners debarred from taking the field, he gives aid to those who go. The men who go leave hostages behind them. The friendship of years causes Yalois to make him the adviser of his wife in property matters. He makes him his own representative. "Thank Heaven!" cries Valois, "my wife's property is safe. No taint from me can attach to her birthright. It is her own by law."

Valois, at Lagunitas, unfolds to the sorrowing padre his departure for the war. Safe in the bosom of the priest, this secret is a heavy load. Valois gains his consent to remain in charge of Lagunitas. The little girl begins to feebly walk. Her infant gaze cannot measure her possessions.

Lovely Dolores Valois listens meekly to her husband's plans. Devoted to Maxime, his will is her only law. The beautiful dark eyes are tinged with a deeper lustre.

Busied with his affairs, Maxime thinks of the future as he handles his papers. Francois Ribaut is the depositary of his wishes. Dolores is as incapable as her child in business. Will God protect these two innocents?

Valois wonders if he will return in defeat like Don Miguel. Poor old Don!

around his tomb the roses creep,--his gentle Juanita by his side.

He hopes the armies of the West will carry the banner, now flying from Gulf to border, into the North. There the legendary friends of the South will hail it.

Alas! pent up in California, Maxime hears not the murmurs of the Northern pines, breathing notes of war and defiance. The predictions of the leaders of the conspiracy are fallacious. Aid and comfort fail them abroad. North of Mason and Dixon's line the sympathizers are frightened.

In his heart he only feels the tumult of the call to the field. It is his pride of race. Tired, weary of the crosses of fortune, he waits only to see the enemy's fires glittering from hill and cliff.

With all his successes, the West has never been his home. Looking out on his far-sweeping alamedas, his thoughts turn fondly back to his native land. He is "going home to Dixie."

CHAPTER XI.

"I'SE GWINE BACK TO DIXIE."--THE FORTUNES OF WAR.--VAL VERDE.

The last weeks of Maxime Valois' stay at Lagunitas drift away. Old "Kaintuck" has plead in vain to go. He yields to Valois' orders not to dream of going with him. His martial heart is fired, but some one must watch the home. Padre Francois Ribaut has all the documents of the family, the marriage, and birth of the infant heir. He is custodian also of the will of Donna Dolores. She leaves her family inheritance to her child, and failing her, to her husband. The two representatives of the departing master know that Philip Hardin will safely guide the legal management of the estate while its chieftain is at the wars.

Donna Dolores and the priest accompany Valois to San Francisco. He must leave quietly. He is liable to arrest. He takes the Mexican steamer, as if for a temporary absence.

It costs Maxime Valois a keen pang of regret, as he rides the last time over his superb domain. He looks around the plaza, and walks alone through the well-remembered rooms. He takes his seat, with a sigh, by his wife's side, as the carriage whirls him down the avenues. The orange-trees are in bloom. The gardens show the rare beauties of midland California. As far as the eye can reach, the sparkle of lovely Lagunitas mirrors the clouds flaking the sapphire sky. Valois fixes his eyes once more upon his happy home. Peace, prosperity, progress, mining exploration, social development, all smile through this great interior valley of the Golden State. No war cloud has yet rolled past the "Rockies." It is the golden youth of the commonwealth. The throbbing engine, clattering stamp, whirling saw, and busy factory, show that the homemakers are moving on apace, with giant strides. No fairer land to leave could tempt a departing warrior. But even with a loved wife and his only child beside him, the Southerner's heart "turns back to Dixie."

Passing rapidly through Stockton, where his old friends vainly tempt him to say, publicly, good-by, he refrains. No one must know his destination. No parting cup is drained.

In San Francisco, Philip Hardin, in presence of Valois' wife and the padre, receives his powers of attorney and final directions. Letters, remittances, and all communications are to be sent through a house in Havana. The old New Orleans family of Valois is well known there. Maxime will be able, by blockade-runners and travelling messengers, to obtain his communications.

The only stranger in San Francisco who knows of Maxime's departure is the old mining partner, Joe Woods. He is now a middle-aged man of property and vigor. He comes from the interior to say adieu to his friend. "Old times" cloud their eyes. But the parting is secret. Federal spies throng the streets.

At the mail wharf the Mexican steamer, steam up, is ready for departure. The last private news from the Texan border tells of General Sibley's gathering forces. Provided with private despatches, and bundles of contraband letters for the cut-off friends in the South, Maxime Valois repairs to the steamer. Several returning Texans and recruits for the Confederacy have arrived singly. They will make an overland party from Guaymas, headed by Valois. Valois, under the orders of the Golden Circle, has been charged with important communications. Unknown to him, secret agents of the government watch his departure. He has committed no overt act. He goes to a neutral land.

The calm, passionless face of Padre Francois Ribaut shows a tear trembling in his eye. He leads the weeping wife ashore from the cabin. The last good-by was sacred by its silent sorrow. Valois' father's heart was strangely thrilled when he kissed his baby girl farewell, on leaving the little party. Even rebels have warm hearts.

Philip Hardin's stern features relax into some show of feeling as Valois places his wife's hands in his. That mute adieu to lovely Dolores moves him. "May God deal with you, Hardin, as you deal with my wife and child," solemnly says Valois. The lips of Francois Ribaut piously add "Amen. Amen."

Padre Francisco comes back to the boat. With French impulsiveness, he throws himself in Valois' arms. He whispers a friend's blessing, a priest's benediction.

The ORIZABA glides out past two or three watchful cruisers flying the Stars and Stripes. The self-devoted Louisianian loses from sight the little knot of dear ones on the wharf. He sees the flutter of Dolores' handkerchief for the last time. On to Dixie! Going home!

Out on the bay, thronged with the ships of all nations, the steamer glides. Its shores are covered with smiling villages. Happy homes and growing cities crown the heights. Past grim Alcatraz, where the star flag proudly floats on the Sumter-like citadel, the boat slowly moves. It leaves the great metropolis of the West, spreading over its sandy hills and creeping up now the far green valleys. It slips safely through the sea-gates of the West, and past the grim fort at the South Heads. There, casemate and barbette shelter the shotted guns which speak only for the Union.

Valois' heart rises in his throat as the sentinel's bayonet glitters in the sunlight. Loyal men are on the walls of the fort. Far away on the Presidio grounds, he can see the blue regiments of Carleton's troops, at exercise, wheel at drill. The sweeping line of a cavalry battalion moves, their sabres flash as the lines dash on. These men are now his foes. The tossing breakers of the bar throw their spray high over bulwarks and guard. In grim determination he watches the last American flag he ever will see in friendship, till it fades away from sight. He has now taken the irrevocable step. When he steps on Mexican soil, he will be "a man without a country." Prudential reasons keep him aloof from his companions until Guaymas is reached. Once ashore, the comrades openly unite. Without delay the party plunges into the interior. Well armed, splendidly mounted, they assume a semi-military discipline. The Mexicans are none too friendly. Valois has abundant gold, as well as forty thousand dollars in drafts on Havana, the proceeds of Lagunitas' future returns advanced by Hardin.

Twenty days' march up the Yaqui Valley, through Arispe, where the filibusters died with Spartan bravery, is a weary jaunt. But high hopes buoy them up. Over mesa and gorge, past hacienda and Indian settlement, they climb passes until the great mountains break away. Crossing the muddy Rio Grande, Valois is greeted by old friends. He sees the Confederate flag for the first time, floating over the turbulent levies of Sibley, still at Fort Bliss.

Long and weary marches; dangers from bandit, Indian, and lurking Mexican; regrets for the home circle at Lagunitas, make Maxime Valois very grave. Individual sacrifices are not appreciated in war-time. As he rides through the Confederate camp, his heart sinks. The uncouth straggling plainsmen, without order or regular equipment, recall to him his old enemies, the nomadic Mexican vaqueros.

There seems to be no supply train, artillery, or regular stores. These are not the men who can overawe the compact California community. Far gray rocky sandhills stretch along the Texan border. Over the Rio Grande, rich mountain scenery delights the eye. It instantly recalls to Valois the old Southern dream of taking the "Zona Libre." Tamaulipas, Coahuila, and Nueva Leon were coveted as a crowning trophy of the Mexican war. Dreams of olden days.

Received kindly by General Sibley, the Louisianian delivers his letters, despatches, and messages. After rest and refreshment, he is asked to join a council of war. There are fleet couriers, lately arrived, who speak of Carleton's column being nearly ready to cross the Colorado. When the General explains his plan of attacking the Federal forces in New Mexico, and occupying Arizona, Valois hastens to urge a forced march down to the fertile Gila. He trusts to Canby timidly holding on to Fort Union and Fort Craig. Alas, Sibley's place of recruiting and assembly has been ill chosen! The animals, crowded on the bare plains, suffer for lack of forage. Recruits are discouraged by the dreary surroundings. The effective strength has not visibly increased in three months. The Texans are wayward. A strong column, well organized, in the rich interior of Texas, full of the early ardor of secession might have pushed on and reached the Gila. But here is only a chafing body of undisciplined men. They are united merely by political sentiment.

General Sibley urges Valois to accompany him in his forward march. He offers him a staff position, promising to release him, then to move to the eastward. Valois' knowledge of the frontier is invaluable, and he cannot pass an enemy in arms. Maxime Valois, with fiery energy, aids in urging the motley command forward. On February 7, 1862, the wild brigade of invasion reaches the mesa near Fort Craig. The "gray" and "blue" meet here in conflict, to decide the fate of New Mexico and Arizona. Feeble skirmishing begins. On the 21st of February, the bitter conflict of Val Verde shows Valois for the first time--alas, not the last!--the blood of brothers mingled on a doubtful field. It is a horrid fight. A drawn battle.

Instead of pushing on to Arizona, deluded by reports of local aid, Sibley straggles off to Santa Fe and Albuquerque. Canby refits his broken forces under the walls of strong Fort Union. Long before the trifling affairs of Glorietta and Peralta, Valois, disgusted with Sibley, is on his way east. He will join the Army of the West. His heart sickens at the foolish incapacity of the border commander. The Texan column melts away under Canby's resolute advance. The few raiders, who have ridden down into Arizona and hoisted the westernmost Confederate flag at Antelope Peak, are chased back by Carleton's strong column. The boasted "military advance on California" is at an end. Carleton's California column is well over the Colorado. The barren fruits of Val Verde are only a few buried guns of McRea's hard-fought battery. The gallantry of Colonel Thos. P. Ochiltree, C.S.A., at Val Verde, under the modest rank of "Captain," is the only remembered historic incident of that now forgotten field. The First Regiment and one battalion of the Second California Volunteer Cavalry, the Fifth California Infantry, and a good battery hold Arizona firmly. The Second Battalion, Second California Cavalry, the Fifth California Cavalry, and Third California Infantry, under gallant General Pat Connor, keep Utah protected. They lash the wild Indians into submission, and prevent any rising.

General Canby and Kit Carson's victorious troops keep New Mexico. They cut the line of any possible Confederate advance. Only Sibley's pompous report remains now to tell of the fate of his troops, who literally disbanded or deserted. An inglorious failure attends the dreaded Texan attack.

The news, travelling east and west, by fugitives, soon announce the failure of this abortive attempt. The golden opportunity of the fall of 1861 never returns.

The Confederate operations west of the Rio Grande were only a miserable and ridiculous farce. Valois, leaving failure behind him, learns on nearing the Louisiana line, that the proud Pelican flag floats no longer over the Crescent City. It lies now helpless under the guns of fearless Farragut's fleet. So he cannot even revisit the home of his youth. Maxime Valois smuggles himself across the Mississippi. He joins the Confederates under Van Dorn. He is a soldier at last.

Here in the circling camps of the great Army of the West, Maxime Valois joins the first Louisiana regiment he meets. He realizes that the beloved Southern Confederacy has yet an unbeaten army. A grand array. The tramp of solid legions makes him feel a soldier, not a sneaking conspirator. He is no more a guerilla of the plains, or a fugitive deserter of his adopted State.

The capture of New Orleans seals the Mississippi. The Confederacy is cut in twain. It is positive now, the only help from the golden West will be the arrival of parties of self-devoted men like himself. They come in squads, bolting through Mexico or slipping through Arizona. Some reach Panama and Havana, gaining the South by blockade runners. He opens mail communication with Judge Hardin, via Havana. He succeeds in exchanging views with the venerable head of his house at New Orleans. It is all gloomy now. Old and despondent, the New Orleans patriarch has sent his youthful son away to Paris. Armand is too young to bear arms. He can only come home and do a soldier's duty later. By family influence, Maxime Valois finds himself soon a major in a Louisiana regiment. He wears his gray uniform at the head of men already veterans. Shiloh's disputed laurels are theirs. They are tigers who have tasted blood. In the rapidly changing scenes of service, trusting to chance for news of his family, Maxime Valois' whole nature is centred upon the grave duties of his station. Southern victories are hailed from the East. The victorious arms of the Confederacy roll back McClellan's great force. Bruised, bleeding, and shattered from the hard-fought fields of the Peninsula, the Unionists recoil. The stars of the Southern Cross are high in hope's bright field. Though Richmond is saved for the time, it is at a fearful cost. Malvern Hill shakes to its base under the flaming cannon, ploughing the ranks of the dauntless Confederates, as the Army of the Potomac hurls back the confident legions of Lee, Johnston, and Jackson. The Army of the Potomac is decimated. The bloody attrition of the field begins to wear off these splendid lines which the South can never replace. Losses like those of Pryor's Brigade, nine hundred out of fifteen hundred in a single campaign, would appall any but the grim Virginian soldiers. They are veterans now. They learn the art of war in fields like Seven Pines and Fair Oaks. Even Pryor, as chivalric in action as truculent in debate, now admits that the Yankees will fight. Fredericksburg's butchery is a victory of note. All the year the noise of battle rolls, while the Eastern war is undecided, for the second Manassas and awful Antietam balance each other. Maxime Valois feels the issue is lost. When the shock of battle has been tried at Corinth, where lion-like Rosecrans conquers, when the glow of the onset fades away, his heart sinks. He knows that the iron-jointed men of the West are the peers of any race in the field.

Ay! In the West it is fighting from the first. Donelson, Shiloh, and Corinth lead up to the awful death shambles of Stone River, Vicksburg, and Chickamauga. These are scenes to shake the nerve of the very bravest.

Heading his troops on the march, watching the thousand baleful fires of the enemy at night, when friend and foe go down in the thundering crash of battle, Valois, amazed, asks himself, "Are these sturdy foes the Northern mudsills?"

For, proud and dashing as the Louisiana Tigers and Texan Rangers prove, steady and vindictive the rugged Mississippians, dogged and undaunted the Georgians, fierce the Alabamans--the honest candor of Valois tells him no human valor can excel the never-yielding Western troops. Their iron courage honors the blue-clad men of Iowa, Michigan, and the Lake States. No hired foreigners there; no helot immigrants these men, whose glittering bayonets shine in the lines of Corinth, as steadily as the spears of the old Tenth Roman Legion--Caesar's pets.

With unproclaimed chivalry and a readiness to meet the foe which tells its own story, the Western men come on. Led by Grant, Sherman, Rosecrans, Sheridan, Thomas, McPherson, and Logan, they press steadily toward the heart of the Confederacy. The rosy dreams of empire in the great West fade away. Farragut, Porter, and the giant captain, Grant, cut off the Trans-Mississippi from active military concert with the rest of the severed Confederacy.

To and fro rolls the red tide of war. Valois' soldierly face, bronzed with service, shows only the steady devotion of the soldier. He loves the cause--once dear in its promise--now sacred in its hours of gloomy peril and incipient decadence. Gettysburg, Vicksburg, and Port Hudson are terrible omens of a final day of gloom. Letters from his wife, reports from Judge Hardin, and news from the Western shores give him only vague hints of the future straggling efforts on the Pacific. The only comforting tidings are that his wife and child are well, by the peaceful shores of Lagunitas. The absence of foreign aid, the lack of substantial support from the Northern sympathizers, and the slight hold on the ocean of the new government, dishearten him. The grim pressure everywhere of the Northern lines tells Valois that the splendid chivalry of the Southern arms is being forced surely backward. Sword in hand, his resolute mind unshaken, the Louisianian follows the Stars and Bars, devoted and never despairing. "Quand meme."

In the long silent days at Lagunitas, the patient wife learns much from the cautious disclosures of Padre Francisco. Her soldier husband's letters tell her the absent master of Lagunitas is winning fame and honor in a dreadful conflict. It is only vaguely understood by the simple Californian lady.

Her merry child is rapidly forgetting the self-exiled father. Under the bowers of Lagunitas she romps in leafy alley and shady bower.

Judge Hardin, grave-faced, cautious, frugal of speech, visits the domain several times. In conference with Padre Francisco and the vigilant "Kaintuck," he adjusts the accumulating business affairs.

Riding over the billowing fields, mounting the grassy hills, threading the matchless forests of uncut timber, he sees all. He sits plotting and dreaming on the porch by the lake side. Thousands of horses and cattle, now crossed and improved, are wealth wandering at will on every side. Hardin's dark eyes grow eager and envious. He gazes excitedly on this lordly domain. Suppose Valois should never come back. This would be a royal heritage. He puts the maddening thought away. Within a few miles, mill and flume tell of the tracing down of golden quartz lodes. The pick breaks into the hitherto undisturbed quartz ledges of Mariposa gold. Is there gold to be found here, too? Perhaps.

Only an old prating priest, a simple woman, and an infant, between him and these thousands of rich acres, should Valois be killed.

Philip Hardin becomes convinced of final defeat, as 1863 draws to a close. The days of Gettysburg and Vicksburg ring the knell of the Confederacy. Even the prestige of Chancellorsville, with its sacred victory sealed with Stonewall Jackson's precious blood, was lost in the vital blow delivered when the columns of Longstreet and Pickett failed to carry the heights of Gettysburg.

The troops slain on that field could never be replaced. Boyhood and old age, alone, were left to fill the vacant ranks. Settling slowly down, the gloomy days of collapse approach.

While Lee skilfully faced the Army of the Potomac, and the Confederacy was drained of men to hold the "sacred soil," the Western fields were lit up by the fierce light of Grant and Sherman's genius. Like destroying angels, seconded by Rosecrans, Thomas, and McPherson, these great captains drew out of the smoke of battle, gigantic figures towering above all their rivals.

Maxime Valois bitterly deplored the uselessness of the war in the trans-Mississippi section of the Confederacy. It is too late for any Western divisions to affect the downward course of the sacred cause for which countless thousands have already died.

The Potomac armies of the Union, torn with the dissensions of warring generals, wait for the days of the inscrutable Grant and fiery Philip Sheridan. In the West, the eagle eye of Rosecrans has caught the weakness of the unguarded roads to the heart of the Confederacy.

Stone River and Murfreesboro' tell of the wintry struggle to the death for the open doors of Chattanooga. Though another shall wear the laurels of victory, it is the proud boast of Rosecrans alone to have divined the open joint in the enemy's harness. He points the way to the sea for the irresistible Sherman. While the fearless gray ranks thin day by day, in march and camp, Valois thinks often of his distant home. Straggling letters from Philip Hardin tell him of the vain efforts of the cowed secessionists of the Pacific Coast. Loyal General George Wright holds the golden coast. Governor and Legislature, Senators and Congressmen, are united. The press and public sentiment are now a unit against disunion or separation.

Colonel Valois looked for some effective action of the Knights of the Golden Circle on the Pacific. Alas, for the gallant exile! Impending defeat renders the secret conspirators cautious. In the cheering news that wife and child are well, still guarded by the sagacious Padre Francois, Valois frets only over the consecutive failures of Western conspiracy. Folly and fear make the Knights of the Golden Circle a timid band. The "Stars and Stripes" wave now, unchallenged, over Arizona and New Mexico. The Texans at Antelope Peak never returned to carry the "Stars and Bars" across the Colorado. Vain boasters!

While Bragg toils and plots to hurl himself on Rosecrans in the awful day of Chickamauga, where thirty-five thousand dying and wounded are offered up to the Moloch of Disunion, Valois bitterly reads Hardin's account of the puerile efforts on the Pacific. It is only boys' play.

All energy, every spark of daring seems to have left the men who, secure in ease and fortune, live rich and unharassed in California. Their Southern brethren in the ranks reel blindly in the bloody mazes of battle, fighting in the field. A poor Confederate lieutenant attempts a partisan expedition in the mountains of California. He is promptly captured. The boyish plan is easily frustrated. Bands of resolute marauders gather at Panama to attack the Californian steamers, gold-laden. The vigilance of government agents baffles them. The mail steamers are protected by rifle guns and bodies of soldiers. Loyal officers protect passengers from any dash of desperate men smuggled on board. Secret-service spies are scattered over all the Western shores. Mails, telegraphs, express, and the growing railway facilities, are in the hands of the government. It is Southern defeat everywhere.

Valois sadly realizes the only help from the once enthusiastic West is a few smuggled remittances. Here and there, some quixotic volunteer makes his way in. An inspiring yell for Jeff Davis, from a tipsy ranchero, or incautious pothouse orator, is all that the Pacific Coast can offer.

The Confederate flag never sweeps westward to the blue Pacific, and the stars and bars sink lower day by day. As the weakness of American commerce is manifest on the sea, Colonel Valois forwards despairing letters to California. He urges attacks from Mexico, Japan, Panama, or the Sandwich Islands, on the defenceless ships loaded with American gold and goods. Unheeded, alas! these last appeals. Unfortunately, munitions of war are not to be obtained in the Pacific. The American fleets, though poor and scattered, are skilfully handled. Consuls and diplomats everywhere aid in detecting the weakly laid plans of the would-be pirates.

Still Valois fumes, sword in hand, at the pusillanimity of the Western sympathizers. They are rich and should be arming. Why do they not strike one effective blow for the cause? One gun would sink a lightly built Pacific liner, or bring its flag down. Millions of gold are being exported to the East from the treasure fields of the West. Though proud of the dauntless, ragged gray ranks he loves, Valois feels that the West should organize a serious attack on some unprotected Federal interest, to save the issue. But the miserable failure of Sibley has discouraged Confederate Western effort. The Confederate Californian grinds his teeth to think that one resolute dash of the scattered tens of thousands lying in camp, uselessly, in Arkansas and Texas, would even now secure California. Even now, as the Confederate line of battle wastes away, desperate Southern men dream of throwing themselves into Mexico as an unwelcome, armed immigration. This blood is precious at home.

Stung by the taunts of Eastern friends, at last Philip Hardin and his co-workers stir to some show of action.

Peacefully loading in San Francisco harbor for Mexico, a heavy schooner is filled with the best attainable fittings for a piratical cruise.

The J.W. Chapman rises and falls at the wharves at half gun-shot from the old U.S. frigate CYANE. Her battery could blow the schooner into splinters, with one broadside. Tackle and gear load the peaceful-looking cases of "alleged" heavy merchandise. Ammunition and store of arms are smuggled on board. Mingling unsuspectedly with the provost guard on the wharves, a determined crew succeed in fitting out the boat. Her outward "Mexican voyage" is really an intended descent on the treasure steamers.

Disguised as "heavy machinery," the rifled cannons are loaded. When ready to slip out of the harbor, past the guard-boats, the would-be pirate is suddenly seized. The vigilant Federal officials have fathomed the design. Some one has babbled. Too much talk, or too much whiskey.

Neatly conceived, well-planned, and all but executed, it was a bold idea. To capture a heavy Panama steamer, gold-laden; to transfer her passengers to the schooner, and land them in Mexico; and, forcing the crew to direct the vessel, to lie in wait for the second outgoing steamer, was a wise plan. They would then capture the incoming steamer from Panama, and ravage the coast of California.

With several millions of treasure and three steamers, two of them could be kept as cruisers of the Confederacy. They could rove over the Pacific, unchallenged. Their speed would be their safety.

Mexican and South American ports would furnish coal and supplies. The captured millions would make friends everywhere. The swift steamers could baffle the antiquated U.S. war vessels on the Pacific. A glorious raid over the Pacific would end in triumph in India or China.

These were the efforts and measures urged by Valois and the anxious Confederates of the East.

It was perfectly logical. It was absolutely easy to make an effective diversion by sea. But some fool's tongue or spy's keen eye ruins all.

When, months after the seizure of the CHAPMAN, Valois learns of this pitiful attempt, he curses the stupid conspirators. They had not the brains to use a Mexican or Central American port for the dark purposes of the piratical expedition. Ample funds, resolute men, and an unprotected enemy would have been positive factors of success. Money, they had in abundance. Madness and folly seem to have ruled the half-hearted conspirators of California. An ALABAMA or two on the Pacific would have been most destructive scourges of the sea. The last days of opportunity glide by. The prosaic records of the Federal Court in California tell of the evanescent fame of Harpending, Greathouse, Rubery, Mason, Kent, and the other would-be buccaneers. The "Golden Circle" is badly shattered.

Every inlet of the Pacific is watched, after the fiasco of the Chapman. She lies at anchor, an ignoble prize to the sturdy old Cyane. It is kismet.

Maxime Valois mourns over the failure of these last plans to save the "cause." Heart-sick, he only wonders when a Yankee bullet will end the throbbings of his unconquerable heart. All is dark.

He fears not for his wife and child. Their wealth is secured. He loses, from day to day, the feelings which tied him once to California.

The infant heiress he hardly knows. His patient, soft-eyed Western wife is now only a placid memory. Her gentle nature never roused the inner fires of his passionate soul. Alien to the Pacific Coast, a soldier of fortune, the ties into which he drifted were the weavings of Fate. His warrior soul pours out its devotion in the military oath to guard to the last the now ragged silken folds of his regimental banner, the dear banner of Louisiana. The eyes of the graceful Creole beauties who gave it are now wet with bitter tears. Beloved men are dying vainly, day by day, under its sacred folds. Even Beauty's spell is vain.

The wild oats are golden once more on the hills of Lagunitas; the early summer breezes waft stray leaf and blossom over the glittering lake in the Mariposa Mountains. Heading the tireless riflemen of his command, Valois throws himself in desperation on the Union lines at Chickamauga. Crashing volley, ringing "Napoleons," the wild yell of the onset, the answering cheers of defiance, sound faintly distant as Maxime Valois drops from his charger. He lies seriously wounded in the wild rush of Bragg's devoted battalions. He has got his "billet."

For months, tossing on a bed of pain, the Louisianian is a sacred charge to his admiring comrades. Far in the hills of Georgia, the wasted soldier chafes under his absence from the field. The beloved silken heralds of victory are fluttering far away on the heights of Missionary Ridge. His faded eye brightens, his hollow cheek flushes when the glad tidings reach him of the environment of Rosecrans. His own regiment is at the front. He prays that he may lead it, when it heads the Confederate advance into Ohio. For now, after Chickamauga's terrific shock, the tide of victory bears northward the flag of his adoration. Months have passed since he received any news of his Western domain. No letters from Donna Dolores gladden him. Far away from the red hills of Georgia, in tenderness his thoughts, chastened with illness, turn to the dark-eyed woman who waits for him. She prays before the benignant face of the Blessed Virgin for her warrior husband. Alas, in vain!

Silent is Hardin. No news comes from Padre Francisco. Nothing from his wife. Valois trusts to the future. The increasing difficulty of contraband mails, hunted blockade-runners, and Federal espionage, cut off his home tidings.

His martial soul thrilled at the glories of Chickamauga, Valois learns that California has shown its mettle on the fiercest field of the West. Cheatham, Brooks, and fearless Terry have led to the front the wild masses of Bragg's devoted soldiery. These sons of California, like himself, were no mere carpet knights. On scattered Eastern fields, old friends of the Pacific have drawn the sword or gallantly died for Dixie. Garnett laid his life down at Rich Mountain. Calhoun Benham was a hero of Shiloh. Wild Philip Herbert manfully dies under the Stars and Bars on the Red River.

The stain of cold indifference is lifted by these and other self-devoted soldiers who battle for the South.

With heavy sighs, the wounded colonel still mourns for the failure to raise the Southern Cross in the West. Every day proves how useless have been all efforts on the Pacific Coast. Virginia is now the "man eater" of the Confederacy. Valois is haunted with the knowledge that some one will retrace the path of Rosecrans. Some genius will break through the open mountain-gates and cut the Confederacy in twain. It is an awful suspense.

While waiting to join his command, he hungers for home news. Grant, the indomitable champion of the North, hurls Bragg from Missionary Ridge. Leaping on the trail of the great army, which for the first time deserts its guns and flags, the blue-clad pursuers press on toward Chattanooga. They grasp the iron gate of the South with mailed hand.

The "Silent Man of Destiny" is called East to measure swords with stately Lee. He trains his Eastern legions for the last death-grapple. On the path toward the sea, swinging out like huntsmen, the columns of Sherman wind toward Atlanta. Bluff, impetuous, worldly wise, genius inspired, Sherman rears day by day the pyramid of his deathless fame. Confident and steady, bold and untiring, fierce as a Hannibal, cunning as a panther, old Tecumseh bears down upon the indefatigable Joe John-ston. Now comes a game worthy of the immortal gods. It is played on bloody fields. The crafty antagonists grapple in every cunning of the art of war. Rivers of human blood make easy the way. The serpent of the Western army writhes itself into the vitals of the torn and bleeding South. Everywhere the resounding crash of arms. Alas, steadfast as Maxime Valois' nature may be, tried his courage as his own battle blade, the roar of battle from east to west tells him of the day of wrath! The yells and groans of the trampled thousands of the Wilderness, are echoed by the despair-ing chorus of the dying myriads of Kenesaw and Dalton. A black pall hangs over a land given up to the butchery of brothers. Mountain chains, misted in the blue smoke of battle, rise unpityingly over heaps of unburied dead from the Potomac to the Mississippi. Maxime Valois knows at last the penalty of the fatal conspiracy. A sacrificed generation, ruined homes, and the grim ploughshare of war rives the fair-est fields of the Land of the Cypress.

Fearless and fate-defying, under ringing guns, crashing volley, and sweeping charge, the Southern veterans only close up the devoted gray ranks. They are thin-ning with every conflict, where Lee and Johnston build the slim gray wall against the resistless blue sea sweeping down.

There is no pity in the pale moon. The cold, steady stars shine down on the upturned faces of the South's best and bravest. No craven blenching when the tat-tered Stars and Bars bear up in battle blast. And yet the starry flag crowns mountain and rock. It sweeps through blood-stained gorges and past battle-scarred defile. On-ward, ever southward. The two giant swordsmen reel in this duel of desperation. Sherman and Johnston may not be withheld. The hour of fate is beginning to knell the doom of the cause. Southern mothers and wives have given up their unreturn-ing brave as a costly sacrifice on the altar of Baal. Valois, once more in command, a colonel now, riding pale and desperate, before his men, sees their upturned glances. The dauntless ranks, filing by, touch his heroic heart. He fears, when Atlanta's ref-uge receives the beaten host, that the end is nigh.

Bereft of news from his home, foreseeing the final collapse in Virginia, assured that the sea is lost to the South, the colonel's mood is daily sadder. His hungry eyes are wolfish in their steady glare. Only a soldier now. His flag is his altar of daily sacrifice.

Port after port falls, foreign flatterers stand coldly aloof, empty magazines and idle fields are significant signs of the end. Useless cotton cannot be sent out or made available, priceless though it be. The rich western Mississippi is now closed as a supply line for the armies. The paper funds of the new nation are mere tokens of unpaid promises, never to be redeemed.

Never to falter, not to shun the driving attacks of the pursuing horse or grappling foot, to watch his battle-flag glittering in the van, to lead, cheer, hope, inspire, and madly head his men, is the second nature of Valois. He has sworn not to see his flag dishonored.

It never occurs to him to ask WHERE his creed came from. His blood thrills with the passionate devotion which blots out any sense of mere right and wrong. His motto is "For Dixie's Land to Death."

CHAPTER XII.

HOOD'S DAY.--PEACHTREE CREEK.--VALOIS' LAST TRUST.--DE
GRESS' BATTERY.--DEAD ON THE FIELD OF HONOR.

A lantern burns dimly before the tent of Colonel Valois on the night of July 21, 1864. Within the lines of Atlanta there is commotion. Myriad lights flicker on the hills. A desperate army at bay is facing the enemy. Seven miles of armed environment mocks the caged tigers behind these hard-held ramparts. Facing north and east, the gladiators of the morrow lie on their arms, ready now for the summons to fall in, for a wild rush on Sherman's pressing lines. It is no holiday camp, with leafy bowers and lovely ladies straying in the moonlight. No dallying and listening to Romeos in gray and gold. No silver-throated bugles wake the night with "Lorena." No soft refrain of the "Suwanee River" melts all the hearts. It is not a gala evening, when "Maryland, my Maryland," rises in grand appeal. The now national "Dixie" tells not of fields to be won. It is a dark presage of the battle morrow. Behind grim redan and salient, the footsore troops rest from the day's indecisive righting. The foeman is not idle; all night long, rumbling trains and busy movements tell that "Uncle Billy Sherman" never sleeps. His blue octopus crawls and feels its way unceasingly. The ragged gray ranks, whose guns are their only pride, whose motto is "Move by day; fight always," are busy with the hum of preparation.

It is a month of horror. North and South stand aghast at the unparalleled butchery of the Wilderness and Spottsylvania. The awful truth that Grant has paved his bloody way to final victory with one hundred thousand human bodies since he crossed the Rapidan, makes the marrow cold in the bones of the very bravest. Sixty thousand foes, forty thousand friends, are the astounding death figures. As if the dark angel of death was not satisfied with a carnage unheard of in modern times, Johnston, the old Marshal Ney of the Confederacy, gives way, in command of the Southern army covering Atlanta, to J.B. Hood. He is the Texan lion. Grizzled Sherman laughs on the 18th of July, when his spies tell him Johnston is relieved. "Replenish every caisson from the reserve parks; distribute campaign ammunition," he says, briefly. "Hood would assault me with a corporal's guard. He will fight by day or night. I know him," Uncle Billy says.

The great Tecumseh feels a twinge as he whips out this verdict. Hood's tactics are fearful. There are thousands of mute witnesses of his own fatal rashness lying at Kenesaw, whose tongues are sealed in death. On that sad clay, Sherman out-Hooded Hood. But the blunt son of Ohio is right. He is a demi-god in intellect, and yet he has the intuition of femininity. He has caught Hood's fighting character at a glance.

There's no time to chaffer over the situation. McPherson, the pride of the army, Thomas, the Rock of Chickamauga, and wary Schofield, draw in the great Union forces. Gallant Howard is in this knightly circle. "Black Jack" Logan, the "Harry Monmouth" of this coming field, connects on the 19th. There has been hot work to-day. Firing in Thomas's front tells the great strategist that Hood has tasted blood. Enough!

Sherman knows how that mad Texan will throw his desperate men to the front, in the snapping, ringing zone of fire and flame. Hooker receives the shock of the onset, reinforced by heavy batteries, whose blazing guns tear lightning-rent lanes through the Confederates. Not a second to lose. The gray swarms are pouring on like mountain wolves.

Fighting sharp and hot, the Union lines reach the strong defences of Peachtree Creek. Here Confederate Gilmer's engineering skill has prepared ditch and fraise, abattis and chevaux-de-frise, with yawning graves for the soon-forgotten brave.

McPherson, Schofield, Howard, Hooker, and Palmer are all in line, deployed with strong reserves.

Anxious Sherman sends clouds of orderly officers and scouts, right and left. Hood's defiant volleys die away. Will the rush come to-day? No; the hours wear away. The night brings quiet along the lines. Though a red harvest lies on the field, it is not the crowning effort of the entire enemy. It is only a rattling day of uneasy, hot-tempered fight.

But the awful morrow is to come. Sherman soon divines the difficulty of fathoming the Texan's real designs. Hood is familiar with the ground. Drawing back to the lines of Atlanta, Hood crouches for a desperate spring. The ridges of the red clay hills, with little valleys running to the Chattahoochee in the west, and Ocmulgee in the east, cover his manoeuvres. Corn and cotton patches, with thick forests between, lie along the extended front. A tangled undergrowth masks the entire movements of the lurking enemy.

Tireless Sherman, expectant of some demoniac rush, learns that the array before him is under Hood, Hardee, and the audacious cavalry leader, Wheeler. Stewart's and Smith's Georgian levies are also in line.

Every disposition is made by the wary antagonists. Sherman, eagle-eyed and prompt to join issue, gains a brief repose before the gray of morning looses the fires of hell. McPherson, young and brilliant, whose splendid star is in its zenith, firmly holds his exposed lines along the railroad between two valleys. In his left and rear, the forest throws out dark shades to cover friend and foe. Between the waiting armies, petty murder stays its hands. The stars sweep to the west, bringing the last morning to thousands. They are now dreaming, perhaps, of the homes they will never see. A thrill of nervous tension keeps a hundred thousand men in vague, dumb expectancy. The coming shock will be terrible. No one can tell the issue.

As the worn Confederate sentinel drags up and down before the tent of Colonel Valois, he can see the thoughtful veteran sitting, his tired head resting on a wasted hand.

Spirit and high soul alone animate now the Louisiana colonel. Hope has fled. Over his devoted head the sentinel stars swing, with neither haste nor rest, toward the occident. They will shine on Lagunitas, smiling, fringed with its primeval pines.

In her sleep, perhaps his little girl calls for him in vain. He is doomed not to hear that childish voice again.

A bundle of letters, carelessly tossed down at head-quarters, have been carried in his bosom during the day's scattering fight. They are all old in their dates, and travel-worn in following the shifting positions of his skeleton regiment. They bring him, at last, nearly a year's news.

Suddenly he springs to his feet, and his voice is almost a shriek. "Sentinel, call the corporal." In a moment, Valois, with quivering lip, says, "Corporal, ask Major Peyton to be kind enough to join me for a few moments."

When his field-officer approaches, anticipating some important charge of duty, sword and revolver in hand, the ghastly face of Valois alarms him.

"Colonel!" he cries. Valois motions him to be seated.

"Peyton," begins Valois, brokenly, "I am struck to the heart."

He is ashy pale. His head falls on his friend's bosom.

"My wife!" He needs not finish. The open letters tell the story. It is death news.

The major clasps his friend's thin hands.

"Colonel, you must bear up. We are fallen on sad, sad days." His voice fails him. "Remember to-morrow; we must stand for the South."

The chivalric Virginian's voice sounds hollow and strange. He sought the regiment, won over by Valois' lofty courage and stern military pride. To-morrow the army is to grapple and crush bold Sherman. It will be a death struggle.

Yes, out of these walls, a thunderbolt, the heavy column, already warned, was to seek the Union left, and strike a Stonewall Jackson blow. Its march will be covered by the friendly woods. The keen-eyed adjutants are already warning the captains of every detail of the attack. Calm and unmoved, the gaunt centurions of the thinned host accepted the honorable charges of the forlorn hope. Valois' powder-seasoned fragment of the army was a "corps d'elite." Peyton wondered, as he watched his suffering colonel, if either would see another sparkling jewel-braided night.

The blow of Hood must be the hammer of Thor.

"To-morrow, yes, to-morrow," mechanically replied Valois. "I will be on duty to-morrow."

"To-night, Peyton," he simply said, "I must suffer my last agony. My poor Dolores! Gone--my wife."

The tears trickled through his fingers as he bowed his graceful head.

"And my little Isabel," he softly said; "she will be an orphan. Will God protect that tender child? "Valois was talking to himself, with his eyes fixed on the dark night-shadows hiding the Federal lines. A stern, defiant gaze.

Peyton shivered with a nervous chill.

"Colonel, this must not be." In the silence of the brooding night, it seems a ghastly call from another world, this message of death.

Valois proudly checks himself.

"Peyton, I have few friends left in this land now. I want you to look these letters over." He hands him several letters from Hardin and from the priest. With tender delicacy, his hands close on the last words of affection from the gentle dark-eyed wife, who brought him the great dowry of Lagunitas, and gave him his little Isabel.

Peyton reads the words, old in date but new in their crushing force of sorrow to the husband. Resting on the stacked arms in front of his tent, the colors of Louisiana and the silken shreds of the Stars and Bars wait for the bugles of reveille calling again to battle.

Dolores dying of sudden illness, cut off in her youthful prime, was only able to receive the last rites of the Church, to smile fondly in her last moments, as she kisses the picture of the absent soldier of the Southern Cross. Francois Ribaut, the French gentleman, writes a sad letter, with no formula of the priest. He knows Maxime Valois is face to face with death, in these awful days of war. A costly sacrifice on the altar of Southern rights may be his fate at any moment.

It is to comfort, not admonish, to pledge every friendly office, that the delicate-minded padre softens the blow. Later, the priest writes of the lonely child, whose tender youth wards off the blow of the rod of sorrow.

Philip Hardin's letter mainly refers to the important business interests of the vast estate. The possibility of the orphanage of Isabel occurs. He suggests the propriety of Colonel Valois' making and forwarding a new will, and constituting a guardianship of the young heiress. In gravest terms of friendship, he reminds Valois to indicate his wishes as to the child, her nurture and education. The fate of a soldier may overtake her surviving parent any day.

Other unimportant issues drop out of sight. Hardin has told of the last attempt to fit out a schooner at a secluded lumber landing in Santa Cruz County. They tried to smuggle on board a heavy gun secretly transported there. An assemblage of desperate men, gathering in the lonely woods, were destined to man the boat. By accident, the Union League discovers the affair. Flight is forced on the would-be pirates.

Valois' lip curls as he tells Peyton of the utter prostration of the last Confederate hope beyond the Colorado. All vain and foolish schemes.

"I wish your advice, Major," he resumes. In brief summing up, he gives Peyton the outline of his family history and his general wishes.

A final result of the hurried conclave is the hasty drawing up of a will. It is made and duly witnessed. It makes Philip Hardin guardian of the heiress and sole executor of his testament. His newly descended property he leaves to the girl child, with directions that she shall be sent to Paris. She is to be educated to the time of her majority at the "Sacred Heart." There in that safe retreat, where the world's storms cannot reach the defenceless child, he feels she will be given the bearing and breeding of a Valois. She must be fitted for her high fortunes.

He writes a fond letter to Father Francisco, to whom he leaves a handsome legacy, ample to make him independent of all pecuniary cares. He adjures that steadfast friend to shield his darling's childhood, to follow and train her budding mind in its development. He informs him of every disposition, and sends the tenderest thanks for a self-devotion of years.

The farewell signature is affixed. Colonel Valois indites to Judge Philip Hardin a letter of last requests. It is full of instructions and earnest appeal. When all is done, he closes his letter. "I send you every document suggested. My heart is sore. I can no longer write. I will lead my regiment to-morrow in a desperate assault. If I give my life for my country, Hardin, let my blood seal this sacred bond between you and me. I leave you my motherless child. May God deal with you and yours as you shall deal with the beloved little one, whose face I shall never see.

"If I had a thousand lives I would lay them down for the flag which may cover me to-morrow night. Old friend, remember a dying man's trust in you and your honor."

When Peyton has finished reading these at Colonel Valois' request, his eyes are moist. To-night the bronzed chief is as tender as a woman. The dauntless soul, strong in battle scenes, is shaken with the memories of a motherless little one. She must face the world alone, God's mercy her only stay.

Colonel Valois, who has explained the isolation of the child, has left his estate in remainder to the heirs of Judge Valois, of New Orleans.

Old and tottering to his tomb is that veteran jurist. The possible heir would be

Armand, the boy student, cut off in Paris. No home-comings now. The ports are all closed.

When all is prepared, Colonel Valois says tenderly: "Peyton, I have some money left at Havana. I will endorse these drafts to you, and give you a letter to the banker there. You can keep them for me. I want you to ride into Atlanta and see these papers deposited. Let there be made a special commission for their delivery to our agent at Havana. Let them leave Atlanta at once. I want no failure if Sherman storms the city. I will not be alive to see it."

Awed by the prophetic coolness of Valois' speech, Peyton sends for his horse. He rides down to the town, where hundreds on hundreds of wounded sufferers groan on every side. Thousands desperately wait in the agony of suspense for the morrow's awful verdict. He gallops past knots of reckless merry-makers who jest on the edge of their graves. Henry Peyton bears the precious packet and delivers it to an officer of the highest rank. He is on the eve of instant departure for the seaboard. Cars and engines are crowded with the frightened people, flying from the awful shock of Hood's impending assault.

This solemn duty performed, the Major rejoins Colonel Valois at a gallop. Lying on his couch, Valois' face brightens as he springs from his rest. "It is well. I thank you," he simply says. He is calm, even cheerful. The bonhomie of his race is manifest. "Major Peyton," he says, pleasantly, "I would like you to remember the matters of this evening. Should you live through this war the South will be in wild disorder. I have referred to your kindness, in my letter to Hardin and in a paper I have enclosed to him. It is for my child. You will have a home at Lagunitas if you ever go to California."

He discusses a few points of the movement of the morrow. There is no extra solemnity in going under fire. They have lived in a zone of fire since Sherman's pickets crossed the open, months ago. But this supreme effort of Hood marks a solemn epoch. The great shops and magazines of Atlanta, the railroad repair works, foundries and arsenals, the geographical importance, studied fortifications, and population to be protected, make the city a stronghold of ultimate importance to the enfeebled South.

If the Northern bayonets force these last doors of Georgia, then indeed the cause is desperate.

When midnight approached, Colonel Valois calmly bade his friend "Good-night." Escorting him to his tent, he whispers, "Peyton, take your coffee with me to-morrow. I will send for you."

Slumber wraps friend and foe alike. All too soon the gray dawn points behind the hills. There is bustle and confusion. Shadowy groups cluster around the waning fires long before daybreak. The gladiators are falling into line. Softly, silently, day steals over the eastern hills. Is it the sun of Austerlitz or of Waterloo?

Uneasy picket-firing ushers in the battle day. Colonel Valois and Major Peyton share their frugal meal. The rattle of picket shots grows into a steady, teasing firing. Well-instructed outpost officers are carrying on this noisy mockery.

Massed behind the circling lines of Atlanta, within the radius of a mile and a half, the peerless troops who DOUBT Hood's ability, but who ADORE his dauntless bravery, are silently massed for the great attack.

The officers of Valois' regiment, summoned by the adjutant, receive their Colonel's final instructions. His steady eye turns fondly on the men who have been his comrades, friends, and devoted admirers. "Gentlemen," he says, "we will have serious work to-day. I shall expect you to remember what Georgia hopes from Louisiana."

Springing to his saddle, he doffs his cap as the head of the regiment files by, in flank movement. The lithe step, steady swing, and lightly poised arms proclaim matchless veterans. They know his every gesture in the field. He is their idol.

As Peyton rides up, he whispers (for the colors have passed), "Henry, if you lead the regiment out of this battle, I ask you never to forget my last wishes." The two friends clasp hands silently. With a bright smile, whose light lingers as he spurs past the springy column, he takes the lead, falcon-eyed, riding down silently into the gloomy forest-shades of death.

A heavy mass of troops, pushing out in swift march, works steadily to the Union left, and gains its ground rapidly. The Seventeenth Corps of Blair, struck in flank, give way. The Sixteenth Union Corps of Dodge are quickly rushed up. The enemy are struck hard. Crash and roar of battle rise now in deafening clamor. Away to the unprotected Union rear ride the wild troopers of Wheeler. The whole left of Sherman's troops are struck at disadvantage. They are divided, or thrown back in confusion toward Decatur. The desperate struggle sways to and fro till late in the day. With a rush of Hood's lines, Murray's battery of regular artillery is captured. The Stars and Bars sweep on in victory.

Onward press the Confederate masses in all the pride of early victory. The Fifteenth Corps, under Morgan L. Smith, make a desperate attempt to hold on at a strong line of rifle pits. The seething gray flood rolls upon them and sends them staggering back four hundred yards. Over two cut-off batteries, the deadly carnage smites blue and gray alike. Charge and countercharge succeed in the mad struggle for these guns. Neither side can use them until a final wave shall sweep one set of madmen far away.

With desperate valor, Morgan L. Smith at last claims the prize. His cheering troops send double canister from the regained batteries into the gray columns of attack. General Sherman, at a deserted house, where he has made his bivouac, paces the porch like a restless tiger. The increasing firing on the left, tells him of this heavy morning attack. A map spread on a table catches his eye from time to time. The waiting crowd of orderlies and staff officers have, one by one, dashed off to reform the lines or strengthen the left. While the firing all along the line is everywhere ominous, the roar on the left grows higher and higher. Out from the fatal woods begin to stream weary squads of the wounded and stragglers. The floating skulkers hover at the edge of the red tide of conflict.

Ha! A wounded aide dashes up with tidings of the ominous gap on the left. That fearful sweep of Wheeler's cavalry to the rear is known at last by the fires of burning trains. With a few brief words of counsel, and a nod of his stately head, McPherson, the splendid light of battle on his brow, gallops away to reform these broken lines. The eye of the chief must animate his corps.

Hawk-eyed Sherman watches the glorious young general as he turns into the forest. A grim look settles on the general's face. He runs his eye over the map. As the tiger's approach is heralded by the clatter of the meaner animals, so from out that forest the human debris tell of Hood's battle hammer crashing down on that left "in air." Is there yet time to reform a battle, now fighting itself in sudden bloody encounters? All is at haphazard. A sigh of relief. McPherson is there. His ready wit, splendid energy, and inspiring presence are worth a thousand meaner souls, in the wild maelstrom of that terrible July day.

Old Marshal Tecumseh, with unerring intuition, knows that the creeping skirmishers have felt the whole left of his position. With the interior lines and paths of the forest to aid, if anything has gone wrong, if gap or lap has occurred, then on those unguarded key-points and accidental openings, the desperate fighters of the great Texan will throw their characteristic fierceness. Atlanta's tall chimneys rise on the hills to the west. There, thousands, with all at stake, listen to the rolling notes of this bloody battle. High in the air, bursting shells with white puffs light up the clouds of musketry smoke. Charging yells are borne down the wind, with ringing answering cheers. The staccato notes of the snapping Parrotts accentuate the battle's din.

Sherman, with cloudy brow, listens for some news of the imperilled left wing. Is the iron army of the Tennessee to fail him now? Seven miles of bayonets are in that great line, from left to right, headed by McPherson, Schofield, and Thomas, the flower of the Union Army.

Looking forward to a battle outside Atlanta, a siege, or a flanking bit of military chesswork, the great Union commander is dragged now into a purely defensive battle. Where is McPherson?

Sherman has a quarter of an hour of horrible misgiving. He saw the mad panic of the first Bull Run. He led the only compact body of troops off that fatal field himself. It was his own brigade. In his first-fought field, he showed the unshakable nerve of Macdonald at Wagram. But he has also seen the fruits of the wild stampede of McCook and Crittenden's divisions since at Chickamauga. It tore the laurels from Rosecrans' brow. Is this to be a panic? Rosecrans' defeat made Sherman the field-marshal of the West.

At Missionary Ridge, even the invincibles of the South fled their lines in sudden impulse, giving up an almost impregnable position. The haughty old artillerist, Braxton Bragg, was forced to officially admit that stampede. He added a few dozen corpses to his disciplinary "graveyards," "pour encourager les autres." Panic may attack even the best army.

Is it panic now swelling on the breeze of this roaring fight? Fast and far his hastily summoned messengers ride. To add a crowning disaster to the confusion of the early morning death grapple, the sun does not touch the meridian before a bleeding aide brings back McPherson's riderless horse. Where is the general? Alas, where?

Dashing far ahead of his staff and orderlies, tearing from wood to wood, to close in the fatal gap and reface his lines--a volley from a squad of Hood's pickets drops the great corps commander, McPherson, a mangled corpse, in the forest. No such individual loss to either army has happened since Stonewall Jackson's untimely end at Chancellorsville.

His rifled body is soon recovered. With super-human efforts it is borne to the house in the clearing and laid at General Sherman's feet.

Lightning flashes of wit traverse Sherman's brain. Every rebel straggler is instantly searched as he is swept in. The invaluable private papers of General McPherson, the secret orders, and campaign plans are found in the haversack of one of the captured skirmishers. These, at least, are safe.

With this blow, comes the news of the Seventeenth Corps being thrown back, far out of its place, by the wild rush of Hood's braves. All goes wrong. The day is lost.

Will it be a Bull Run?

No! The impetuous Logan tears along his lines. "Black Jack's" swarthy face brings wild cheers from the men, who throw themselves madly on the attacking lines, seeking vengeance. The Fifteenth Corps' rifles are sounding shotted requiem salvos for their lost leader. The Seventeenth holds on and connects. The Sixteenth Corps, struck heavily in flank by the victorious Confederates, faces into line of battle to the left. It grimly holds on, and pours in its leaden hail. Smith's left flank doubled back, joining Leggett, completes the reformed line. From high noon till the darkness of the awful night, a general conflict rages along the whole front. War in its grim horror.

Sherman, casting a wistful glance on the body of McPherson, stands alert. He is as bristling as a wild boar at bay. Sherman at his best.

Is this their worst? No, for at four in the afternoon, a terrific sally from Atlanta throws the very flower of the assailants on the bloody knoll, evermore to be known as "Leggett's Hill." There is madness and demoniac fury in the way those gray columns struggle for that ridge.

In vain does Hood send out his bravest stormers to crown the wished-for position of Leggett.

Sherman is as sure of Atlanta now, as if his eagles towered over its domes.

Drawing to the left the corps of Wood, massing Schofield with twenty heavy guns playing on Hood's charging columns, Sherman throws Wood, backed by John A. Logan's victorious veterans, on the great body of the reeling assailants. The final blow has met its stone wall, in the lines of Leggett. The blue takes up the offensive, with wild cheers of triumph. They reach "Uncle Billy's" ears.

Some decisive stroke must cut the tangle of the involved forces. When Hood sees that his devoted troops have not totally crushed the Union left, when his columns reel back from Leggett's Hill, mere fragments, he knows that even his dauntless men cannot be asked to try again that fearful quest. It is checkmate!

But Wheeler is still careering in destruction around Sherman's rear parks, and ravaging his supplies. Hood persists in his desperate design to pierce the Union lines somewhere. He throws away his last chance of keeping an army together. His fiery valor bade him defend Atlanta from the OUTSIDE. He now sends a last thunderbolt crashing on the Decatur road.

During the day Valois' regiment has been thrown in here and there. The stern colonel gazes with pride on the seasoned fighters at their grim work.

But it is after four when Colonel Valois is ordered to mass his regiment, followed by the last reserve, and lead it to the front in the supreme effort of this awful day. His enemy in front is a Union battery, which has been a flail to the Southern army.

In dozens of encounters the four heavy twenty-pound Parrotts of De Gress have been an object of the maddest attack. Superbly handled, in the best equipment, its high power, long range, and dashing energy have given to this battery the rank in the West, which John Pelham's light artillery gained under Lee's eyes in Virginia. The pride of Sherman's artillery is the famous battery of De Gress. To-day it has been dealing out death incessantly, at half musket-range. It has swept rank on rank of the foes away. Now, with the frenzy of despair, General Hood sends a forlorn column to pierce the Union lines, carry the road, and take those renowned guns. A lull betokens the last rush.

Riding to the front, Colonel Valois reins up beside Major Peyton. There is only time for a few last directions. A smile which haunts Peyton for many a long day, flashes on Maxime Valois' stern lips. He dashes on, waving his sword, and cries in his ringing voice,

"Come on, boys, for Louisiana!"

Springing like panthers into the open, the closed ranks bound toward the fated guns at a dead run. Ha! There was a crashing salvo. Now, it is load and fire at will. Right and left, fire pours in on the guns, whose red flashes singe the very faces of the assailants. Peyton's quick eye sees victory wavering. Dashing towards the guns he cheers his men. As he nears the battery the Louisiana color-bearer falls dead. Henry Peyton seizes the Pelican flag, and dashes on over friends, dead and dying, as his frightened steed races into the battery.

There, every horse is down. The guns are now silent. A knot of men, with clubbed rammers, bayonet thrusts, and quick revolver shots, fight for the smoking cannon. A cheer goes up. De Gress's guns are taken. Peyton turns his head to catch a glimpse of Colonel Valois. Grasping the star-spangled guidon of the battery with his bridle hand, Valois cuts down its bearer.

A wild yell rises as a dozen rebel bayonets are plunged into a defiant fugitive, for he has levelled his musket point-blank and shot Valois through the heart.

The leader's frightened charger bounds madly to the front, and the Louisiana colonel falls heavily to the ground.

Clasped in his clenched hands, the silken folds of the captured battery flag are dyed with his blood. A dozen willing arms raise the body, bearing it to one side, for the major, mindful of the precious moments, yells to "swing the guns and pass the caissons." In a minute, the heavy Parrotts of De Gress are pouring their shrapnel into the faces of the Union troops, who are, three hundred yards away, forming for a rush to recapture them.

As the cannon roar their defiance to the men who hold them dear, Peyton bends over Maxime Valois. The heart is stilled forever. With his stiffening fingers clutching his last trophy, the "Stars and Stripes," there is the light of another world shining on the face of the dead soldier of the Southern Cross. Before sending his body to the rear, Henry Peyton draws from Valois' breast a packet of letters. It is the last news from the loved wife he has rejoined across the shadowy river. United in death. Childish Isabel is indeed alone in the world. A rain of shrieking projectiles and bursting shells tells of the coming counter-charge.

Drawing back the guns by hand to a cover for the infantry, and rattling the caissons over a ridge to screen the ammunition boxes, the shattered rebel ranks send volleys into the faces of the lines of Schofield, now coming on at a run.

The captured Parrotts ring and scream. One over-heated gun of the battery bursts, adding its horrors to the struggle. Logan's men are leaping over the lines to right and left, bayoneting the gunners. The Louisianians give way and drift to the rear. The evening shadows drop over crest, wood, and vale. When the first stars are in the skies Hood's shattered columns stream back into Atlanta. The three guns of De Gress have changed hands again. Even the bursted piece falls once more under the control of the despairing Union artillery captain. He has left him neither men, horses, fittings, nor harness available--only three dismantled guns and the wreck of his fourth piece. But they are back again! Sherman's men with wildest shouts crowd the field. They drive the broken remnants of the proud morning array under the guns of the last lines of the doomed city. Dare-devil Hood has failed. The desperate dash has cost ten thousand priceless men. The brief command of the Texan fighter has wrecked the invaluable army of which Joe Johnston was so mindful.

McPherson, who joined the subtlety of Stonewall to the superb bearing of Sidney Johnston, a hero born, a warrior, and great captain to be, lies under the stars in the silent chambers of the Howard House.

General Sherman, gazing on his noble features, calm in death, silently mourns the man who was his right hand. Thomas, Schofield, Howard, Logan, and Slocum stand beside the dead general. They bewail the priceless sacrifice of Peachtree Creek.

In the doomed city of Atlanta, there is gloom and sadness. With the fragments of the regiment which adored him, a shattered guard of honor, watching over him with yet loaded guns, in charge of the officers headed by Major Peyton, the body of Maxime Valois rests within the Southern lines.

For the dear land of his birth he had abandoned the fair land of his choice. With the captured banner of his country in his hand, he died in the hour of a great personal triumph, "under the Stars and Bars." Game to the last.

High-souled and devoted, the son of Louisiana never failed the call of his kinsmen. He carried the purest principles to the altar of Secession.

Watching by the shell from which the dauntless spirit had fled in battle and in storm, Henry Peyton feels bitterly that the fate of Atlanta is sealed. He knows the crushing of their weak lines will follow. He can picture Sherman's heavy columns taking city after city, and marching toward the blue sea.

The end is approaching. A gloomier darkness than the night of the last battle broods over the Virginian. With pious reverence, he hastens to arrange the few personal matters of his chief. He knows not the morrow. The active duties of command will soon take up all his time. He must keep the beloved regiment together.

For, of the two or three companies left of a regiment "whose bayonets were once a thousand," Henry Peyton is the colonel now. A "barren honor," yet inexpressibly dear to him.

In the face of the enemy, within the lines held hard by the reorganizing fragments of yesterday's host, the survivors bury the brave leader who rode so long at their head. Clad in his faded gray, the colonel lies peacefully awaiting the great Reveille.

When the sloping bayonets of the regiment glitter, for the last time, over the ramparts their generous blood has stained in fight, as the defeated troops move away, many a stout heart softens as they feel they are leaving alone and to the foe the lost idol of their rough worship.

Major Peyton preserves for the fatherless child the personal relics of his departed friend. Before it is too late, he despatches them to the coast, to be sent to Havana, to await Judge Hardin's orders at the bankers'. The news of the fate of Colonel Valois, and the last wishes of the dead Confederate, are imparted in a letter to Judge Hardin by Peyton.

In the stern realities of the last retreat, fighting and marching, after the winter snows have whitened the shot-torn fields around Atlanta; sick of carnage and the now useless bloodshed, Colonel Peyton leads his mere detachment to the final scene of the North Carolina surrender. Grant's iron hand has closed upon Petersburg's weakened lines. Sheridan's invincible riders, fresh from the Shenandoah, have shattered the steadfast at Five Forks.

Gloomy days have fallen, also, on the cause in the West. The despairing valor of the day at Franklin and the assault on Nashville only needlessly add to. the reputation for frantic bravery of the last of the magnificent Western armies of the Confederacy. Everywhere there are signs of the inevitable end. With even the sad news of Appomattox to show him that the great cause is irretrievably lost, there are bitter tears in Henry Peyton's eyes when he sees the flags of the army he has served with, lowered to great Sherman in the last surrender.

The last order he will ever give to them turns out for surrender the men whose reckless bravery has gilded a "Lost Cause" with a romantic halo of fadeless glory. Peyton sadly sheathes the sword he took from Maxime Valois' dead hands. Southward, he takes his way. Virginia is now only a graveyard and one vast deserted battle-field. The strangers' bayonets are shining at Richmond. He cannot revisit the scenes of his boyhood. A craving seizes him for new scenes and strange faces. He yearns to blot out the war from his memory. He dreams of Mexico, Cuba, or the towering Andes of South America. His heart is too full to linger near the scenes where the red earth lies heaped over his brethren of the sword. Back to Atlanta he travels, with the returning fragments of the men who are now homeward bound. All is silent now. From wood and hill no rattling fire wakes the stillness of these days. The blackened ruins and the wide swath cut by Sherman tell him how true was the prediction that the men of the Northwest would "hew their way to the Gulf with their swords." He finds the grave of Valois, when dismantled and crippled Atlanta receives him again. Standing there, alone, the pageantry of war has rolled away. The battle-fields are covered with wild roses. The birds nest in the woods where Death once reigned supreme. High in the air over Atlanta the flag of the country waves, on the garrison parade, with not a single star erased.

On his way to a self-appointed exile, the Virginian has seen the wasted fields, blackened ruins, and idle disheartened communities of the conquered, families brought to misery, and the young arms-bearing generation blotted out. Hut and manor-house have been licked up by the red torch of war. The hollow-eyed women, suffering children, and dazed, improvident negroes, wander around aimlessly. Bridges, mills and factories in ruins tell of the stranger's torch, and the crashing work of the artillery. Tall, smokeless chimneys point skywards as monuments of desolation.

Bowed in defeat, their strongholds are yet occupied by the blue-coated victors. All that is left of the Southern communities lingers in ruined homes and idle marts. They now are counting the cost of attempted secession, in the gloom of despair.

The land is one vast graveyard. The women who mourn husbands and lovers stray over fields of strife, and wonder where the loved one sleeps. Friend and foe, "in one red burial blent," are lying down in the unbroken truce of death.

Atlanta's struggle against the restless Sherman has been only wasted valor, a bootless sacrifice. Her terrific sallies, lightning counter-thrusts, and final struggles with the after-occupation, can be traced in the general desolation, by every step of the horrible art of war.

Here, by the grave of his intrepid comrade, Henry Peyton reviews the past four years. His scars and wasted frame tell him of many a deadly fray, and the dangers of the insane fight for State rights.

The first proud days of the war return. Hopes that have failed long since are remembered. The levy and march to the front, the thousand watch-fires glittering around the unbroken hosts, whose silken-bordered banners tell of the matchless devotion of the women clinging blindly to the cause.

Peyton thinks now of the loved and lost who bore those flags, to-day furled forever, to the front, at Bull Run, Shiloh, the Seven Days, Groveton, Fredericksburg, Chancellorsville, Chickamauga, and Spottsylvania.

The foreign friends in Europe, the daring rovers of the sea who carried the Stars and Bars from off New York to Singapore and far Behring Straits. What peerless leaders. Such deep, sagacious statesmen. The treasures of the rich South, the wealth of King Cotton, all wasted uselessly. A popular devotion, which deeply touched the magnanimous Grant in the supreme hour of victory, has been lavished on the altar of the Confederacy where Davis, Lee, and Jackson were enthroned. Fallen gods now, but still majestic and yet revered.

Peyton thinks with an almost breaking heart of all these sacrifices for the Lost Cause. By his friend's grave he feels that an awful price has been paid for the glories of the short-lived Confederacy.

The noble-hearted Virginian dares not hope that there may yet be found golden bands of brotherhood to knit together the children of the men who fought under gray and blue. Frankly acknowledging the injustice of the early scorn of the Northern foe, he knows, from glances cast backward over the storied fields, the vigor of the North was under-estimated. The men of Donelson, Antietam, Stone River, Vicksburg, awful Gettysburg, of Winchester, and Five Forks, are as true and tried as ever swung a soldier's blade.

He has seen the country's flag of stars stream out bravely against the tide of defeat. If American valor needs a champion the men who saw the "Yankees" at Seven

Pines, Gaines Mill, Marye's Heights, and holding in fire and flame the batteries of Corinth and Knoxville, will swear the embittered foes were worthy of each other.

The defeated Confederate veteran, as he plucks a rose from the grass growing over the gallant Valois, bitterly remembers the useless sacrifices of the whole Southern army to the "Virginia policy." A son of the "old State" himself, he can feel now, in the sorrow and silence of defeat, that the early triumphs of the war were wasted. The great warlike generation was frittered away on the Potomac.

Devoted to Lee, he still mourns the lost months of the fall of '61, when, flushed with triumph, the Confederates could have entered Washington. Then Maryland would have risen "en masse." Foreign lands would have been won over. An aggressive policy even in 1862, after the Peninsula, might have changed the final result. The dead Californian's regrets for the abandonment of all effort in the Pacific, the cutting-off and uselessness of the great trans-Mississippi region, all return to him in vain sorrow.

By Maxime Valois' grave, Peyton wonders if the battle-consecrated blood of the sons has washed away the sins of the fathers. He knows not of the brighter days, when the past shall seem a vision of romance. When our country will smile in peace and brotherhood, from ocean to ocean. Sadly he uncovers his head. He leaves Maxime Valois lying in the proud silence of the soldier's grave--"dead on the field of honor."

To New Orleans Colonel Peyton repairs. On making search, he finds that Judge Valois has not survived the collapse of the Confederacy. His only son is abroad, in Paris. The abandoned plantations and family property are under the usual load of debt, taxes, and all the legal confusion of a change of rulers.

Peyton thanks the dead soldier in his heart for the considerable legacy of his unused balances. He is placed beyond immediate necessity. He leaves the land where the Southern Cross met defeat. He wishes to wander over Cuba, Mexico, and toward the West. At Havana, he finds that the documents and articles forwarded by the agents to Judge Hardin have been duly sent though never acknowledged.

The letters taken from Colonel Valois' body he seals in a packet. He trusts that fate may lead him some day westward. They are too precious to risk. He may some day tell the little lady of Lagunitas, of the gallant father whose thoughts, before his last battle, were only for the beloved "little one." She is confided, as a trust, from the dying to Judge Hardin. She is surely safe in the sheltering care of Valois' oldest friend. A "Southern gentleman."

Peyton for years can bring back the tender solemnity of Maxime Valois' face, as he reads his charge to Hardin.

"And may God deal with you and yours, as you deal with me and mine."

The devoted father's appeal would touch a heart of stone.

The folly of not beginning active war in the West; the madness of not seizing California at the outset; the rich prizes of the Pacific left ungathered, for has not Semmes almost driven Yankee ships from the sea with the Alabama, and does not Waddell, with the cockle-shell Shenandoah, burn and destroy the entire Pacific whaling fleet? The free-booter sails half around the world, unchallenged, after the war. Oh, coward Knights of the Golden Circle! Fools, and blind, to let California slip from your grasp!

Maxime Valois was right. Virginian rule ruined the Confederacy. Too late, too late!

Had Sidney Johnston lived; had Robert E. Lee been willing to leave sacred Virginia uncovered for a fortnight in the days before he marshalled the greatest army the Southerners ever paraded, and invaded the North boldly, a peace would have resulted.

Peyton thinks bitterly of the irreparable loss of Sidney Johnston. He recalls the death of peerless Jackson. Jackson, always aggressive, active, eager to reach for the enemy, and ever successful.

Wasted months when the prestige was with the South, the fixed determination of Lee to keep the war in Virginia, and Davis's deadly jealousy of any leading minds, seem to have lost the brightest chances of a glorious success.

Peyton condemns the military court of Davis and the intrenched pageantry of Lee's idle forces. The other armies of the Confederacy fought, half supplied, giving up all to hold the Virginia lines. He cannot yet realize that either Sherman or Grant might have baffled Sidney Johnston had he lived. Lee was self-conscious of his weakness in invasion. He will not own that Philip Sheridan's knightly sword might have reached the crest of the unconquered Stonewall Jackson.

Vain regret, shadowy dreams, and sad imaginings fill Colonel Peyton's mind. The thrilling struggles of the Army of the West, its fruitless victories, and unrewarded heroism make him proud of its heroes. Had another policy ruled the Confederate military cabinet, success was certain. But he is now leaving his friend's grave.

The birds are singing in the forest. As the sun lights up the dark woods where McPherson died, into Henry Peyton's war-tried soul enters the peace which broods over field and incense-breathing trees. Far in the East, the suns of future years may bring happier days, when the war wounds are healed. The brothers of the Union may find a nobler way to reach each other's hearts than ball or bayonet. But he cannot see these gleams of hope.

BOOK IV.
A LOST HEIRESS.--MILLIONS AT STAKE.

CHAPTER XIII.

MOUNT DAVIDSON'S MAGIC MILLIONS.--A CALIFORNIA PLUTOCRACY.--THE PRICE OF A CRIME.

Philip Hardin's library in San Francisco is a place for quiet labors. A spider's parlor. September, 1864, hides the enchanted interior with deeper shades from the idle sight-seer.

Since the stirring days of 1861, after the consecutive failures of plot, political scheme, and plan of attack, the mysterious "chief of the Golden Circle" has withdrawn from public practice. A marked and dangerous man.

It would be an insult to the gallant dead whose blood watered the fields of the South, for Philip Hardin to take the "iron-clad oath" required now of practitioners.

Respected for his abilities, feared by his adversaries, shunned for his pro-secession views, Philip Hardin walks alone. No overt act can be fastened on him, Otherwise, instead of gazing on Alcatraz Island from his mansion windows, he might be behind those frowning walls, where the 15-inch Columbiads spread their radial lines of fire, to cross those of the works of Black Point, Fort Point, and Point Blunt. Many more innocent prisoners toil there. He does not wish to swell their number. Philip Hardin dares not take that oath in open court. His pride prevents, but, even were he to offer it, the mockery would be too patent.

A happy excuse prevents his humiliation. Trustee of the vast estate of Lagunitas, he has also his own affairs to direct. It is a dignified retirement.

Another great passion fills his later days. Since the wandering Comstock and Curry, proverbially unfortunate discoverers, like Marshall, pointed to hundreds of millions for the "silver kings," along Mount Davidson's stony, breast, he gambles daily. The stock board is his play-room.

The mining stock exchange gives his maturer years the wilder excitements of the old El Dorado.

Washoe, Nevada Territory, or the State of Nevada, the new "Silverado" drives all men crazy. A city shines now along the breast of the Storey County peaks, nine thousand feet above the sea. The dulness of California's evolution is broken by the rush to Washoe. Already the hardy prospectors spread out in that great hunt for treasure which will bring Colorado, Idaho, and Montana, crowned aspirants, bearing gifts of gold and silver, to the gates of the Union. The whole West is a land of hidden treasures.

Speculation's mad fever seized on Hardin from the days of 1860. Shares, stocks, operations, schemes, all the wild devices of hazard, fill up his days with exciting successes and damning failures.

His name, prestige, and credit, carry him to the front. As in the early days, his cool brain and nerve mark him as a desperate gamester. But his stakes are now gigantic.

Secure in his mansion house, with private wires in his study, he operates through many brokers and agents. His interrupted law business is transferred to less prominent Southern advocates.

Philip Hardin's fine hand is everywhere. Reliable dependants, old prospecting friends and clients, keep him informed by private cipher of every changing turn of the brilliant Virginia City kaleidoscope.

Hardin gambles for pleasure, for vanity, and for excitement. Led on by his desire to stand out from the mass of men, he throws his fortune, mixed with the funds of Lagunitas, into the maelstrom of California Street. Success and defeat alternate.

It is a transition time. While war rages in the East, the California merchant kings are doubling fortunes in the cowardly money piracy known as California's secession. The "specific contract act" is the real repudiation of the government's lawful money. This stab in the back is given to the struggling Union by the well-fed freedom shriekers of the Union League. They howl, in public, over their devotion to the interests of the land.

The future railroad kings of the Pacific, Stanford, Hopkins, Crocker, Huntington, Colton, and their allies, are grasping the gigantic benefits flowing from the Pacific Railroad, recommended by themselves as a war measure. Heroes.

The yet uncrowned bonanza kings are men of obscure employment, or salaried miners working for wages which would not in a month pay their petty cash of a day in a few years.

Quiet Jim Flood, easy O'Brien, sly Jones, sturdy Mackay, and that guileless innocent, "Jim Fair," are toiling miners or "business men." Their peculiar talents are hidden by the obscurity of humdrum, honest labor.

Hands soon to sway the financial sceptre, either mix the dulcet cocktail, swing the pick, or else light with the miner's candle the Aladdin caves to which they grope and burrow in daily danger, deep hidden from public view. These "silver kings" are only in embryo.

These two groups of remarkable men, the future railroad princes, and the budding bonanza kings, represent cunning, daring, energy, fortitude, and the remarkable powers of transition of the Western resident.

The future land barons are as yet merely sly, waiting schemers. They are trusting to compound interest, rotten officials, and neglected laws to get possession of ducal domains. The bankers, merchant princes, and stock operators are writing their names fast in California's strange "Libro d'oro." All is restlessness. All is a mere waiting for the turbid floods of seething human life to settle down. In the newer discoveries of Nevada, in the suspense of the war, the railroads are yet only half finished, croaked at mournfully by the befogged Solons of the press. All is transition.

It is only when the first generation of children born in California will reach maturity in the 'eighties; only when the tide of carefully planned migration from North and South, after the war, reaches the West, that life becomes regular. Only when the railways make the new State a world's thoroughfare, and the slavery stain is washed from our flag, that civilization plants the foundations of her solid temples along the Pacific.

There is no crystallization until the generation of mere adventurers begin to drop into graves on hillside and by the sea. The first gold-seekers must pass out from active affairs before the real State is honestly builded up.

No man, not even Philip Hardin, could foresee, with the undecided problems of 1860, what would be the status of California in ten years, as to law, finance, commerce, or morals.

A sudden start might take the mass of the people to a new Frazer River or another Australia. They might rush to the wilds of some frontier treasury of nature, now unknown.

Even Philip Hardin dared not dream that humble bar-keepers would blossom out into great bank presidents, that signatures, once potent only on the saloon "slate," would be smiled on by "friend Rothschild" and "brother Baring." The "lightning changes" of the burlesque social life of Western America begin to appear. It is a wild dream that the hands now toiling with the pick or carrying the miner's tin dinner-pail, would close in friendship on the aristocratic palm of H.R.H. Albert Edward, the Prince of Wales. The "chambermaid's own" romances would not dare to predict that ladies bred to the broom and tub or the useful omnipotent "fry pan," would smile on duchesses, crony with princesses, or regulate their visiting lists by the "Almanach de Gotha."

Their great magician is Gold. In power, in pleasing witchery of potent influence; insidious flattery of pleasure; in remorseless persecution of the penniless, all wonders are its work. Ariel, Mephisto, Moloch, thou, Gold! King Gold! and thy brother, Silver!

While Philip Hardin speculated from his lofty eyrie, the San Francisco hills are now covered with the unsubstantial palaces of the first successful residents. He dared not dream that the redwood boxes called mansions, in which the wealthy lived in the days of '60, would give way to the lordly castles of "Nob Hill."

These castles, whether of railroad tyrant, bonanza baron, or banking conspirator, were yet castles in the air.

Perched in lofty isolation now, they architecturally dominate the meaner huts below. Vulgar monuments of a social upheaval which beggars the old stories of fairy changelings, of Sancho Panza, of "Barney the Baron," or "Monte Cristo."

In the days of '60, Philip Hardin is too busy with plot and scheme, with daily plunging, and dreaming over the fate of Lagunitas, to notice the social elevation of the more aspiring male and female adventurers. The rising tide of wealth grows.

Judicious use of early gained riches, trips to Europe, furtive lessons, the necessities of the changed station, and an unlimited cheek and astounding adaptability change the lucky men and women whom fortune's dower has ennobled. They are all now "howling swells."

Some never reach as high as the "Monarchs of Mount Davidson," who were pretty high up at the start, nearly a mile and a half. In many cases, King Midas's Court shows very fairly scattered promotions.

Society's shoddy geometry gives a short-cut for "my lady's maid" to become "my lady." She surely knows "how to dress." The lady who entertains well, in some cases does so with long experience as a successful professional cook.

Some who dropped into California with another woman's husband, forget, while rolling in their carriages, that they ever had one of their own. Children with no legal parents have not learned the meaning of "filius nullius." From the bejewelled mass of vigorous, keen upstarts, now enriched by stocks, the hardy children of the great bonanzas, rises the chorus, "Let the past rest. We have passed the gates of Gold."

To the "newer nobility of California," is given local golden patents. They cover modest paternal names and many shady personal antecedents.

In a land without a past, the suddenly enriched speculators reign in mart and parlor. They rule society and the Exchange. In a great many cases, a judicious rearrangement of marriage proves that the new-made millionnaires value their recently acquired "old wines" and "ancient pictures," more than their aging wives. They bring much warmth of social color into the local breezy atmosphere of this animated Western picture, these new arrangements of Hymen.

Hardin, plunging into the general madness of stock speculation, destined to reign for twenty years, keeps his own counsel. He sneers not at the households queened over by the "Doubtful Loveliness" of the "Rearranged Aristocracy of the Pacific." He has certain twinges when he hears the laughing girl child at play in the bowers of his park. While the ex-queen of the El Dorado, now a marvel of womanly beauty, gazes on that dancing child, she cannot yet see, among the many flashing gems loading her hands, the plain circlet of a wedding ring.

No deeper consecration than the red blood of the murdered gambler ever sealed the lawless union of the "Chief of the Golden Circle" with the peerless "Empress of

Rouge et Noir."

Her facile moods, restrained passions, blind devotion, and self-acquired charms of education, keep Philip Hardin strangely faithful to a dark bond.

Luxury, in its most insidious forms, woos to dreamy enjoyment the not guile-less Adam and Eve of this hidden western Paradise.

There is neither shame nor the canker of regret brooding over these "children of knowledge," who have tasted the clusters of the "Tree of Life."

Within and without, it is the same. Philip Hardin is not the only knave and unpunished murderer in high place. His "Gulnare" is not the only lovely woman here, who bears unabashed the burden of a hideous past. A merit is peculiar to this guilty, world-defying pair. They seek no friends, obtrude on no external circles, and parade no lying sham before local respectability.

It is not so with others. The bench, the forum, the highest places, the dazzling daily displays of rough luxury, are thronged by transformed "Nanas" and resolute climbers of the social trapeze. The shameless motto flaunts on their free-lance banners, golden-bordered:

"Pour y parvenir."

Philip Hardin smiles, on the rare occasions when he enters the higher circles of "society," to see how many fair faces light up, in strange places, with a smile of recognition. How many rosy lips are closed with taper fingers, hinting, "Don't ask me how I got here; I AM! here!"

In his heartless indifference to the general good, he greets the promoted "la-dies" with grave courtesy. It is otherwise with the upstart men. His pride of brain and life-long station makes him haughtily indifferent to them. He will not grovel with these meaner human clods.

A sardonic grin relaxes his dark visage as he sees them go forth to "shine" in the East and "abroad."

Why should not the men of many aliases, the heroes of brawl and murder, of theft and speculation, freely mix with the more polished money sharks swarming in the Eastern seas of financial piracy?

"Arcades ambo!" Bonanza bullion rings truer than the paper millions of shoddy and petroleum. The alert, bright free-lances of the West are generally more interest-ing than the "shoddy" magnates or "contract" princes of the war. They are, at least, robust adventurers; the others are only money-ennobled Eastern mushrooms.

The Western parvenu is the more picturesque. The cunning railroad princes have, at least, built SOMETHING. It is a nobler work than the paper constructions of Wall Street operators. It may be jeered, that these men "builded better than they knew." Hardin feels that on one point they never can be ridiculed, even by Eastern magnate, English promoter, or French financier. They can safely affirm they grasped all they could. They left no humble sheaf unreaped in the clean-cut fields of their work. They took all in sight.

Hardin recognizes the clean work of the Western money grabbers, as well and truly done. The railroad gang, bonanza barons, and banking clique, sweep the threshing floor. Nothing escapes them.

He begins to feel, in the giant speculations of 1862 and 1863, that luck can desert even an old gamester, at life's exciting table. He suffers enormously, yet Lagunitas's resources are behind him.

In the long fight of the street, victory perches with the strongest battalions. Philip Hardin cannot know that men toiling by the day in obscure places now, will yet exchange cigars with royal princes. They will hobnob with the Hapsburgs. They will enter racing bets in the jewelled notebooks of grand dukes. They copy the luxuries, the inborn vices of the blue blood of Europe's crowned Sardanapalian autocrats.

From saloon to salon, from kitchen to kirmess, from the faro table to the Queen's drawing-room, from the canvas trousers of the miner to Poole's creations, from the calico frock of the housemaid to Worth's dazzling masterpieces, from making omelets to sneering at operas, the great social lightning-change act goes on.

Philip Hardin loves his splendid home, where the foot of Hortense Duval sinks in the tufted glories of Persia and the Wilton looms. He does not marvel to see ex-cattle-drovers, promoted waiters, lucky lemonade-sellers, and Pike County discoverers, buying gold watch-chains by the pound. They boast huge golden timepieces, like young melons. Their diamond cluster pins are as resplendent as crystal door-knobs.

Fair hands, fresh from the healthful contact of washing-soda, wave recognition to him from coupe or victoria. In some cases these are driven by the millionnaire himself, who insists on "holding the ribbons."

The newspapers, in the recherche society columns, refer to the grandeur of the "Gold Hill" outfit, the Virginia City "gang," the Reese River "hummers," or the Eberhardt "crowd." These are the Golden Horde.

These lucky children of fortune mingle with the stock-brokers, who, resplendent in attire, and haughty of demeanor, fill the thousand offices of speculation. They disdain the meaner element, as they tool their drags over the Cliff Road to bathe in champagne, and listen to the tawdry Phrynes and bedraggled Aspasias who share their vulture feast of the moment.

It is a second descent of male and female harpies. Human nature, loosened from long restraint by the war, has flooded the coast with the moral debris of the conflict. It is a reign of the Bacchanals.

"After all," thinks Philip Hardin, as he sees these dazzling rockets rise, with golden trails, into the social darkness of the Western skies, "they are really the upper classes here. Their power of propulsion to the zenith is inherent in themselves. If they mingle, in time, with the aristocratic noblesse of Europe, they may infuse a certain picturesque element." Hardin realizes that some of the children of these millionnaires of a day will play at school with young princes, their girls will marry titles, and adorn their smallest belongings with excrescent coronets and coats of arms, won in the queer lottery of marriage.

"It is well," the cold lawyer muses. "After all, many of the aristocracy of Europe are the descendants of expert horse-thieves, hired bravos, knights who delighted to roast the merchant for his fat money-bags, or spit the howling peasant on their spears. Many soft-handed European dames feel the fiery blood burning in their ardent bosoms. In some cases, a reminder of the beauty whose easy complaisance caught a monarch's smile and earned an infamous title. Rapine, murder, lust, oppression, high-handed bullying, servile slavishness in every vile abandonment, have bred up delicate, dreamy aristocrats. Their ancestors, by the two strains, were either red-handed marauders, or easy Delilahs."

The God-given title to batten in luxury, is one which depends now on the possession of golden wealth. It finally burns its gleaming pathway through every barrier.

With direct Western frankness, the Pacific "jeunesse doree" will date from bonanza or railroad deal. Spoliated don, stolen franchise, giant stock-job, easy political "coup de main," government lands scooped in, or vast tracts of timber stolen under the law's easy formalities, are their quarterings. Whiskey sellers, adventuresses, and the minor fry of fighting henchmen, make up the glittering train of these knights. The diamond-decked dames of this "Golden Circle" exclaim in happy chorus, as they sit in the easy-chairs of wealth's thronging courts:

"This is the way we long have sought, And mourned because we found it not."

But riding behind Philip Hardin is the grim horseman, Care. He mourns his interrupted political career. The end of the war approaches. His spirited sultana now points to the lovely child. Her resolute lips speak boldly of marriage.

Hardin wonders if any refluent political wave may throw him up to the senate or the governor's chair. His powers rust in retirement. He fears the day when his stewardship of Lagunitas may be at an end.

He warily determines to get rid of Padre Francisco as soon as possible. The death of Donna Dolores places all in his hands. As he confers with the quick-witted ex-queen of the El Dorado, he decides that he must remove the young Mariposa heiress to San Francisco. It is done. Philip Hardin cannot travel continually to watch over a child.

"Kaintuck" and the sorrowing padre alone are left at Lagunitas. The roses fall unheeded in the dead lady's bower. On this visit, when Hardin takes the child to the mansion on the hill, he learns the padre only awaits the return of Maxime Valois, to retire to France. Unaware of the great strength of the North and East, the padre feels the land may be held in the clutches of war a long period. He would fain end his days among the friends of his youth. As he draws toward old age, he yearns for France. Hardin promises to assist the wishes of the old priest.

After Padre Francisco retires to the silent cottage by the chapel, Hardin learns from "Kaintuck" a most momentous secret. There are gold quartz mines of fabulous richness on the Lagunitas grant. Slyly extracting a few tons of rock, "Kaintuck" has had these ores worked, and gives Philip Hardin the marvellous results.

Hardin's dark face lights up: "Have you written Colonel Valois of this?" "Not a word," frankly says "Kaintuck."

"Judge, I did not want to bring a swarm of squatters over our lines. I thought to tell you alone, and you could act with secrecy. If they stake off claims, we will have a rush on our hands."

Hardin orders the strictest silence. As he lies in the guest chamber of Lagunitas, Philip Hardin is haunted all night by a wild unrest. If Lagunitas were only his. There is only Valois between him and the hidden millions in these quartz veins. Will no Yankee bullet do its work?

The tireless brain works on, as crafty Philip Hardin slumbers that night. Visions of violence, of hidden traps, of well-planned crime, haunt his dreams. Only "Kaintuck" knows. Secretly, bit by bit, he has brought in these ores. They have been smuggled out and worked, with no trace of their real origin. No one knows but one. Though old "Kaintuck" feels no shadow over his safety, the sweep of the dark angel's wing is chilling his brow. He knows too much.

When Hardin returns to San Francisco he busies himself with Lagunitas. His brow is dark as he paces the deck of the Stockton steamer. Hortense Duval has provided him with a servant of great discretion to care for the child. Marie Berard is the typical French maid. Deft, neat-handed, she has an eye like a hawk. Her little pet weaknesses and her vices give spice to an otherwise colorless character.

The boat steams down past the tule sloughs. Hardin's cigar burns late on the deck as he plots alone.

When he looks over his accumulated letters, he seizes eagerly a packet of papers marked "Havana." Great God!

He has read of Sherman's occupation of Atlanta. The struggle of Peachtree Creek brought curses on Tecumseh's grizzled head. Now, with a wildly beating heart, he learns of the death of Colonel Valois among the captured guns of De Gress. As the last pages are scanned, he tears open the legal documents. The cold beads stand out on his brow. He is master now. The king is dead!

He rings for Madame Duval. With shaking hand, he pours a draught from the nearest decanter. He is utterly unnerved. The prize is at last within his grasp. It shall be his alone!

Lighting a fresh cigar he paces the room, a human tiger. There is but one frail girl child between him and Lagunitas, with its uncoined millions. He must act. To be deep and subtle as a thieving Greek, to be cold and sneaking as an Apache, to be as murderous as a Malay creeping, creese in hand, over the bulwarks of a merchantman,--all that is to be only himself. Power is his for aye.

But to be logically correct, to be wise and safe in secret moves. Time to think? Yes. Can he trust Hortense Duval? Partly. He needs that devilish woman's wit of hers. Will he tell her all? No. Professional prudence rules. A dark scheme has formulated itself in his brain, bounding under the blow of the brandy.

He will get Hortense out of the State, under the pretext of sending the colonel's child to Paris. The orphan's education must be brilliant.

He will have no one know of the existence of Valois' mine. If "Kaintuck" were only gone. Yes! Yes! the secret of the mines. If the priest were only in France and locked up in his cloister. The long minority of the child gives time to reap the golden harvest.

A sudden thought: the child may not live! His teeth chatter. As he paces the room, Hortense enters. She sees on his face the shadow of important things.

"What has happened, Philip?" she eagerly asks.

"Sit down, Hortense. Listen to me," says Hardin, as he sees the doors all secure.

Her heart beats fast. Is this the end of all? She has feared it daily.

"How would you like to live in Paris?" he ejaculates.

He watches her keenly, pacing to and fro. A wild hope leaps up. Will he retire, and live his days out abroad? Is the marriage to come at last?

"Philip, I don't understand you," she murmurs. Her bosom heaves within its rich silks, under its priceless laces. The sparkling diamonds in her hair glisten, as she gazes on his inscrutable face. Is this heaven or hell? Paradise or a lonely exile? To have a name at last for her child?

"Colonel Valois was killed at the battles near Atlanta. I have just received from the Havana bankers the final letters of Major Peyton, his friend." Hardin speaks firmly.

"Under the will, that child Isabel inherits the vast property. She must be educated in France. Some one must take care of her."

Hortense leans over, eagerly. What does he mean? "There is no one but me to look after her. The cursed Yankees will probably devastate the South. I dare not probate his will just now. There is confiscation and all such folly."

Philip Hardin resumes his walk. "I do not wish to pay heavy war taxes and succession tax on all this great estate. I must remain here and watch it. I must keep the child's existence and where-abouts quiet. The courts could worry me about her removal. Can I trust you, Hortense?" His eyes are wolfish. He stops and fixes a burning glance on her. She returns it steadily.

"What do you wish me to do?" she says, warily.

It will be years and years she must remain abroad.

"Can I trust you to go over with that child, and watch her while I guard this great estate? You shall have all that money and my influence can do for you. You can live as an independent lady and see the great world."

She rises and faces him, a beautiful, expectant goddess. "Philip, have I been true to you these years?"

He bows his head. It is so! She has kept the bond.

"Do I go as your wife?" Her voice trembles with eagerness.

"No. But you may earn that place by strictly following my wishes." He speaks kindly. She is a grand woman after all. Bright tears trickle through her jewelled fingers. She has thrown herself on the fauteuil. The woman of thirty is a royal beauty, her youthful promise being more than verified. She is a queen of luxury.

"Listen to me, Hortense," says Hardin, softly. He seats himself by her side and takes the lovely hands in his. His persuasive voice flows like honey. "I am now surrounded by enemies. I am badly compromised. I am all tied up. I fear the Union League, the government spies, and the damned Yankee officers here. One foolish move would utterly ruin me. If you will take this child you can take any name you wish. No one knows you in Paris. I will have the bankers and our Southern friends vouch for you in society. I will support you, so you can move even in the Imperial circles. If you are true to me, in time I will do as you wish. I dare not now." He is plausible, and knows how to plead. This woman, loving and beloved, cannot hold out.

"Think of our child, Philip," cries Hortense, as she throws herself on his breast. He is moved and yet he lies.

"I do at this very moment, Hortense. I am not a rich man, for I have lost much for the South. These Yankee laws keep me out of court. I dare not get in their power. If I hold this estate, I will soon be able to settle a good fortune on Irene. I swear to you, she shall be my only heiress except yourself. You can take Irene with you and give her a superb education. You will be doing a true mother's duty. I will place such a credit and funds for you that the future has no fears. When I am free to act, 'when this foolish war is over,' I can come to you. Will you do as I wish?"

"Philip, give me till to-morrow to think. I have only you in the world." The beautiful woman clings to him. He feels she will yield. He is content to wait.

While they talk, the two children chatter under the window in childish glee.

"Hortense, you must act at once! to-morrow! The steamer leaves in three days. I wish you to go by Panama direct to France. New York is no place for you. I will have much to arrange. I will give you to-night. Now leave me, for I have many papers to draw up."

In her boudoir, Hortense Duval sits hours dreaming, her eyes fixed on vacancy. All the hold she has on Hardin is her daily influence, and HIS child. To go among strangers. To be alone in the world. And yet, her child's future interests. While Hardin paces the floor below, or toils at his cunningly worded papers, she feels she is in the hands of a master.

Philip Hardin's late work is done. By the table he dreams over the future. Hortense will surely work his will. He will divest himself of the priest. He must open these mines. He will get rid of "Kaintuck;" but how?

Dark thoughts come to him. He springs up aghast at the clatter when his careless arm brushes off some costly trifles. With the priest gone forever and the child in Paris, he has no stumbling block in his way but "Kaintuck." There are ways; yes, ways.----!----!----!----!

"He must go on a journey; yes, a long, long journey." Hardin stops here, and throwing himself on his couch, drifts out on the sea of his uneasy dreams.

Morning proves to him Hortense is resigned; an hour's conclave enlightens her as to the new life. Every contingency will be met. Hortense, living in wealth's luxurious retirement, will be welcomed as Madame Natalie de Santos, everywhere. A wealthy young widow, speaking French and Spanish, with the best references. She will wear a discreet mask of Southern mystery, and an acknowledged relationship to families of Mexico and California. Her personal appearance, tact, and wealth will be an appropriate dower to the new acquisition of the glittering Capital of Pleasure. She is GOOD ENOUGH for Paris.

Rapidly, every preparation moves on. The luggage of Madame de Santos is filled with the varied possessions indicating years of elegance. Letters to members of the

Confederate court circle at Paris are social endorsements. Wealth will do the rest.

Hardin's anxiety is to see the heiress lodged at the "Sacred Heart" at Paris. In his capacity as guardian, he delegates sole power to Madame Natalie de Santos. She alone can control the little lady of Lagunitas. With every resource, special attentions will be paid to the party, from Panama, on the French line. The hegira consists of the two children, Marie Berard, and the nameless lady, soon to be rebaptized "Natalie de Santos." Not unusual in California,--!--a golden butterfly.

Vague sadness fills Hortense Duval's heart as she wanders through her silent mansion, choosing these little belongings which are dear to her shadowed heart. They will rob a Parisian home of suspicious newness. The control of the heiress as well as their own child, the ample monetary provision, and the social platform arranged for her, prove Hardin's devotion. It is the best she can do.

True, he cannot now marry with safety. He has promised to right that wrong in time.

There has been no want of tenderness in his years of devotion. Hortense Duval acknowledges to herself that he dares not own her openly, as his wife, even here. But in Paris, after a year or so. Then he could come, at least as far as New York. He could meet her, and by marriage, legitimize his child. Her child. The tiger's darling.

A sudden thought strikes her. Some other woman!--Some one of REAL station and blood. Ah, no! She shivers slightly as she paces the room. No corner of the earth could hide him from her vengeance if he betrays her.

The dinner of the last evening is a serious feast. As Hortense ministers to the dark master of the house, she can see he has not fully disclosed his ultimate plans. It is positive the child must be hidden away at Paris from all. Hardin enjoins silence as to the future prospects of the orphan. The little one has already forgotten her father. She is rapidly losing all memories of her sweet mother.

In the silence of these last hours, Philip Hardin speaks to the woman who has been his only intimate in years.

"Hortense, I may find a task for you which will prove your devotion," he begins with reluctance.

"What is it, Philip?" she falters.

He resumes. "I do not know how far I may be pushed by trouble. I shall have to struggle and fight to hold my own. I am safe for a time, but I may be pushed to the wall. Will you, for the sake of our own child, do as I bid you with that Spanish brat?"

At last she sees his gloomy meaning. Is it murder? An orphan child!

"Philip," she sobs, "be careful! For MY SAKE, for YOUR OWN." She is chilled by his cold designs.

"Only at the last. Just as I direct, I may wish you to control the disappearance of that young one, who stands between me and our marriage."

She seizes his hands: "Swear to me that you will never deceive me."

"I do," he answers huskily.

"On the cross," she sternly says, flashing before his startled eyes a jewelled crucifix. "I will obey you--I swear it on this--as long as you are true." She presses her ashy lips on the cross.

He kisses it. The promise is sealed.

In a few hours, Hortense Duval, from the deck of the swift Golden Gate, sees the sunlight fall for the last time, in long years, on San Francisco's sandy hills.

With peculiar adroitness, in defence of her past, for the sake of her future position, she keeps her staterooms; only walking the decks with her maid occasionally at night. No awkward travelling pioneer must recognize her as the lost "Beauty of the El Dorado." A mere pretence of illness is enough.

When safely out of the harbor of Colon, on the French steamer, she is perfectly free. Her passage tickets, made out as Madame de Santos, are her new credentials.

She has left her old life behind her. Keen and self-possessed, with quiet dignity she queens it on the voyage. When the French coast is reached, her perfect mastery of herself proves she has grown into her new position.

Philip Hardin has whispered at the last, "I want you to get rid of your maid in a few months. It is just as well she should be out of the way."

When out of Hardin's influence, reviewing the whole situation, Hortense, in her real character, becomes a little fearful. What if he should drop her? Suppose he denies her identity. He can legally reclaim the "Heiress of Lagunitas." Hortense Duval well knows that Philip Hardin will stop at nothing. As the French coast nears, Hortense mentally resolves NOT to part with Marie Berard. Marie is a valuable witness of the past relations. She is the only safeguard she has against Hardin's manifold schemes. So far there is no "entente cordiale" between mistress and maid. They watch each other.

By hazard, as the children are brought out, ready for the landing, Hortense notices the similarity of dress, the speaking resemblance of the children. Marie Berard, proud of their toilettes, remarks, "Madame, they are almost twins in looks."

Hortense Duval's lightning mind conceives a daring plan. She broods in calm and quiet, as the cars bear her from Havre to Paris. She must act quickly. She knows Hardin may use more ways of gaining information than her own letters. His brain is fertile. His purse, powerful.

Going to an obscure hotel, she procures a carriage. She drives alone to the Convent of the Sacre Coeur. With perfect tranquillity she announces her wishes. The Mother Superior, personally, is charmed with Madame de Santos. A mere mention of her banking references is sufficient. Blest power of gold!

Madame Natalie de Santos is in good humor when she regains her apartment. On the next morning, after a brief visit to her bankers, who receive her "en princesse," she drives alone with her OWN child to the Sacred Heart. While the little one prattles with some engaging Sisters, Hortense calmly registers the nameless child of sin as ISABEL VALOIS, THE HEIRESS OF LAGUNITAS. A year's fees and payments are made. A handsome "outfit allowance" provides all present needs suited to the child's station. Arranging to send the belongings of the heiress to the convent, Hortense Duval buries her past forever in giving to her own child the name and station of the heiress of Lagunitas. To keep a hold on Hardin she will place the other child where that crafty lawyer can never find her. Her bosom swells with pride. Now, at last, she can control the deepest plans of Philip Hardin. But if he should demand their own child? He has no legal power over the nameless one--not even here. Marriage first. After that, the secret. It is a MASTER STROKE.

Hortense Duval thinks only of her own child. She cares nothing for the dead Confederate under the Georgia pines. Gentle Dolores is sleeping in the chapel grounds at Lagunitas. Isabel Valois has not a friend in the world!

But, Marie Berard must be won and controlled. Why not? It is fortune for her to be true to her liberal mistress. Berard knows Paris and has friends. She will see them. If the maid be discharged, Hortense loses her only witness against Hardin; her only safeguard. As Madame de Santos is ushered to her rooms, she decides to act at once, and drop forever her past. But Marie?

Marie Berard wonders at the obscure hotel. Her brain finds no reason for this isolation. "Ah! les modes de Paris." Madame will soon emerge as a lovely vision.

In the years of her service with Hortense Duval, Marie has quietly enriched herself. She knows the day of parting comes in all unlawful connections. Time and fading charms, coldness and the lassitude of habit, eat away the golden chain till it drops off. "On se range enfin."

The "femme de chambre" knows too much to ever think of imposing on Judge Hardin. He is too sly. It is from Madame de Santos the golden stream must flow.

Self-satisfied, Marie Berard smiles in her cat-like way as she thinks of a nice little house in Paris. Its income will support her. She will nurse this situation with care. It is a gold mine.

There is no wonderment in her keen eyes when Madame de Santos returns without the child she took away. A French maid never wonders. But she is astonished when her mistress, calling her, calmly says, pointing to the lonely orphan:

"Marie, I wish you to aid me to get rid of this child. Do you know any one in Paris whom we can trust?"

"Will Madame kindly explain?" the maid gasps, her visions of that snug house becoming more definite.

"Sit down, Marie," the newly christened Madame de Santos commands. "I will trust you. You shall be richly rewarded."

The Frenchwoman's eyes glitter. The golden shower she has longed for, "Auri sacra fames."

"You may trust me perfectly, Madame."

"I wish you to understand me fully. We must act at once. I will see no friends till this girl is out of the way. Then I shall at once arrange my household."

"Does the young lady not go to the convent?" says the astonished servant, a trifle maliciously.

"Certainly not," coldly says Hortense. "My own child shall be the heiress of that fortune. She is already at the Sacred Heart."

Marie Berard's keen eye sees the plot. An exchange of children. The nameless child shall be dowered with millions. Her own future is assured.

"Does any one know of this plan?" the maid eagerly asks.

"Only you and I," is the response.

Ah! Revenge on her stately tyrant lover. The maid dreams of a golden shower. That snug hotel. It is a delicious moment. "What do you wish me to do, Madame?" Marie is now cool.

"Find a place, at once, where the child can be well treated in a 'bourgeois' family. I want you to place her as if she were your own. I wish no one to ever see me or know of me in this matter."

The maid's eyes sparkle. Fortune's wheel turns. "And I shall be--" she pauses.

"You may be suspected to be the mother. No one can learn anything from the child. I wish her to be raised in ignorance."

Madame de Santos is a genius in a quiet way. It is true, the prattling heiress, on the threshold of a new life, speaks only Spanish and a little English. She has forgotten her father. Even now her mother fades from her mind. A few passing months will sweep away all memories of Lagunitas. The children are nearly the same age, and not dissimilar.

"And the Judge?" murmurs the servant.

"I will take care of that," sharply says Hortense.

"Madame, it is a very great responsibility," begins the sly maid, now confidante. There is a strong sharp accent on the "very."

"I will pay you as you never dreamed of being paid." Madame Natalie is cool and quiet. Gold, blessed gold!

"It is well. I am yours for life," says Marie Berard. The two women's eyes meet. They understand one another. Feline, prehensile nerves.

Then, action at once. Hortense hands the woman a package of bank-notes. "Leave here as if for a walk. Take a 'fiacre' on the street, and go to your friends. You tell me you have some discreet ones. Tell them you have a child to take care of. Say no more. They will guess the rest. I want the child to be left to-morrow morning. After your return we can arrange her present needs. The rest you can provide through your friends. I want you to see the child once a week, not oftener. Go."

In ten minutes Marie Berard is rolling away to her advisers. Her letter has already announced her arrival. She knows her Paris. If a French maid has a heart history, hers is a succession of former Parisian scenes.

Madame Natalie de Santos closes the doors. While her emissary is gone she examines the child thoroughly. Not a single blemish or peculiar mark on the girl, save a crossed scar on her left arm, between the wrist and elbow. Some surgical operation of trifling nature has left a mark in its healing, which will be visible for many years.

Making careful mental note, the impatient woman awaits her servant's return.

Seated, she watches the orphan child trifling with her playthings. Hortense Duval feels no twinge of conscience. Her own child shall be lifted far beyond the storms of fate. If Hardin acts rightly, all is well. If he attempts to betray her, all the better. She will guard the heiress of Mariposa with her life. She shall become a "bourgeoise."

Should Hardin die before he marries her, the base-born child is then sure of the millions. She will make her a woman of the world. When the great property is safely hers, then she can trust HER OWN daughter.

As to the poor orphan, buried in Paris, educated as a "bourgeoise," she will never see her face, save perhaps, as a passing stranger. The child can be happy in the solid comforts of a middle-class family. It is good enough for her.

And Marie Berard. She needs her, at all cost, as a protection, the only bulwark against any dark scheme of Hardin's. Her tool, and her one witness.

Ten years in the mansion on the hills of San Francisco have given her an insight into Philip Hardin's desperate moves on the chessboard of life. Love, faith, truth, she dares not expect. A lack of fatherly tenderness to the child he has wronged; his refusal to put a wedding ring on her own finger, tell her the truth. She knows her hold is slight. But NOW the very millions of Lagunitas shall fight against him. Move for move in the play. Blow for blow, if it comes to a violent rupture.

Hortensc Duval might lose her hold on cold Philip Hardin. The scheming beauty smiles when she thinks how true Marie Berard will be to the new Madame de Santos. A thorough adventuress, she can count on her fellow-conspirator. Two smart women, with a solid golden bond, united against a distant, aging man.

Marie returns, her business-like manner showing no change. "I have found the family," she says. "They will take the child at once."

In the evening every arrangement is made for an early departure. It is a rare day's work.

Marie Berard conducts the friendless child to its new home, in the morning hours. The luggage and belongings are despatched. All is over. Safe at last.

Free to move, as soon as the maid returns, Hortense at once leaves her modest quarters. The bills are all paid. Their belongings are packed as for departure. To the Hotel Meurice, by a roundabout route, mistress and maid repair. Hortense Duval is no more. A new social birth.

Madame de Santos, in superb apartments, proceeds to arrange her entree into future social greatness. A modern miracle.

No one has seen the children together in Paris. On the steamer not a suspicion was raised. Natalie de Santos breathes freely. A few days of preparation makes Madame "au fait" in the newest fashions. Her notes, cartes de visite, dazzling "batterie de toilette," and every belonging bear crest, monogram, and initial of the new-born Senora Natalie.

Securely lodged in an aristocratic apartment, Madame de Santos receives her bankers, and the members of the Southern circle, to whom the Judge has given her the freemasonry of his influence. Madame de Santos is now a social fact, soon to find her old life a waning memory. The glittering splendors of the court gaieties are her everyday enjoyments.

Keenly watching all Californians, protected by her former retirement, her foreign appearance and glamour of wealth impose on all. She soon almost forgets herself and that dark past before the days of the El Dorado. She is at last secure within wealth's impregnable ramparts, and defies adverse fate.

An apartment on the Champs Elysees is judiciously chosen by her bankers. Marie Berard, with her useful allies, aids in the selection of the exquisite adornment. Her own treasures aid in the "ensemble."

The servants, the equipage of perfect appointment, all her surroundings bespeak the innate refinement of the woman who has for long years pleased even the exacting Hardin.

Natalie de Santos has not neglected to properly report by telegraph and mail to the guardian of the person and future millions of Col. Valois' only child.

Her attitude toward society is quiet, dignified, without haste or ostentation. A beautiful woman, talented, free, rich, and "a la mode," can easily reach the social pleasures of that gaudy set who now throng the Tuileries.

There is not a care on Natalie de Santos' mind. Her own child is visited, with a growing secret pleasure. She thrives in the hands of the gentle ladies of the Sacred Heart.

Regularly, Marie Berard brings reports of the other child, whose existence is important for the present.

Madame de Santos, discreetly veiled, finds time to observe the location and movements of the orphan. Marie Berard's selection has been excellent.

"Louise Moreau" is the new name of the changeling heiress, now daily becoming more contented in her new home.

Aristide Dauvray has a happy household. A master decorative workman, only lacking a touch of genius to be a sculptor, his pride is in his artistic handiwork. His happiness in his good wife Josephine. His heart centres in his talented boy.

To educate his only son Raoul, to be able to develop his marked talent as an artist, has been Aristide's one ambition. The proposition to take the girl, and the liberal payments promised, assure the artistic future of Raoul. Marie Berard has appreciated that the life of this orphan child is the measure of her own golden fortunes. Good Josephine becomes attached to the shy, sweet little wanderer, who forgets, day by day, in the new life of Cinderella, her babyish glimpses of any other land.

Natalie de Santos is safe. Pressing her silken couch, she rests in splendor. Her letters from Hardin are clear, yet not always satisfactory. Years of daily observance have taught her to read his character. As letter after letter arrives she cons them all together. Not a word of personal tenderness. Not an expression which would betray any of their secrets. With no address or signature, they are full only in directions. He is called for a length of time to Lagunitas, to put the estate in "general order."

Removed from the sway of Hardin, Natalie relies upon herself. Her buoyant wings bear her on in society. Recognized as an opponent of the North, she meets those lingering Southern sympathizers who have little side coteries yet in glittering Paris.

Adulation of her beauty and sparkling wit fires her genius. Her French is classic. The sealed book of her youth gives no hint of where her fine idiom came from. Merrily Marie Berard recounts to the luxurious social star the efforts of sly dames and soft-voiced messieurs to fathom the "De Santos'" past.

Marie Berard is irreproachable; never presuming. She can wait.

Madame Natalie's stormy past has taught her to trust no one. It is her rule from the first that no one shall see Isabel Valois, the pet of the Sacred Heart Convent, but herself. Little remains in a month or two, with either child, of its cradle memories. The months spent by the two girls in mastering a new language are final extinguishers of the past.

Without undue affectation of piety, Madame de Santos gives liberally. The good nuns strive to fit the young heiress for her dazzling future.

Keenly curious of the dangers of the situation, Natalie writes Hardin that she has sent her own child away to a country institution, to prevent awkward inquiry. As months roll on, drawn in by the whirlpool of pleasure, Natalie de Santos' letters become brief. They are only statements of affairs to her absent "financial agent."

Hardin's letters are acknowledgments of satisfactory news, and directions regarding the education of the child. He does not refer to the future of the woman who ruled his home so long. No tenderness for his own child appears. He is engrossed in BUSINESS, and she in PLEASURE. Avarice is the gentlemanly passion of his later years. "Royal days of every pleasure" for the brilliant woman; she, ambitious and self-reliant, lives only for the happy moments.

And yet, as Natalie de Santos sweeps from palace ball or the opera, she frames plans as to the future control of Hardin. To keep the child he fears, where his agency can reach her, is her aim. To place the child he would ignore, where millions will surround her, is her ambition. With Marie Berard as friend, confidante, agent, and spy, she can keep these two children apart. Hortense Duval and Natalie Santos can defy the world.

Distrust of Hardin always burns in her breast. Will he dare to attempt her life; to cut off her income; to betray her? When the work of years is reflected in her own child's graces and charms, will the man now aging ever give its mother the name of wife? Her fears belie her hopes.

She must guard her own child, and conceal the other. He may live and work out his schemes. If he acts well, she will be ready to meet him. If not, the same.

But she has sworn in her heart of hearts, the orphan shall live. If necessary to produce her, she alone knows her hiding place. If fortune favors, the properties shall descend to her own child.

The year 1865 opens with the maddest gaieties. Though France is drained of men and treasure for a foolish war in Mexico, glittering streets, rich salons, mad merry-makings and imperial splendor do not warn gay Lutetia she is tottering toward the dawning war-days of gloom. The French are drunk with pleasure.

Marie Berard has now a nice little fund of ringing napoleons securely invested, and that hoard is growing monthly. Natalie de Santos gives freely, amply. The maid bides her time for a great demand. She can wait.

A rare feminine genius is Natalie de Santos. The steady self-poise of her nature prevents even a breath of scandal. Frank, daring, and open in her pleasures, she individualizes no swain, she encourages no one sighing lover. Her name needs no defence save the open record of her social life. A solid, undisturbed position grows around her. The dear-bought knowledge of her youth enables her to read the vapid men and women around her.

As keen-eyed as a hawk, Madame Natalie watches the scholar of the Sacred Heart. She takes good care, also, to verify the substantial comfort and fair education of little Louise Moreau.

With silent lips she moves among the new associates of her later days. Madame de Santos' position moves toward impregnability, as the months roll on. A "lionne" at last.

CHAPTER XIV.

A MARIPOSA BONANZA.--NATALIE DE SANTOS BORN IN PARIS.--
THE QUEEN OF THE EL DORADO JOINS THE GALLIC "FOUR HUN-
DRED."

Philip Hardin's days are busy after the steamer bears away his "Ex-Queen of the El Dorado." There are his tangled finances to arrange; giant speculations to follow up. The Lagunitas affairs are pressing. That hidden mine!

Hardin sets his house in order. The establishment is reduced. He has, now, peace for his schemes. No petticoat rule now. No prying eyes. As the winter rain howls among his trees, he realizes that the crash of the Confederacy will bring back clouds of stragglers from the ruin yet to come. He must take legal possession of Lagunitas. He has a good reason. Its hidden gold will give him power.

His public life is only cut off for a time. Gold is potent; yes, omnipotent! He can bide his time. He must find that mine. He has now two points to carry in his game. To rid himself of the padre is easy, in time. To disembarrass himself of old "Kaintuck" is another thing.

His face grows bitter as he thinks of the boundless wealth to be reached in Lagunitas's glittering quartz beds. The property must remain in his care.

If the heiress were to die, the public administrator might take it. He knows he is not popular. His disloyalty is too well known. Besides, Valois' death is not yet officially proven. He has kept his counsel. No one has seen the will. But the returning wave of Confederates may bring news. The dead colonel was of too great local fame to drop unheeded into his grave.

His carefully prepared papers make him the representative of Colonel Valois. He is legal guardian of the child. He will try and induce "Kaintuck" to quit the rancho. Then he will be able to open the mines. If the Confederacy totters to its fall, with the control of that wealth he may yet hold the highest place on the coast.

Dreaming over his cigar, he knows that legislatures can be bought, governors approached, and high positions gained, by the adroit use of gold. Bribery is of all times and places.

Telegraphing to "Kaintuck" to meet him near Stockton, at the station, with a travelling carriage, the Judge revolves plans to rid himself of this relic of the Valois regime.

His stay at Lagunitas will be for some weeks. He has now several agents ready to open up the mines.

A liberal use of the income of Lagunitas has buoyed up his sinking credit. But his stock-gambling has been desperately unlucky. Hardin revolves in his mind the displacement of old "Kaintuck." The stage sweeps down the San Joaquin to the station, where his team awaits him. An unwonted commotion greets him there. His arrival is opportune. In the room which is the office, bar, and billiard-room of the little hostelry, poor old "Kaintuck" lies dying, when the Judge dismounts. It is the hand of fate.

During the hours of waiting, a certain freedom, induced by copious draughts of fiery Bourbon, caused the old foreman to injudiciously "Hurrah for Jeff Davis." He gave free vent to his peculiar Southern opinions.

A sudden quarrel with a stranger results in a quick resort to weapons. Benumbed with age and whiskey, the old trapper is shot while tugging at his heavy "Colt."

Before the smoke cleared away the stranger was far away. Dashing off, he spurred his horse at full speed into the chaparral. No one dared, no one cared, to follow a desperate man riding for his life.

Hardin orders every attention to the sufferer. Old "Kaintuck" is going out alone on the dark river.

Hardin, steeled to scenes like this, by an exciting life, blesses this opportune relief. "Kaintuck" is off his hands forever. Before the Judge leaves, a rude examination by a justice precedes the simple obsequies of the dead ranger.

One more red mound by the wayside. A few pencilled words on a shingle mark the grave, soon to be trampled down by the feet of cattle and horses. So, one by one, many of the old pioneers leave the theatre of their aimless lives.

The Judge, happy at heart, bears a grave face. He drives into Lagunitas. Its fields looked never so fair. Seated in the mansion house, with every luxury spread out before him, his delighted eye rests on the diamond lake gleaming in the bosom of the fair landscape. It already seems his own.

He settles in his easy-chair with an air of conscious lordship. Padre Francisco, studiously polite, answers every deft question. He bears himself with the self-possession of a man merely doing his duty.

Does the priest know of the hidden gold mines? No. A few desultory questions prove this. "Kaintuck's" lips are sealed forever in death. The secret is safe.

Padre Francisco does not delay his request to be allowed to depart. As he sips his ripe Mission claret, he tells Judge Hardin of the desire of years to return to France. There are now no duties here to hold him longer. He desires to give the Judge such family papers as are yet in his charge. He would like practical advice as to his departure. For he has grown into his quiet retreat and fears the outer world.

With due gravity the lawyer agrees in the change. He requests the padre to permit him to write his San Francisco agent of the arrival of the retiring missionary.

"If you will allow me," he says, "my agent shall furnish your passage to Paris and arrange for all your wants."

Padre Francisco bows. It is, after all, only his due.

"When will you wish to leave?" queries Hardin.

"To-morrow, Judge. My little affairs are in readiness."

During the evening the light of the good priest glimmers late in the lonely little sacristy. The chapel bell tolls the last vespers, for long years, at Lagunitas.

All the precious family papers are accepted by the Judge when the padre makes ready for his departure. The priest, with faltering voice, says early mass, with a few attendants. Delivering up the keys of the sacristy, chapel, and his home to the Judge, he quietly shares the noonday meal.

If there is sadness in his heart his placid face shows it not. He sits in the lonely room replete with memories of the past.

He is gone for a half hour, after the wily Judge lights his cigar, to contemplate the rich domain which shall be his, from the porch of the old home. When the priest returns, it is from the graves of the loved dead. He has plucked the few flowers blooming there. They are in his hand.

His eyes are moist with the silent tears of one who mourns the useless work of long years. They have been full of sadness, separation, spiritual defeat, and untimely death. Even Judge Hardin, merciless as he is, feels compassion for this lonely man. He has asked nothing of him. The situation is delicate.

"Can I do anything for you, Father Francisco?" says Hardin, with some real feeling. He is a gentleman "in modo." The priest may be penniless. He must not go empty-handed.

"Nothing, thank you, save to accept my adieux and my fondest blessing for the little Isabel."

He hands Judge Hardin the address of the religious house to which he will retire in Paris.

"I will deliver to your agent the other papers and certificates of the family. They are stored for safety at the Mission Dolores church."

"My agent will have orders to do everything you wish," remarks the Judge, as the carriage drives up for the priest.

Hardin arises, with a sudden impulse. The modest pride of this grave old French gentleman will not be rudely intruded on. He must not, he shall not, go away entirely empty-handed. The lawyer returns with an envelope, and hands it to the padre.

"From the colonel," he says. "It is an order for ten thousand dollars upon his San Francisco bankers."

"I will be taken care of by those who sent me here," simply remarks the padre.

Hardin flushes.

"You can use it, father, in France, for the poor, for the friendless; you will find some worthy objects."

The priest bows gravely, and presses the hand of the lawyer. With one loving look around the old plaza, the sweeping forest arches, and the rolling billows of green, he leaves the lonely lake gleaming amid its wooded shores. Its beauty is untouched by the twenty long years since first he wandered by its shores. A Paradise in a forest. His few communicants have said adieu. There is nothing to follow him but the incense-breathing murmurs of the forest branches, from fragrant pine and stately redwood, sighing, "Go, in God's name."

Their wind-wafted voices speak to him of the happy past. The quiet, saddened, patient padre trusts himself as freely to his unknown future, as a child in its mother's cradling arms. In his simple creed, "God is everywhere."

So Francois Ribaut goes in peace to spend a few quiet days at the Mission Dolores church. He will then follow the wild ocean waves back to his beloved France. "Apres vingt ans." A month sees him nearing the beloved shores.

Walking the deck, he thinks often of that orphan child in Europe. He remembers, strangely, that the Judge had neglected to give him any clew to her present dwelling. Ah! he can write. Yes, but will he be answered? Perhaps. But Judge Hardin is a cunning old lawyer.

Disembarrassed of the grave priest, Hardin at once sends orders for his prospectors. A new man appears to superintend the grant.

It is with grim satisfaction he reflects that the hand of fate has removed every obstacle to his control. His fiery energy is shown by the rapidity with which hundreds of men swarm on ditch and flume. They are working at mill and giant water-wheels. They are delving and tracing the fat brown quartz, gold laden, from between the streaks of rifted basalt and porphyry.

There is no one to spy, none to hinder now. Before the straggling veterans of Lee and Johnston wander back to the golden West, the quartz mine of Lagunitas yields fabulous returns.

The legacy of "Kaintuck" was wonderful. The golden bars, run out roughly at the mine, represented to Hardin the anchor of his tottering credit. They are the basis of a great fortune, and the means of political prestige.

When the crash came, when the Southern flags were furled in the awful silence of defeat and despair, the wily lawyer, safe in Lagunitas, was crowning his golden fortunes.

Penniless, broken in pride and war-worn, the survivors of the men whom he urged into the toils of secession, returned sadly home, scattering aimlessly over the West. Fools of fortune.

Philip Hardin, satisfied with the absence of the infant heiress, coldly stood aloof from the ruin of his friends.

As the months ran on, accumulating his private deposits, Judge Hardin, engrossed in his affairs, grew indifferent even to the fate of the woman he had so long cherished. His unacknowledged child is naught to him.

It was easy to keep the general income and expenses of the ranch nearly even in amount.

But the MINE was a daily temptation to the only man who knew its real ownership. It must be his at any cost. Time must show the way. He must have a title.

Hardin looked far into the future. His very isolation and inaction was a proof of no overt treason. With the power of this wealth he might, when a few years rolled away, reach lofty civic honors. Young at sixty, as public men are considered, he wonders, looking over the superb estate, if a high political marriage would not reopen his career. In entertaining royally at San Francisco and Sacramento, with solid and substantial claims in society, he may yet be able to place his name first in the annals of the coast. A senator. Why not? Ambition and avarice.

With prophetic insight, he knows that sectional rancor will not long exist in California. Not really, in the war, a divided community, a debatable land, there will be thousands of able, hardy men, used to excitement, spreading over the West. It is a land of easy and liberal opinion. Business and the mine's affairs cause him to visit San Francisco frequently. He reaches out for all men as his friends. Seated in his silent parlors, walking moodily through the beautiful rooms, haunted with memories of the splendid "anonyma" whose reign is yet visible, he dreams of his wasted past, his lonely future. Can he repair it? Enveloped in smoke wreaths, from his portico he surveys the thousand twinkling city lights below. He is careless of the future movements of his Parisian goddess.

It cost Philip Hardin no heart-wrench to part with voluptuous Hortense Duval. Partners in a crime, the stain of "French Charlie's" blood crimsoned their guilty past. An analytical, cold, all-mastering mind, he had never listened to the heart. He supposed Hortense to be as chilly in nature as himself. Yet she writes but seldom. Taught by his profession to dread silence from a woman, he casually corresponds with several trusted friends of the Confederate colony in France. What is her mystery? Madame Natalie de Santos is now a personage. The replies tell him of her real progress in the glittering ranks of the capital, and her singularly steady life. As the months roll on, he becomes a little anxious. She is far too cool and self-contained to suit him. He wishes women to lean on him and to work his will. Does she intend to establish a thorough position abroad, and claim some future rights? Has she views of a settlement? Who knows?

Hardin sees too late, that in the control of both children, and her knowledge of his past, she is now independent of his mere daily influence. The millions of Lagunitas mine cannot be hidden. If he recalls the heiress, will "Natalie de Santos" be as easily controlled as "Hortense Duval"?

And his own child, what of her? Hardin dares not tie himself up by acknowledging her claims. If he gives a large sum to the girl, it will give his "sultana" a powerful weapon for the future.

Is she watching him through spies? She betrays no anxiety to know anything, save what he imparts. He dare not go to Paris, for fear of some public scandal and a rupture. He must confirm his position there. What new friends has she there?

Ah! He will wait and make a final settlement of a handsome fortune on the child. He will provide a future fixed income for this new social star, now, at any rate, dependent on her obedience. Reports, in due form, accompany the occasional communications forwarded from the "Sacred Heart" as to the heiress. This must all be left to time.

With a deep interest, Hardin sees the cessation of all hostilities, the death of Lincoln, the disbandment, in peace, of the great Union armies.

Bayonets glitter no more upon the crested Southern heights. The embers of the watchfires are cold, gray ashes now. The lonely bivouac of the dead is the last holding of the foughten fields.

While the South and East is a graveyard or in mourning, strange to say, only a general relief is felt in the West. The great issue easily drops out of sight. There are here no local questions, no neighborhood hatreds, no appealing graves. Happy California! happy, but inglorious. The railway approaches completion. A great activity of scientific mining, enterprises of scope and local development, urge the Western communities to action. The bonanza of Lagunitas gives Judge Hardin even greater local prominence. He establishes his residence at the old home in the Sierras.

With no trusted associates, he splits and divides the funds from the mine, placing them in varied depositories. He refrains from an undue appearance of wealth or improvement at the rancho itself. No one knows the aggregates, the net returns, save himself. Cunning old robber.

To identify himself with the interior and southern part of the State, he enters the higher body of the Legislature. His great experience and unflagging hospitalities make him at once a leader.

Identified with State and mining interests, he engages public attention. He ignores all contention, and drops the question of the Rebellion. A hearty welcome from one and all, proves that his commanding talents are recognized.

There are no relatives, no claims, no meddlesome legatees to question the disposition of Colonel Valois' estate. His trusteeship is well known, and his own influence is pre-eminent in the obscure District Court having control of the legal formalities.

Hardin is keenly watchful of all returning ex-Confederates who might have been witnesses of Maxime Valois' death. They do not appear. His possession is unchallenged. His downy couch grows softer daily.

He has received the family papers left by the departing padre. They are the baptismal papers of the little heiress. The last vouchers.

Hardin, unmoved by fear, untouched by sympathy, never thinks of the lowly grave before the ramparts of Atlanta. The man lies there, who appealed to his honor, to protect the orphaned child, but he is silent in death.

He decides to quietly strip the rancho of its great metallic wealth. He will hold the land unimproved, to be a showing in future years should trouble come as to the settlement of the estate.

With the foresight of the advocate, Hardin fears the Valois heirs of New Orleans. He must build up his defensive works in that quarter. From several returned "Colonels" and "Majors" he hears of the death of old Judge Valois.

The line of the family is extinct, save the boy in Paris, who has been lost sight of. A wandering artist.

A sudden impulse seizes him. He likes not the ominous silence of Natalie as to important matters.

Selecting one of his law clerks (now an employee of the estate), he sends him to Paris, amply supplied with funds, to look up the only scion left of the old family. He charges his agent to spare neither money nor time in the quest. A full and detailed report of Madame de Santos' doings and social surroundings is also ordered.

"Mingle in the circles of travelling Americans, spend a little money, and find out what you can of her private life," are his orders. He says nothing of the heiress.

In the gay season of 1866, Hardin, still bent on the golden quest in the hills, reads with some astonishment, the careful "precis" of his social spy. He writes:

"I have searched Paris all over. The old Confederate circles are scattered now. They are out of favor at the imperial court. Even Duke Gwin, the leader of our people, has departed. His Dukedom of Sonora has gone up with our Confederacy. From one or two attaches of the old Confederate agency, I learned that the boy Armand Valois is now sixteen or seventeen years old, if living. He was educated in one of the best schools here, and is an artist by choice. When his father died he was left without means. I understand he intended to make a living by selling sketches or copying pictures. I have no description of him. There are thousands of young students lost in this maze. I might walk over him in the Louvre and not know him. If you wish me to advertise in the journals I might do so."

"Fool," interjects Hardin, as he reads this under the vines at Lagunitas. "I don't care to look up an heir to Lagunitas. One is enough."

"Now for Madame de Santos: I have by some effort worked into the circle of gayety, where I have met her. She is royally beautiful. I should say about thirty-five. Her position is fixed as an 'elegante.'" Her turnout in the Bois is in perfect taste. She goes everywhere, entertains freely, and, if rumor is true, is very rich. She receives great attention, as they say she is guardian of a fabulously wealthy young girl at one of the convents here.

"Madame de Santos is very accomplished, and speaks Spanish, French, and English equally well. I have made some progress in her acquaintance, but since, by accident, she learned I was from California she has been quite distant with me. No one knows her past, here. It is supposed she has lived in Mexico, and perhaps California. The little feminine 'Monte Cristo' is said to be Spanish or Mexican. Madame Santos' reputation is absolutely unblemished. In all the circle of admirers she meets, she favors but one. Count Ernesto de Villa Rocca, an Italian nobleman, is quite the 'ami de maison.'

"I have not seen the child, save at a distance. Madame permits no one to meet her. She only occasionally drives her out, and invariably alone with herself.

"She visits the convent school regularly. She seems to be a vigilant wide-awake woman of property. She goes everywhere, opera, balls, theatres, to the Tuileries. She is popular with women of the best set, especially the French. She sees very few

Americans. She is supposed to be Southern in her sympathies. Her life seems to be as clear as a diamond. She has apparently no feminine weaknesses. If there is a sign of the future, it is that she may become 'Countess de Villa Rocca.' He is a very fine fellow, has all the Italian graces, and has been in the 'Guardia Nobile.' He is desperately devoted to Madame, and to do him justice, is an excellent fellow, as Italian counts go.

"By the way, I met old Colonel Joe Woods here. He entertained me in his old way. He showed me the sights. He has become very rich, and operates in New York, London, and Paris. He is quite a swell here. He is liberal and jolly. Rather a change from the American River bar, to the Jockey Club at Paris. He sends you remembrances.

"I shall wait your further orders, and return on telegraph. I cannot fathom the household mysteries of the Madame. When all Paris says a woman is 'dead square,' we need not probe deeper. There is no present sign of her marrying Villa Rocca, but he is the first favorite."

"So," muses the veteran intriguer Hardin, as he selects a regalia, "my lady is wary, cautious, and blameless. Danger signals these. I must watch this Villa Rocca. Is he a 'cavalier servente'? Can he mean mischief? She would not marry him, I know," he murmurs.

The red danger signal's flash shows to Hardin, Marie Berard standing by the side of Natalie and the two girls. Villa Rocca is only a dark shade of the background as yet.

He smiles grimly.

The clicking telegraph key invokes the mysterious cable. For two days Judge Philip paces his room a restless wolf.

His prophetic mind projects the snares which will bring them all to his feet. He will buy this soubrette's secrets.

A French maid's greed and Punic faith can be counted on always.

With trembling fingers he tears open the cipher reply from his spy. He reads with flaming eyes:

"Have seen girl; very knowing. Says she can tell you something worth one hundred thousand francs. Will not talk now. Money useless at present. She wants your definite instructions, and says, wait. Cable me orders."

Hardin peers through the grindstone, and evolves his orders. He acts with Napoleon's rapidity. His answer reads:

"Let her alone. Tell her to notify Laroyne & Co., 16 Rue Vivienne, when ready to sell her goods. Wait orders."

Hardin revolves in his busy brain every turn of fortune's wheel.

Has Natalie an intrigue?

Is she already secretly married? Is the heiress of Lagunitas dead?

The labors of his waking hours and the brandy bottle only tell him of an unfaithful woman's vagaries; a greedy lover's plots, or the curiosity of the dark-eyed maid, whose avarice is above her fidelity.

Bah! she will tattle. No woman can resist it; they all talk.

But this Italian cur; he must be watched.

The child! Pshaw; she is a girl in frocks. But Villa Rocca is a needy man of brains and nerve; he must be foiled.

Now, what is her game? Hardin must acknowledge that she is true to her trust, so far.

The Judge walks over to his telegraph office, for there is a post, telegraph, and quite a mining settlement now on the Lagunitas grant.

He sends a cable despatch to Paris to his agent, briefly:

"Stop work. Report acceptable. Come back. Take your time leisurely, East. Well pleased."

He does not want any misplaced zeal of his spy to alarm Natalie. As the year 1866 rolls on, the regular reports, business drafts and details as to Isabel Valois are the burden of the correspondence. Natalie's heart is silent. Has she one? She has not urged him to come back; she has not pressed the claims of her child. His agent returns and amplifies the general reports, but he has no new facts.

The clerk drops into his usual life. He is not curious as to the Madame. "Some collateral business of the Judge, probably," is his verdict.

While the stamps rattle away in the Lagunitas quartz mills, Judge Hardin takes an occasional run to the city by the bay. The legislative season approaches. Senator Hardin's rooms at the Golden Eagle are the centre of political power. Railroads are worming their way into politics. Franchises and charters are everywhere sought. Over the feasts served by Hardin's colored retainers, he cements friendships across old party lines.

As Christmas approaches in this year, the Judge receives a letter from Natalie de Santos which rouses him from his bed of roses. He steadies his nerves with a glass of the best cognac, as he reads this fond epistle:

I have waited for you to refer to the future of our child. I will not waste words. If you wished to make me happy, you would have, before now, provided for her. I do not speak of myself. You have been liberal enough to me. I am keeping up the position you indicated. My child is now old enough to ask meaning questions, to be informed of her place in the world and to be educated for it. You spoke of a settlement for her. If anything should happen to me, what would be her future? Isabel will be of course, in the future, a great lady. There is nothing absolutely my own. I am dependent on you. What I asked you, Philip, you have not given me: the name of wife. It is for her, not for myself, I asked it. I have made myself worthy of the position I would hold. You know our past. I wish absolutely now, to know my child's destiny. If you will not do the mother justice, what will you do for the child? Whose name shall she bear? What shall she have?

Philip, I beg you to act in these matters and to remember that, if I once was Hortense Duval, I now am NATALIE DE SANTOS.

Danger signals. Red and flaring they burn before Hardin's steady eyes. What does she mean? Is her last clause a threat? Woman! Perfidious woman!

Hardin tosses on a weary couch several nights before he can frame a reply. It is not a money question. In his proud position now, forming alliances daily with the new leaders of the State, he could not stoop to marry this woman. Never. To give the child a block sum of money would be only to give the mother more power. To settle an income on her might be a future stain on his name. Shall he buy off Natalie de Santos? Does she want money alone? If he did so, would not Villa Rocca marry her and he then have two blackmailers on his hands? To whom can he trust Isabel Valois if he breaks with Natalie? The girl is growing, and may ask leading questions. She must be kept away. In a few years she not only will be marriageable, but at eighteen her legal property must be turned over.

And to give up the Lagunitas quartz lead? Hardin's brow is gloomy. He uses days for a decision. The letter makes him very shaky in his mind. Is the "ex-Queen of the El Dorado" ready to strike a telling blow?

He remembers how tiger-like her rage when she drew her dagger over the hand of "French Charlie." She can strike at need, but what will be her weapon now?

He sets the devilish enginery of his brain at work. His answer to Natalie de Santos is brief but final:

"You may trust my honor. I shall provide a fund as soon as I can, to be invested as you direct, either in your name or the other. You can impart to the young person what you wish. In the meantime you should educate her as a lady. If you desire an additional allowance, write me. I have many burdens, and cannot act freely now. Trust me yet awhile."

Philip Hardin feels no twinge as he seals this letter. No voice from the grave can reach him. No proof exists in Natalie de Santos' hands to verify her story.

As for Lagunitas, and orphan Isabel, he pores over every paper left by the unsuspicious Padre Francisco. He smiles grimly. It was a missionary parish. Its records have been all turned over to him. He quietly destroys the whole mass of papers left at Lagunitas by the priest. As for the marriage papers of her parents and certificate of baptism of Isabel, he conceals them, ready for destruction at a moment's notice.

He will wait till the seven years elapse before filing legal proof of Maxime Valois' death.

Securing from the papers of the old mansion house, materials, old in appearance, he quietly writes up a bill of sale of the quartz lead known as the Lagunitas mine, to secure the forty thousand dollars advanced by him to Maxime Valois, dated back to 1861. Days of practice enable him to imitate the signature of Valois. He appends the manual witness of "Kaintuck" and "Padre Francisco." They are gone forever; one in the grave, one in a cloister.

This paper he sends quietly to record. It attracts no attention. "Kaintuck" is dead. Valois sleeps his last sleep. From a lonely cell in a distant French monastery, Padre Francisco will never hear of this.

As for Isabel Valois, he has a darker plot than mere theft and forgery, for the future.

The years to come will strengthen his possession and drown out all possible gossip.

Natalie de Santos must hang dependent on his bounty. He will not arm her with weapons against himself. He knows she will not return to face him in California. His power there is too great. If she dares to marry any one, her hold on him is lost. She must lie to hide her past. Hardin smiles, for he counts upon a woman's vanity and love of luxury. The veteran lawyer sums up the situation to himself. She is powerless. She dares not talk. Time softens down all passions. When safe, he will give the child some funds, but very discreetly.

And to bury the memory of Maxime Valois forever is his task.

Broadening his political influence, Hardin moves on to public prominence. He knows well he can bribe or buy judge and jury, suppress facts, and use the golden hammer in his hands, to beat down any attack. Gold, blessed gold!

The clattering stamps ring out merry music at Lagunitas as the months sweep by.

CHAPTER XV.

AN OLD PRIEST AND A YOUNG ARTIST.--THE CHANGELINGS.

As a thoroughfare of all nations, nothing excels the matchless Louvre. Though the fatal year of 1870 summons the legions of France under the last of the Napoleons to defeat, Paris, queen of cities, has yet to see its days of fire and flame. The Prussians thunder at its gates. It is "l'annee terrible. "Dissension and rapine within. The mad wolves of the Commune are yet to rage over the bloody paths of the German conqueror.

Yet a ceaseless crowd of strangers, a polyglot procession of all ages and sexes, pours through these wonderful halls of art.

In the sunny afternoons of the battle year, an old French priest wanders through these noble galleries. Pale and bowed, Francois Ribaut dreams away his waning hours among the priceless relics of the past. These are the hours of release from rosary and breviary. The ebb and flow of humanity, the labors of the copyists, the diverse types of passing human nature, all interest the padre.

He has waited in vain for responses to his frequent letters to Judge Hardin. Perhaps the Judge is dead. Death's sickle swings unceasingly. The little heiress may have returned to her western native land. He waits and marvels. He finally sends a last letter through the clergy at Mission Dolores. To this he receives a response that they are told the young lady has returned to America and is being educated in the Eastern States.

With a sigh Francois Ribaut abandons all hopes of seeing once more the child he had baptized, the orphaned daughter of his friend. She is now far from him. He feels assured he will never cross the wild Atlantic again.

Worn and weary, waiting the approach of old age, he yet participates, with a true Frenchman's patriotism, in the sorrows of "l'annee terrible." Nothing brightens the future! Human nature itself seems giving way.

All is disaster. Jacques Bonhomme's blood waters in vain his native fields. Oh, for the great Napoleon! Alas, for the days of 1805!

As he wanders among the pictures he makes friendly acquaintance with rising artist and humble imitator. The old padre is everywhere welcome. His very smile is a benediction.

He pauses one day at the easel of a young man who is copying a Murillo Madonna. Intent upon his work, the artist politely answers, and resumes his task. Spirited and artistic in execution, the copy betokens a rare talent.

Day after day, on his visits, the padre sees the glowing canvas nearing completion. He is strangely attracted to the resolute young artist.

Dark-eyed and graceful, the young painter is on the threshold of manhood. With seemingly few friends or acquaintances, he works unremittingly. Padre Francisco learns that he is a self-supporting art-student. He avows frankly that art copying brings him both his living and further education.

Francois Ribaut is anxious to know why this ardent youth toils, when his fellows are in the field fighting the invaders. He is astonished when the young man tells him he is an American.

"You are a Frenchman in your language and bearing," says the priest doubtfully.

The young artist laughs.

"I was educated here, mon pere, but I was born in Louisiana. My name is Armand Valois."

The old priest's eyes glisten.

"I knew an American named Valois, in California. He was a Louisianan also."

The youth drops his brush. His eyes search the padre's face. "His name?" he eagerly asks.

"He was called Maxime Valois," says the priest, Sadly. "He went into the Southern war and was killed."

The artist springs from his seat. Leading the priest to a recessed window-seat, he says, quietly:

"Mon pere, tell me of him. He was my cousin, and the last of my family. I am now the only Valois."

Padre Francisco overstays his hour of relaxation. For the artist learns of the heroic death of his gallant kinsman, and all the chronicles of Lagunitas.

"But you must come to me. I must see you often and tell you more," concludes the good old priest. He gives Armand his residence, a religious establishment near Notre Dame, where he can spend his days under the shadows of the great mystery-haunted fane.

Armand tells the priest his slender history.

Left penniless by his aged father's death, the whirlwind of the Southern war swept away the last of his property. Old family friends, scattered and poor, cannot help him. He has been his own master for years. His simple annals are soon finished. He tells of his heart comrade, Raoul Dauvray (his senior a few years), now fighting in the Army of the Loire. The priest learns that the young American remained, to be a son in the household, while Raoul, a fellow art-student of past years, has drawn his sword for France.

Agitated by the discovery, Padre Francisco promises to visit the young man soon. It seems all so strange. A new romance! Truly the world is small after all. Is it destiny or chance?

In a few weeks, Francois Ribaut is the beloved of that little circle, where Josephine Dauvray is the household ruler. Priest and youth are friends by the memory of the dead soldier of the Confederacy. Armand writes to New Orleans and obtains full details of the death, in the hour of victory, of the gallant Californian. His correspondent says, briefly, "Colonel Henry Peyton, who succeeded your relative in command of the regiment, left here after the war, for Mexico or South America. He has never been heard from. He is the one man who could give you the fullest details of the last days of your kinsman--if he still lives."

Thundering war rolls nearer the gates of Paris. The horrible days of approaching siege and present danger, added to the gloom of the national humiliation, make the little household a sad one. Padre Francisco finds a handsome invalid officer one day at the artist's home. Raoul Dauvray, severely wounded, is destined to months of inaction. There is a brother's bond between the two younger men. Padre Francisco lends his presence to cheer the invalid. Father and mother are busied with growing cares, for the siege closes in.

The public galleries are now all closed. The days of "decheance" are over. France is struggling out of the hands of tyranny under the invaders' scourge into the nameless horrors of the Commune.

It is impossible to get away, and unsafe to stay. The streets are filled with the mad unrest of the seething population. By the side of the young officer of the Garde Mobile, Francois Ribaut ministers and speeds the recovery of the chafing warrior. Thunder of guns and rattle of musketry nearer, daily, bring fresh alarms. Armand Valois has thrown away the palette and is at last on the ramparts with his brother artists, fighting for France. The boy has no country, for his blood is as true to the Lost Cause as the gallant cousin who laid down his life at Atlanta. He can fight for France, for he feels he has no other country now. It has been his foster-mother.

Bright and helpful, demure and neat-handed, is the little nurse, who is the life of the household. Padre Francisco already loves the child. "Louise Moreau" is a pretty, quiet little maiden of twelve. Good Josephine Dauvray has told the priest of the coming of the child. He listens to the whole story. He sighs to think of some dark intrigue, behind the mask of this poor child's humble history. He gravely warns Josephine to tell him all the details of this strange affair. The motherly care and protection of Josephine has rendered the shy child happy. She knows no home but her little nest with the Dauvrays. Her education is suited to her modest station in life. The substantial payments and furtive visits of the woman who is responsible for her, tell the priest there is here a mystery to probe.

Josephine casts down her eyes when Pere Francois asks her sternly if she has not traced the woman who is the only link between her charge and the past. Interest against duty.

"I have followed her, mon pere, but I do not know her home. She comes irregularly, sometimes on foot, sometimes in a carriage. I have always lost all traces. She must have friends here, but I cannot find them, for she was sent to us by others to give this child a home."

"This must be looked into," murmurs the priest.

He interrogates the soldier and also Armand when he returns from the lines, as the siege drags slowly on. They know nothing save the fact of the child's being friendless. It may be right; it may be wrong. "Voila tout." It's the way of Paris.

The priest is much disturbed in mind. Since his conversations with Armand

Valois he feels a vague unrest in his heart as to the young artist's rights in Lagunitas. Does none of that great estate go to Armand? Is this equitable? There must be some share of the domain, which would legally descend to him. In the days of the convalescence of Raoul Dauvray, the two friends of the soldier-artist, now waiting the orders for the great attack, commune as to his rights. It would not be well to disturb him with false hopes.

The gentle old priest tells Raoul the whole story of Lagunitas.

"Mon pere," says the sculptor, "I think there is something wrong with the affairs of that estate. This great Judge may wish you out of the way. He may wish to keep Armand out of his rights. He is deceiving you. It would be well, when brighter days come, that Armand should go to the western land and see this man."

"But he is poor," Raoul sighs, "and he cannot go."

"If he writes to the 'avocat,' the man will be on his guard."

Pere Francois takes many a pinch of snuff. He ponders from day to day. When the fatal days of the surrender of Paris come, Armand returns saddened and war-worn, but safe. The victorious columns of the great German "imperator" march under the Arc de Triomphe. Their bayonets shine in the Bois de Boulogne. Thundering cannon at Versailles bellow a salute to the new-crowned Emperor of Germany.

The days of the long siege have been dreadful. Privation, the streams of wounded, and the dull boom of the guns of the forts are sad witnesses of the ruin of war.

When to the siege and the shame of surrender, the awful scenes of the Commune are added, each day has a new trial. Raoul is well enough to be out, now. The two young men guard the household. Aristide Dauvray is gloomily helpless at his fireside. Armand busies himself in painting and sketching. Pere Francois' visits are furtive, for the priest's frock is a poor safeguard now. Already the blood of the two murdered French generals, Lecomte and Clement-Thomas, cries to heaven for vengeance against rash mutiny.

Raoul Dauvray foresees the downfall of the socialistic mob. After consultation, he decides to take a place where he can protect the little household when the walls are stormed. He escapes by night to the lines of the Versaillese.

For, maddened Paris is now fighting all France. In his capacity of officer, he can at once insure the personal safety of his friends when the city is taken.

The red flag floats on the Hotel de Ville. The very streets are unsafe. Starvation faces the circle around Aristide Dauvray's hearth. Mad adventurers, foolish dreamers, vain "bourgeois" generals, head the Communists. Dombrowski, Cluseret, Flourens, the human tigers Ferre and Lullier, Duval, Bergeret, and Eudes, stalk in the stolen robes of power. Gloomy nights close sad and dreary days. From Issy and Vanvres huge shells curve their airy flight, to carry havoc from French guns into French ranks.

Hell seems to have vomited forth its scum. Uncanny beings lurk at the corners. Wild with cognac and absinthe, the unruly mob commits every wanton act which unbridled wickedness can suggest. Good men are powerless, and women exposed to every insult. Public trade is suspended. Robbery and official pillage increase. The creatures of a day give way quickly to each other. Gallant Rossell, who passed the Prussian lines to serve France, indignantly sheathes his sword. He is neither a Nero nor a mountebank.

Alas, for the talented youth! a death volley from his old engineer troops awaits him at the Buttes de Chaumont. To die the dishonored death of a felon, a deserter!

Alas, for France: bright of face and hard of heart! Tigress queen, devouring your noblest children.

While Thiers proclaims the law, he draws around him the wreck of a great army. A bloody victory over demented brethren hangs awful laurels on the French sword: De Gallifet, Vinoy, Ducrot, L'Admirault, Cissey, D'Aurelle de Palladines, Besson and Charrette surround the unlucky veteran, Marshal McMahon, Duc de Magenta. General Le Flo, the Minister of War, hurls this great army against the two hundred and fifty-two battalions of National Guards within the walls of Paris. These fools have a thousand cannon.

Down in the Bois de Boulogne, the fighting pickets pour hissing lead into the bosoms of brothers. From the heights where the brutal Prussian soldiery grinned over the blackened ruins of the ill-starred Empress Eugenie's palace of St. Cloud, the cannon of the Versaillese rain shot and shell on the walls of defenceless Paris.

Pere Francois is a blessing in these sad and weary days. Clad "en bourgeois," he smuggles in food and supplies. He cheers the half-distracted Josephine. Armand Valois keeps the modest little maiden Louise, fluttering about the home studio which he shares with Raoul. Their casts and models, poor scanty treasures, make their modest sanctum a wonder to the girl. Her life's romance unfolds. Art and dawning love move her placid soul. The days of wrangling wear away. An occasional smuggled note from Raoul bids them be of cheer. Once or twice, the face of Marie Berard is seen at the door for a moment.

Thrusting a packet of notes in Josephine's hand, she bids her guard the child and keep her within her safe shelter.

The disjointed masses of Communists wind out on April 3d of the terrible year of '71, to storm the fortified heights held by the Nationalists.

Only a day before, at Courbevoie, their bayonets have crossed in fight. Mont Valerien now showers shells into Paris. Bergeret, Duval, and Eudes lead huge masses of bloodthirsty children of the red flag, into a battle where quickening war appalls the timid Louise. It makes her cling close to Armand. The human family seems changed into a pack of ravening wolves. Pouring back, defeated and dismayed, the Communists rage in the streets. The grim fortress of Mont Valerien has scourged the horde of Bergeret. Duval's column flees; its defeated leader is promptly shot by the merciless Vinoy. Fierce De Gallifet rages on the field--his troopers sabring the socialists without quarter.

Flourens' dishonored body lies, riddled with bullets, on a dung heap at St. Cloud.

Eudes steals away, to sneak out and hide his "loot" in foreign lands. Red is the bloody flail with which McMahon thrashes out Communism.

The prisoned family, joined by Pere Francois, now a fugitive, day by day shudder at the bedlam antics and reign of blood around them.

Saintly Archbishop Darboy dies under the bullets of the Communists. His pale face appeals to God for mercy.

Vengeance is yet to come. The clergy are now hunted in the streets! Plunder and rapine reign! Orgies and wild wassail hold a mocking sway in the courts of death. Unsexed women, liberated thieves, and bloodthirsty tramps prey on the unwary, the wounded, or the feeble. On April 30th, the great fort of Issy falls into the hands of the government. Blazing shells rain, in the murky night air, down on Paris. Continuous fighting from April 2d until May 21st makes the regions of Auteuil, Neuilly, and Point du Jour a wasted ruin.

Frenzied fiends drag down the Colonne Vendome where the great Corsican in bronze gazed on a scene of wanton madness never equalled. Not even when drunken Nero mocked at the devastation of the imperial city by the Tiber, were these horrors rivalled.

Down the beautiful green slopes into the Bois de Boulogne, the snaky lines of sap and trench bring the octopus daily nearer to the doomed modern Babylon. Flash of rifle gun and crack of musketry re-echo in the great park. It is now shorn of its lovely trees, where man and maid so lately held the trysts of love. A bloody dew rains on devoted Paris.

A fateful Sunday is that twenty-first of May when the red-mouthed cannon roar from dawn till dark. At eventide, the grim regulars bayonet the last defenders of the redoubts at the Point du Jour gates. The city is open to McMahon.

The lodgment once made, a two nights' bombardment adds to the horrors of this living hell.

On the twenty-third, Montmartre's bloody shambles show how merciless are the stormers. Dombrowski lies dead beside his useless guns. All hope is lost. Murder and pillage reign in Paris.

Behind their doors, barricaded with the heavier furniture, the family of Aristide Dauvray invoke the mercy of God. They are led by Pere Francois, who thinks the awful Day of Judgment may be near. Humanity has passed its limits. Fiends and furies are the men and women, who, crazed with drink, swarm the blood-stained streets.

In their lines, far outside, the stolid Prussians joke over their beer, as they learn of the wholesale murder finishing red Bellona's banquet. "The French are all crazy." They laugh.

The twenty-fourth of May arrives. Paris is aflame. Battle unceasing, storm of shell, rattle of rifles, and cannon balls skipping down the Champs Elysees mark this fatal day. A deep tide of human blood flows from the Madeleine steps to the Seine. The river is now filled with bodies. Columns of troops, with heavy tramp and ringing platoon volleys, disperse the rallying squads of rebels, or storm barricade after barricade. Squadrons of cavalry whirl along, and cut down both innocent and guilty.

After three awful days more, the six thousand bodies lying among the tombs of Pere la Chaise tell that the last stronghold of the Commune has been stormed. Belleville and Buttes de Chaumont are piled with hundreds of corpses. The grim sergeants' squads are hunting from house to house, bayoneting skulking fugitives, or promptly shooting any persons found armed.

The noise of battle slowly sinks away. Flames and smoke soar to the skies: the burnt offering now; the blood offering is nearly over.

Thirty superb palaces of the municipality are in flames. Under Notre Dame's sacred roof, blackened brands and flooded petroleum tell of the human fiends' visit.

The superb ruins of the Tuileries show what imperial France has been. Its flaming debris runs with streams of gold, silver, and melted crystal.

Banks, museums, and palaces have been despoiled. Boys and old crones trade costly jewels in the streets for bread and rum. The firing parties are sick of carnage.

Killing in cold blood ceases now, from sheer mechanical fatigue.

On the twenty-eighth, a loud knocking on the door of the house brings Aristide Dauvray to the door. A brief parley. The obstructions are cleared. Raoul is clasped in his father's arms. Safe at last. Grim, bloody, powder-stained, with tattered clothes, he is yet unwounded. A steady sergeant and half-dozen men are quickly posted as a guard. They can breathe once more. This help is sadly needed. In a darkened room above, little Louise Moreau lies in pain and silence.

Grave-faced Pere Francois is the skilful nurse and physician. A shell fragment, bursting through a window, has torn her tender, childish body.

Raoul rapidly makes Armand and his father known to the nearest "poste de garde." He obtains protection for them. His own troops are ordered to escort drafts of the swarming prisoners to the Orangery at Versailles. Already several thousands of men, women, and children, of all grades, are penned within the storied walls. Here the princesses of France sported, before that other great blood frenzy, the Revolution, seized on the Parisians.

With a brief rest, he tears himself away from a mother's arms, and departs for the closing duties of the second siege of Paris. The drawing in of the human prey completes the work.

Safe at last! Thank God! The family are able to look out to the light of the sun again. They see the glittering stars of night shine calmly down on the slaughter house, the charnel of "Paris incendie." The silence is brooding. It seems unfamiliar after months of siege, and battle's awful music.

In a few days the benumbed survivors crawl around the streets. Open gates enable provisions to reach the half-famished dwellers within the walls. Over patched bridges, the railways pour the longed-for supplies into Paris. Fair France is fruitful, even in her year of God's awful vengeance upon the rotten empire of "Napoleon the Little."

Pere Francois lingers by the bedside of the suffering girl. She moans and tosses in the fever of her wound. Her mind is wandering.

A slender, girlish arm wanders out of the coverlid often. She lies, with flushed cheeks and eyes strangely bright.

Tenderly replacing the innocent's little hands under the counterpane, Francois Ribaut starts with sudden surprise.

He fastens his gaze eagerly on the poor girl's left arm.

Can there be two scars like this?

The sign of the cross.

He is amazed. The little Spanish girl, from whose baby arm he extracted a giant poisonous thorn, bore a mark like this,--a record of his own surgery.

At far Lagunitas, he had said, playfully to Dolores Valois:

"Your little one will never forget the cross; she will bear it forever."

For the incision left a deep mark on baby Isabel Valois' arm.

The old priest is strangely stirred. He has a lightning flash of suspicion. This girl has no history; no family; no name. Who is she?

Yet she is watched, cared for, and, even in the hours of danger, money is provided for her. Ah, he will protect this poor lamb. But it is sheer madness to dream of her being his lost one. True, her age is that of the missing darling. He kneels by the bed of the wounded innocent, and softly quavers a little old Spanish hymn. It is a memory of his Californian days.

Great God! her lips are moving; her right hand feebly marks his words, and as he bends over the sufferer, he hears "Santa Maria, Madre de Dios."

Francois Ribaut falls on his knees in prayer. This nameless waif, in her delirium, is faltering words of the cradle hymns, the baby lispings of the heiress of Lagunitas.

A light from heaven shines upon the old priest's brow.

Is it, indeed, the heiress!

He can hear his own heart beat.

The wearied, hunted priest feels the breezes from the singing pines once more on his fevered brow. Again he sees the soft dark eyes of Dolores as they close in death, beautiful as the last glances of an expiring gazelle. Her dying gaze is fixed on the crucifix in his hand.

"I will watch over this poor lonely child," murmurs the old man, as he throws himself on his knees, imploring the protection of the Virgin Mother mild.

Sitting by the little sufferer, softly speaking the language of her babyhood, the padre hears word after word, uttered by the girl in the "patois" of Alta California.

And now he vows himself to a patient vigil over this defenceless one. Silence, discretion, prudence. He is yet a priest.

He will track out this mysterious guardian.

In a week or so, a normal condition is re-established in conquered Paris. Though the yellowstone houses are pitted with the scourge of ball and mitraille, the streets are safe. Humanity's wrecks are cleared away. Huge, smoking ruins tell of the mad barbarity of the floods of released criminals. The gashed and torn beauties of the Bois de Boulogne; battered fortifications, ruined temples of Justice, Art, and Commerce, and the blood-splashed corridors of the Madeleine are still eloquent of anarchy.

The reign of blood is over at last, for, in heaps of shattered humanity, the corses of the last Communists are lying in awful silence in the desecrated marble wilderness of Pere la Chaise.

The heights of Montmartre area Golgotha. Trade slowly opens its doors. The curious foreigner pokes, a human raven, over the scenes of carnage. Disjointed household organizations rearrange themselves. The railway trains once more run regularly. Laughter, clinking of glasses, and smirking loiterers on the boulevards testify that thoughtless, heartless Paris is itself once more. "Vive la bagatelle."

Francois Ribaut at last regains his home of religious seclusion. Louise is convalescent, and needs rest and quiet. There is no want of money in the Dauvray household. The liberal douceurs of Louise Moreau's mysterious guardian, furnish all present needs.

"Thank God!" cries Pere Frangois, when he remembers that he has the fund intact, which he received from the haughty Hardin.

He can follow the quest of justice. He has the means to trace the clouded history of this child of mystery. A nameless girl who speaks only French, yet in her wandering dreams recalls the Spanish cradle-hymns of lost Isabel.

Already the energy of the vivacious French is applied to the care of what is left, and the repair of the damages of the reign of demons. The rebuilding of their loved "altars of Mammon" begins. The foreign colony, disturbed like a flock of gulls on a lonely rock, flutters back as soon as the battle blast is over. Aristide Dauvray finds instant promotion in his calling. The hiding Communists are hunted down and swell the vast crowd of wretches in the Orangery.

Already, all tribunals are busy. Deportation or death awaits the leaders of the revolt.

Raoul Dauvray, whose regiment is returned from its fortnight's guard duty at Versailles, is permitted to revisit his family. Peace now signed--the peace of disgrace--enables the decimated Garde Mobile to be disbanded. In a few weeks, he will be a sculptor again. A soldier no more. France needs him no longer in the field.

By the family Lares and Penates the young soldier tells of the awful sights of Versailles. The thousand captured cannon of the Communists, splashed with human blood, the wanton ruin of the lovely grounds of the Bois, dear to the Parisian heart, and all the strange scenes of the gleaning of the fields of death show how the touch of anarchy has seared the heart of France. Raoul's adventures are a nightly recital.

"I had one strange adventure," says the handsome soldier, knocking the ashes from his cigar. "I was on guard with my company in command of the main gate of the Orangery, the night after the crushing of these devils at Montmartre. The field officer of the day was away. Among other prisoners brought over, to be turned into that wild human menagerie, was a beautiful woman, richly dressed. She was arrested in a carriage, escaping from the lines with a young girl. Their driver was also arrested. He was detained as a witness.

"She had not been searched, but was sent over for special examination. She was in agony. I tried to pacify her. She declared she was an American, and begged me to send at once for the officers of the American Legation. It was very late. The best I could do was to give her a room and put a trusty sergeant in charge. I sent a messenger instantly to the American Legation with a letter. She was in mortal terror of her life. She showed me a portmanteau, with magnificent jewels and valuables. I calmed her terrified child. The lady insisted I should take charge of her jewels and papers. I said:

"'Madame, I do not know you.'

"She cried, 'A French officer is always a gentleman.'

"In the morning before I marched off guard, a carriage with a foreign gentleman and one of the attaches of the United States Embassy, came with a special order from General Le Flo for her release. She had told me she was trying to get out of Paris with her child, who had been in a convent. It was situated in the midst of the fighting and had been cut off. Passing many fearful risks, she was finally arrested as 'suspicious.'

"She persists in saying I saved her life. She would have been robbed, truly, in that mad whirl of human devils penned up there under the chassepots of the guards on the walls. Oh! it was horrible."

The young soldier paused.

"She thanked me, and was gracious enough not to offer me a reward. I am bidden to call on her in a few days, as soon as we are tranquil, and receive her thanks."

"I have never seen such beauty in woman," continues the officer.

"A Venus in form; a daughter of the South, in complexion,--and her thrilling eyes!"

Gentle Louise murmurs, "And the young lady?"

"A Peri not out of the gates of Paradise," cries the enthusiastic artist.

"What is she? who is she?" cried the circle. Even Pere Francois lifted his head in curiosity. Raoul threw two cards on the table. A dainty coronet with the words,

{Madame Natalie de Santos, 97 Champs Elysees.}

appeared on one; the other read,

{Le Comte Ernesto Villa Rocca, Jockey Club.}

"And you are going to call?" said Armand.

"Certainly," replies Raoul. "I told the lady I was an artist. She wishes to give me a commission for a bust of herself. I hope she will; I want to be again at my work. I am tired of all this brutality."

That looked-for day comes. France struggles to her feet, and loads the Teuton with gold. He retires sullenly to where he shows his grim cannons, domineering the lovely valleys of Alsace and the fruitful fields of Lorraine.

Louise Moreau is well now. The visits of her responsible guardian are resumed. Adroit as a priest can be, Pere Francois cannot run down this visitor. Too sly to call in others, too proud to use a hireling, in patience the priest bides his time.

Not a word yet to the fair girl, who goes singing now around the house. A few questions prove to Francois Ribaut that the girl has no settled memory of her past. He speaks, in her presence, the language of the Spaniard. No sign of understanding. He describes his old home in the hills of Mariposa. The placid child never raises her head from her sewing.

Is he mistaken? No; on her pretty arm, the crucial star still lingers.

"How did you get that mark, my child?" he asks placidly.

"I know not, mon pere; it has been there since I can remember."

The girl drops her eyes. She knows there is a break in her history. The earliest thing she can remember of her childhood is sailing--sailing on sapphire seas, past sculptured hills. Long days spent, gazing on the lonely sea-bird's flight.

The priest realizes there is a well-guarded secret. The regular visitor does not speak TO the child, but OF her.

Pere Francois has given Josephine his orders, but there is no tripping in the cold business-like actions of the woman who pays.

Pere Francois is determined to take both the young men into his confidence. He will prevent any removal of this child, without the legal responsibility of some one. If they should take the alarm? How could he stop them? The law! But how and why?

Raoul Dauvray is in high spirits. After his regiment is disbanded, he is not slow to call at the splendid residence on the Champs Elysees. In truth, he goes frequently.

The splendors of that lovely home, "Madame de Santos"' gracious reception, and a royal offer for his artistic skill, cause him to feel that she is indeed a good fairy.

A modelling room in the splendid residence is assigned him. Count Villa Rocca, who has all an Italian's love of the arts, lingers near Natalie de Santos, with ill-concealed jealousy of the young sculptor. To be handsome, smooth, talented, jealous--all this is Villa Rocca's "metier." He is a true Italian.

CHAPTER XVI.

NEARING EACH OTHER.--THE VALOIS HEIRS.

Paris is a human hive. Thousands labor to restore its beauty. The stream of life ebbs and flows once more on the boulevards. The galleries reopen. Armand labors in the Louvre. He finished the velvet-eyed Madonna, copied after Murillo's magic hand. He chafes under Raoul's laurels. The boy would be a man. Every day the sculptor tells of the home of the wealthy Spaniard. The girl is at her convent again. Raoul meets Madame Natalie "en ami de maison."

He tells of Count Villa Rocca's wooing. Marriage may crown the devotion of the courtly lover.

The bust in marble is a success. Raoul is in the flush of glory. His patroness directs him to idealize for her "Helen of Troy."

Armand selects as his next copy, a grand inspiration of womanly beauty. He, too, must pluck a laurel wreath.

Under the stress of emulation, his fingers tremble in nervous ardor. He has chosen a subject which has myriad worshippers.

Day by day, admirers recognize the true spirit of the masterpiece.

Throngs surround the painter, who strains his artistic heart.

A voice startles him, as the last touches are being laid on:

"Young man, will you sell this here picture?"

"That depends," rejoins Armand. His use of the vernacular charms the stranger.

"Have you set a price?" cries the visitor, in rough Western English.

"I have not as yet," the copyist answers.

He surveys the speaker, a man of fifty years, whose dress and manner speak of prosperity in efflorescent form.

The diamond pin, huge watch-chain, rich jewelled buttons, and gold-headed cane, prove him an American Croesus.

"Well, when it's done, you bring it to my hotel. Everyone knows me. I will give you what you want for it. It's way up; better than the original," says the Argonaut, with a leer at its loveliness.

He drops his card on the moist canvas. The nettled artist reads,

{{Colonel Joseph Woods, California. Grand Hotel.}}

on the imposing pasteboard.

The good-humored Woods nods.

"Yes sir, that's me. Every one in London, Paris, and New York, knows Joe Woods.

"Good at the bank," he chuckles.

"What's your name?" he says abruptly.

Armand rises bowing, and handing his card to the stranger:

"Armand Valois."

Woods whistles a resounding call. The "flaneurs" start in astonishment.

"Say; you speak English. By heavens! you look like him. Did you ever know a Colonel Valois, of California?" He gazes at the boy eagerly.

"I never met him, sir, but he was the last of my family. He was killed in the Southern war."

"Look here, young man, you pack up them there paint-brushes, and send that picture down to my rooms. You've got to dine with me to-night, my boy. I'll give you a dinner to open your eyes."

The painter really opens his eyes in amazement.

"You knew my relative in California?"

"We dug this gold together," the stranger almost shouts, as he taps his huge watch-chain. "We were old pardners," he says, with a moistened eye.

There was a huskiness in the man's voice; not born of the mellow cognac he loved.

No; Joe Woods was far away then, in the days of his sturdy youth. He was swinging the pick once more on the bars of the American River, and listening to its music rippling along under the giant pines of California.

The young painter's form brought back to "Honest Joe" the unreturning brave, the chum of his happiest days.

Armand murmurs, "Are you sure you wish this picture?"

"Dead sure, young man. You let me run this thing. Now, I won't take 'no.' You just get a carriage, and get this all down to my hotel. You can finish it there. I've got to go down to my bank, and you be there to meet me. You'll have a good dinner; you bet you will. God! what a man Valois was. Dead and gone, poor fellow!

"Now, I'm off! don't you linger now."

He strides to his carriage, followed by a crowd of "valets de place." All know Joe Woods, the big-souled mining magnate. He always leaves a golden trail.

Armand imagines the fairy of good luck has set him dreaming. No; it is all true.

He packs up his kit, and sends for a coupe. Giving orders as to the picture, he repairs to the home of the Dauvrays for his toilet. He tells Pere Francois of his good fortune.

"Joe Woods, did you say," murmurs the priest. "He was a friend of Valois. He is rich. Tell him I remember him. He knows who I am. I would like to see him."

There is a strange light in Francois Ribaut's eye. Here is a friend; perhaps, an ally. He must think, must think.

The old priest taps his snuff-box uneasily.

In a "cabinet particulier" of the Grand Hotel restaurant, Woods pours out to the young man, stories of days of toil and danger; lynching scenes, gambling rows, "shooting scrapes," and all kaleidoscopic scenes of the "flush days of the Sacramento Valley."

Armand learns his cousin's life in California. He imparts to the Colonel, now joyous over his "becassine aux truffes" and Chambertin, the meagre details he has of the death of the man who fell in the intoxicating hour of victory on fierce Hood's fiercest field.

Colonel Joe Woods drains his glass in silence.

"My boy," he suddenly says, "Valois left an enormous estate; don't you come in anywhere?"

"I never knew of his will," replies Armand. "I want you, Colonel, to meet my old friend Pere Francois, who was the priest at this Lagunitas. He tells me, a Judge

Hardin has charge of all the property."

Joe Woods drops the knife with which he is cutting the tip of his imperial cigar.

"By Heavens! If that old wolf has got his claws on it, it's a long fight. I'll see your Padre. I knew him. Now, my boy," says Colonel Joe, "I've got no wife, and no children," he adds proudly.

"I'll take you over to California with me, and we'll see old Hardin. I'm no lawyer, but you ought to hear of the whole details. We'll round him up. Let's go up to my room and look at your picture."

Throwing the waiter a douceur worthy of his financial grade, the new friends retire to the Colonel's rooms.

Here the spoils of the jeweler, the atelier, and studio, are strangely mingled. Joe Woods buys anything he likes. A decanter of Bourbon, a box of the very primest Havanas, and a business-like revolver, lying on the table, indicate his free and easy ways.

Letters in heaps prove that "mon brave Colonel Woods" is even known to the pretty free-lances who fight under the rosy banner of Venus Victrix.

In hearty terms, the Californian vents his enthusiasm.

"By the way, my boy, I forgot something." He dashes off a check and hands it to the young painter.

"Tell me where to send for a man to frame this picture in good shape," he simply says.

He looks uneasily at the young man, whose senses fail him when he sees that the check is for five thousand francs.

"Is that all right?" he says cheerfully, nudging Armand in the ribs. "Cash on delivery, you know. I want another by and by. I'll pick out a picture I want copied. I'm going to build me a bachelor ranch on Nob Hill: Ophir Villa." He grins over some pet "deal" in his favorite Comstock. Dulcet memories.

For Colonel Joe Woods is a man of "the Golden Days of the Pacific." He too has "arrived."

The boy murmurs his thanks. "Now look here, I've got to run over to the Cafe Anglais, and see some men from the West. You give me your house number. I'll come in and see the padre to-morrow evening.

"Stay; you had better come and fetch me. Take dinner with me to-morrow, and we'll drive down in a hack."

The Colonel slips his pistol in its pocket, winks, takes a pull at the cocktail of the American, old Kentucky's silver stream, and grasps his gold-headed club. He is ready now to meet friend or foe.

Joy in his heart, good humor on his face, jingling a few "twenties," which he carries from habit, he grasps a handful of cigars, and pushes the happy boy out of the open door.

"Oh! never mind that; I've got a French fellow sleeping around here some-where," he cries, as Armand signals the sanctum is unlocked. "He always turns up if any one but HIMSELF tries to steal anything. He's got a patent on that," laughs the "Croesus of the American River."

Armand paints no stroke the next day. He confers with Pere Francois. He is paralyzed when the cashier of the "Credit Lyonnais" hands him five crisp one-thou-sand-franc notes. Colonel Joe Woods' check is of international potency. It is not, then, a mere dream.

When the jovial Colonel is introduced to the family circle he is at home in ten minutes. His good nature carries off easily his halting French. He falls into sudden friendship with the young soldier-sculptor. He compliments Madame Josephine. He pleases the modest Louise, and is at home at once with Padre Francisco.

After a friendly chat, he says resolutely:

"Now, padre, you and I want to have a talk over our young friend here. Let us go up to his room a little."

Seated in the boy's studio, Woods shows the practical sense which carried him to the front in the struggle for wealth.

"I tell you what I'll do," he says. "I'm going out to the coast in a month or so. I'll look this up a little. If I want our young friend here, I'll send you a cable, and you can start him out to me. My banker will rig him out in good style. Just as well he comes under another name. See? Padre, you take a ride with me to-morrow. We will talk it all over."

The Californian's questions and sagacity charm the padre. He is now smoking one of those blessed "Imperiales." An innocent pleasure.

They rise to join the circle below. A thought animates the priest.

Yes, he will confer with the clear-headed man and tell him of the child below, whose pathway is unguarded by a parent's love.

Around the frugal board Colonel Joe enters into the family spirit. He insists on having Raoul come to him for a conference about his portraiture in marble.

"I have just finished a bust of Madame de Santos, the beautiful Mexican lady," remarks Raoul.

Colonel Joe bounds from his chair. "By hokey, young man, you are a bonanza. Do you know her well?" he eagerly asks.

The sculptor tells how he saved her from the bedlam horrors of the Orangery.

The miner whistles. "Well, you control the stock, I should say. Now, she's the very woman, Gwin, and Erlanger, and old Slidell, and a whole lot told me about. I want you to take me up there," he says.

"I will see Madame de Santos to-morrow," remarks Raoul, diplomatically.

"Tell her I'm a friend of her Southern friends. They're scattered now. Most of them busted," says Wood calmly. "I must see her. See here, padre; we'll do the thing in style. You go and call with me, and keep me straight." The priest assents.

In gayest mood the Colonel bids Raoul come to him for this most fashionable call. Claiming the padre for breakfast and the ride of the morrow, he rattles off to his rooms, leaving an astounded circle.

Golden claims to their friendly gratitude bound them together.

Colonel Joe has the "dejeuner a deux" in his rooms. He says, "More homelike, padre, you know," ushering the priest to the table. Under the influence of Chablis, the Californians become intimate.

Raoul arrives with news that Madame de Santos will be pleased to have the gentlemen call next day in the afternoon. After an arrangement about the bust, the horses, champing before the doors, bear the elders to the Bois, now beginning to abandon its battle-field appearance.

Long is their conference on that ride. Pere Francois is thoughtful, as he spends his evening hour at dominoes with Aristide Dauvray. His eyes stray to fair Louise, busied with her needle. At last, he has a man of the world to lean on, in tracing up this child's parentage. Raoul and Armand are deep in schemes to enrich Joe's queer collection, the nucleus of that "bachelor ranch," "Ophir Villa."

In all the bravery of diamonds and goldsmithing the Westerner descends from his carriage, at the doors of Madame de Santos, next day.

Pale-faced, aristocratic Pere Francois is a foil to the "occidental king." Mind and matter.

Waiting for the Donna, the gentlemen admire her salon.

Pictures, objets d'art, dainty bibelots, show the elegance of a queen of the "monde."

"Beats a steamboat," murmurs Colonel Joe, as the goddess enters the domain.

There is every grace in her manner. She inquires as to mutual friends of the "Southern set." Her praises of Raoul are justified in the beautiful bust, a creation of loveliness, on its Algerian onyx pedestal.

Colonel Joe Woods is enchanted. He wonders if he has ever seen this classic face before.

"I drive in the Bois," says madame, with an arch glance.

She knows the Californian is a feature of that parade, with his team. Paris rings with Colonel Joe's exploits.

"No poor stock for me," is Colonel Joe's motto.

With a cunning glance in his eyes, the miner asks: "Were you ever in California, madame?"

Her lips tremble as she says, "Years ago I was in San Francisco."

Colonel Joe is thoughtful. His glance follows madame, who is ringing a silver bell.

The butler bows.

"I shall not drive this afternoon," she says.

With graceful hospitality, she charms Pere Francois. Chat about the Church and France follows.

The gentlemen are about to take their leave. Madame de Santos, observing that Pere Francois speaks Spanish as well as French, invites him to call again. She would be glad to consult him in spiritual matters.

Colonel Joe speaks of California, and asks if he may be of any service.

"I have no interests there," the lady replies with constraint.

Passing into the hall, Pere Francois stands amazed as if he sees a ghost.

"What's the matter, padre?" queries Colonel Joe as they enter their carriage.

"Did you see that maid who passed us as we left the salon?" remarks the padre.

"Yes, and a good-looking woman too," says the Californian.

"That woman is the guardian of Louise Moreau," the padre hastily replies.

"Look here! What are you telling me?" cries the Colonel.

"There's some deviltry up! I'm sorry I must leave. But how do you know?" he continues.

The priest tells him about artful Josephine, whose womanly curiosity has been piqued. He has seen this person on her visits. Useless to trace her. Entering an arcade or some great shop, she has baffled pursuit. Through the Bois, the friends commune over this mystery.

"I'll fix you out," says Woods, with a shout. "I've got a fellow here who watched some people for me on a mining deal. I'll rip that household skeleton all to pieces. We'll dissect it!"

He cries: "Now, padre, I'm a-going to back you through this affair," as they sit in his rooms over a good dinner. Colonel Joe has sent all his people away. He wants no listeners. As he pours the Cliquot, he says, "You give me a week and I'll post you. Listen to me. You can see there is an object in hiding that child. Keep her safely guarded. Show no suspicion. You make friends with the lady. Leave the maid dead alone. Take it easy, padre; we'll get them. I'll tell my bankers to back you up. I'll take you down; I'll make you solid.

"All I fear is they will get frightened and take her off. You people have got to watch her. They'll run her off, if they suspect. Poor little kid."

"It's strange," says the miner; "they could have put this poor little one out of the way easy. But they don't want that. Want her alive, but kept on the quiet. I suppose there's somebody else," he mutters.

"By Jove! that's it. There's property or money hanging on her existence. Now, padre, I'll talk plain. You priests are pretty sly. You write your people about this child. I'll see you have money. My banker will work the whole municipality of Paris for you."

"That's it; we've got it." The miner's fist makes the glasses rattle, as he quaffs his wine.

"Don't lose sight of her a minute. Don't show your hand."

The priest rolls home in Joe's carriage. He busies himself the next days with going to the bank, conferring with his fellows, and awaking the vigilance of Josephine.

It is left to the priest and his ally from the ranks of "Mammon" to follow these tangled threads. The younger men know nothing, save the injunctions to Josephine.

Ten days after this visit, Colonel Joe, who has run over to London, where he closed some financial matters of note, sends post-haste to Pere Francois this note:

"Come up, padre. I've got a whole history for you. It will make your eyes open. I want you to talk to the detective."

Even the Californian's horses are not quick enough to-day for the priest.

Ushered in, he finds Colonel Joe on the broad grin.

Accepting a cigar, his host cries, "We've struck it rich. A mare's nest. Now, Vimont, give my friend your report."

Joe Woods smokes steadily, as Jules Vimont reads from his note-book:

"Madame Natalie de Santos arrived in Paris with two young girls, one of whom is at the Sacre-Coeur under the name of Isabel Valois; the other is the child who is visited by Marie Berard, her maid. She is called Louise Moreau."

Pere Francois listens to this recital. The detective gives a description of the beautiful stranger, and at length.

Joe interrogates. The priest gravely nods until the recital is finished. Vimont shuts his book with a snap and disappears, at a nod from the miner. The friends are alone.

Pere Francois is silent. His face is pale. Joe is alarmed at his feeling. Forcing a draught of Bourbon on the padre, Joe cries, "What is the matter?"

"I see it now," murmurs the priest. "The children have been changed. For what object?"

He tells Woods of the proofs gained in days of Louise's illness.

"Your little friend is the heiress of Lagunitas?" Woods asks.

"I am sure of it. We must prove it."

"Leave that to me," bursts out Joe, striding the room, puffing at his cigar.

"How will you do it?" falters the priest.

"I will find the father of the other child," Joe yells. "I am going to California. I will root up this business. I have a copy of Vimont's notes. You write me all you remember of this history. Meanwhile, not a word. No change in your game. You make foothold in that house on the Elysees.

"There was no railroad when these people came here. I will get the lists of passengers and steamer reports, I have friends in the Pacific Mail."

Joe warms up. "Yes, sir. I'll find who is responsible for that extra child. The man who is, is the party putting up for all this splendor here. I think if I can stop the money supplies, we can break their lines. I think my old 'companero,' Judge Hardin, is the head-devil of this deal.

"It's just like him.

"Now, padre, I have got something to amuse me. You do just as I tell you, and we'll checkmate this quiet game.

"We are not on the bedrock yet, but we've struck the vein. Don't you say a word to a living soul here.

"I'll have that maid watched, and tell Vimont to give you all the particulars of her cuttings-up.

"She's not the master-mind of this. She has never been to the convent. There's a keynote in keeping these girls apart. I think our handsome friend, Madame de Santos, is playing a sharp game." In two days he has vanished.

In his voyage to New York and to the Pacific, Joe thinks over every turn of this intrigue. If Hardin tries to hide Armand Valois' fortune, why should he dabble in the mystery of these girls?

Crossing the plains, where the buffalo still roam by thousands, Woods meets in the smoking-room many old friends. A soldierly-looking traveller attracts his attention. The division superintendent makes Colonel Peyton and Colonel Woods acquainted. Their friendship ripens rapidly. Joe Woods, a Southern sympathizer, has gained his colonelcy by the consent of his Western friends. It is a brevet of financial importance. Learning his friend is a veteran of the "Stars and Bars," and a Virginian, the Westerner pledges many a cup to their common cause. To the battle-torn flag of the Confederacy, now furled forever.

As the train rattles down Echo Canyon, Peyton tells of the hopes once held of a rising in the West.

Woods is interested. When Peyton mentions "Maxime Valois," the Croesus grasps his hand convulsively.

"Did you serve with him?" Joe queries with eagerness. "He was my pardner and chum."

"He died in my arms at Peachtree Creek," answers Peyton.

Joe embraces Peyton. "He was a game man, Colonel."

Peyton answers: "The bravest man I ever saw. I often think of him, in the whirl of that struggle for De Gress's battery. Lying on the sod with the Yankee flag clutched in his hand, its silk was fresh-striped with his own heart's blood. The last sound he heard was the roar of those guns, as we turned them on the enemy."

"God! What a fight for that battery!" The Californian listens, with bated breath, to the Virginian. He tells him of the youthful quest for gold.

The war brotherhood of the two passes in sad review. Peyton tells him of the night before Valois' death.

Joe Woods' eyes glisten. He cries over the recital. An eager question rises to his lips. He chokes it down.

As Peyton finishes, Woods remarks:

"Peyton, I am going to get off at Reno, and go to Virginia City. You come with me. I want to know about Valois' last days."

Peyton is glad to have a mentor in the West. He has gained neither peace nor fortune in wandering under the fringing palms of Latin America.

Toiling up the Sierra Nevada, Woods shows Peyton where Valois won his golden spurs as a pathfinder.

"I have a favor to ask of you, Peyton," says Joe. "I want to hunt up that boy in Paris. I'm no lawyer, but I think he ought to have some of this great estate. Now, Hardin is a devil for slyness. I want you to keep silent as to Valois till I give you the word. I'll see you into some good things here. It may take time to work my game. I don't want Hardin to suspect. He's an attorney of the bank. He counsels the railroad. He would spy out every move."

"By the way, Colonel Woods," Peyton replies, "I have the papers yet which were found on Valois' body. I sealed them up. They are stained with his blood. I could not trust them to chances. I intended to return them to his child. I have never examined them."

Joe bounds from his seat. "A ten-strike! Now, you take a look at them when we reach 'Frisco.' If there are any to throw a light on his affairs, tell me. Don't breathe a word till I tell you. I will probe the matter. I'll break Hardin's lines, you bet." The speculator dares not tell Peyton his hopes, his fears, his suspicions.

San Francisco is reached. Peyton has "done the Comstock." He is tired of drifts, gallery, machinery, miners, and the "laissez-aller" of Nevada hospitality. The comfort of Colonel Joe's bachelor establishment places the stranger in touch with the occidental city.

Received with open arms by the Confederate sympathizers, Peyton is soon "on the stock market." He little dreams that Joe has given one of his many brokers word to carry a stiff account for the Virginian. Pay him all gains, and charge all losses to the "Woods account."

Peyton is thrilled with the stock gambling of California Street. Every one is mad. Servants, lawyers, hod carriers, merchants, old maids, widows, mechanics, sly wives, thieving clerks, and the "demi-monde," all throng to the portals of the "Big Board." It is a money-mania. Beauty, old age, callow boyhood, fading manhood, all chase the bubble values of the "kiting stocks."

From session to session, the volatile heart of San Francisco throbs responsive to the sliding values of these paper "stock certificates."

Woods has departed for a fortnight, to look at a new ranch in San Joaquin. He does not tell Peyton that he lingers around Lagunitas. He knows Hardin is at San Francisco. A few hours at the county seat. A talk with his lawyer in Stockton completes Joe's investigations. No will of Maxime Valois has ever been filed. The estate is held by Hardin as administrator after "temporary letters" have been renewed. There are no accounts or settlements. Joe smiles when he finds that Philip Hardin is guardian of one "Isabel Valois," a minor. The estate of this child is nominal. There is no inventory of Maxima Valois' estate on file. County courts and officials are not likely to hurry Judge Philip Hardin.

On the train to San Francisco, Woods smokes very strong cigars while pondering if he shall hire a lawyer in town.

"If I could only choose one who would STAY bought when I BOUGHT> him, I'd give a long price," Joe growls. With recourse to his great "breast-pocket code," the Missourian runs over man after man, in his mind. A frown gathers on his brow.

"If I strike a bonanza, I may have to call in some counsel. But I think I'll have a few words with my friend Philip Hardin."

Woods is the perfection of rosy good-humor, when he drags Hardin away from his office next day to a cosey lunch at the "Mint."

"I want to consult you, Judge," is his excuse. Hardin, now counsel for warring giants of finance, listens over the terrapin and birds, to several legal posers regarding Joe's affairs. Woods has wide influence. He is a powerful friend to placate. Hardin, easy now in money matters, looks forward to the United States Senate. Woods can help. He is a tower of strength.

"They will need a senator sometime, who knows law, not one of those obscure MUD-HEADS," says Hardin to himself.

Colonel Joe finishes his Larose. He takes a stiff brandy with his cigar, and carelessly remarks:

"How's your mine, Judge?"

"Doing well, doing well," is the reply.

"Better let me put it on the market for you. You are getting old for that sort of bother."

"Woods, I will see you by and by. I am trustee for the Valois estate. He left no will, and I can't give a title to the ranch till the time for minor heirs runs out. So I am running the mine on my own account. Some outside parties may claim heirship."

"Didn't he leave a daughter?" says Woods.

"There is a girl--she's East now, at school; but, between you and me, old fellow, I don't know if she is legitimate or not. You know what old times were."

Colonel Joe grins with a twinge of conscience. He has had his "beaux-jours."

"I will hold on till the limitation runs out. I don't want to cloud the title to my mine, with litigation. It comes through Valois."

"You never heard of any Eastern heirs?" Joe remarks, gulping a "stiffener" of brandy.

"Never," says Hardin, reaching for his hat and cane. "The Judge died during the war. I believe his boy died in Paris. He has never turned up. New Orleans is gone to the devil. They are all dead."

"By the way, Judge, excuse me." Woods dashes off a check for Hardin. "I want to retain you if the 'Shooting Star' people fool with my working the 'Golden Chariot;' I feel safe in your hands."

Even Hardin can afford to pocket Joe's check. It is a prize. Golden bait, Joseph.

Woods says "Good-bye," floridly, to his legal friend. He takes a coupe at the door. "Cute old devil, Hardin; I'll run him down yet," chuckles the miner. Joe is soon on his way to the Pacific Mail Steamship office.

Several gray-headed officials greet the popular capitalist.

He broaches his business. "I want to see your passenger lists for 1865." He has notes of Vimont's in his hand. While the underlings bring out dusty old folios, Joe distributes his pet cigars. He is always welcome.

Looking over the ancient records he finds on a trip of the Golden Gate, the following entries:

Madame de Santos,
Miss Isabel Valois,
Marie Berard and child.

He calls the bookkeeper. "Can you tell about these people?"

The man of ink scans the entry. He ponders and says:

"I'll tell you who can give you all the information, Colonel Joe. Hardin was lawyer for this lady. He paid for their passages with a check. We note these payments for our cash references. Here is a pencil note: 'CK Hardin.' I remember Hardin coming himself."

"Oh, that's all right!" says the Argonaut.

An adjournment of "all hands," to "renew those pleasing assurances," is in order.

"Ah, my old fox!" thinks Woods. "I am going to find out who gave Marie Berard that other child. But I won't ask YOU. YOUR TIME IS TOO VALUABLE, Judge Philip Hardin."

He gives his driver an extra dollar at the old City Hall.

Joe Woods thinks he is alone on the quest. He knows not that the Archbishop's secretary is reading some long Latin letters, not three blocks away, which are dated in Paris and signed Francois Ribaut. They refer to the records of the Mission Dolores parish. They invoke the aid of the all-seeing eye of the Church as to the history and rights of Isabel Valois.

Pere Ribaut humbly begs the protection of his Grace for his protege, Armand Valois, in case he visits California.

Philip Hardin, in his office, weaving his golden webs, darkened here and there with black threads of crime, is deaf to the cry of conscience. What is the orphaned girl to him? A mere human puppet. He hears not the panther feet of the avengers of wrong on his trail. Blind insecurity, Judge Hardin.

Woods has seized Captain Lee, and taken him out of his sanctum to the shades of the "Bank Exchange."

The great detective captain, an encyclopedia of the unwritten history of San Francisco, regards Woods with a twinkle in his gray eye. The hunted, despairing criminal knows how steady that eye can be. It has made hundreds quail.

Lee grins over his cigar. Another millionaire in trouble. "Some woman, surely." The only question is "What woman?"

The fair sex play a mighty part in the mysteries of San Francisco.

"Lee, I want you to hunt up the history of a woman for me," says the old miner.

The captain's smile runs all over his face. "Why, Colonel Joe!" he begins.

"Look here; no nonsense!" says Joseph, firmly. "It's a little matter of five thousand dollars to you, if you can trace what I want."

There is no foolishness in Lee's set features. He throws himself back, studying his cigar ash. That five thousand dollars is an "open sesame."

"What's her name?"

Joseph produces his notes.

"Do you remember Hardin sending some people to Panama, in '65?" begins the Colonel. "Two women and two children. They sailed on the GOLDEN GATE."

"Perfectly," says the iron captain, removing his cigar. "I watched these steamers for the government. He was a Big Six in the K.G.C., you remember, Colonel Joe?"

Joe winces; that Golden Circle dinner comes back, when he, too, cheered the Stars and Bars.

"I see you do remember," says Lee, throwing away his cigar. "Now be frank, old man. Tell me your whole game."

Woods hands him the list of the passengers. He is keenly eying Lee.

"Who was that Madame de Santos?" he says eagerly.

"Is it worth five thousand to know?" says the detective, quietly.

"On the dead square," replies Joe, "Cash ready."

"Do you remember the 'Queen of the El Dorado'?" Lee simply says.

"Here! Great God, man!" cries Lee, for Joe Woods' fist comes down on the table. Flying cigars, shattered glasses, and foaming wine make a rare havoc around.

"By God!" shouts the oblivious Joe," the woman Hardin killed 'French Charlie' for."

"The same," says Lee, steadily, as he picks some splintered glass out of his goatee. "Joe, you can add a suit of clothes to that check."

"Stop your nonsense," says the happy Joe, ringing for the waiter to clear away the wreck of his cyclonic fist. "The clothes are O.K."

"Where did she come from to take that boat?" demands Woods.

"From Hardin's house," says Lee.

A light breaks in on Colonel Joe's brain.

"And that woman with her?"

"Was her maid, who stayed with her from the time she left the El Dorado, and ran the little nest on the hill. The mistress never showed up in public."

"And the child who went with the maid?" Joe's voice trembles.

"Was Hardin's child. Its mother was the 'Queen of the El Dorado.'"

Woods looks at Lee.

"Can you give me a report, from the time of the killing of 'French Charlie' down to the sailing?"

"Yes, I can," says the inscrutable Lee.

"Let me have it, to-morrow morning. Not a word to Hardin."

"All right, Colonel Joe," is the answer of silent Lee.

Joseph chokes down his feelings, orders a fresh bottle of wine, some cigars, and calls for pen and ink.

While the waiter uncorks the wine, Joe says: "What do you pay for your clothes, Lee?"

"Oh, a hundred and fifty will do," is the modest answer. "That carries an overcoat."

Joe laughs as he beautifies a blank check with his order to himself, to pay to himself, five thousand one hundred and fifty dollars, and neatly indorses it, "Joseph Woods." "I guess that's the caper, Captain," he says. This "little formality" over, the wine goes to the right place THIS TIME.

"Now I don't want to see you any more till I get your reminiscences of that lady," remarks Joe, reaching for his gold-headed club.

"On time, ten o'clock," is the response of the police captain.

"Have you seen her since, Joe? She was a high stepper," muses the Captain. He has been a great connoisseur of loveliness. Many fair ones have passed under his hands in public duty or private seance.

"That's my business," sturdy Joe mutters, with an unearthly wink. "You give me back my check, old man, and I'll tell you what *I* know."

Lee laughs. "I'm not so curious, Colonel."

They shake hands, and the gray old wolf goes to his den to muse over what has sent Joe Woods on a quest for this "fallen star."

Lee wastes no time in mooning. The check is a "pleasing reality." The memories of Hortense Duval are dearer to Joe than to him. His pen indites the results of that watchful espionage which covers so many unread leaves of private life in San Francisco.

There is an innocent smile on Woods' face when he strolls into his own office and asks Peyton to give him the evening in quiet. Strongly attracted by the Virginian, Woods has now a double interest in his new friend.

In the sanctum, Woods says, "Peyton, I am going to tell you a story, but you must first show me the papers you have kept so long of poor Valois."

Peyton rises without a word. He returns with a packet.

"Here you are, Woods. I have not examined them yet. Now, what is it?"

"You told me Valois made a will before he died, Peyton," begins Woods.

"He did, and wrote to Hardin. He wrote to the French priest at his ranch."

Woods starts. "Ha, the damned scoundrel! Go on; go on." Joe knows Pere Francois never got that letter. "I read those documents. His letter of last wishes to Hardin. When I was in Havana, I found Hardin never acknowledged the papers."

Woods sees it all. He listens as Peyton tells the story.

"We have to do with a villain," says Joe. "He destroyed the papers or has hidden them. Colonel, open this packet." Joe's voice is solemn.

With reverent hand, Peyton spreads the papers before the miner. There are stains upon them. Separating them, he arranges them one by one. Suddenly he gives a gasp.

"My God! Colonel Joe, look there!"

Woods springs to his side.

It is a "message from the dead."

Yes, lying for years unread, between the last letters of his wife and the tidings of her death, is an envelop addressed:

Major Henry Peyton,
Fourteenth Louisiana Inf'y,
C.S.A."

Tears trickle through Peyton's fingers, as he raises his head, and breaks the seal.

"Read it, Major," says Woods huskily. He is moved to the core of his heart. It brings old days back.

Peyton reads:

Atlanta--In the field,
July 21, 1864.

My Dear Peyton:--I am oppressed with a strange unrest about my child! I do not fear to meet death to-morrow. I feel it will take me away from my sadness. I am ready. Our flag is falling. I do not wish to live to see it in the dust. But I am a father. As I honor you, for the brotherhood of our life together, I charge you to watch over my child. Hardin is old; something might happen to him. I forgot a second appointment in the will; I name you as co-executor with him. Show him this. It is my dying wish. He is a man of honor. I have left all my estate to my beloved child, Isabel Valois. It is only right; the property came by my marriage with my wife, her dead mother. In the case of the death of my child, search out the heirs of Judge Valois and see the property fairly divided among them. Hardin is the soul of honor, and will aid you in all. I desire this to be a codicil to my will, and regarded as such. I could not ask you to ride out again for me this wild night before my last battle.

The will you witnessed, is the necessary act of the death of my wife. If you live through the war, never forget

Your friend and comrade, MAXIME VALOIS.

P.S. If you go to California, look up Joe Woods. He is as true a man as ever breathed, and would be kind to my little girl. Padre Francisco Ribaut married me at Lagunitas to my Dolores. Good-bye and good-night. M.V.

The men gaze at each other across the table, touched by this solemn voice sweeping down the path of dead years. That lonely grave by the lines of Atlanta seemed to have opened to a dead father's love. Peyton saw the past in a new light. Valois' reckless gallantry that day was an immolation. His wife's death had unsettled him.

Joe Woods' rugged breast heaved in sorrow as he said, "Peyton, I will stand by that child. So help me, God! And he thought of me at the last--he thought of me!" The old miner chokes down a rising sob. Both are in tears.

"Look here, Colonel!" said Woods briskly. "This will never do! You will want to cheer up a little, for your trip, you know."

"Trip?" says the wondering Virginian.

"Why, yes," innocently remarks Joseph Woods. "You are going to New Orleans to look up about the Valois boy. Then you are to see those bankers at Havana, and get proof before the Consul-General about the documents. I want you to send your affidavit to me. I've got a lawyer in New York, who is a man. I'll write him. You can tell him all. I'm coming on there soon. After you get to New York from Havana, you will go to Paris and stay there till I come."

Peyton smiles even in his sadness. "That's a long journey, but I am yours, Colonel. Why do I go to Paris?"

"You are going to answer the letter of that dead man," impressively remarks Joseph.

"How?" murmurs Peyton.

"By being a father to his lonely child and watching over her. There's two girls there. You can keep an eye on them both. I'll trap this old scoundrel here. You've got to leave this town. He might suspect YOU when I start MY machinery.

"I'll plow deep here. I'll meet you in New York. Now, I want you to take to-morrow's train. I'll run your stock account, Colonel Henry," Woods remarks, with a laugh.

The next day, Peyton speeds away on his errand after receiving the old miner's last orders. His whispered adieu was: "I'm going to stand by my dead pardner's kid, for he thought of me at the last."

CHAPTER XVII.

WEAVING SPIDERS.--A COWARD BLOW.--MARIE BERARD'S DOOM.

Peyton's good-bye rings in Woods' ears as the train leaves. The boxes and parcels forced on the Confederate veteran, are tokens of his affection. The cognac and cigars are of his own selection. Joe's taste in creature comforts is excellent, and better than his grammar.

On the ferry, Joe surveys San Francisco complacently from the steamer.

"I've got those documents in the vaults. I'll have Peyton's evidence. I rather fancy Captain Lee's biography will interest that dame in Paris. I will prospect my friend Hardin's surroundings. He must have some devil to do his dirty work. I will do a bit of 'coyote work' myself. It's a case of dog eat dog, here."

Joseph classes all underhand business as "coyote work." He appreciates the neatness with which that furtive Western beast has taken his boots, soap, his breakfast and camp treasures under his nose.

Invincible, invisible, is the coyote.

"By Heavens! I'll make that old wolf Hardin jump yet!" Joseph swears a pardonable oath.

After writing several telling letters to the Padre and Vimont, he feels like a little stroll. He ordered Vimont to guard Louise Moreau at any cost. "No funny business," he mutters.

"If she's the girl, that scoundrel might try to remove her from this world," thinks Joseph. "As for the other girl, he's got a tiger cat to fight in the 'de Santos.'"

Colonel Woods beams in upon the clerks of Judge Hardin. That magnate is absent. The senatorial contest is presaged by much wire-pulling.

"I don't see the young man who used to run this shebang," carelessly remarks the Croesus.

"Mr. Jaggers is not here any longer," smartly replies his pert successor, to whom the fall of Jaggers was a veritable bonanza.

"What's the matter with him?" says Woods. "I wanted him to do a job of copying for me."

The incumbent airily indicates the pantomime of conveying the too frequent Bourbon to his lips.

"Oh, I see! The old thing," calmly says Woods. "Fired out for drinking."

The youth nods. "He is around Montgomery Street. You 'most always will catch him around the 'old corner' saloon."

Joseph Woods is familiar with that resort of bibulous lawyers. He wanders out aimlessly.

While Barney McFadden, the barkeeper, surveys Colonel Joseph swallowing his extra cocktail, he admires himself in the mirror. He dusts off his diamond pin with a silk handkerchief.

"Jaggers! Oh, yes; know him well. In back room playing pedro. Want him?"

Woods bows. The laconic Ganymede drags Jaggers away from his ten-cent game.

Impelled by a telegraphic wink, Barney deftly duplicates the favorite tipple of the Californian. The Golden State has been sustained in its growth, by myriads of cocktails. It is the State coat of arms.

"Want to see me? Certainly, Colonel." Jaggers is aroused.

In a private room, Jaggers wails over his discharge. His pocket is his only fear. Otherwise, he is in Heaven. His life now, is all "Cocktails and poker!" "Poker and cocktails!" It leaves him little time for business. Woods knows his man--a useful tool.

"Look here, Jaggers; I know your time is valuable." Jaggers bows gravely; he smells a new twenty-dollar piece; it will extend his "cocktail account." "I want you to do some business for me." Jaggers looks stately.

"I'm your man, Colonel," says Jaggers, who is, strange to say, very expert in his line. The trouble with Jaggers is, the saloon is not near enough to Judge Hardin's office. The OFFICE should be in the SALOON. It would save useless walking.

"I want you to search a title for me," says Colonel Joe, from behind a cloud of smoke. Jaggers sniffs the aroma. Joseph hands him several "Excepcionales."

Jaggers becomes dignified and cool. "Is there money in it, Colonel?" he says, with a gleam of his ferret eyes.

"Big money," decisively says Woods.

"I'm very busy now," objects Jaggers. He thinks of his ten-cent ante in that pedro game.

"I want you to give me your idea of the title to the Lagunitas mine. I am thinking of buying in," continues Joe. "I'll give you five hundred dollars, in cold twenties, if you tell me what you know."

"How soon?" Jaggers says, with a gasp.

"Right off!" ejaculates Woods, banging the bell for two more cocktails.

Jaggers drains the fiery compound. He whispers with burning breath in Woods' ears:

"Make it a cool thousand, and swear you'll look out for me. I'll give the thing dead away. You know what a son-of-a-gun Hardin is?"

Woods bows. He DON'T know, but he is going to find out. "I'll give you a job in my mine (the Golden Chariot), as time-keeper. You can keep drunk all your life, except at roll-call. If Hardin hunts you up there, I'll have the foreman pitch him down the shaft. Is this square?"

"Honor bright!" says Jaggers, extending his palm. "Honor bright!" says Joseph, who dares not look too joyous.

Jaggers muses over another cocktail. "You go to the bank, and get a thousand dollars clean stuff. Give me a coupe. I'll give you the things you want, in half an hour. I've got 'em stowed away. Don't follow me!"

Woods nods, and throws him a double-eagle. "I'll be here when you come back. Keep sober till we're done. I'll give you a pass to Virginia City, so you can finish your drunk in high altitudes. It's healthier, my boy!" Joe winks.

Jaggers is off like a shot. Colonel Joseph walks two blocks to the bank. He returns with fifty yellow double-eagles.

"Got to fight coyote style to catch a coyote!" is the murmur of Colonel Woods to his inward monitor. "It's for the fatherless kid."

"Barney," impressively says Joseph, "make me a good cocktail this time! Send 'em in, ANY WAY, when that young man returns. His life is insured. *I* have to work for a living. Make one for yourself. YOU are responsible."

Barney's chef d'oeuvre wins a smile from the genial son of Missouri. As the last drops trickle down his throat, Jaggers enters. He has had external cocktails. He is flushed, but triumphant.

"Colonel, you're a man of honor. There's your stuff." He throws an envelope on the table.

Joseph Woods opens the packet. "Just count that, young man, while I look at these."

He peruses the papers handed him, with interest. Jaggers follows him.

"This is all you have. Anything else in the office?" says Woods.

"Not a scratch. Colonel, I thought they would come in handy." Jaggers' work is done.

"Take care of your money, my lad. It is yours," says Woods. He rings for Barney, and indites a note to his foreman at the "Golden Chariot." "You better get up there, to-night, Jaggers," he says, handing him the note and a pass. "Your appointment is only good for that train. You give that note to Hank Daly. He'll supply you all the whiskey you want, free. By the way, the boys up there play poker pretty well. Now you keep cool, or you'll get shot as well as lose your money. Don't you forget to stay there, if it's ten years till I want you. Daly will have orders for you.

"If you come back here, Hardin will kill you like a dog, if he finds this out."

"And you?" murmurs Jaggers, who is imbibing the stirrup cup.

"Oh, I'll look out for that!" remarks cheerful Joe Woods. Armed with substantial "persuaders," Jaggers leaves with an agent of Barney's. He has orders to see Jaggers and his "baggage," started for Virginia City.

Jaggers beams. Joe Woods never drops a friend. His future smiles before him. Exit Jaggers.

Woods reads the documents. One is a press copy of a letter dated January, 1864, addressed to Colonel Maxime Valois, from Hardin, asking him to sell him the quartz claims on the Lagunitas grant.

The answer of Valois is written while recovering from his wounds. It reads:

"TALLULAH, GEORGIA, March 1, 1864.

"MY DEAR HARDIN: I have your letter, asking me to sell you the quartz leads on the Lagunitas grant. I am still suffering from my wound, and must be brief.

"I cannot do this. My title is the title of my wife. I have no right to dispose of her property by inheritance, without her consent. She has my child to look after. As the ranch income may fail some day, I will not cut off her chances to sell. It is her property. I would not cloud it. I will join my regiment soon. If the war ends and I live to return, I will arrange with you. I have no power to do this, now, as my wife would have to join in the sale. I will not ask her to diminish the value of the tract. I leave no lien on this property. My wife and child have it free from incumbrance if I die.

"Address me at Atlanta, Georgia.

"YOURS, MAXIME VALOIS."

"I think I hold four aces now, Mr. Philip Hardin," says Woods, contemplating himself in the mirror over the bar as he settles with the gorgeous Barney.

"By the way," remarks Woods, "Barney; if that young man owes you a bill, send it around to my office." Barney escorts his visitor to the door, bowing gratefully. Woods departs in a quandary.

"I guess I'll gather up all my documents, and take a look over things. New York is the place for me to get a square opinion."

When Woods reaches New York he meets Peyton, successful in his tour for evidence. On consultation with Judge Davis, his adviser, Woods sends Peyton to Tallulah. It is likely Valois' papers may be found, for the Colonel "joined" hurriedly on the last advance of Sherman. Colonel Joseph imparts his ideas to his counsel. A certified copy of the transfer recorded by Hardin, of the Lagunitas mine, is sent on by Jaggers, directed in his trip by Hank Daly from the mine.

In five days a despatch from Tallulah gladdens the miner, who longs for Paris:

"Found and examined baggage. Original letter in my hands. Coming with all. Many other papers.

"PEYTON."

On the Virginian's arrival Judge Davis instructs the friends. Woods insists on Peyton taking joint charge of the quest for the orphan's fortune.

"Hardin is responsible under his trusteeship. You can't force Peyton on him as co-executor. He has concealed the will. A suit now would warn the villain and endanger the child's life. Take the certified copy of the transfer to Paris. Get the priest's deposition that the document is forged; then guard the girl as if she were your life. In a few years the heiress will be entitled to claim her estate. Keep the child near Paris, but change her residence often. Watch the maid and Madame de Santos. Follow them to California. Produce the girl you claim to be the heiress. I will give you a letter to an advocate in Paris, who will close up the proof. Beware of Hardin! If he suspects, the child's life may be in danger!"

"I'll kill him myself if there is any foul play!" roars Joe Woods.

"My dear Colonel, that would not bring the child back," remarks Judge Davis, smiling at his handsome counsel fee. "Count on me! Use the cable."

On the Atlantic the guardians agree on their duties. "I will interview Madame de Santos when I close some business in London," says Woods grimly.

Peyton, with credentials to Padre Francisco, speeds from Liverpool to Paris. He arrives none too soon.

Philip Hardin's villany strikes from afar!

Judge Hardin, passing the county seat, on his way to the mine, looks in to obtain his annual tax papers. A voluble official remarks:

"Going to sell your mine, Judge?"

"Certainly not, sir," replies the would-be Senator, with hauteur.

"Excuse me. You sent for certified copies of the title. We thought you were putting it on the market."

Hardin grows paler than his wont. Some one has been on the trail. He asks no questions. His cipher-book is at San Francisco. Who is on the track? He cannot divine. The man applying was a stranger who attracted no attention. The Judge telegraphs to the mine for his foreman to come to San Francisco. He returns to his house on the hill. From his private safe he extracts the last letters of Natalie de Santos.

Since her urgent appeal, she has been brief and cold. She is waiting. Is this her stroke? He will see. Has anyone seen the child and made disclosures? His heart flutters. He must now placate Natalie. The child must be quickly removed from Paris. He dare not give a reason. No, but he can use a bribe.

After several futile attempts he pens this cipher:

Remove child instantly to Dresden. Telegraph your address on arrival. Definite settlement as you wished. Remember your promise. Directions by mail. Imperative.

PHILIP.

Hardin chafes anxiously before a reply reaches him. When he reads it, he rages like a fiend. It clearly reads:

I will not obey. Marry me first. Come here. Keep your oath. I will keep my promise. A settlement on the other child is no safeguard to me. She must have a name. Letters final. Useless to telegraph. HORTENSE.

When Hardin's rage subsides, he reviews the situation in his palace. He is safe for years from an accounting, yet it is coming on. If he brings the heiress to California, it will precipitate it. Secret plans for the Senate of the United States are now maturing. Marriage with Hortense. Impossible. His friends urge his giving his name to an ambitious lady of the "blue blood" of his Southern home. She is a relative of the head of the Democratic capitalists. This is a "sine qua non." The lady has claims on these honors. It has been a secret bargain to give his hand in return for that seat. Hortense talks madness. Never.

As for facing her, he dare not. He has established her. She is too subtle to risk herself out of the lines she has found safe. Who can be the "Deus ex machina"?

Ah, that Italian meddler, Villa Rocca! Hardin weaves a scheme. He will wait her letters. If the Italian is his enemy, he will lure him to California and then----

Ah, yes, till then, patience--the patience of the tiger crouching at the water-pool for his coming prey.

Peyton loses no time in Paris. He reaches the home of Aristide Dauvray. He is welcomed by the circle. The young artists are busy with brush and modelling tool. Woods' patronage has been a blessing. The fame of his orders has been extended by the exhibition of the works ordered by him. His bankers have directed the attention of the travelling Americans to the young man.

Louise Moreau is no longer a bud, but an opening rose. So fair is she, so lovely, that Armand feels his heart beat quicker when the girl nears his canvas to admire his skill. By the direction of Pere Francois, she leaves the house no more for her lessons. There is a secret guard of loving hearts around her.

Pere Francois meets Peyton with open arms. They are to be joint guardians over the innocent child of destiny.

At Peyton's hotel, the men commune. It is not strange that the ex-Confederate is comfortably settled opposite the Dauvray mansion! In an exchange of opinion with the able Josephine, it is agreed that one of the young men or the Colonel shall be always at hand.

Woods meditates a "coup de maitre." He intends, on his arrival, to remove the girl Louise where no malignity of Hardin can reach her, to some place where even Marie Berard will be powerless. He will force some one to show a hand. Then, God keep the villain who leaves his tree to fight in the open! It is war to the death. Woods directs Peyton to use his bankers and the police, telegraphing him at London. He has a fear they have been followed to Europe. The bankers understand that Peyton and the priest are Woods' ambassadors.

Marie Berard comes no more to the home of her charge. Her letters are sent by a commissionaire. Peyton reads in this a danger signal. The soldier is on the watch for treachery. His quiet habits are easily satisfied. He has his books, daily journals, and also French lessons from charming Louise.

It is sunny splendor at the house on the Champs Elysees, where Natalie de Santos moves in her charmed circle of luxury. While Peyton waits for the "Comstock Colonel," an anxious woman sits in her queenly boudoir.

Natalie's beauty is ravishing. The exquisite elegance of her manner is in keeping with the charms of the shining loveliness which makes her a cynosure in the "Bois."

Face to face with a dilemma, the fair "chatelaine" racks her brain for a new expedient. Her woman's wit is nonplussed.

Villa Rocca DEMANDS, URGES, PLEADS, SUES for marriage. Is it love? Of all her swains he is the only one who touches her heart. At his approach, her tell-tale pulse beats high. She dare not yet quit Hardin. There is a campaign before her. To force Hardin to marry her, even secretly, is the main attack. He is now old. Then, to establish her daughter as the heiress of Lagunitas. After Hardin's death, marriage with Villa Rocca. That is the goal. But how to restrain his lover-like ardor.

She smiles at her reflection in the glass. She knows "the fatal gift of beauty." It is another woman than the "queen of the gambling hell" who smiles back at her. The pearls on her neck rise and fall. Hardin! Ah, yes; his possible treachery! Would he dare to take the convent pupil away from her? Perhaps.

A devilish smile plays on her lips. She will let him steal his own child; the other, the REAL Lady of Lagunitas, he never shall know. Gods! If he should be aware of it. It must be prevented. Whom can she trust? No one.

Villa Rocca? Triumph shines in her eyes! She must definitely promise him marriage in these happy years, and give him the child as a gage. He can hide her in his Italian hills. He really has a bit of a castle under the olive-clad hills of Tuscany.

But Marie Berard. She must outwit that maid. When the child is gone, Marie's power ceases. No one will ever believe her. A few thousand francs extra will satisfy the greedy soubrette.

Seizing her pen, she sends a note to the club where baccarat and billiards claim Villa Rocca's idle hours. He meets her in the Bois de Boulogne, now splendid in transplanted foliage. His coupe dismissed, they wander in the alleys so dear to lovers. There is triumph in her face as they separate. A night for preparation; next day, armed with credentials in "billets de banque," Villa Rocca will lure the girl to her mysterious guardian who will be "sick" near Paris. Once under way, Villa Rocca will not stop till the girl is in his Italian manor.

With bounding heart, he assents. He has now Natalie's promise to marry him. They are one in heart.

"I am yours to the death," he says.

While Natalie sips her chocolate next morning, a carriage draws up before Aristide Dauvray's home. Josephine is busied with the household. Louise, singing like a lark, gayly aids her foster-mother. Aristide is far away. He toils at the new structures of beauty. Arm in arm, the young artists are taking a long stroll.

A gentleman of elegant appearance descends, with anxious visage. The peal of the bell indicates haste. Josephine receives her visitor. He curtly explains his visit. The guardian of Louise Moreau needs her instant presence. She is ill, perhaps dying. In her excitement, Josephine's prudence is forgotten. To lose the income from the child, to hazard the child's chances of property. "But the child must go: at once!" Josephine is awed and flurried. As she hastily makes preparation, a ray of suspicion darts through her mind. Who is this messenger?

"I think I had better accompany you," cries Josephine. Then, "her house," to be left to only one feeble old servant.

"Ah, ciel! It is terrible."

"Madame, we have no time to lose. It is near the train time. We will telegraph.

You can follow in two hours," the stranger remarks, in silken voice.

The visitor urges. The girl is cloaked and bonneted. Josephine loses her head. "One moment,"--she rushes for her hat and wrap; she will go at once, herself.

As she returns, there is a muffled scream at the door of the coupe.

"Mon Dieu!" Josephine screams. "My child! my Louise!" The coupe door is closing.

A strong voice cries to the driver, "Allez vite!"

As "Jehu" is about to lash his horses, an apparition glues him to his seat.

A gray-haired man points an ugly revolver at his head.

"Halt!" he says. The street is deserted. Villa Rocca opens the door. A strong hand hurls him to the gutter. Louise is urged from the coach. She is in her home again!

Peyton turns to grasp the man, who picks himself from the gutter. He is ten seconds too late. The carriage is off like a flash; it turns the corner at a gallop. Too cool to leave the fort unguarded, Peyton enters the salon. He finds Josephine moaning over Louise, who has fainted.

In a half-hour, Pere Francois and the young men are a bodyguard on duty. Peyton drives to the bank, and telegraphs Woods at London:

"Come instantly! Attempt to abduct, prevented by me! Danger! PEYTON."

The next night, in the rooms of the miner, the padre and Peyton hold a council of war. An engine waits at the "Gare du Nord." When sunlight gilds once more Notre Dame, Peyton enters the car with a lady, clad in black. A maid, selected by Joseph Vimont, is of the party. "Monsieur Joseph" himself strolls into the depot. He jumps into the cab with the engineer. "Allons!" They are off.

From forty miles away a few clicks of the telegraph flash the news to Woods. The priest knows that Peyton and his ward are safely "en route." "Tres bien!"

It is years before the light foot of Louise Moreau presses again the threshold of her childhood's home. In a sunny chateau, near Lausanne, a merry girl grows into a superb "Lady of the Lake." She is "Louise Moreau," but Louise "en reine." She rules the hearts of gentle Henry Peyton and the "autocrat of the Golden Chariot." It is beyond the ken of "Natalie de Santos," or Philip Hardin, to pierce the mystery of that castle by the waters of the Swiss lake.

Visions of peace lend new charms to the love of the pure-souled girl who wanders there.

Louise is not always alone by Leman's blue waters. Colonel Peyton is a thoughtful, aging man, saddened by his fiery past.

He sees nothing. He dreams of the flag which went down in battle and storm. The flag of which Father Ryan sang--"in fond recollection of a dead brother"--the ill-fated stars and bars:

"Furl that banner, for 'tis weary,
Round its staff 'tis drooping dreary.
Furl it, fold it, it is best;
For there's not a man to wave it--
And there's not a sword to save it--
And there's not one left to lave it
In the blood which heroes gave it;
And its foes now scorn and brave it;
Furl it, hide it; let it rest."

But younger and brighter eyes than his own, dimmed with battle smoke, look love into each other. Louise and Armand feel the throbbing whispers of the lake in their own beating hearts.

Far above them there, the silver peaks lift unsullied altars to the God of nature, life, and love.

And as the rosy flush of morning touches the Jungfrau, as the tender light steals along the sunlit peaks of the Alps, so does the light of love warm these two young hearts. Bounding pulse and melting accent, blush of morning on rosy peak and maiden's cheek, tell of the dawning day of light and love.

Shy and sweet, their natures mingle as two rivulets flowing to the sea. Born in darkness and coldness, to dance along in warmth and sunlight, and mingle with that great river of life which flows toward the unknown sea.

In days of bliss, in weeks of happiness, in months of heart growth, the two children of fortune drink in each other's eyes the philter of love. They are sworn a new Paul and Virginia, to await the uncertain gifts of the gods. The ardor of Armand is reflected in the tender fidelity of graceful Louise, who is a radiant woman now.

While this single car flies out of Paris, a "mauvais quart d'heure" awaits Ernesto de Villa Rocca, at the hands of Natalie.

Bounding from her seat, she cries, "Imbecile fool, you have ruined both of us! The girl is lost now!"

In an hour the Italian evolves a new plan. Marie Berard shall herself find and abduct the child! The Comte de Villa Rocca will escort them to the Italian tower, where Natalie's dangerous ward will be lost forever to Hardin.

But Marie must now be placated! Natalie de Santos smiles as she points to a plump pocket-book.

"A magic sceptre, a magnetic charm, my dear Count." Her very voice trickles with gold.

While Ernesto Villa Rocca and his promised bride dine in the lingering refinement of a Parisian table, they await the return of the baffled Marie. The maid has gone to arrange the departure of Louise. No suspicion must be awakened! Once under way, then silence!--quietly enforced. Ah, chloroform!

There was no etiquette in the sudden return of the pale-faced maid; she dashed up, in a carriage, while the lovers dallied with the dessert.

"Speak, Marie! What has happened?" cries Natalie, with a sinking heart.

"Madame, she is gone! Gone forever!"

Madame de Santos bounds to the side of the defeated woman. "If you are lying, beware!" she hisses. Her hand is raised. There is a dagger flashing in the air. Villa Rocca wrests it from the raging woman's hand. "No folly, Madame! She speaks the truth!"

Marie stubbornly tells of her repulse. Josephine was "not alone!" Blunt Aristide elbowed her out of the house, saying:

"Be off with you! The girl is gone! If you want to know where she is, apply to the police. Now, don't show your lying face here again! I will have you arrested! You are a child stealer! You and your ruffian had better never darken this door. Go!"

Natalie de Santos sinks back in her chair. Her teeth are chattering. A cordial restores her nerves. Count Villa Rocca lingers, moody and silent.

What powerful adversary has baffled them?

"Marie, await me in my room!" commands Natalie. In five minutes the roll of rubber-tired wheels proves that madame and the count have gone out. "To the opera?" "To the theatre?" The sly maid does not follow them. Her brain burns with a mad thirst for vengeance. Her hoard must now be completed. "Has she been tricked?" "Thousand devils, no!"

Softly moving over the driveway, Natalie eagerly pleads with Villa Rocca. Her perfumed hair brushes his cheek. Her eyes gleam like diamonds, as they sweep past the brilliantly lighted temples of pleasure. She is Phryne and Aspasia to-night.

Villa Rocca is drunk with the delirium of passion. His mind reels.

"I will do it," he hoarsely murmurs. Arrived at the "porte cochere," the count lifts his hat, as madame reenters her home.

There is a fatal glitter in Natalie's eyes, as she enters alone her robing room.

When madame is seated in the freedom of a wonderful "robe de chambre," her face is expectant, yet pleasant. Marie has fulfilled every duty of the evening.

"You may go, Marie. I am tired. I wish to sleep," remarks the lady, nonchalantly.

"Will madame pardon me?"

Marie's voice sounds cold and strange. Ah, it has come, then! Natalie has expected this. What is the plot?

Natalie looks her squarely in the eyes. "Well?" she says, sharply.

"I hope madame will understand that I close my duties here to-night!" the maid slowly says.

"Indeed?" Madame lifts her eyebrows.

"I would be glad to be permitted to leave the house to-morrow."

"Certainly, Marie!" quietly rejoins Natalie. "You may leave when you wish. The butler will settle your account. I shall not ring for you to-morrow." She leans back. Checkmate!

"Will madame excuse me?" firmly says the maid, now defiantly looking her mistress in the eyes. "The butler can probably not settle my little account."

"What is it?" simply asks Madame de Santos.

"It is one hundred thousand francs," firmly replies the woman.

"I shall not pay it! decidedly not!" the lady answers.

"Very good. Judge Hardin might!"

The maid moves slowly to the door.

"Stay!" commands Natalie. "Leave my house before noon to-morrow. You can come here with any friend you wish at this hour to-morrow night. You will have your money. How do you wish it?"

"In notes," the maid replies, with a bow. She walks out of the room. She pauses at the threshold. "Will madame ask Georgette to look over the property of madame?"

"Certainly. Send her to me!"

Marie Berard leaves her world-wearied mistress, forever, and without a word.

When the other maid enters, madame finds need for the assistant. "You may remain in my apartment and occupy the maid's couch. I may want you. I am nervous. Stay!"

The under-maid is joyous at her promotion. Madame de Santos sleeps the sleep of the just. Happy woman!

Marie Berard rages in her room, while her mistress sleeps in a bed once used by a Queen of France.

The ticking clock drives her to madness. She throws it into the court-yard.

Spurned! foiled! baffled!

Ah, God! She will have both fortunes. She remembers that little paper of years ago.

Yes, to find it now. Near her heart. By the candle, she reads the cabalistic words:

"Leroyne & Co., 16 Rue Vivienne."

Was it an imprudence to speak of Hardin? No, it was a mere threat. Marie's cunning eyes twinkle. She will get this money here quietly. Then, to the bank--to the bank! Two fortunes at one "coup."

But she must see Jules! Jules Tessier! He must help now; he must help. And how? He is at the Cafe Ney.

Yet she has often slipped out with him to the "bals de minuit." A friend can replace him; servants keep each others' secrets. Victory!

She must see him at once. Yes, Jules will guide her. He can go to the bank, after she has received her money. And then the double payment and vengeance on madame!

Like lightning, she muffles herself for the voyage. A coupe, ten minutes, and above all--a silent exit. All is safe; the house sleeps. She steals to her lover. Jules Tessier starts, seeing Marie in the ante-room at the Cafe Ney. There are, even here, curious spies.

Marie's eyes are flashing; her bosom heaves. "Come instantly, Jules! it is the hour. My coupe is here."

"Mon Dieu, in an instant!" The sly Jules knows from her shaken voice the golden hoard is in danger.

In a few moments he is by her side in the coupe. "Where to?" huskily asks the head-waiter.

"To the 'bal de minuit.' We can talk there."

"Allons! au Jardin Bullier," he cries.

Before the "fiacre" stops, Jules has an idea of the situation. Ah! a grand "coup." Jules is a genius!

Seated in a bosky arbor, the two talk in lowest tones over their chicken and Burgundy.

There is a noisy party in the next arbor, but a pair of dark Italian eyes peer like basilisks through the leaves of the tawdry shade. The lovers are unconscious of the listener.

With joint toil, the pair of lovers prepare a letter to Leroyne & Co., bankers, 16 Rue Vivienne.

Marie's trembling hand draws the paper from her bosom. She knows that address by heart.

"Give it to me, Marie," he pleads, "for safety." A FRENCHWOMAN can deny her lover nothing.

"Now, listen, 'ma cherie,'" Jules murmurs. "You get the one treasure. To-morrow I go to the bank, the telegraph, you understand, but not till you have the other money safe." Her eyes sparkle. A double fortune! A double revenge! A veritable "coup de Machiavelli."

"And I must go, dearest. I wait for you to-morrow. You get your money; then I am off to the bank, and we will secure the rest. Bravo!"

Jules snaps his fingers at the imbeciles. He sees the "Hotel Tessier" rising in cloudland.

"Press this proud woman hard now. Be careful. I will pay the coupe; we might be followed."

While Jules is absent, Marie dreams the rosy dreams of fruition. Love, avarice, revenge!

Down through the entrance, they saunter singly. Both are Parisians. After a square or two brings them to night's obscurity, parting kisses seal the dark bond; Judge Hardin shall pay after madame; Marie's velvet hand grips Jules' palm in a sinful compact.

Home by the usual way, past Notre Dame, and Jules will discreetly watch her safety till she reaches the omnibus.

She knows not when she reaches Notre Dame that Tessier lies behind her, stunned upon the sidewalk, his pockets rifled, and his senses reeling under brutal blows. Her heart is blithe, for here, under the shade of Notre Dame, she is safe. Twenty steps bring her to the glaring street. Yet the avenger has panther feet.

Out of the shadow, in a moment, she will be. "Oh, God!" the cry smothers in her throat. Like lightning, stab after stab in her back paralyzes her.

Bubbling blood from her quivering lips, Marie falls on her face. A dark shadow glides away, past buttress and vaulted door.

Is it Villa Rocca's ready Italian stiletto?

BOOK V.
REAPING THE WHIRLWIND.

CHAPTER XVIII.

JOE WOODS SURPRISES A LADY.--LOVE'S GOLDEN NETS.

When a cab is halted, the horses shying at a prostrate body, knots of street loungers gather at the cries of the discoverers of Marie Berard's body. The "sergents de ville" raise the woman. Her blood stains the sidewalk, in the shadow of the Church of Christ. Twinkling lights flicker on her face. A priest passing by, walks by the stretcher. He is called by his holy office to pray for the "parting soul."

It is Pere Francois. He has been in Notre Dame. To the nearest hospital the bearers trudge. It is only a few rods. When the body is examined, the pale face is revealed. Pere Francois clasps his hands.

It is, indeed, the mysterious guardian of Louise, stabbed and dying. It is the hand of fate!

Breathing faintly, the poor wretch lies prone. There is no apparent clue to her assailant. She is speechless. It has not been robbery; her valuables are intact. Hastily anointing her, Pere Francois departs. He promises to return in the morning. He hastens to the nearest cabstand, and whirls away to Colonel Woods' hotel. Whose hand has dealt this blow? The financier is startled at the priest's face. Joseph has been jocular since the safe departure of Louise.

He listens. A prodigious whistle announces his feelings. "Padre," says he, "if that Frenchwoman is alive to-morrow, you must see her. Find out all she knows. I'll turn out at daybreak, and watch Madame Santos' house myself. I think that handsome 'she devil' had something to do with this.

"Got done with the maid. No more use for her. Now, my dear friend, I will be here to-morrow when you show up. We will interview the madame. She's the spider in this game."

Woods sleeps like a man in a tossing storm. He knows from the padre's repeated visits at the Santos mansion that dying Marie holds the secret of these two children's lives. If she could only talk.

All night the miner battles for Valois' unknown child.

Up with the lark, Joe sends his "French fellow" for detective Vimont. "Voila! un grand proces."

Vimont sees gold ahead.

By eight o'clock, ferret eyes are watching the Santos mansion, the home of discreet elegance.

A stunning toilet is made by Joseph, in the vain hope of impressing the madame. He will face this Lucrezia Borgia "in his raiment of price." He has a dim idea, that splendid garb will cover his business-like manner of coming to "first principles."

A happy man is he at his well-ordered dejeuner, for though Joe is no De Rohan or Montmorençy, yet he eats like a lord and drinks like a prince of the blood. He is the "first of his family"--a golden fact.

He revenges himself daily for the volunteer cuisine of the American River. Often has he laughed over haughty Valois' iron-clad bread, his own flinty beans, the slabs of pork, cooked as a burnt offering by slow combustion. Only one audacious Yankee in the camp ever attempted a pie. That was a day of crucial experiment, a time of bright hopes, a period of sad failure.

Vimont reports at noon. A visit from Villa Rocca of a half-hour. Sauntering up the Elysees, after his departure, the count, shadowed carefully, strolled to his club. He seemed to know nothing. The waxen mask of Italian smoothness fits him like a glove. He hums a pleasant tune as he strolls in. The morning journals? Certainly; an hour's perusal is worthy the attention of the elegant "flaneur." Ah! another murder. He enjoys the details.

Pere Francois enters the colonel's rooms, with grave air. While Vimont frets over his cigar, in the courtyard, the story of Marie Berard is partly told.

She will not live through the night. At her bedside, Sisters of Charity twain, tell the beads and watch the flickering pulse of the poor lost girl. The police have done their perfunctory work. They are only owls frightened by sunlight. Fools! Skilful fools! She knows nothing of her assailant. Her feeble motions indicate ignorance. She must have rest and quiet. The saddened Pere Francois can not disguise from Woods that he suspects much. Much more than the police can dream in their theories.

What is it? Hopes, fears, the rude story of a strange life, and upon it all is the awful seal of the confessional. For, Marie Berard has unfolded partly, her own life-story. Joe Woods clasps the padre's hands.

"You know which of these children is a million-heiress, and which a pauper?"

The padre's eyes are blazing. He is mute. "Let us trust to God. Wait, my friend," says Pere Francois solemnly. Before that manly voice, the miner hushes his passionate eagerness. Violence is vain, here.

It seems to him as if the dead mother of an orphan child had placed her hand upon his brow and said: "Wait and hope!"

Monte Cristo's motto once more.

The padre eyes the Comstock colonel under his thin lashes.

"My friend"--his voice trembles--"I can tell you nothing yet, but I will guide you. I will not see you go wrong."

"Square deal, padre!" roars Joseph, with memories of gigantic poker deals. Irreverent Joe.

"Square deal," says the priest, solemnly, as he lays an honest man's hand in that of its peer. He knows the Californian force of this appeal to honor. Joseph selects several cigars. He fusses with his neckgear strangely.

"Vamos, amigo," he cries, in tones learned from the muleteers of the far West.

Once in the halls of "Madame de Santos," Colonel Joe is the pink of Western elegance. The acute sense of the Missourian lends him a certain dignity, in spite of his gaudy attire.

Under fire, this Western pilgrim can affect a "sang froid" worthy of Fontenoy.

Radiant in white clinging "crepe de Chine," her "prononcee" beauty unaccentuated by the baubles of the jeweller, Madame de Santos greets the visitors.

A blue circle under her eyes tells of a vigil of either love or hate. Speculation is vain. The "monde" has its imperial secrets.

Who can solve the equation of womanhood? Colonel Joseph is effusive in his cheery greeting. "My dear madame, I am glad to be in Paris once more." He would charm this sphinx into life and warmth. Foolish Joseph.

"We all are charmed to see you safely returned," murmurs the madame. The padre is studying the art treasures of the incomparable "Salon de Santos."

"I have some messages from a friend of yours," continues Joseph, strangely intent upon the narrow rim of his hat.

"Ah, yes! Pray who remembers me so many years?"

Joseph fires out the answer like a charge of canister from a Napoleon gun: "Philip Hardin."

The lady's lips close. There is a steely look in her eyes. Her hand seeks her heaving bosom. Is there a dagger there?

"Useless, my lady." There are two men here. The padre is intent upon a war picture of Detaille. His eyes catch a mirror showing the startled woman.

"And--what--did--Mr.--Philip--Hardin say?" the lady gasps.

"He asked me if you remembered Hortense Duval, the Queen of the El--" Natalie reels and staggers, as if shot.

"By God, Lee was right!" cries Woods. He catches her falling form. The first and only time he will ever hold her in his arms.

"Padre, ring the bell!" cries the excited miner.

The clock ticks away noisily in the hall. The wondering servants bear madame to her rooms. All is confusion. A fainting fit.

"Let's get out of here," whispers Woods, frightened by his own bomb-shell.

"Stay till we get a message of formality," murmurs the diplomatic padre. "It would look like violence or insult to leave abruptly. No one here must suspect." Joe nods gloomily and wipes his brows.

The stately butler soon expresses the regrets of madame. "A most unforeseen affair, an assault upon one of her discharged servants, has tried her nerves. Will Colonel Woods kindly excuse madame, who will send him word when she receives again?"

"Colonel Woods will decidedly excuse madame." He returns to his hotel. He grieves over the dark shadows cast upon her suffering loveliness. "By the gods! It's a shame SHE IS WHAT SHE IS," he murmurs to his cigar. Ah, Joseph! entangled in the nets of Delilah.

In a few days the spacious apartments of Colonel Woods have another tenant. Bag and baggage he has quietly departed for the Pacific Slope. Pere Francois runs on to Havre. He waves an adieu from the "quai." It would not be possible to prove that Colonel Joe has not gone to Switzerland. That is not the question, however. But the padre and the colonel are now sworn allies. Joseph is the bearer of a letter to the Archbishop of California. It carries the heart and soul of Pere Francois. The great Church acts now.

"My dear old friend," says Woods in parting, "I propose to keep away from Paris for a couple of years and watch Philip Hardin's handling of this great estate. Peyton will bring the girl on, when her coming of age calls for a legal settlement of the estate. I don't want to strike that woman down until she braves me.

"I'm going to lure Madame de Santos over to California. If she wants to watch me, I will be on deck every time there. I'll bring Peyton and Louise Moreau over to San Francisco. I will never lose sight of that child. Judge Davis shall now run my whole game. I don't ask you who killed that woman, padre, but I will bet the de Santos knows the hand which struck the blow.

"By leaving you, Vimont, to watch her, you may be yet able to catch our man. We'll let her bring forward the heiress of Lagunitas, whom she stowed away in the convent. Don't spare the cash, padre. You can use what you want from my bankers. They will cable me at once, at your wish. Good-bye." Joe Woods is off. His mind is bent on a great scheme.

Pere Francois thinks of the unavenged murder of the poor maid-servant. She is now sleeping the last sleep in Pere la Chaise. Paris has its newer mysteries already, to chase away her memory--only one more unfortunate.

Joe gets news after his arrival at the Golden Gate. "I will tell you, my dear friend, that a large sum of money was due to this woman from Madame de Santos. She was to have it the next day. I can not see who would kill her to prevent her getting money from a prosperous mistress. She was making her a final present on leaving her service. Madame de Santos openly admits she intended to give her a considerable sum of money. She has acted with commendable kindness as to her funeral. All is quiet. The police are baffled." This is the priest's letter.

"I cannot, at present, reveal to you all I learned from the dying penitent. I need a higher permission. I have given you an order to receive the original Valois marriage papers, and the baptismal and birth certificates of Isabel Valois. She is the only child of Maxime and Dolores Valois. Louise Moreau is the real heiress, in my opinion, but we must prove it. I shall come to San Francisco to watch the sequel of the guardianship of the rightful heiress.

"One person ALONE can now positively swear to this child. I shall watch that defiant woman, until she goes to California."

High life in Paris rolls on golden wheels as always. Ernesto Villa Rocca is a daily visitor at the Santos residence. A change has been inaugurated by the death of Marie Berard.

There is a lovely girl there now, whose beauty shines out even by the side of Natalie the peerless. The heiress is at home. Not even to Villa Rocca does Natalie confide herself. The disappearance of Louise Moreau startles her yet. The sudden death of Marie brings her certain advantages in her once dangerous position. She has no fear to boldly withdraw the blooming Isabel Valois, so called, from the "Sacre Coeur," now she has learned that the legal control of the child can only be taken from her by Hardin himself. He will never dare to use open force as regards her. No! fear will restrain him. The dark bond of the past prevents.

But by fraud or artifice, yes! To defeat any possible scheme, she surrounds the young girl with every elegance of instruction and accomplishment. She watches her like a tigress guarding its young, But by her side, in her own home, the young "claimant" will be surely safe. Hardin fears any public denouncement of his schemes. Open scandal is worse than secret crime, in the high circles he adorns.

Count Ernesto Villa Rocca does not plead immediately for madame's hand. Wise Italian. "Chi va piano va sano." Since the fateful evening when he promised to do a certain deed of blood for Natalie, his ardor has chilled a little. "Particeps criminis." He revolves the whole situation. With cool Italian astuteness, he will wait a few months, before linking himself to the rich lady whose confidential maid was so mysteriously murdered. There has been no hesitation, on his part, to accept a large sum of money from Natalie. Besides, his eye rests with burning admiration on the young girlish beauty. Her loveliness has the added charms of untold millions, in her future fortune. A prize. Does he dare? Ernesto Villa Rocca cannot fathom the mysterious connection between the guardian siren and her charge. Would he be safe to depend upon Madame de Santos' fortune? He knows not. Has not the young girl a greater value in his eyes?

Seated in the boudoir of Natalie, with bated breath, Villa Rocca has told Natalie what he expects as a reward for freeing her from Marie.

Natalie hails the expiration of the minority of the "daughter of the Dons." The millions will now fall under her own control. Power!--social power! concrete power!

The most urgent appeals to her from Hardin cannot make her leave France. Hardin storms. He threatens. He implores. He cannot leave California and go to France himself. The wily wretch knows that Natalie THERE will have a local advantage over him. Month after month glides away. Swordplay only. Villa Rocca, dallying with Natalie, gloats over the beauties of the ward.

Armand Valois, by invitation of Colonel Peyton, has decided to spend a year or so in Switzerland and Germany, painting and sketching. Louise Moreau soons becomes a proficient amateur artist. She wanders on the lovely shores of the lake, with the gifted young American. Love weaves its golden web. Joined heart and soul, these children of fortune whisper their love by the throbbing bosom of the lake.

It is with the rare genius of her sly nature, a happy thought, that Madame de Santos requests the chivalric Raoul Dauvray to instruct her own ward in modelling and sketching. It will keep her mind busy, and content the spirited girl. She must save her from Villa Rocca. Dauvray is also a painter of no mean talent. A studio is soon arranged. The merry girl, happy at her release from convent walls, spends pleasant hours with the ex-Zouave. Drifting, drifting daily down happy hours to the knowledge of their own ardent feelings.

Natalie absolutely debars all other visitors from meeting her young ward. Only her physician and Pere Francois can watch these studio labors. She fears Hardin's emissaries only.

Many visits to the studio are made by Villa Rocca. He is a lover of the "beaux-arts."

The days fly by pleasantly. Natalie is playing a cool game now. Pere Francois and Raoul Dauvray are ever in her charmed circle. She dare not refuse the friendship of the inscrutable priest. She watches, cat-like, for some sign or token of the absent Louise Moreau. Nothing. Colonel Joseph's sagacity has arranged all communication from the Swiss lakes, through his trusted banker. It is a blind trail.

Vimont, eying Natalie and Villa Rocca keenly, reports that he cannot fathom their relations. Guilty lovers? No. There is no obstacle at all to their marriage. Then why not a consummation? "Accomplices?" "In what crime?" "Surely none!" The count is of station undoubted. A member of the Jockey Club. Natalie de Santos speaks frankly to Pere Francois of her obligations to the dead woman. That mysterious assailant still defies the famed police of Paris.

Yet around Madame de Santos a web of intrigue is woven, which even her own keen eyes do not ferret out.

Strange woman-heart. Lonely and defiant, yet blind, she thinks she guards her control of the budding heiress, "Isabel Valois." Waiting?

In the studio, handsome Raoul Dauvray bends glowing eyes on the clay which models the classic beauty of Isabel Valois. The sabre scar on his bronzed face burns red as he directs the changes of his lovely model. Neither a Phryne nor an Aphrodite, but "the Unawakened Venus."

A dreamy light flickers in her eyes, as she meets the burning gaze of an artist lover.

Fighting hard against the current, the heiress of millions affects not to understand.

It is "Monsieur Raoul," "Mademoiselle Isabel;" and all the while, their hearts beat in unison.

Raoul, soldier-artist, Frenchman, and lover, dissembles when Villa Rocca is present. There is a strange constraint in the girl's dark eyes, as her idle hands cross themselves, in unconscious pose, when they are alone.

"Lift your eyes a little, mademoiselle. Look steadily at me," is his gentle request. He can hear the clock tick as if its beat was the fail of a trip hammer.

When even his fastidious task can no longer delay, he says, as the afternoon sun gilds the dome of the Invalides, throwing down his graver, "Je n'en puis plus, mademoiselle. It is finished. I will release you now."

As Raoul throws the cloth over the clay model, Isabel passes him with a gasp, and gazes with set face from the window.

His bursting heart holds him back. There is no longer an excuse.

"And I shall see you no more, Monsieur Raoul?" the heiress of millions softly says.

"Not till this is in marble, mademoiselle. A poor artist does not mingle in your own gay world."

"But a soldier of France is welcome everywhere," the girl falters.

A mist rises to Raoul's eyes. He bears the cross of the Legion of Honor on his breast. The perfume from her hair is blown across his face. "Les violettes de Parme." The artist sinks in the soldier.

Springing to the window, the girl's assenting hand, cold as ice, is clasped in his palm.

"Isabel!" he cries. She trembles like a leaf. "May the soldier ask what the artist would not dare?" He is blind with passion.

The lovely dark-eyed girl turns a splendid face upon him, her eyes filled with happy tears, and cries:

"Captain, you saved my life!"

The noisy clock ticks away; the only sound beside its clang is the beating hearts which close in love's first embrace, when the soldier knows he has won the heart of the Pearl of Paris.

"Your rank, your millions, your guardian! The Count Villa Rocca, my enemy!" he hoarsely whispers.

The clinging beauty hands him the ribbon from her throat.

"Claim me with this!" she cries as his arms enfold her.

The dream of young love; first love; true love.

Every obstacle fades away: Lagunitas' millions; proud guardian; scheming duenna; watchful Villa Rocca. The world is naught to the two whose arms bind the universe in love's golden circle,

Raoul murmurs to the glowing maiden in his arms:

"And can you trust me?"

The splendid beauty clasps him closer, whispering softly:

"A Spanish girl loves once and to the death."

"But, darling," she falters, as her arms cling closer, "we must wait and hope!"

A letter from Philip Hardin arrives, in the gayest midwinter of a rejuvenated Paris. The time for decisive action has arrived. Natalie revolves every clause of Hardin's proposition in her mind.

In less than a year the now blooming Isabel will be eighteen years of age. The accounting--

Hardin is trying now to cut the legal Gordian knot. His letter reads as follows:

I have determined to make you a proposition which should close all our affairs. It should leave no cause for complaint. I need Isabel Valois here, You will not trust yourself in America with our past relations unsettled. I shall not force you, but I must do my duty as guardian.

You are worthy of a settlement. No one knows you here now. Marry Villa Rocca. Come here with Isabel. I will give you jointly a fortune which will content you. I will settle upon your child the sum of one hundred thousand dollars, to be paid over to her use when of age. If you marry Villa Rocca now, I will give him the drafts for the child's money. If you decide to marry him, you may ask him to visit me here, as your agent. I will show him where your own property is located, to the extent of half a million dollars. This is to be turned over to you and him jointly, when you are man and wife. This will satisfy his honor and his rank. Otherwise, I shall soon cease my remittances. You may not be willing to do as I wish, but the heiress must be returned to me, or you and your child will remain without means.

Your marriage will be my safeguard and your own establishment. Tell Villa Rocca any story of your life; I will confirm and prove it. I shall name my bankers as trustee to join with any person you name for your child. The principal to be paid over to her on her marriage, to her own order. She can take any name you choose, except mine. If this is satisfactory, cable to me, "Accepted; agent coming." Send a letter by your agent, with a private duplicate to me, with your wishes. HARDIN.

Natalie stands face to face with a life's decision. Can she trust Villa Rocca? By the dark bond of crime between them she must. A poor bond of crime. And the millions of Lagunitas. To yield them up. A terrible temptation.

In her boudoir, Villa Rocca sums up with lightning flashes, the merits of this proposition. It is partly unfolded to him by the woman, who holds his pledge to marry her. "She must settle her affairs." It is a good excuse. He smiles, as he says:

"Madonna mia, in whose name will this property be placed, if I make you Countess Villa Rocca?"

"In our joint names, with benefit to the survivor," she replies.

"If arranged in even sums on each of us, with a reversion to me, if you die childless, I will accept. I will go to California, and bring the deposit for the missing child. I can make every arrangement for your lawyer. We can go over together and marry there, when you restore the heiress next year to her guardian." A bargain, a compact, and a bond of safety. It suits both.

The lady despatches to Hardin her acceptance of his proposal. In preparing a letter to the Judge she gives her "fiance" every instruction. She permits him to mail the duplicate, carefully compared.

In a week, Count Ernesto is tossing on the billows of the Atlantic. He is a fashionable Columbus. He is sufficiently warned to be on his guard in conversation with the wily Hardin. Natalie is far-seeing.

Villa Rocca laughed as he embraced his future bride. "Trust an Italian, in finesse, cara mia."

It is arranged between the two that Hardin is to have no hint of the character, appearance, or whereabouts of the child who receives the bounty. The letter bears the name of "Irene Duval" as the beneficiary of the fund. A system of correspondence is devised between them. Villa Rocca, using his Italian consul at San Francisco as a depositary, will be sure to obtain his letters. He will write to a discreet friend in Paris. Perhaps a spy on herself, Natalie muses.

Still she must walk hand in hand with Villa Rocca, a new sharer of her secret. But HE dare not talk.

When these two have said their last adieux, when Natalie sums up her lonely thoughts, she feels, with a shudder for the future, that not a shade of tenderness clings around this coming marriage. Mutual passion has dissipated itself. There is a self-consciousness of meeting eyes which tells of that dark work under the gloomy buttresses of Notre Dame. Murder--a heavy burden!

Can they trust each other? They MUST. The weary secret of unpunished crime grows heavier, day by day. In losing a tyrant, in the maid, will she not gain a colder master in the man she marries? Who knows?

Natalie Santos realizes that she has no legal proof whose hand struck that fatal blow. But Villa Rocca can expose her to Hardin. A fatal weakness. The anxious woman realizes what her false position and idle luxury cost in heartache. It is life!

The roses turn to ashes on her cheeks as she paces her lonely rooms. Restless and weary in the Bois, she is even more dull and "distraite" in society. The repression of her secret, the daily presence of the daughter she dares not own, all weary her heart and soul. She feels that her power over Hardin will be gone forever when the heiress enters upon her rights. Has the child learned to love another? Her life is barren, a burning waste.

Money, with its myriad luxuries, must be gained by the marriage with Villa Rocca. To see her child inherit an honored name, and in possession of millions, will be revenge enough upon Philip Hardin. He never shall know the truth while he lives. Once recognized, Isabel Valois cannot be defeated in her fortune. Marie is dead. The only one who might wish to prove the change of the two children, Hardin himself, knows not. He must take her word. She is invincible.

Pere Francois becomes a greater comfort to her daily. The graceful priest brings with him an air of peace into the gaudy palace on the Elysees. She softens daily.

Raoul Dauvray has finished the artistic labors of his commissions. He is now only an occasional visitor. If he has the love of the heiress he dares not claim her yet. The fiery Zouave chafes in vain. Natalie holds him off. Pere Francois whispers, "Wait and hope!"

With the blindness of preoccupation, Natalie sees not how the tendrils of "first love" have filled the girl's heart. The young soldier-artist rules that gentle bosom. Love finds its ways of commune. Marriage seems impossible for years. Isabel must mount her "golden throne" before suitors can come to woo. A sculptor! The idea is absurd.

Not a single trace is left of "Louise Moreau." Natalie's lip curls as she fathoms the motive of the girl's disappearance. Friends of Marie Berard's have probably secreted her, as a part of the old scheme of blackmail upon her. Did the secret die with her? It is fight now. She muses: "Now they may keep her. The seal of the grave is on the only lips which could tell the story of Lagunitas." Villa Rocca even, does not know who the child was! His evidence would be valueless.

If--yes, if the Dauvray household should seek to fathom the history of the waif, how like an everyday history is the story in reply:

"Marie Berard wished to disembarrass herself of her fatherless child. She yet wished to hold some claim on the future in its behalf. That explains Louise Moreau's motives." There is a high wall of defence around her whole position. Her own child dead; but where, or how? She must invent. Walls have been scaled, my Lady of the Castle Dangerous. The enemy is mining under your defences, in silence.

With Villa Rocca's nerve and Italian finesse, even Hardin can be managed. If HE should die, then the dark secret of her child's transformation is safe forever!

Days fly by. Time waits for no aching hearts. There is a smile of satisfaction on the lovely face of Natalie. She peruses the letters from Hardin and the count. They announce the arrangement of the dower for the absent "Irene Duval." Villa Rocca is in San Francisco. The count forwards one set of the drafts, without comments. He only says he will bring the seconds, and thirds of exchange himself, He is going to come "home."

He announces his departure to the interior with Judge Hardin. He wishes to see the properties and interests held for Madame de Santos by her lawyer.

In a month he will be on his homeward way; Judge Hardin has loyally played his part. Villa Rocca's letters prove his respect for a bride who brings him a half million. The letters warm visibly. Even an Italian count can be impressed by solid wealth. Natalie de Santos's lips curl in derision of man. Her clouded history is now safe. Yes, the golden glitter of her ill-gotten fortune will cover all inquiry as to the late "Senor de Santos," of shadowy memory. She IS safe!

It is only a fair exchange of courtesy. She has not investigated the family stories of the noble Villa Rocca.

Cool, suave, polished; accepted at the clubs as a man of the world; an adept with rapier and pistol; Ernesto Villa Rocca bears his social coronet as bravely as the premier duke of France--always on guard!

"Does she love this man?" Natalie looks in her glass. From girlhood she has been hunted for her beauty. Now a fortune, title, and the oblivion of years will aid her in reigning as a mature queen. A "mondaine" with no entanglements. Paradise opens.

Liberal in works of charity, the adventuress can glide easily into religion. Once her feet firmly planted, she will "assume that virtue, if she have it not."

"And then--and after all!" The last tableau before the curtain falls. The pall of sable velvet. Natalie shudders. She remakes her toilet and drives to the opera.

"After all, social life is but a play." Her heart beats high with pride. Villa Rocca's return with the funds will be only a prelude to their union. But how to insure the half million? "How?"

The count's greed and entire union in interest with her will surely hold him faithful,

She will marry Ernesto as soon as he returns. She can trust him with the heiress until the property is settled on the married lovers.

Hardin, when Jules Tessier's addled brains are restored by careful nursing, receives a document from Leroyne & Co., which rouses his inmost soul.

Jules Tessier, handsome brute, chafes under the loss of the double blackmail. "Two hundred thousand francs," and his Marie.

To add to his anguish, he knows not where or under what name, Marie has deposited her own golden hoard. The "Hotel Tessier" has gone to Cloudland with the other "chateaux en Espagne"--the two payments are lost! Jules rages at knowing that even the savings of murdered Marie are lost to him. Even if found, they cannot be his by law. The ruffians who robbed him of everything, have left no trace.

The two weeks passed tossing on a hospital bed, have been lost to the police. Dimly Jules remembers the sudden assault. Crashing blows raining down upon him! Not a scrap of paper is left. The fatal letter to Leroyne & Co. is gone.

The police question the artful Jules.

He holds the secret of Leroyne & Co. to himself.

He may yet get a handsome bribe to tell even the meagre facts he knows. Marie Berard's case is one of the reigning sensations. Her lips are now sealed in death.

The baffled police only see in the visit to the "bal de minuit," a bourgeois intrigue of ordinary character.

Jules dares not tell all. He fears the stern French law. Tossing on his bed of pain, his only course is to secretly visit Leroyne & Co.

The bereaved lover feels that the parties who followed him, were directed by some malign agency which is fraught with future danger for him.

The poniard of darkness may reach his heart, if he betrays his designs.

Strongly suspecting Natalie de Santos, yet he knows her revenge struck through meaner hands than her own.

He has no proof. Not a clue. Villa Rocca is to him unknown. He fears to talk.

He hobbles forth to his vocation, and dares not even visit Marie's grave.

Spies may track him as on that fatal night. And even Leroyne's bank may be watched.

He must take this risk, for his only reward lies in that mysterious address.

Jules, in workman's blouse, spends an hour with the grave-faced banker of the Rue Vivienne.

When he emerges, he has ten one-thousand-franc notes in his waist-lining and the promise of more.

The banker knows the whole story of Jules' broken hopes; of the promised reward; the double crime.

He directs Jules Tessier to further await orders at the cafe, and to ignore the whole affair.

A significant hint about going forth at night makes Jules shudder. And the cipher cablegram gives Hardin the disjointed facts of Marie's death! His one ally gone. Her lips sealed forever.

Musing in his library, Hardin's clear head unravels this intrigue. The Paris police know not the past history of the actors in this drama. Jules is simply greedy and thick-headed. Leroyne & Co. are passionless bankers.

But Hardin gathers up the knotted threads and unravels all.

Accustomed to weigh evidence, to sift facts, his clear mind indicates Natalie de Santos as the brain, Villa Rocca as the striking assassin of this plot.

It is all aimed at him.

"Ah, yes!" the chafing lawyer muses, as he walks the legal quarter-deck of his superb library. "Villa Rocca and Natalie are lovers. The girl tried to blackmail them. She was trapped and put out of the way.

"Marie Berard dead--one dangerous ally gone. Villa Rocca and Natalie are the only two who know all. Her mind is his now.

"Ah, I have it!" with a devilish sneer. "I will separate these two billing and cooing lovers. If I get Villa Rocca here, he will never get back to France.

"When he is out of the way, Natalie can prove nothing.

"If she comes here I will treat her story as that of an insane woman."

Hardin draws a glass with shaking hand.

"Yes; a private asylum."

As for the heiress, there are plans in his mind he dare not whisper.

Illegitimacy and other reasons may bar her rights. The heiress knows nothing and she has not a paper.

Some outsider must fight this case.

In Hardin's dreams he sees his enemies at his feet. On Ernesto Villa Rocca's handsome face is the pallor of death. Lagunitas and its millions are his by right of power and cunning.

Marie Berard's avenger is thousands of miles away from her grave, and his cunning plan already woven to ensnare the Italian when off his guard. Yet Hardin's blood boils to feel that "the secret for a price" is buried in Marie Berard's grave. Toss as he may, his dreams do not discover the lost secret. Even Philip Hardin may meet a Nemesis.

Villa Rocca, slain by a well-contrived accident, died for a secret he knew not.

His own hand slew the woman who knew alone of the changelings, save the bright and defiant ex-queen of the El Dorado.

Dark memories hover around some of the great mines of the Pacific. Giant stock operations resulted from a seeming accidental fire. A mine filled with water by mysterious breakage of huge pumps. Hoisting machinery suddenly unmanageable; dashing to their doom unsuspecting wretches. Imprisoned miners, walled up in rich drifts, have died under stifling smoke, so that their secrets would die with them.

Grinning Molochs of finance have turned markets on these ghastly tricks.

Madame de Santos may never suspect how a steel spike adroitly set could cut a rope and dash even a noble Villa Rocca to his doom, carrying down innocent men as a mask to the crime.

In the clear sky of Natalie's complacency, a lightning stroke of the gods brings her palace of delight crashing down around her. Nemesis!

The telegraph flashes across the prairies, far beneath the Atlantic; the news of Villa Rocca's death arrives. Hardin's cable is brief. It is all-sufficient. Her trembling limbs give way. She reads:

SAN FRANCISCO.

Count Ernesto killed while visiting a mine, with friends. Accident of hoisting machinery. I was not there. Leave to-night for the place. Telegraph your wishes. Remain. Wait my reports. Write fully in a few days.

HARDIN.

She is all alone on earth. This is a crushing blow. No one to trust. None to advise, for she has leaned on Ernesto. Her mind reels under this blow. Pere Francois is her only stay. The sorrow of these days needs expression.

Villa Rocca's gay letters continue to arrive. They are a ghastly mockery of these hours. Hardin can cast her off now, and claim the heiress.

Hardin's full account dispels any suspicion of foul play. After a visit to the interior, the count went to see some interesting underground workings. By a hazard of mining life, a broken rope caused the death of the visitor, with several workmen, and a mine superintendent who was doing the honors. Death waited at the foot of the shaft for the noble stranger.

Hundreds of days, on thousands of trips like this, the princes of the Comstock have risked their own lives in the perils of the yawning pits. These dark holes blown out of the mountain rocks have their fearful death-rolls to show.

It is the revenge of the gnomes. Every detail points to a frank explanation. Journals and reports, with letters from the Italian consul, lifted the sad tragedy above any chance of crime or collusion. It is kismet.

Hardin's letter was manly. In it, he pledged his honor to carry out the agreement, advising Natalie to select a friend to accompany her to California with the heiress, as soon as she could travel. His banker had orders to supply funds.

"I suggest, in view of this untimely accident, you would sooner have your funds settled on you in Europe. It shall be as you wish. You may rely on me," so ran the closing lines.

The parted strands of the hoisting cable cannot reveal whether it was cut or weakened, yet Hardin knows. It was his devilish masterpiece.

Days of sadness drag down the self-reliant adventuress. Whom can she trust now? Dare she confide in Pere Francois?

A simple envelope addressed in a scrawling hand, and postmarked San Francisco, drives all sorrow from her heart. The tiger is loosened in her nature. She rages madly. A newspaper slip contains the following, in flaming prominence:

"THE UNITED STATES SENATE.

"The choice of the Legislature for U. S. Senator will undoubtedly fall upon that distinguished jurist Judge Hardin, who is now supported by the railroad kings and leading financiers of the coast.

"It is rumored that Judge Hardin will, in the event of his election, contract a matrimonial alliance with one of our leaders of society. His bride will entertain extensively in the national capital."

A paper bears pithy advice:

"Come out and strike for your rights. You will find a friend to back you up. Don't delay."

Natalie recognizes Joe Woods in this. He is the only man knowing half the secret. Tossing on her pillow, the Queen of the El Dorado suffers the tortures of the Inferno. Now is the time to strike Hardin. Before the great senatorial contest. Before this cruel marriage. She will boldly claim a secret marriage. The funds now in the Paris bank are safe. She can blast his career. If she does not take the heiress out, her chances vanish. And once there, what will not Hardin do? What is Woods' motive? Jealousy. Revenge. Hatred.

Ah, the priest! She will unbosom herself to Pere Francois. She will urge him to accompany her and the girl to San Franciso. He will be a "background." And his unrivalled calmness and wisdom. Pere Francois only knows her as the "elegante" of the Champs Elysees. She feels that Woods has been wisely discreet.

Summoning the ecclesiastic, Madame de Santos tells the story of her claims upon Hardin.

The old Frenchman passes his rosary beads, with a clinking sound, as he listens to the half-truths told him.

"And your child?" he queries.

"I have placed her secretly where Hardin cannot reach her. She will be produced if needed."

There is a peculiar smile in the priest's face. "Madame, I will accompany you on one condition."

"Name it," cries the siren, "I will furnish money, and every comfort for you. It shall be my duty to reward you."

The priest bows gravely.

"I wish to have a resolute man with our party. My young friend, Raoul Dauvray, has a lion's courage. Let him go with us. I do not wish Judge Hardin to know of my presence in San Francisco. Dauvray will guard you with his life."

"I agree to your wishes!" says madame thoughtfully. And loyal Raoul will fight for her and his hoped-for bride. In a month there is a notable departure from Paris. Madame de Santos, Mademoiselle Isabel Valois, with their maids, and Raoul, "en cavalier." On the same steamer, Pere Francois travels. He affects no intimacy with the distinguished voyagers. His breviary takes up all his time. Arrived at New York, Pere Francois leaves for San Francisco several days in advance of the others.

It is singular that he goes no farther than Sacramento. The legislature is about to assemble. Joseph Woods, as State senator, is launched in political life. The robust miner laughs when he is asked why he accepts these cheap honors.

"I'm not too old to learn some new tricks," he cheerfully remarks. His questions soon exhaust Pere Francois' stock of answers.

A day's conference between the friends leads to a series of Napoleon-like mandates of the mining Croesus. Telegraph and cable bear abroad to the shores of the Lake of Geneva the summons which brings Peyton, with Armand Valois and the lovely blooming "Louise Moreau," secretly to the Pacific. Natalie knows nothing of these pilgrims. Quietly reaching San Francisco, by a local train, Pere Francois becomes again Padre Francisco. He rests his weary head under the hallowing sounds of the well-remembered bells of the past at the Mission Dolores.

Natalie de Santos rubs her eyes in wonder at the queen city of the West, with its conquered hills and vanished sand-dunes. Whirled away to a secure quiet retreat in a convent, selected by Pere Francois, the heiress and her young guardian are safe from even Hardin's wiles.

Pere Francois at New York has conferred a day with Judge Davis, and bids his new charge be calm and trust to his own advice. Isabel Valois is in a maze of new impressions, and bewildered by a strange language.

Bravely attired, and of a generous port, Raoul Dauvray installs himself in one of the palatial hotels which are the pride of the occidental city. Colonel Joseph Woods is conspicuously absent.

When the fatigue of travel is over, Natalie de Santos quietly summons Philip Hardin to the interview she dreads. She has been prepared by Pere Francois for this ordeal. Yet her tiger blood leaps up in bubbling floods. She will at last face the would-be traitor, and upbraid him. Oh, for one resolute friend!

It is in another convent that lovely "Isabel Valois" is concealed. The heiress longs to burst her bonds. Is not Raoul near her? Assured of a necessity for patience, the wayward beauty bides her time. Every day the roses she caresses, whisper to her of the ardent lover who sighs near her in vain.

Philip Hardin steels himself to face the woman he intends to trick and deceive at the very last. There are such things as insane asylums in California, if she makes any hubbub.

But he has a "coup d'etat" in his mind. The old schemer will bring Natalie to terms. Flattery first; fear afterwards.

"And they are face to face once more."

CHAPTER XIX.

LOVERS ONCE.--STRANGERS NOW.--FACE TO FACE.

Ushered into a private room, the soulless Hardin's iron nerves fail him. His heart leaps up wildly when royal "Madame de Santos" approaches silently. Heavens! Her startling beauty is only mellowed with time. Another woman than the Hortense Duval of old stands before him. A goddess. She has grown into her new role in life.

"Hortense!" he eagerly cries, approaching her.

"Spare me any further deceit, Philip," she coldly replies. Seating herself, she gazes at him with flaming eyes! She is a queen at bay!

He is startled. A declaration of war. No easy mastery now.

"Where is your charge?" Hardin queries.

"Where you will not see her, until we understand each other," rejoins the determined woman. Her steady glance pierces his very soul. Memories of old days thrill his bosom.

"What do you mean by all this?" Hardin's nerve returns. He must not yield to mortal.

The woman who queened it over his home, extends a jewelled hand with an envelop. "Explain this," she sharply cries.

The Judge reads it. It is the announcement of his double senatorial and matrimonial campaign.

"Is there any foundation for that report?" Madame de Santos deliberately asks.

"There is," briefly rejoins the lawyer. He muses a moment. What devil is awakened in her now? This is no old-time pleading suppliant.

"Then you will not see Isabel until you have settled with me and provided the funds promised before the death of the count."

"Ah!" sneers the old advocate; "I understand you NOW, madame. Blood money!"

"Partly," remarks Madame de Santos. "I also insist upon your giving up this marriage."

Hardin springs from his chair. Age has robbed him of none of his cold defiance. He will crush her.

"You dare to dream of forcing me to marry you?" His eyes have the glitter of steel.

"You need not give up the senate, but you must marry me, privately, and give your own child a name. Then I will leave, with the funds you will provide. You can separate from me afterward by the mere lapse of time. There will be no publicity needed."

"Indeed!" Hardin snarls, "A nice programme, You have had some meddling fool advise you; some later confidant; some protector."

"Exactly so, Judge," replies the woman, her bosom heaving in scorn and defiance. "We have lived together. We are privately married now by law! Philip, you know the nameless girl you have never asked for is your own child."

Hardin paces the floor in white rage. He gazes sternly in her eyes. She regards his excited movements, glaring with defiant eyes. A tigress at bay.

"I will end this here, madame! In two weeks Isabel Valois will be eighteen. If she is not forthcoming I will invoke the law. If I am forced to fight you, you will not have a cent from me. I will never marry you! I decline to provide for you or yours, unless you yield this girl up. You must leave the country before the senatorial election. That is my will."

Natalie faces her old lover. Tyrant of her heart once, he is now a malignant foe!

"Philip Hardin," she pleads, "look out of that window. You can see the house my child was born in--YOUR home, OUR home! Philip, give that child a name; I will leave you in peace forever!" There is the old music in her velvet voice.

"Never!" cries the Judge. "Give up the girl you took away. Leave at once. I will secure your fortune. You cannot force me. You never could. You cannot now!" He glares defiance to the death.

His eyes tell the truth. He will not yield,

"Then God help you, Philip," the woman solemnly says. "You will never reach the Senate! You will never live to marry another woman!"

"Do you threaten me, you she-devil?" snarls Hardin, alarmed at the settled, resolute face. "I have a little piece of news for you which will block your game, my lady. There is no proof of the legitimacy of the child, Isabel Valois. A claim has already been filed by a distant Mexican relative of the Peraltas. The suit will come up soon. If the girl is declared illegitimate, you can take her back to France, and keep her as a beggar. You are in my hands!" He chuckles softly.

"Philip Hardin, you are a liar and a monster. This is your conspiracy. Now, show yourself a thief, also." Natalie retorts. The words cut the proud man like a lash.

He seizes her jewelled wrist. He is beside himself.

"Beware," she hisses. "By the God who made me, I'll strike you dead."

He recoils.

She is once more the queen of the El Dorado. Her ready knife is flashing before his eyes. "You have a fearful reckoning to answer. You will meet your match yet at the game of Life!" she cries.

But, Natalie de Santos is stunned by his devilish plot to rob the despoiled orphan even of her name. He reads her face. "I will give you a day to think this over. I will come to-morrow." Hardin's voice rings with ill-concealed triumph.

"Not ten minutes will you give me. I tell you now I will crush you in your hour of victory, if I die to do it. Once more, will you marry me and give your child a name?" She rises and paces room, a beautiful fury.

"You have your answer," he coldly replies.

"Then, may the plundered orphan's curse drag you down to the hell you merit," is Natalie's last word as she walks swiftly out of the door. She is gone.

He is alone. Somethings rings with dull foreboding in his ears as his carriage rolls away. An orphan's curse! A cold clammy feeling gnaws at his heart. An orphan's curse!

Ah! from the tomb of buried years the millionaire hears the voice of Maxime Valois and shudders:

"May God deal with you as you deal with my child."

At home, in his library, where the silken rustling of that woman's dress has thrilled him in bygone years, the old Judge drinks a glass of cognac and slowly recovers his mental balance.

Through smoke-clouds he sees the marble chamber of the Senate of the Great Republic. He must move on to the marriage, he has deferred until the election. It is a pledge of twenty votes in joint ballot.

As for the girl Isabel, why, there is no human power to prove her legitimacy now. That priest. Bah! Dead years ago. Silence has rolled the stone over his tomb.

Hardin has foreseen for years this quarrel with Natalie de Santos. But she can prove absolutely nothing. He will face her boldly. She is ALONE in the world. He can tear the veil aside and blacken her name.

And yet, as evening falls, his spirit sinks within him. He can not, will not, marry the woman who has defied him. What devil, what unseen enemy put her on his track again? If he had never trusted her. Ah, too late; too late!

Secretly he had laid his well-devised mines. The judge in Mariposa is weighted down with a golden bribe. The court officials are under his orders. But who is the unknown foe counselling Natalie? He cannot fathom it. Blackmail! Yes, blackmail.

In three days Hardin is at Sacramento. His satellites draw up their cohorts for the senatorial struggle. If the legislature names him senator, then his guardianship will be quickly settled before the Mariposa Court. There, the contest will be inaugurated, which will declare Isabel Valois a nameless child of poverty. This is the last golden lock to the millions of Lagunitas, The poor puppet he has set up to play the contestant is under his control. He had wished to see Natalie homeward bound before this denouement. It must be. He muses. Kill her! Ah, no; too dangerous. He must FOIL her.

But her mad rage at his coming marriage. Well, he knew the ambitious and stately lady who aspired to share his honors would condone the story of his early "bonnes fortunes." What could lonely Natalie do at the trial? Nothing. He has the Court in his pocket. He will brave her rage.

Hardin writes a final note, warning the woman he fears, to attend with the heiress on the day of the calling for his accounting.

Marvels never cease. He tears open the answer, after two sleepless nights. She simply replies that the young Lady of Lagunitas will be delivered to him on the appointed day. He cannot read this riddle. Is it a surrender in hopes of golden terms? He knows not of Pere Francois' advice.

He smiles in complacent glee. He has broken many a weak woman's nerve: she is only one more.

While he ponders, waiting that reply, Natalie Santos, with heavy heart, tells the priest the story of her tryst with her old lover.

Pere Francois smiles thoughtfully. He answers: "Be calm. You will be protected. Trust to me. I will confer with our advisers. Not a word to Isabel of impending trouble."

The little court-house at Mariposa is not large enough for the crowd which pours in to see the Lady of Lagunitas when the fated day approaches. It is the largest estate in the country. A number of strangers have arrived. They are targets for wild rumors. Several grave-looking arrivals are evidently advocates. There is "law" in their very eyebrows.

Raoul Dauvray escorts Madame de Santos and the girl whose rumored loveliness is famous already. Philip Hardin, with several noted counsel, is in readiness. Pere Francois is absent. There is an elderly invalid, with an Eastern party of strangers, who resembles him wonderfully.

On the case being reached, there is a busy hum of preparation. One or two professional-looking men of mysterious identity quietly take their places at the bar. In the clerk's offices there is also a bevy of strangers. By a fortuitous chance, the stalwart form of Colonel Joe Woods illuminates the dingy court-room. His business is not on the calendar, He sits idly playing with a huge diamond ring until the "matter of the guardianship of Isabel Valois" is reached.

Several lawyers spring to their feet at once. A queer gleam is in Joe Woods' eye as he nods carelessly to Hardin. They are both Knights of the Golden Circle.

Judge Hardin's counsel opens the case, Hardin passes Natalie in the court-room, with one last look of warning and menace. There is no quiver to her eyelids. The graceful figure of a veiled young girl is beside her.

When Hardin's advocate ceases, counsel rises to bring the contest for the heirship of Lagunitas to the judicial notice of the Court.

The Judge is asked to stay the confirmation of the guardian's accounts and reports. His Honor blandly asks if the young lady is in court.

"Let Isabel Valois take the stand," is the direction.

Judge Hardin arises and passing to Natalie Santos, whose glittering eyes are steadily fixed on his, in an inscrutable gaze, leads the young lady beside her to the stand. Natalie has whispered a few words of cheer.

All eyes are fixed upon the beautiful stranger, who is removing a veil from a face of the rarest loveliness. There is a sensation.

Philip Hardin rises to his feet, ghastly pale, as Joseph Woods quietly leads up to the platform a slight, girlish form. It is another veiled woman, who quietly seats herself beside the claimant.

There is amazement in the court-room, "His Honor," with a startled glance at Judge Hardin, who is gazing vacantly at the two figures before him, says, "Which of these young ladies is Miss Isabel Valois?"

A voice is heard. It is one of the strange counselors speaking.

Hardin hears the words, as if each stabbed him to the heart.

"Your Honor, we are prepared to show that the last young lady who has taken the stand, is Miss Isabel Valois."

There is consternation in the assembly. Hardin's veins are knotted on his forehead. He stares blankly at the two girls. His eyes turn to Natalie de Santos. She is gazing as if the grave had given up its dead. Her cheeks whiten to ashes. Pere Francois, Henry Peyton, and Armand Valois enter and seat themselves quietly by the side of the man who is speaking. What does this all mean? No one knows. The lawyer resumes.

"We will show your Honor, by the evidence of the priest who baptized her, and by the records of the church, that this young lady is the lawful and only child of Maxime Valois and Dolores Peralta. We have abundant proof to explain the seeming paradox. We are in a position to positively identify the young lady, and to dispose of the contest raised here to-day, as to the marriage of the parents of the real heiress."

Philip Hardin has sprung to his lawyers. They are amazed at the lovely apparition of another Isabel Valois. At the bidding of the Court, Louise Moreau's gentle face appears.

"And who is the other young lady, according to your theory?" falters the astounded judge, who cannot on the bench receive the support of his Mephistopheles.

"We will leave that to be proved, your Honor! We will prove OUR client to be Isabel Valois. We will prove the other lady not to be. It remains for the guardian, who produces her, to show who she may be." The lawyer quietly seats himself.

There is a deadlock. There is confusion in court. Side by side are seated two dark-eyed girls, in the flush of a peerless young womanhood. Lovely and yet unlike in facial lines, they are both daughters of the South. Their deep melting eyes are gazing, in timid wonder, at each other. They are strangers.

"What is the name of your witness?" the judge mechanically questions. The lawyer calmly answers, "Francois Ribaut (known in religion as 'Padre Francisco'), who married the father and mother of this young lady, and also baptized her."

A faint sob from Natalie breaks the silence. Her eyes are filled with sudden tears. She knows the truth at last. The priest has risen. Hardin looks once more upon that pale countenance of the padre which has haunted his dreams so long. "Is it one from the dead?" he murmurs. But, with quick wit, his lawyer demands to place on the witness stand, the lady charged with the nurture of "Isabel Valois." Philip Hardin gazes wolfishly at the royal beauty who is sworn. A breathless silence wraps the room.

The preliminary questions over, while Hardin's eyes rove wildly over the face of the woman he has cast off, the direct interrogatory is asked:

"Do you know who this young lady is?" says the attorney, with a furtive prompting from Hardin. "I do!" answers the lady, with broken voice.

Before another question can be asked, the colleagues of Hardin's leading lawyer hold a whispered colloquy with their chief.

There is a breathless silence in the court. The principal attorney for the guardian asks the Court for a postponement of two weeks.

"We were prepared to meet an inquiry into the legitimacy of the ward of our client. This production of another claimant to the same name, is a surprise to us. On account of the gravity of this matter, we ask for a stay."

No objection is heard. His Honor, anxious himself to have time to confer with the would-be senator, adjourns the hearing for two weeks.

Before Hardin could extricate himself from the circle of his advisers, the long-expected girl he has seen for the first time has disappeared with Madame de Santos.

He has no control over her now. Too late!

His blood is bounding through his veins. He has been juggled with. By whom? Natalie, that handsome fiend. And yet, she was paralyzed at the apparition of the second beauty, who has also vanished.

He must see Natalie at once before she can frame a new set of lies. After all, the MINE is safe.

As he strides swiftly across the plaza, the thought of the senatorial election, and the lady whom he has to placate, presses on his mind.

As for the election, he will secure that. If Natalie attempts exposure, he will claim it to be a blackmail invention of political enemies. Ha! Money! Yes, the golden arguments of concrete power. He will use it in floods of double eagles.

He will see Natalie on her way to Paris before the second hearing. Yes, and send some one out of the State to watch her as far as New York. He must buy her off.

A part of the money in hand; the rest payable at Paris to her own order. She must be out of the way.

Mariposa boasts two hotels. The avoidance of Hardin's friends brings all the strangers, perforce, together in the other. They have been strangely private in their habits.

Philip Hardin's brow is set. It is no time for trifling. He sends his name up to Madame de Santos. She begs to be excused. "Would Judge Hardin kindly call in the evening?"

This would be after a council of war of his enemies. It must be prevented. He pens a few words on a scrap of paper, and waits with throbbing pulses,

"Madame will receive him." As he walks upstairs, he realizes he has to face a reckoning with Joe Woods. He will make that clumsy-headed Croesus rue the day. And yet Woods is in the State Senate, and may oppose his election.

With his eyes fixed on the doors of Natalie's apartment, he does not notice Woods gazing at him, from the end of the hall, in the open door of the portico.

Natalie motions him to a seat as he enters. He looks at her in amazement. She is not the same woman who entered that court-house. He speaks. The sound of his own voice makes him start.

"What is all this devil's tomfoolery? Explain it to me. Are you mad?" His suppressed feelings overmaster him. He gives way to an imprudent rage.

"Are you ready to marry me? Are you ready to keep the oath you swore to stand by me?" Her dark eyes burn into his heart. She is calm, but intense in her demand.

"Tell me the truth or I'll choke it out of you," he hisses, grasping her rudely.

His rashness breaks the last bond between them. A shriek from the struggling woman echoes through the room.

The door flies open.

Hardin is hurled to the wall, reeling blindly.

The energetic voice of Joe Woods breaks the silence. "You are a mean dog, but, by God, I did not think you'd strangle a woman."

Hardin has struggled to his feet. In his hand, flashes a pistol.

Joe Woods smiles.

"Trying the old El Dorado dodge, Judge, won't work. Sit down now. Listen to me. Put up that shooting iron, or I'll nail you to the wall."

His bowie knife presses a keen point to Hardin's breast. It is checkmate.

Natalie Santos is buried in the cushions of her chair. She is sobbing wildly. Shuffling feet are at the door. The fracas has been overheard.

Joe Woods quietly opens it. He speaks calmly. "The lady has fainted. It's all right. Go away."

Through the door a girl's lovely face is seen, in frightened shyness. "I'll send for you, miss, soon," Colonel Joe remarks, with awkward sympathy.

He seats himself nonchalantly.

"Now, Hardin, I've got a little account to settle with you. I'll give you all the time you want. But I'll say right here before this lady, I know you are under an obligation to treat her decently.

"I remember her at the El Dorado!"

Hardin springs to his feet. Natalie raises her tearful eyes.

"Keep cool, Judge," continues the speaker. "You used to take care of her. Now I'm a-going to advise her in her little private affairs. I want you to let her severely alone. I want you to treat her as she deserves; like a woman, not a beast. You can finish this interview with her. I'm a-going out. If you approach her after this, without my presence or until she sends for you, I'll scatter your brains with my old six-shooter. I shall see she gets a square deal. She's not going to leave California till this whole business is cleared up. You hear me." Joe's mood is dangerous.

"Now go ahead with your palaver, madame. I'm not going to leave the house. I know my business, and I'll stand by you as long as my name is Joe Woods. When you're done I want you to see me, and see my lawyer."

There is silence. Natalie's eyes give the stalwart miner a glance of unutterable thankfulness.

She has met a man at last.

Her bosom heaves with pride, her eyes beam on rough old Joe. Woods has taken out an unusually long cigar. He lights it at the door, and leisurely proceeds to smoke it on the upper veranda.

When his foot-fall dies away, Hardin essays to speak. His lips are strangely dry. He mutters something, and the words fail him. Natalie interrupts, with scorn: "Curse you and your money, you cowardly thief. You have met your match at last. I trusted to your honor. Your hands were on my throat just now. I have but one word to say to you now. Go, face that man out there!" Hardin is in a blind rage.

His legal vocabulary finds no ready phrase of adieu. His foot is on the top stair. Joe Woods says carelessly:

"Judge, you and I had better have a little talk to-night." Ah, his enemy! He knows him at last. Hardin hoarsely mutters: "Where? when?"

"When you please," says Woods.

"Ten, to-night; your room. I'll bring a friend with me." Hardin nods, and passes on, crossing the square to his hotel. He must have time for thought; for new plans; for revenge; yes, bloody revenge.

Colonel Joseph Woods spends an hour in conference with Peyton and Father Francois. Their plans are all finished.

Judge Davis, who is paralyzed by the vehemence of California character, caresses his educated whiskers. He pets his eye-glasses, while the three gentlemen confer. He is essentially a man of peace. He fears he may become merely a "piece of man" in case the appeal to revolvers, or mob law, is brought into this case. They do things differently in New York.

While the two lovely girls are using every soothing art of womanly sympathy to care for Natalie, it begins to dawn upon each of them that their futures are strangely interlinked. The presence of Madame de Santos seals their lips. They long for the hour when they can converse in private. They know now that the redoubtable Joe Woods has TWO fatherless girls to protect instead of ONE.

Natalie Santos, lying on her couch, watches these young beauties flitting about her room. "Does the heiress, challenged in her right, dream of her real parentage?" A gleam of light breaks in on the darkness of her sufferings. Why not peace and the oblivion of retirement for her, if her child's future is assured in any way? Why not?

Looking forward hopefully to a conference with Colonel Joe, she fears only the clear eyes of old Padre Francisco. "Shall she tell him all?" In these misgivings and vain rackings of the mind, she passes the afternoon. She yields to her better angel, and gives the story of her life to the patient priest.

Armand Valois and Raoul Dauvray have a blessed new bond of brotherhood. They are both lovers. With Padre Francisco, they are a guard of honor, watching night and day the two heiresses.

They share the secret consciousness of Natalie de Santos that Joe Woods has in store some great stroke.

Judge Davis, Peyton, and the resolute Joe are the only calm ones in the settlement. For, far and wide the news runs of racy developments. In store, saloon, and billiard lounging-place, on the corners, and around the deserted court-room, knots of cigar-smoking scandal-mongers assuage their inward cravings by frequent resort to the never-failing panacea--whiskey. Wild romances are current, in which two great millionaires, two sets of lawyers, duplicate heiresses, two foreign dukes, the old padre and the queenly madame are the star actors in a thrilling local drama, which is so far unpunctuated by the crack of the revolver.

It is a struggle for millions, and the clash of arms will surely come.

There has been no great issue ever resolved in Mariposa before the legal tribunal, which has not added its corpses to the mortuary selections lying in queer assortment on the red clay hillsides.

"Justice nods in California while the pistols are being drawn."

Hardin, closeted with his lawyers, suspends their eager plotting, to furtively confer in private with the judge.

When the first stars sweep into the blue mountain skies, and a silver moon rises slowly over the pine-clad hills, Joseph Woods summons all his latent fascinations to appease Madame Natalie de Santos. The sturdy Missourian has had his contretemps with Sioux and Pawnee. He has faced prairie fires, stampeded buffalo herds, and met dangers by flood and field. Little personal discussions with horse thieves, some border frays, and even a chance encounter on a narrow trail with a giant grizzly, have tried his nerve. But he braces with a good stiff draught of cognac now. He fears the wily and fascinating Natalie. He is at heart a would-be lady's man. Roughness is foreign to his nature, but he will walk the grim path of duty.

When he thinks of flinching, there rises on his memory the lonely grave where Peyton laid Maxime Valois to rest on the bloody field of Peachtree Creek, with the stars and bars lying lightly on his gallant breast. And he calmly enters the presence of the once famous siren.

There is a mute entreaty in her eyes, as she motions him to a seat.

Joseph toys nervously with the huge diamond, which is a badge "de rigueur" of his rank and grade as a bonanza king.

"I do not wish to agitate or distress you, madame," begins Joe, and his voice is very kind.

"I broke out a little on Hardin; all bluff, you know. Just to show him a card. Now will you trust and let me help you? I mean to bring you out all right. I can't tell you all I know. I am going to fight Hardin on another quarrel. It will be to the death. I can just as well square your little account too, if you will trust me. Will you let me handle your movements, up to the legal issue. After that you are free. I'll give you the word of an honest man, you shall not suffer. Will you trust me?"

Joe's big eyes are looking very appealingly in hers.

Without a word, she places her hand in his. "I am yours until that time, but spare me as much as you can--the old histories, you know," her voice falters. She is a woman, after all.

"Now see here, madame! I swear to you I am the only private man in California who knows your secret, except Hardin, now. I got it in the days long past. No one shall know your identity." He fixes a keen glance on her: "Is there anyone else you wish to spare?" he softly says.

"Yes." She is sobbing now. "It is my child. Don't let her know that awful past."

Joseph's eyes are filled with manly sorrow. He whispers with eagerness:

"Her father is"--

"Philip Hardin," falters the woman, whose stately head is now bowed in her hands.

"I'll protect that child. She shall never want a friend, if you do one thing," Joe falters.

Natalie raises a white face to his.

"What is it?" she huskily whispers.

"Will you swear, in open court, which of these two girls is your own child, if I ask you to?" He is eager and pleading.

She reads his very soul. She hesitates. "And you will protect the innocent girl, against his wrath?" There is all a mother's love in her appeal.

"Both of you. I swear it. You shall not want for money or protection," Joe solemnly says.

"Then, I will!" Natalie firmly answers.

He springs to her side.

"Does Hardin know which girl is his daughter?"

"He does not!" Natalie says slowly.

There is a silence; Joe can hear his own heart beat. Victory at last.

"I have nothing to ask you, except to see no one but myself, Padre Francisco, or my lawyer. If Hardin wants to see you, I'll be present. Now I am going to see him to-night. You will be watched over night and day. I am going to have every precaution taken. I shall be near you always. Rest in safety. I think I can save you any opening up of the old days.

"I will see you early."

Her hands clasp his warmly! She says: "Colonel, send Pere Francois to me. I will tell him all you need to know. He will know what to keep back."

"That's right," cries Joseph, warmly. "I know how to handle Hardin now. You can bank on the padre. He's dead game."

"And your reward?" Natalie whispers, with bowed head.

A wild thought makes the blood surge to Joe's brain. He slowly stammers, "My reward?" His eyes tell him he must make no mistake. A flash of genius.

"You will square my account, madame, if you make no objection to the immediate marriage of your daughter to Dauvray. He's a fine fellow for a Frenchman, and she shall never know this story. She'll have money enough. I'll see to that." Joe's voice is earnest.

Natalie's arms are stretched to him in thanks. "In God's name, be it, my noble friend."

Joe dares not trust himself longer.

He retires, leaving Natalie standing, a splendid statue, with shining, hopeful eyes. Her blessing follows him; sin-shadowed though she be, it reaches the Court of Heaven.

Natalie, in silent sorrow, sees her labor of years brushed away. Her child can never be the heiress of Lagunitas. Fate has brought the gentle Louise Moreau to the very threshold of her old home. It is Providence. Destiny. The all-knowing Pere Francois reveals to her how strangely the life-path of the heiress has been guarded. "My daughter," the priest solemnly says, "be comforted. Right shall prevail. Trust me, trust Colonel Woods. Your child may fall heir yet to a name and to her own inheritance. The ways of Him who pardons are mysterious." He leaves her comforted and yet not daring to break the seal of silence to the lovely claimants.

While Pere Francois confers with Natalie, as the moon sails high in heaven over the fragrant pines, Woods and Peyton exchange a few quiet words over their cigars.

By the repeater which Joe consults it is now a quarter of ten. The two gentlemen stroll over the grassy plaza. By a singular provincial custom each carries a neat navy revolver, where a hand could drop easily on it. Joe also caresses his favorite knife in his overcoat pocket.

In five minutes they are seated with Philip Hardin in his room. There is an air of gloomy readiness in Hardin which shows the unbending nature of the man. He is alone. Woods frankly says: "Judge Hardin, I wish you to know my friend, Mr. Henry Peyton. If anything should happen to me, he knows all my views. He will represent me. As you are alone, I will ask Mr. Peyton to wait for me below."

Henry Peyton bows and passes downstairs, where he is regarded as an archangel of the enemy. For the Hardin headquarters are loyal to their great chief. The man who controls the millions of Lagunitas is surrounded by his loyal body-guard at Mariposa.

When the two men are alone, Woods waits for Hardin to speak. He is silent.

There is a gulf between them which never can be bridged. Joseph feels he is no match for Hardin in chicanery, but he has his little surprise in store for the lawyer. It is an armed truce.

"Hardin, I've come over to-night to talk a little politics with you," begins Joseph. His eye is glued on the Judge's, who steadily returns the glance.

CHAPTER XX.

JUDGE HARDIN MEETS HIS MATCH.--A SENATORIAL ELECTION.--IN A MARIPOSA COURT-ROOM.--THE TRUST FULFILLED AT LA-GUNITAS.

Y̤ou need not trouble yourself about my political aspirations, sir," haughtily remarks Hardin, glaring at the stolid visitor, who calmly continues. "I don't allow no trouble, Jedge," Woods drawls. "I'll play my cards open. I run this here joint convention, which makes or breaks you. I'm dead-flat plain in my meaning. I can burst up your election as United States Senator, unless you and me can make 'a deal.'"

"Your terms?" sneers Hardin, with a glance at Joe's hand in his pocket, "Toujours pret" is Joseph's motto.

"Oh, my terms! I'll be open, Jedge. I leave this here lawsuit between us, to our lawyers. I will fight you fair in that. You will find me on the square."

"Do you threaten me, sir?" demands Hardin.

"Now, make your own game." Joe's brow darkens. "Hardin, I want you to hear me out; you can take it then, in any shape you want to. Fight or trade." Woods' old Missouri grit is aroused.

"Go on," says Hardin, with a rising gorge.

"You're talking marriage." Joe's sneer maddens Hardin." I tell you now to settle old scores with the lady whom I found in your hands to-night. If you don't, you're not going to the Senate."

Hardin gathers himself. Ah, that hand in the pocket!

"Don't make a mistake, Jedge," coldly interjects Woods. "Drop that gun. We're no bravos."

"I positively decline to have any bargain with you on my private matters. After you leave this room, you can look out for yourself, if you cross my path," hisses the Judge, his face pale and ghastly.

"Now, Jedge," Joe snaps out, "watch your own scalp. Hardin, I'll not dodge you. You are going on the wrong road. We split company here. But there's room enough in California for you and me. As for any 'shooting talk,' it's all bosh. You will get in a hot corner, unless you hear me out. I tell you now, to acknowledge your child by that woman. Save your election; save yourself, old man.

"She'll go off to France, but you've got to give her child a square name and a set-out."

"Never!" yells Hardin, forgetting himself, as with blind rage he points to the door.

"All right," says Joseph, coolly. "You'll never be senator till you send for me. You have fair warning. My cards are face-up on the table." Hardin, speechless with rage, sees him disappear.

Peyton and Joe Woods walk over the silent plaza, with the twinkling stars sweeping overhead. They exchange but few words. They seek the rest of their pillows. Joe's prayers consist of reloading his revolvers.

The last watcher in Mariposa is Hardin, the hate of hell in his heart. A glass of neat brandy is tossed off. He throws himself heavily on the bed. The world is a torment to him now. "On to Sacramento" is his last thought. Money, in hoards and heaps, will drown this rich booby's vain interference. For, legislatures sell senatorial honors in California openly like cabbage in a huckster's wagon, only at higher prices.

Before the gray squirrels are leaping on the madronas and nutty oaks next dawn of day, Hardin is miles away towards the State capital. His legal forces remain. He takes one trusty agent, to distribute his golden arguments.

When Woods leisurely finishes his breakfast he strolls under the pines with Pere Francois. There are also two youthful couples. They are reading lessons, not of law, but of love, in each other's shining eyes as they wander in the lonely forest paths.

Seated by a dashing mountain brook which runs past the town, Pere Francois gravely informs Joe that Natalie de Santos has given him the dark history of her chequered life. Though the seal of the confessional protects it, he has her consent to supply Woods and Judge Davis with certain facts. Her sworn statements will verify these if needed.

After a long interview with Madame de Santos, Colonel Joseph follows Hardin to Sacramento. He has one or two resolute friends with him as a guard against the coarse Western expedient of assassination. He knows Hardin's deft touches of old.

As the stage rattles around dizzy heights, below massy cliffs, swinging under the forest arches, the Missouri champion reasons out that Hardin's hands are tied personally as regards a bloody public quarrel, by the coming senatorial fight. To pluck the honors of the Senate at last from a divided State, is a testimony to the lawyer's great abilities. Joe thinks, with a sigh of regret, that some mere animated money-bag may sit under the white dome, and misrepresent the sovereign State of California. "Well, if Hardin won't bend, he's got to break." The miner puffs his cigar in search of wisdom.

Single-minded and unswerving, Woods goes directly to his splendid rooms at the "Golden Eagle," on reaching Sacramento.

The capital city of the State is crowded with legislators and attaches. The lobby banditti, free lances, and camp followers of the annual raid upon the pockets of the people are on guard. While his meal is being served in his parlor, he indites a note to Hardin's political Mark Antony. It will rest with him to crown a triumph or deliver his unheard oration over the body of a politically dead Caesar. The billet reads:

"I want you instantly, on a matter deciding Hardin's election. You can show him this."

In half an hour, over burgundy and the ever-flowing champagne, Woods, feeling his visitor in good humor, fires his first gun. He begins with half-shut eyes, in a genial tone:

"Harris, I have sent for you to tell you Hardin and me have locked horns over some property. Now I won't vote for him, but I'll hold off my dogs. I won't work against him if he signs a sealed paper I'm goin' to give you. If he don't, I'll open out, and tell an old yarn to our secret nominating caucus. I am solidly responsible for the oration. He will be laid out. It rests only with his friends then, to spread this scandal. He has time to square this. It does not hang on party interests. I am a man of my word, you know. Now, I leave it to you to consider if he has any right to ask his friends to back him in certain defeat. See him quick. If he tells you to hear the story from me, I will tell you all. If he flies the track, I am silent until the caucus. THEN, I will speak, if I'm alive. If I am dead, my pard will speak for me. My death would seal his utter ruin. I can stand the consequences. He has got to come up to the captain's office and settle." The astounded Harris gloomily muses while Woods quietly inscribes a few lines on a sheet of paper. He seals the envelop, and hands it to Senator Harris.

"I won't leave this camp, Harris, till I get your answer," calmly remarks Joseph. He refuses to waste more words in explanation. "See Hardin," is his only phrase. "It's open war then between him and me."

Harris, with a very grave face, enters the private rooms of Judge Hardin at the Orleans Hotel.

Hardin listens, with scowling brow as black as night. He tears open the envelop! His faithful henchman wonders what can bring night's blackness to Judge Hardin's face.

The lines are a careful acknowledgment of the paternity of the girl child of "Natalie de Santos," born at San Francisco and now about eighteen years of age. It closes with a statement of her right to inherit as a lawful heiress from him.

"I will shoot that dog on sight, if he carries out this threat," deliberately says Hardin.

"Judge," coldly replies his lieutenant, "does this note refer to public affairs, or to party interests?"

"Private matters!" replies Hardin, his eyes flashing.

"Then, let me say, I will keep silent in this matter. I shall ask you to name some other man to handle your candidacy before the Legislature. Joe Woods is honest, and absolutely of iron nerve. You can send for any of your other friends, and choose a man to take my place. I won't fight Joe. Woods never lied in his life.

"If you will state that you have adjusted this difference with him, I am at your service. Let me know your decision soon. He waits for me. In all else, I am yours, as a friend, but I will not embroil the State now for a mere private feud. Send for me, Judge, when you have decided."

In the long and heated conferences of the night, before the sun again pours its shimmering golden waves on the parched plains of Sacramento, Hardin finds no one who will face the mysterious situation.

Harris finds the patient Joe playing seven-up with a couple of friends, and his pistols on the table.

"All right, Harris; let him think it over." Joe nods, and continues his game.

Calmly expectant, when Harris sends his name up next morning, Joe Woods is in very good humor. The gathering forces are anxious for the hour when a solemn secret party caucus shall name the man to be officially balloted in as Senator of the United States for six years. The term is not to begin for three months, but great corporations, the banks, with their heaped millions, and all the mighty high-priests of the dollar-god, need that sense of security which Hardin's ability will give to their different schemes. Their plans can be safely laid out then.

In simple straightforwardness, Harris hands Woods a sealed envelop, without a word.

In the vigils of one awful night, Philip Hardin knows that he must fence off the maddened woman who seems to have a mysterious hold upon his destiny at this crisis. What force impels her?

Hardin has enjoined Harris to have Woods repeat his pledge of "non-opposition."

"Did you see the Jedge sign this here paper?" says Woods dryly, as he inspects the signature. His face is solemn.

"I did," Harris answers.

"Then just write your name here as witness," Joseph briskly says, handing him a pen, and covering the few lines of the document, leaving only Philip Hardin's well-known signature visible.

Harris hesitates. Joe's eyes are blazing; no foolery now! Harris quietly signs. The name of Joseph Woods is added, at once, with the date.

"Harris," says Joseph, "you're a man of honor. I pledge you now I will not make public the nature of this document. Hardin can grab for the Senate now, if you boys can elect him. I'll not fight him."

Harris retires in silence. The day is saved. Though the election is within three days, Joseph Woods finds private business so pressing that his seat is vacant, when Philip Hardin is declared Senator-elect. The pledge has been kept. Not a rumor of the secret incident reaches the public. The cautious Joseph is grateful for not being obliged to shorten Hardin's life.

Fly as fast as Hardin may to Mariposa, Joe Woods is there before him. The telegraph bears to every hamlet of the Golden State the news of the senatorial choice.

Philip Hardin, seated on the porch of the old mansion at Lagunitas, reads the eulogies crowding the columns of fifty journals.

From San Diego to Siskiyou one general voice hails the new-made member of that august body, who are now so rapidly giving America "Roman liberties."

The friend of Mammon, nurtured in conspiracy, skilled in deceit, Hardin, the hidden Mokanna, grins behind his silver veil.

His deep-laid plans seem all safe now. The local meshes of his golden net hold the District Judge firmly. It will be easy to postpone, to weary out, to harass this strange faction. He has stores of coin ready. They are the heaped-up reserves of his "senatorial ammunition." And yet Joe Woods, that burly meddling fool. To placate Natalie! To induce her to leave at once for Paris! How shall this be done? Ha! The marriage is her dream in life! He is elected now. He fears not her Southern rival. The ambitious political lady aspirant! He can explain to her now in private, To give Natalie an acknowledgment of a private marriage will content her. Then his bought Judge can quietly grant a separation for desertion, after Natalie has returned to France. She will care nothing for the squabble over the acres of Lagunitas, if well paid. As for the priest, he may swear as strongly as he likes. The girl will surely be declared illegitimate. He has destroyed all the papers. Valois' will is never to see the light. If deception has been practiced he cares not. Senatorial privilege raises him too high for the voice of slander.

He has the golden heart of these hills now to himself.

Yes, he will fool the priest and divide his enemies. The money for Natalie will be deposited in Paris banks. The principal to be paid her in one year, on condition of never again coming to the United States. Long before that time he will be legally free and remarried. Hardin rubs his hands in glee. Neither reporter nor the public will ever see the divorce proceedings. That is easily handled in Mariposa.

In his local legal experience, he has many times seen wilder schemes succeed. Spanish grants have been shifted leagues to suit the occasion. Boundaries are removed bodily. Witnesses are manufactured under golden pressure. The eyes of Justice are blinded with opaque weights of the yellow treasure.

But he must work rapidly. It is now only a short week to the trial. The court-house and records are regularly watched. Not a move indicates any prying into the matter beyond the mere identity of the heiress. But who has set up the other claimant?

It would be madness for Natalie to raise this quarrel! Some schemers have imposed a strange girl on the other party. Hardin recalls Natalie's wild astonishment at the apparition of another "Isabel Valois."

And the second girl did not even know who Natalie was. What devil's work is this?

Hardin decides to "burn his ships." Alone in the home of the Peraltas, he prepares for a campaign "a l'outrance." That crafty priest might know too much. The evening before his departure he burns up every paper at the ranch which would cause any remark, even in case of his death. Next morning, as he rides out of Lagunitas, he gazes on the fair domain. The last thing he sees is the chapel cross. A chill suddenly strikes him. He gallops on. Rapidly journeying to Mariposa, he installs himself in the headquarters of his friends. His ablest counsel has provided the bought Judge, with full secret instructions to meet every contingency.

Sober and serious in final judgment, Philip Hardin quickly summons a discreet friend. He requests a last personal interview with Natalie de Santos. The ambassador is received by good-humored Joe Woods. He declines an interview, by the lady's orders, unless its object is stated.

Hardin requests that some friend other than the Missouri miner, may be named to represent Natalie.

His eyes gleam when the selection is made of Pere Francois. Just what he would wish.

It lacks now but three days of the final hearing. An hour after the message, Hardin and the priest are seated, in quiet commune. There are no papers. There is no time lost, none to lose. No witnesses, no interlopers.

Hardin opens his proposals. The priest seems tractable. "I do not wish to refer to any present legal matters. I speak only of the past. I will refer only to the future of 'Madame de Santos.' You may say to her that if she will grant me a brief interview, I feel I can make her a proposition she will accept, as very advantageous. In justice to her, I cannot communicate its details, even to you. But if she wishes to advise with you, I have no objection to giving you the guarantees of my provision for her future.

You shall know as much of our whole arrangement as she wishes you to. She can have you or other friends, in an adjoining room. You can be called in to witness the papers, and examine the details."

The grave priest returns in half an hour. Hardin ponders uneasily. The priest plays an unimpassioned part. "Madame de Santos will receive Judge Hardin on his terms, with the condition, that if there is any exciting difference, Judge Hardin will retire at once, and not renew his proposals." Hardin accepts. Now for work.

Side by side, the new-made senator and the old priest walk across the plaza. Success smiles on Hardin.

Local quid-nuncs mutter "Compromise," as they seek the spiritual consolation of the Magnolia Saloon and Palace Varieties. Is there to be no pistol practice after all?

Alas, these degenerate days! The camp has lost its glory. Betting has been two to one that Colonel Joe Woods riddles the Judge before the trial is over.

Now these bets will be off. A fraud on the innocent public. The decadence of Mariposa.

Yet, Hardin is not easy. In the first struggle of his life with a priest, Hardin feels himself no match for his passionless antagonist. The waxen mask of the Church hides the inner soul of the man.

Only when Pere Francois turns his searching gaze on the Judge, parrying every move, does the lawyer feel how the immobility of the clergyman is proof against his wiles and professional ambushes.

Pere Francois conducts Hardin into the room whence Natalie dismissed him, in her roused but sadly wounded spirit. She is there, waiting. Her face is marble in pallor.

With a grave bow, the old ecclesiastic retires to an adjoining room and leaves them alone. There is a writing table.

"Madame, to spare you discussion," Hardin remarks seriously, "I will write on two sheets of paper what I ask and what I offer. You may confer with your adviser. I will retire. You can add to either anything you propose. We can then, at once, observe if we can approach each other."

Natalie's stately head bows assent in silence. In five minutes Hardin hands her the two sheets.

Natalie's face puzzles him. Calm and unmoved, she looks him quietly in the eyes, as if in a mute farewell. She has simply uttered monosyllables, in answer to his few explanations.

Hardin walks up and down upon the veranda, while Natalie, the priest, and Colonel Joe scan the two sheets. His heart beats quickly while the trio read his proposals.

They are simple enough. What he gets and what he gives. Madame de Santos is to absent herself from the trial. She is to leave Isabel Valois, her charge, with the priest. She is to be silent as to the entire past.

Hardin's lawyers are to stipulate, in case of Isabel Valois being defeated in any of her rights, she shall be free to receive a fund equal to that settled on the absent child of Natalie. Her freedom comes with her majority in any case.

Judge Hardin offers, on the other hand:

To give a written recognition of the private marriage, and to fully legalize the absent Irene.

To admit her to his succession, and to surrender all control to the mother.

On condition of Natalie de Santos ceasing all marital claims and disappearing at once, she is to receive five hundred thousand dollars, in bankers' drafts to her order in Paris, six months after the legal separation.

Hardin's tread re-echoes on the porch. His mind is busied. Is he to have a closing career of unsullied honor in the Senate? He is yet in a firm, if frosty age. A dignified halo will surround his second marriage. It is better thus. Peace and silence at any cost. And Lagunitas' millions to come. The mine--his dear-bought treasure. It is coming, Philip Hardin. Peace and rest? it will be peace and silence. He starts! The black-robed priest is at the door. Father Francois has now resumed his soutane.

"Will you kindly enter?" he says.

Hardin, with unmoved face, seats himself opposite Natalie. Pere Francois remains.

"I will accept your terms, Judge Hardin," she steadily says, "with the addition that the advice of Judge Davis be at my service regarding the papers, and that I leave to-morrow for San Francisco.

"You are to send an agent, also. The money to be transferred by telegraph, payable absolutely to me at Paris, by my bankers, at the appointed time. Your agent may accompany me to the frontier of the State. I will leave as soon as the bankers acknowledge the transfer.

"In case of any failure on your part, the obligation to keep silent ceases. I retain the marriage papers."

Hardin bows his head. The priest is silent. In a few moments, the senator-elect says:

"I agree to all." His senatorial debut pictures itself in his mind.

Madame de Santos rises, "I authorize Pere Francois to remain with you, on my behalf. Let the papers be at once prepared. I am ready to leave to-morrow morning. I only insist the two papers which would affect my child, be duplicated, and both witnessed by our lawyers."

Hardin bows assent. Natalie de Santos walks toward the door of her rooms. Her last words fall on his ear: "Pere Francois will represent me in all." She is going. Hardin springs to the door: "And I shall see you again?" His voice quivers slightly. Old days throng back to his memory. "Is it for ever?" His iron heart softens a moment.

"I pray God, never! Philip Hardin, you are dead to me. The past is dead. I can only think of you with your cruel grasp on my throat!" She is gone.

As the door closes, Hardin buries his face in his hands. Thoughts of other days are rending his heart-strings.

Before three hours, the papers are all executed. The morning stage takes Natalie de Santos, with the priest, and guarded by Armand Valois, away from the scene of the coming legal battle.

In the early gray of the dawn, Philip Hardin only catches a glimpse of a muffled form in a coach. He will see the mother of his child no more. With a wild dash, the stage sweeps away. It is all over.

His agent, in a special conveyance, is already on the road. He has orders to telegraph the completion of the transfer. He is to verify the departure for New York, of the ex-queen of the El Dorado.

On the day of the hearing, the court-house is crowded. Pere Francois and Armand Valois have not yet returned. Both sides have received, by telegraph, the news of the completion of the work. By stipulation, the newly-acknowledged marriage is not to be made public.

Hardin, pale and thoughtful, enters the court with his supporters. There is but one young lady present. With her, Peyton, Judge Davis, and Joseph Woods are seated. Raoul Dauvray seats himself quietly between the two parties.

When the case is reached, there is the repression of a deathly silence. Hardin, by the advice of his lawyers, will stand strictly on the defensive. He has decided to acknowledge his entire readiness to close his guardianship. He will leave the heirship to be finally adjusted by the Court. The Court is under his thumb.

His senatorial duties call for this relief. It will take public attention from the unpleasant matter. Rid of the burden of the ranch, still the "bonanza of Lagunitas" will be his, as always.

The great lawyer he relies on states plausibly this entire willingness to such a relief, and requests the Court to appoint a successor to the distinguished trustee. Hardin feels that he has now covered his past with a solid barrier. Safe at last. No living man can roll away the huge rock from the "tomb of the dead past." It would need a voice from the grave. He can defy the whole world. No thought of his dead friend haunts him.

When the advocate ceases speaking, while the Judge ponders over the disputed heirship, and the contest as to the legitimacy of Maxime Valois' child, when clearly identified, Judge Davis rises quietly to address the Court. Philip Hardin feels a slight chill icing down his veins, as he notes the gravity of the Eastern lawyer's manner. Is there a masked battery?

"Your Honor," begins Davis, "we oppose any action tending to discharge or relieve the present guardian of Isabel Valois.

"A most important discovery of new matters in the affairs of this estate, makes it my duty to lay some startling facts before your Honor."

There is a pause. Hardin's heart flutters madly. He sees a stony look gather on Joe Woods' face. There is a peculiar grimness also in the visage of the watchful Peyton. Everyone in the room is on the alert. Crowding to the front, Hardin is elbowed by a man who seats himself in a chair reserved by Judge Davis.

His eyes are blinded for a moment. Great Heavens! It is his old law-clerk. The wily and once hilarious Jaggers.

He is here for some purpose. That devil Woods' work.

Hardin's hand clutches a revolver in his pocket. He glares uneasily at Joe Woods, at Peyton, at the ex-clerk. He breathlessly waits for the solemn voice of Davis:

"We propose, your Honor, to introduce evidence that the late Maxime Valois left a will. We propose to prove that the estate has been maladministered. We will prove to your Honor that a gigantic fraud has been perpetrated during the minority of the child of Colonel Valois. The most valuable element of the estate, the Lagunitas mine, has been fraudulently enjoyed by the administrator."

Hardin springs to his feet. He is forced into his chair by his counsel. There is the paleness of death on his face, but murder lurks in his heart. Away with patience now. A hundred eyes are gazing in his direction. The Judge is anchored, in amazement, on the bench. Woods and Peyton are facing Hardin, with steady defiance.

As he struggles to rise, he feels his blood boiling like molten iron.

He has been trapped by this devil, Woods. Davis resumes: "I shall show your Honor, by the man who held Colonel Valois in his arms on the battlefield as he lay dying, that a will was duly forwarded to the guardian and administrator, who concealed it. I will also prove, your Honor, that Colonel Valois repeated that will in a document taken from his dead body, in which he acknowledged his marriage, and the legitimacy of his true child. I will file these papers, and prove them by testimony of the gallant officer who buried him, and who succeeded to his regiment."

A deep growl from Hardin is heard. He knows now who Peyton is. What avenging fiends are on his track? But the mine, the mine is safe. Always the mine, The deeds will hold. Davis resumes, his voice ringing cold and clear:

"I shall also prove by documents, concealed by the administrator, that Maxime Valois never parted with the title to the Lagunitas mine; that the millions have been stolen, which it has yielded. I will bring in the evidence of the clerk who received these last letters from the absent owner in the field, that they are genuine. They state his utter inability to sell the mine, as the whole property belonged to his wife."

There is a blood-red film before Hardin's eyes now. Prudence flies after patience. It is his Waterloo. All is lost, even honor.

"I venture to remind your Honor, that even if the daughter, whom I produce here, is proved illegitimate, that she takes the whole property, including the mine, as the legal heir of her mother, under the laws of California." A murmur is suppressed by the clerk's hammer.

There is an awful silence as Judge Davis adds: "I will further produce before your Honor, Armand Valois, the only other heir of the decedent, to whom the succession would fall by law. He is named in the will I will establish, made twelve hours before the writer was killed at the battle of Peachtree Creek.

"I am aware," Judge Davis concludes, "that some one has forged the titles to the Lagunitas mine. I will prove the forgery to have been executed in the interest of Philip Hardin, the administrator, whom I now formally ask you to remove pending this trial, as a man false to his trust. He has robbed the orphan daughter of his friend. He deceived the man who laid his life down for the cause of the South, while he plotted in the safe security of distant California homes. Colonel Valois was robbed by his trusted friend."

A mighty shudder shakes the crowd. Men gaze at each other, wildly. The blinking Judge is dazed on the bench he pollutes. Before any one can draw a breath in relief, Hardin, bending himself below the restraining arms, springs to his feet and levels a pistol full at Joe Woods' breast.

"You hound!" he yells. His arm is struck up; Raoul Dauvray has edged every moment nearer the disgraced millionaire. The explosion of the heavy pistol deafens those near. When the smoke floats away, a gaping wound tells where its ball crashed through Hardin's brain. Slain by his own hand. Dead and disgraced. The senatorial laurels never touch his brow!

In five minutes the court is cleared. An adjournment to the next day is forced by the sudden tragedy. The wild mob are thronging the plaza.

Silent in death lies the man who realized at last how the awful voice of the dead Confederate called down the vengeance of God on the despoiler of the orphan.

The telegraph, lightning-winged, bears the news far and wide. By the evening Pere Francois and Armand Valois return. In a few hours Natalie de Santos turns backward. The swift wheels speeding down the Truckee are slower than the electric spark bearing to the ex-queen of the El Dorado, the wife of a day, the news of her legal widowhood.

Henry Peyton brings back the traveller, whose presence is now absolutely needed.

A lonely grave on the red hillside claims the last remains of the dark Chief of the Golden Circle. Few stand by its yawning mouth, to see the last of the man whose name has been just hailed everywhere with wild enthusiasm.

Unloved, unhonored, unregretted, unshriven, with all his imperfections on his head, he waits the last trump. Alone in death, as in life.

In the brief and formal verification of all these facts, the Court finds an opportunity to at once establish the identity of the heiress of Lagunitas. For, there is no contest now.

In formal devotion to the profession, Hardin's lawyer represents the estate of the dark schemer.

The legal tangles yield to final proofs.

There is a family party at Lagunitas once more. Judge Davis and Peyton guard the interests of the girl who has only lost the millions of Lagunitas to inherit a fortune from the father who scorned to even gaze upon her face. Joseph Woods joyfully guides the beautiful heiress of the domain, who kneels besides the grave of Dolores Peralta, her unknown mother, with her lover by her side. The last of the Valois stand there, hand in hand. She is Louise Moreau no more.

Pere Francois is again in his old home by the little chapel, where twenty years ago he raised his voice in the daily supplication for God's sinful children.

While Raoul Dauvray and Armand ride in voyages of discovery over the great domain, the two heiresses are happy with each other. There is no question between them. They are innocent of each other's sorrows. They now know much of the shadowy past with its chequered romance. The transfer of all the mine and its profits to the young girl, who finds the domain in the hills a fairyland, is accomplished.

Judge Davis hies himself away to the splendid excitement of his Eastern metropolitan practise. His "honorarium" causes him to have an added and tender feeling for the all-conquering Joe Woods. Henry Peyton is charged with the general supervision of the Lagunitas estate. He is aided by a mine superintendent selected by that wary old Argonaut, Joe.

Natalie de Santos leaves the refuge of lovely Lagunitas in a few weeks. There is a shadow resting on her heart which will never be lifted. In vain, beside the old chapel, seated under the giant rose-vines, Pere Francois urges her to witness the marriage of her daughter. Under the care of Joseph Woods, she leaves for San Francisco. Her daughter, who is soon to take a rightful name, learns from Pere Francois the agreed-on reasons of her absence. Natalie will not make a dark background to the happiness to come. Silence and expiation await her beyond the surges of the

Atlantic.

Joseph Woods and Pere Francois have buried all awkward references to past history. Irene Dauvray will never know the story of the lovely "Queen of the El Dorado."

There are no joy bells at Lagunitas on the day when the old priest unites Armand and Isabel Valois in marriage. The same solemn consecration gives gallant Raoul Dauvray, the woman he adores. It is a sacrament of future promise. Peyton and Joe Woods are the men who stand in place of the fathers of these two dark-eyed brides. It is a solemn and tender righting of the old wrongs. A funeral of the past--a birth of a brighter day, for all.

The load of care and strife has been taken from the shoulders of the three elders, who gravely watch the four glowing and enraptured lovers.

In a few weeks, Raoul Dauvray and his bride leave for San Francisco. Fittingly they choose France for their home. In San Francisco, Joseph Woods leads the young bride through the silent halls of the old house on the hill. The Missourian gravely bids the young wife remember that it was here her feet wandered over the now neglected paths.

Joseph Woods convoys the departing voyagers to the border of the State. The ample fortune secured to them, will engage his occasional leisure in advice as to its local management.

Natalie de Santos goes forth with them. Her home in Paris awaits her. The Golden State knows her no more. Her feet will never wander back to the shores where her stormy youth was passed.

A lover's pilgrimage to beloved Paris and the old castle by the blue waters of Lake Geneva claims the Lord and Lady of Lagunitas. For, they will return to dwell in the mountains of Mariposa. Before they cross the broad Atlantic, they have a sacred duty to perform. It is to visit the grave of the soldier of the Lost Cause and lay their wreaths upon the turf which covers his gallant breast.

The old padre sits on the porch of his house at Lagunitas. He waits only for the last solemn act. Henry Peyton is to follow the travellers East, and remove the soldier of the gray to the little chapel grounds of Lagunitas.

When Padre Francisco has seen the master come home, and raised his weakening voice in requiem over the friend of his youth, he will seek once more his dear

Paris, and find again his cloistered home near Notre Dame.

He has, as a memorial of mother and daughter, a deed of the old home of Philip Hardin. It is given to the Church for a hospital. It is well so. None of the living ever wish to pass again its shadowed portals.

While waiting the time for their departure, the priest and Henry Peyton watch the splendid beauties of Lagunitas, in peaceful brotherhood. The man of war and the servant of peace are drawn towards each other strangely.

The Virginian often gazes on the sword of Maxime Valois, hanging now over the hearthplace he left in his devotion to the Lost Cause. He thanks God that the children of the old blood are in the enjoyment of their birthright.

Padre Francisco, telling his beads, or whiling an hour away with his breviary, begins to nod easily as the lovely summer days deepen in splendor. He is an old man now, yet his heart is touched with the knowledge of God's infinite mercy as he looks over the low wall to where the roses bloom around: the grave of Dolores Valois.

He hopes to live yet to know, that gallant father and patient mother will live over again in the happy faces of the children of their orphaned child.

In the United States of America, at this particular juncture, no happier man than Colonel and State Senator Joseph Woods can be found. His mines are unfailing in their yield; his bachelor bungalow, in its splendor, will extinguish certain ambitious rivals, and he is freed from the nightmare of investigating the tangled web of the mysterious struggle for the millions of Lagunitas. He is confirmed in his resolve to remain a bachelor.

"I have two home camps now, one in Paris and one in California, where I am a sort of a brevet father. I won't be lonely," Joe merrily says.

Joseph's cheery path in life is illuminated by his gorgeous diamonds, and roped in with his massive watch-chains. More precious than the gold and gems is the rough and ready manhood of the old Argonaut. He seriously thinks of eschewing the carrying of weapons, and abandoning social adventures, becoming staid and serene like Father Francois.

He often consoles himself in his loneliness by the thought that Henry Peyton is also a man without family. "I will capture Peyton when he gets the young people in good shape, and they are tired of Paris style," Joe muses. "He's a man and a brother, and we will spend our old days in peace together."

One haunting, sad regret touches Colonel Joe's heart. He learns of the intention of Natalie to spend her days in retirement and in helping others.

Thinking of her splendid beauty, her daring struggle for her friendless child's rights, and all that is good of the only woman he ever could have desperately loved, he guards her secret in his breast. He dare not confess to his own heart that if there had been an honorable way, he would fain have laid his fortune at the feet of the peerless "Queen of the El Dorado."

Francois Ribaut, walking the deck of the steamer, gazes on the great white stars above him. The old man is peaceful, and calmly thankful. The night breezes moan over the lonely Atlantic! As the steamer bravely dashes the spray aside, his heart bounds with a new happiness. Every hour brings the beloved France nearer to him. Looking back at the life and land he leaves behind him, the old priest marvels at the utter uselessness of Philip Hardin's life. Apples of Sodom were all his treasures. His wasted gifts, his dark schemes, his sly plans, all gone for naught. Blindly driven along in the darkness of evil, his own hand pulled down his palace of sin on his head. And even "French Charlie" was avenged by the murderer's self-executed sentence. "Vengeance is mine, saith the Lord; I will repay." The innocent and helpless have wandered past each dark pitfall dug by the wily Hardin, and enjoy their own. Pere Francois, with his eyes cast backward on his own life path, feels that he has not fought the good fight in vain. His gentle heart throbs in sympathy, filled with an infinite compassion for the lonely Natalie de Santos. Sinned against and sinning. A free lance, with only her love for her child to hallow and redeem her. Her own plans, founded in guile, have all miscarried. Blood stains the gold bestowed on her by Philip Hardin's death. Her life has been a stormy sea. Yet, to her innocent child, a name and fortune have been given by the hand of Providence. In turning away her face from the vain and glittering world she has adorned, the chase and plaything of men, one pure white flower will bloom from the red ashes of her dead life. The unshaken affection of the child for whom she struggled, who can always, in ignorance of the dark past, lift happy eyes to hers and call her in love, by the holy name of mother. With bowed head and thankful heart, Padre Francisco's thoughts linger around beautiful Lagunitas. Its groves and forest arches, its mirrored lake, its smiling beauties and fruitful fields, return to him. The old priest murmurs: "God made Lagunitas; but man made California what it has been."

A land of wild adventure, of unrighted wrongs. A land of sad histories, of many shattered hopes. Fierce waves of adventurers swept away the simple early folk. Lawless license, flaunting vice, and social disorganization made its early life as a State, one mad chaos.

The Indians have perished, rudely despoiled. The old Dons have faded into the gray mists of a dead past. The early Argonauts have lived out the fierce fever of their wild lives. To the old individual freebooters, a new order of great corporate monopolies and gigantic rough-hewn millionaires succeeds. There is always some hand on the people's throat in California. Yet the star of hope glitters.

Slowly, through all the foamy restless waves of transient adventurers the work of the homebuilders is showing the dry land decked with the olive branches of peace.

The native sons and daughters of the Golden West, bright, strong, self-reliant and full of promise, are the glittering-eyed young guardians of the Golden Gate. Born of the soil, with life's battle to fight on their native hills, may they build around the slopes of the Pacific, a State great in its hearths and homes. The future shines out. The gloomy past recedes. The sunlight of freedom sparkles on the dreamy lake of Lagunitas!

The Codes Of Hammurabi And Moses
W. W. Davies

QTY

The discovery of the Hammurabi Code is one of the greatest achievements of archaeology, and is of paramount interest, not only to the student of the Bible, but also to all those interested in ancient history...

Religion   **ISBN:** *1-59462-338-4*   **Pages:132**

MSRP $12.95

The Theory of Moral Sentiments
Adam Smith

QTY

This work from 1749. contains original theories of conscience amd moral judgment and it is the foundation for systemof morals.

Philosophy   **ISBN:** *1-59462-777-0*   **Pages:536**

MSRP $19.95

Jessica's First Prayer
Hesba Stretton

QTY

In a screened and secluded corner of one of the many railway-bridges which span the streets of London there could be seen a few years ago, from five o'clock every morning until half past eight, a tidily set-out coffee-stall, consisting of a trestle and board, upon which stood two large tin cans, with a small fire of charcoal burning under each so as to keep the coffee boiling during the early hours of the morning when the work-people were thronging into the city on their way to their daily toil...

Pages:84

Childrens   **ISBN:** *1-59462-373-2*   *MSRP $9.95*

My Life and Work
Henry Ford

QTY

Henry Ford revolutionized the world with his implementation of mass production for the Model T automobile. Gain valuable business insight into his life and work with his own auto-biography... "We have only started on our development of our country we have not as yet, with all our talk of wonderful progress, done more than scratch the surface. The progress has been wonderful enough but..."

Pages:300

Biographies/   **ISBN:** *1-59462-198-5*   *MSRP $21.95*

The Art of Cross-Examination
Francis Wellman

QTY

I presume it is the experience of every author, after his first book is published upon an important subject, to be almost overwhelmed with a wealth of ideas and illustrations which could readily have been included in his book, and which to his own mind, at least, seem to make a second edition inevitable. Such certainly was the case with me; and when the first edition had reached its sixth impression in five months, I rejoiced to learn that it seemed to my publishers that the book had met with a sufficiently favorable reception to justify a second and considerably enlarged edition. ..

Pages:412

Reference   ISBN: *1-59462-647-2*   *MSRP $19.95*

On the Duty of Civil Disobedience
Henry David Thoreau

QTY

Thoreau wrote his famous essay, On the Duty of Civil Disobedience, as a protest against an unjust but popular war and the immoral but popular institution of slave-owning. He did more than write—he declined to pay his taxes,   and was hauled off to gaol in consequence. Who can say how much this refusal of his hastened the end of the war and of slavery ?

Law   ISBN: *1-59462-747-9*   **Pages:48**

MSRP $7.45

Dream Psychology Psychoanalysis for Beginners
Sigmund Freud

QTY

Sigmund Freud, born Sigismund Schlomo Freud (May 6, 1856 - September 23, 1939), was a Jewish-Austrian neurologist and psychiatrist who co-founded the psychoanalytic school of psychology. Freud is best known for his theories of the unconscious mind, especially involving the mechanism of repression; his redefinition of sexual desire as mobile and directed towards a wide variety of objects; and his therapeutic techniques, especially his understanding of transference in the therapeutic relationship and the presumed value of dreams as sources of insight into unconscious desires.

Pages:196

Psychology   ISBN: *1-59462-905-6*   *MSRP $15.45*

The Miracle of Right Thought
Orison Swett Marden

QTY

Believe with all of your heart that you will do what you were made to do. When the mind has once formed the habit of holding cheerful, happy, prosperous pictures, it will not be easy to form the opposite habit. It does not matter how improbable or how far away this realization may see, or how dark the prospects may be, if we visualize them as best we can, as vividly as possible, hold tenaciously to them and vigorously struggle to attain them, they will gradually become actualized, realized in the life. But a desire, a longing without endeavor, a yearning abandoned or held indifferently will vanish without realization.

Pages:360

Self Help   ISBN: *1-59462-644-8*   *MSRP $25.45*

www.bookjungle.com *email: sales@bookjungle.com fax: 630-214-0564 mail: Book Jungle PO Box 2226 Champaign, IL 61825*

QTY

The Rosicrucian Cosmo-Conception Mystic Christianity *by Max Heindel*   ISBN: *1-59462-188-8*   **$38.95**
The Rosicrucian Cosmo-conception is not dogmatic, neither does it appeal to any other authority than the reason of the student. It is: not controversial, but is: sent forth in the, hope that it may help to clear...   *New Age/Religion Pages 646*

Abandonment To Divine Providence *by Jean-Pierre de Caussade*   ISBN: *1-59462-228-0*   **$25.95**
"The Rev. Jean Pierre de Caussade was one of the most remarkable spiritual writers of the Society of Jesus in France in the 18th Century. His death took place at Toulouse in 1751. His works have gone through many editions and have been republished...   *Inspirational/Religion Pages 400*

Mental Chemistry *by Charles Haanel*   ISBN: *1-59462-192-6*   **$23.95**
Mental Chemistry allows the change of material conditions by combining and appropriately utilizing the power of the mind. Much like applied chemistry creates something new and unique out of careful combinations of chemicals the mastery of mental chemistry...   *New Age Pages 354*

The Letters of Robert Browning and Elizabeth Barret Barrett 1845-1846 vol II   ISBN: *1-59462-193-4*   **$35.95**
by Robert Browning and Elizabeth Barrett   *Biographies Pages 596*

Gleanings In Genesis (volume I) *by Arthur W. Pink*   ISBN: *1-59462-130-6*   **$27.45**
Appropriately has Genesis been termed "the seed plot of the Bible" for in it we have, in germ form, almost all of the great doctrines which are afterwards fully developed in the books of Scripture which follow...   *Religion/Inspirational Pages 420*

The Master Key *by L. W. de Laurence*   ISBN: *1-59462-001-6*   **$30.95**
In no branch of human knowledge has there been a more lively increase of the spirit of research during the past few years than in the study of Psychology, Concentration and Mental Discipline. The requests for authentic lessons in Thought Control, Mental Discipline and...   *New Age/Business Pages 422*

The Lesser Key Of Solomon Goetia *by L. W. de Laurence*   ISBN: *1-59462-092-X*   **$9.95**
This translation of the first book of the "Lemegton" which is now for the first time made accessible to students of Talismanic Magic was done, after careful collation and edition, from numerous Ancient Manuscripts in Hebrew, Latin, and French...   *New Age/Occult Pages 92*

Rubaiyat Of Omar Khayyam *by Edward Fitzgerald*   ISBN:*1-59462-332-5*   **$13.95**
Edward Fitzgerald, whom the world has already learned, in spite of his own efforts to remain within the shadow of anonymity, to look upon as one of the rarest poets of the century, was born at Bredfield, in Suffolk, on the 31st of March, 1809. He was the third son of John Purcell...   *Music Pages 172*

Ancient Law *by Henry Maine*   ISBN: *1-59462-128-4*   **$29.95**
The chief object of the following pages is to indicate some of the earliest ideas of mankind, as they are reflected in Ancient Law, and to point out the relation of those ideas to modern thought.   *Religion/History Pages 452*

Far-Away Stories *by William J. Locke*   ISBN: *1-59462-129-2*   **$19.45**
"Good wine needs no bush, but a collection of mixed vintages does. And this book is just such a collection. Some of the stories I do not want to remain buried for ever in the museum files of dead magazine-numbers an author's not unpardonable vanity..."   *Fiction Pages 272*

Life of David Crockett *by David Crockett*   ISBN: *1-59462-250-7*   **$27.45**
"Colonel David Crockett was one of the most remarkable men of the times in which he lived. Born in humble life, but gifted with a strong will, an indomitable courage, and unremitting perseverance...   *Biographies/New Age Pages 424*

Lip-Reading *by Edward Nitchie*   ISBN: *1-59462-206-X*   **$25.95**
Edward B. Nitchie, founder of the New York School for the Hard of Hearing, now the Nitchie School of Lip-Reading, Inc, wrote "LIP-READING Principles and Practice". The development and perfecting of this meritorious work on lip-reading was an undertaking...   *How-to Pages 400*

A Handbook of Suggestive Therapeutics, Applied Hypnotism, Psychic Science   ISBN: *1-59462-214-0*   **$24.95**
by Henry Munro   *Health/New Age/Health/Self-help Pages 376*

A Doll's House: and Two Other Plays *by Henrik Ibsen*   ISBN: *1-59462-112-8*   **$19.95**
Henrik Ibsen created this classic when in revolutionary 1848 Rome. Introducing some striking concepts in playwriting for the realist genre, this play has been studied the world over.   *Fiction/Classics/Plays 308*

The Light of Asia *by sir Edwin Arnold*   ISBN: *1-59462-204-3*   **$13.95**
In this poetic masterpiece, Edwin Arnold describes the life and teachings of Buddha. The man who was to become known as Buddha to the world was born as Prince Gautama of India but he rejected the worldly riches and abandoned the reigns of power when...   *Religion/History/Biographies Pages 170*

The Complete Works of Guy de Maupassant *by Guy de Maupassant*   ISBN: *1-59462-157-8*   **$16.95**
"For days and days, nights and nights, I had dreamed of that first kiss which was to consecrate our engagement, and I knew not on what spot I should put my lips..."   *Fiction/Classics Pages 240*

The Art of Cross-Examination *by Francis L. Wellman*   ISBN: *1-59462-309-0*   **$26.95**
Written by a renowned trial lawyer, Wellman imparts his experience and uses case studies to explain how to use psychology to extract desired information through questioning.   *How-to/Science/Reference Pages 408*

Answered or Unanswered? *by Louisa Vaughan*   ISBN: *1-59462-248-5*   **$10.95**
Miracles of Faith in China   *Religion Pages 112*

The Edinburgh Lectures on Mental Science (1909) *by Thomas*   ISBN: *1-59462-008-3*   **$11.95**
This book contains the substance of a course of lectures recently given by the writer in the Queen Street Hail, Edinburgh. Its purpose is to indicate the Natural Principles governing the relation between Mental Action and Material Conditions...   *New Age/Psychology Pages 148*

Ayesha *by H. Rider Haggard*   ISBN: *1-59462-301-5*   **$24.95**
Verily and indeed it is the unexpected that happens! Probably if there was one person upon the earth from whom the Editor of this, and of a certain previous history, did not expect to hear again...   *Classics Pages 380*

Ayala's Angel *by Anthony Trollope*   ISBN: *1-59462-352-X*   **$29.95**
The two girls were both pretty, but Lucy who was twenty-one who supposed to be simple and comparatively unattractive, whereas Ayala was credited, as her Bombwhat romantic name might show, with poetic charm and a taste for romance. Ayala when her father died was nineteen...   *Fiction Pages 484*

The American Commonwealth *by James Bryce*   ISBN: *1-59462-286-8*   **$34.45**
An interpretation of American democratic political theory. It examines political mechanics and society from the perspective of Scotsman James Bryce   *Politics Pages 572*

Stories of the Pilgrims *by Margaret P. Pumphrey*   ISBN: *1-59462-116-0*   **$17.95**
This book explores pilgrims religious oppression in England as well as their escape to Holland and eventual crossing to America on the Mayflower, and their early days in New England...   *History Pages 268*

QTY

The Fasting Cure by *Sinclair Upton*　　　　　　　　ISBN: *1-59462-222-1*　**$13.95**
In the Cosmopolitan Magazine for May, 1910, and in the Contemporary Review (London) for April, 1910, I published an article dealing with my experiences in fasting. I have written a great many magazine articles, but never one which attracted so much attention... New Age/Self Help/Health Pages 164

Hebrew Astrology by *Sepharial*　　　　　　　　　ISBN: *1-59462-308-2*　**$13.45**
In these days of advanced thinking it is a matter of common observation that we have left many of the old landmarks behind and that we are now pressing forward to greater heights and to a wider horizon than that which represented the mind-content of our progenitors...　Astrology Pages 144

Thought Vibration or The Law of Attraction in the Thought World　ISBN: *1-59462-127-6*　**$12.95**

by *William Walker Atkinson*　　　　　　　　　　　　　*Psychology/Religion Pages 144*

Optimism by *Helen Keller*　　　　　　　　　　　ISBN: *1-59462-108-X*　**$15.95**
Helen Keller was blind, deaf, and mute since 19 months old, yet famously learned how to overcome these handicaps, communicate with the world, and spread her lectures promoting optimism. An inspiring read for everyone...　Biographies/Inspirational Pages 84

Sara Crewe by *Frances Burnett*　　　　　　　　　ISBN: *1-59462-360-0*　**$9.45**
In the first place, Miss Minchin lived in London. Her home was a large, dull, tall one, in a large, dull square, where all the houses were alike, and all the sparrows were alike, and where all the door-knockers made the same heavy sound...　Childrens/Classic Pages 88

The Autobiography of Benjamin Franklin by *Benjamin Franklin*　ISBN: *1-59462-135-7*　**$24.95**
The Autobiography of Benjamin Franklin has probably been more extensively read than any other American historical work, and no other book of its kind has had such ups and downs of fortune. Franklin lived for many years in England, where he was agent...　Biographies/History Pages 332

Name	
Email	
Telephone	
Address	
City, State ZIP	

☐ **Credit Card**　　　　　☐ **Check / Money Order**

Credit Card Number	
Expiration Date	
Signature	

Please Mail to:　Book Jungle
PO Box 2226
Champaign, IL 61825
or Fax to:　　　630-214-0564

ORDERING INFORMATION
web*: www.bookjungle.com*
email*: sales@bookjungle.com*
fax*: 630-214-0564*
mail*: Book Jungle PO Box 2226 Champaign, IL 61825*
or PayPal *to sales@bookjungle.com*

Please contact us for bulk discounts

DIRECT-ORDER TERMS

**20% Discount if You Order
Two or More Books**
Free Domestic Shipping!
Accepted: Master Card, Visa,
Discover, American Express

www.ingramcontent.com/pod-product-compliance
Lightning Source LLC
Chambersburg PA
CBHW081143020726
47504CB00009B/1985